Courting Poppy Tidemore
Lords of Honor Series

Copyright © 2019 by Christi Caldwell

For more information about the author:
www.christicaldwellauthor.com
christicaldwellauthor@gmail.com
Twitter: @ChristiCaldwell
Or on Facebook at: Christi Caldwell Author

For first glimpse at covers, excerpts, and free bonus material, be sure to sign up for my monthly newsletter!

Printed in the USA.

Cover Design and Interior Format
© THE KILLION GROUP, INC.

Courting Poppy Tidemore

Lords
OF
Honor

5

CHRISTI CALDWELL

A REGENCY DUET
Rogues Rush In

MEMOIR: NON-FICTION
Uninterrupted Joy

DEDICATION

For every reader who ever asked about Poppy Tidemore.

PROLOGUE

Two and a half years earlier
London, England

OH, HELL.

Tristan Poplar, the Earl of Maxwell, had stumbled into it now.

He'd come upon a lady. Not just any lady, however...but rather, one who was *crying*.

He'd always been useless with weeping women. It was, in short, the only type of women he was rubbish around. If he could throw jewels and dresses to make a lady stop, he would.

What was worse? The weepy lady he'd discovered in his host's conservatory was, in fact, Lady Poppy Tidemore. She was the sister-in-law to his best friend, Christian Villiers, the Marquess of St. Cyr, and had become a de facto friend.

As such, the last thing he could do for either of those reasons was to simply leave her here alone.

He glanced over his shoulder. Mayhap he should retrieve her sister. He could be gone and have the young woman here in hardly any time. Or he could always fetch St. Cyr. Or the mother. Or... in short, *anyone* other than himself. Yes, that was the decidedly safer option, given that the alternative was being caught alone with the young lady.

This, however, was a vulnerable, defeated Poppy, with her hands in front of her and her shoulders shaking. Poppy with whom he chatted often at summer picnics and chance meetings in Hyde

Park—about dogs. Poppy whom he fished with.

He took a step forward…

Poppy peeked over. "*You.*"

As one of society's most notorious rogues, detached annoyance was an altogether unfamiliar state to find himself in.

Tristan opened and then closed his mouth as several realizations came to him all at once: one, not only was the chit annoyed at his being here…but two, she'd decidedly not been crying.

The lady angled to face him.

Her bodice down.

"Oh, good God in heaven," he strangled out. His face afire, Tristan squeezed his eyes shut, and promptly knocked into Lord Smith's wrought-iron plant stand.

A porcelain planter crashed down, raining glass and soil upon the stone floor.

"Have a care, Maxwell," Poppy groused. "Or you'll see me ruined."

"I'll see you ruined? I'll see you *ruined*? You're the one with a gaping gown." If one wished to be precise, *that* would actually be the culprit behind her demise. Nay, in truth, all he needed was one inopportune visit from her overprotective brother, and brother-in-law, and he'd be done for. There'd be no hasty marriage, but rather a bullet at sunrise. Two of them.

"Aww, you are *blushing.* That is adorable, Tristan."

"I'm not adorable," he said indignantly. "Kittens and pups are adorable. And even if I was red in the face, which I am not," he said hastily, "it would be with entirely good reason."

"Tsk, tsk. For shame, one would expect with your reputation, you'd be better at this tryst business. Why, it is even in your name."

"I am," he said automatically into his palms, his voice muffled to his own ears. Or he was. With the right women, and certainly not with this woman.

She snorted, as if she'd followed the silently self-deprecating thoughts.

Either way, the last thing he intended to do is provide a laundry list of all his past scandalous endeavors. "Is your gown righted?" he asked impatiently when Poppy returned to whatever earlier task had occupied her focus.

"It is."

Tristan let his arms fall to his side. And here he'd believed she was crying.

Crying. As if fearless, spirited Poppy Tidemore could ever be brought to tears.

Just then, the lady picked up a cloth from Lord Smith's table and dipped the fabric into the watering fountain. He rubbed his brow. It *really* wasn't his business. *She* wasn't his business. And yet, she was St. Cyr's business and thereby, by default, Tristan's. He peered into the dimly lit gardens. By the saints. "You're dampening your dress," he hissed.

Poppy favored him with an impressive scowl. "You're still here."

Why, the chit was annoyed by *his* presence? Which could only mean... Spinning on his heel, he yanked the door shut, and locked it.

"Maxwell," she exclaimed. "What is wrong with you—?"

"You are meeting someone." He'd kill the bastard. Poppy Tidemore was as off-limits as any one of Tristan's own sisters.

She rolled her eyes. "I've greater sense than to sneak off with some rogue."

He eyed her dubiously.

A mischievous grin turned her lips up into a saucy smile. "If I did, I'd certainly not find myself caught."

"Dead. I'd kill the bastard dead." St. Cyr would expect him to do nothing less in the name of their friendship.

"I daresay the whole 'death' part would be the expected outcome of the whole 'killing' business."

"You're making light of this?" Tristan balled his hands.

"Oh, stuff and nonsense." Her smile dipped. "When did *you* go all proper on me?"

Since he'd stumbled upon her waiting about for some scoundrel. "This isn't about me, Poppy," he said, exasperated as ever by the chit. "This is about—"

Poppy fully faced him and all the anger went out of him. "Oh." A sizeable splotch of pink marred the bodice of her gown.

Over the years, every Tidemore girl who'd made her Come Out had been forced into voluminous white dresses as if the color and sheer size of their skirts alone was enough to hold scandal at bay. As such, at her debut, Poppy had managed the impossible feat not a single one of the three Tidemore sisters to proceed her had managed—she wasn't attired solely in white.

"At least it's not white," she said with her usual Poppy optimism. No, it was certainly not white.

"Well, not entirely *white*," she said under her breath.

Drip.

Lemonade slipped down her waist and with that, Poppy dismissed Tristan once more.

"Poppy, since when did you begin drinking *lemonade*?"

The lady despised the milquetoast drink, as she'd called it. It was a detail she'd shared by some lakeside over fishing at St. Cyr's country estate…when she'd tried—and succeeded in—convincing Tristan to allow her a sip from his flask.

"I haven't begun drinking lemonade, Tristan," she said as if he'd lost his mind and deserved a prompt trip to Bedlam, which given the way his head spun whenever he was in the minx's company, was likely not far from the mark.

"Then how did you spill the drink on yourself."

Poppy looked up. "Careful, Maxwell." She thinned her eyes into slits that oozed danger. "I'm not the clumsy sort."

He opened his mouth to point out that the first time he'd come across her, she'd been knocked on her buttocks in Hyde Park, but time had taught him enough to refrain from pointing out that detail. "Then, how—?"

"Someone tossed it at me." With a sigh, she set to work wiping at her bodice. "Are you happy? Someone tossed it at me."

He opened and closed his mouth several times. "Someone *tossed it*?" he finally managed.

Poppy paused mid-wiping and released a long sigh. "*Tossssed.*" She managed to stretch that single, overly emphasized syllable into five. "As in 'to throw', 'to hurl', 'to—'"

"I well know what the word tossed means," he interrupted.

"Trust me, Maxwell, I've tossed enough objects and items at my siblings through the years that I can quite determine when the act is deliberate." Her scowl deepened. "And when it is *not*."

Who in blazes could possibly hold ill feelings for Poppy Tidemore? Spirited. Always smiling. Well, except, now; now she was managing an impressive scowl. "I'm sure whoever did so," Tristan began, using the same tones he affected when dealing with his mother or sisters' upset, "did so entirely by—*oomph*."

The soggy rag she'd thrown hit his chest, and then landed on his feet with a *plop*.

Poppy lifted an arched brow. "Accident?"

He dusted the remnants of that sopping cloth from his jacket. "I see your point," he muttered. Only…on the heel of that came the knowledge that someone had deliberately hurt her. Fury crackled to life. "Who is responsible?"

Poppy glanced up from her stained gown, and he forced himself to relax the tense muscles in his face into a small half grin. "Lady Kathryn Delaney."

The Diamond of the First Water. "What in blazes issue could she have with you?"

"My family."

Tristan cocked his head.

"She had…words to say about my family."

Ah, of course. Loyal as she was spirited. He dropped his hip atop the work table. "And you no doubt took offense."

"I undoubtedly did."

He grinned. "I trust you told her where to go?"

Poppy curled her lips slowly up at the corners in that minx's grin that likely accounted for the grey at her brother's temples. "With very specific directions on how she might find herself there."

Tristan tossed his head back and laughed. Another debutante might be filled with tears at how the stain had come to be there. Never Poppy. She'd go toe-to-toe with the king himself if she felt one she'd loved had been wronged.

Poppy joined in laughing; and hers was a full, colorful expression of mirth that compelled another to join. The sound of it honest and so different from any lady of his acquaintance. He dusted amusement from the corners of his eyes. "God, you're refreshing, Poppy Tidemore," he said, after his hilarity had abated.

Her eyes softened. It was not an unfamiliar look he'd received from other women…but never from this woman.

Tristan hurriedly straightened. "You should return," he croaked. "We should both return." He grimaced. "*Not* together." He swiped his palms down toward the ground. Not unless he wished to face her brother at dawn. She furrowed her brow. "You should take yourself off." *Now.* As it was, society would dearly love to feast upon a scandal involving another Tidemore girl.

And just like that, the dangerous warmth that had been in her eyes was replaced by a keen sharpness. "Why, you're trying to be rid of me."

"Not at all," he said smoothly. Not *technically*. He was trying to rid both of them of one another's company before scandal came raining down.

"Listen here," she said, stabbing a finger in his direction. "And listen well." She proceeded to march in his direction, and Tristan, who'd earned a reputation of only ever advancing into the fieriest battle, did something he'd never done before—he retreated. "I found this hiding place in our host's home first, Tristan Poplar." Oh, hell, not even his own mother dragged out his full name when displeased. The backs of his legs knocked into a stool, and he toppled into the seat. Even in partial repose, he was several inches taller than the petite spitfire, and yet, she still somehow managed to stare down the length of her pert nose at him. "There are infinitely more locations a gentleman can steal for himself."

He knew ending this exchange and being on his way, and seeing that she was on hers, was the wisest course. The safest one. Only, in all the years he'd known the lady, she'd always managed to stir his damned curiosity. "And what places are those?"

Without missing a beat, Poppy proceeded to tick off a list on her gloveless fingers. "The billiards room. Lord Smith's offices. The stables. Lord Smith's dungeons."

He sat up straighter. "Dungeons? Surely you jest?"

"They were part of an original structure that he kept and—" She eyed him suspiciously. "Are you funning me?"

Tristan marked an X over his chest. "I wouldn't dream of it." It was another lie. Over the years, Poppy had proven more fun to tease than even his own mother and sisters. Granted, they didn't have quite the same…zest for life that Poppy Tidemore—or any Tidemore, for that matter—did.

Poppy gave a toss of her dark curls. "Either way, there are countless places you can safely seek out for your tryst where no one would dare look for you, thus you shouldn't go about taking mine. Now, shoo." Like she was trying to be rid of a bothersome cat, she gave a little flick of her fingers.

And it was precisely then that he knew he'd no intention of abandoning this exchange.

Tristan stretched his feet out, and crossed them at the ankles; the movement forced the minx back several steps. "And what makes you believe I'm here for…for…?" God help him. Even with his bid to tease, he couldn't manage to utter that word. Not in front of this woman.

"A tryst?" she supplied with a mischievous grin.

His ears went hot. "*That*," he settled for.

"For your roguish reputation, you're shockingly prudish."

Prudish? That charge was certainly…a first. "I don't have a reputation." At least not one that she should know about, anyway.

Switching to her opposite hand, Poppy went on to tick off another list. "There's been the widow at the Opera House."

"Gossip," he scoffed. Accurate gossip, but he'd sooner lop off his own arm than concede to those indiscretions to a young lady. "I'd trust a Tidemore wouldn't take everything written in the scandal sheets as fact."

"I saw you," she said flatly.

Tristan coughed into his hand. "Ah…I see." *Checkmate.*

"Shall I go on?" she drawled, lifting a thin black brow.

"No." He'd rather wandered himself down a path he'd no business walking. "I'd rather you didn'—"

"There was the serving girl at the Hell and Sin Club," she continued over him.

Alas, the bloodthirsty minx was determined to stomp all over him in this battle. "Your sister talks too much," he mumbled, glancing up at the ceiling. Past Poppy's shoulder. Anywhere but at her.

"And there was your mistress at Madame Archambault's." Poppy drifted forward, stalking around his chair so that she circled him. "You do recall our meeting—?"

"I recall," he croaked. Tristan adjusted his previously flawless cravat.

"Where I was being fitted for my trousseau and you were accompanying your mistress?"

The most out of the way modiste *would* have been the place Poppy had found herself. "Very well." He eyed the exit covetously. "You were…are…indeed entitled to your suspicions. This time, however, was not one of those times."

Poppy leaned in, peering at his face as if searching for his every truth. She sank back on her heels. "Then what *are* you doing here?"

she asked quietly, all earlier teasing gone.

"I despise balls." There it was…the truth.

Poppy rocked back on her heels. "You?" she shot back, incredulously.

Abandoning his negligent pose, Tristan pushed to his feet. "Yes, me." Because given his reputation, the world would only expect him to be in the midst of the crowd. Loving every moment of the noisy, thrilling crush of a ballroom.

"You, the adored, charming, always-sought-after Earl of Maxwell?"

Flashing a grin, he drifted over to her. "Is that what I am? Adored? Charming?"

The minx swatted him on the chest. "Oh, hush. Save your rogue's smile for another, Maxwell."

Except, with the pale moon's glow slashing through the conservatory windows, it didn't escape his notice that a blush bloomed on Poppy's cheeks. He opened his mouth to tease her once more… but when their eyes met, the very somber and very un-Poppy-like glint froze the levity on his lips.

Shoving his hands behind his back, he wandered over to the little work station she'd set herself up by the fountain. "The balls and soirees eventually grow tiring."

"They do," she murmured, gliding toward him.

"The noise. The inanity. It was once—"

"Thrilling?" she ventured, speaking as one who knew.

He nodded, and stared down at the fountaining water. "Thrilling," he murmured, his gaze on his visage in the pond. Upon his return from Waterloo years earlier, he'd welcomed the inanity. For it had proved a distraction. A desperately needed one. He'd relished each dalliance, for those very reasons. At thirty, time had aged him, and reminded him how…empty it all was.

"I…never knew you felt that way," she ventured, hesitantly…as if she believed he might still be feeding her a line.

"I didn't always," he confessed. How easy it had always been to talk to Poppy. There'd been no messy entanglement. No fawning. Just…an unfettered honesty that only a girl was capable of. Only, that bluntness had followed her into womanhood.

"What changed?"

Life. Him. Everything.

Tristan sank onto the step leading into the watering fountain. "Here," he urged, motioning her back to her seat.

She hesitated, and then in further un-Poppy like fashion, complied without complaint. Tristan took one of Lord Smith's work rags.

"What are you...?" Her words trailed off as he brought that cloth toward the front of her dress.

He hesitated. Though there were years of friendship and history between them, Poppy Tidemore was still a lady. "May I?"

With her eyes wide in her face, Poppy nodded.

"Now, the first step to cleaning a stain is blot the area. Like so." He dabbed at the mark. Tristan continued to dip the fabric in the fountain and then blot. "The secret is to remove the excess moisture from the fabric."

"I was attempting to rinse it."

He paused, eyeing the wide splotch on the waist of her gown. "Uh...I see that. One needs to remove the stain first." Gathering up another cloth, he dipped it into the fountain, and soaked it. "Next," he explained, as he rang out the excess water, "one rinses."

"You've experience with laundering your own garments?" She directed that question to his bent head.

He may as well have hung a star for the awe coating her voice.

His lips twitched.

Only Poppy Tidemore. Any other lady would long for baubles and pretty compliments. Poppy would admire and appreciate a person who could clean a garment.

"In war, a soldier learns all manner of skills that he wouldn't have otherwise acquired," he murmured. They fell into an easy silence as he tended her gown. When he'd finished with the cloth, he set it aside. He leaned forward to blow on the damp article...

The air crackled and hissed, thrumming with tension.

And he, who'd been previously absorbed in helping little Poppy Tidemore right her gown, noted a sea of details that had failed to escape him: the lace trim of her neckline. The rise and fall of her chest. The gentle swell of her breasts; cream swells that would fit perfectly in his palms.

He struggled to swallow.

Did he imagine the slight increase in her breathing, a faint rasp?

Or mayhap that was his own.

Look away. Run. Run as far and as fast as your damned legs might carry you.

"Are you all right?" she asked, pressing the back of her hand to his forehead. And the concern in her voice sent reality rushing back.

Cad. I am an utterly depraved cad.

"Fine," he managed gruffly. He gave his head a slight, disgusted shake. What momentary madness had overtaken him? "You should return," he said, coming to his feet. "There's a sea of suitors, I trust, awaiting you."

With a snort, Poppy lifted her dance card.

He frowned.

Why...why...? "It's empty."

"You always did have a tendency for stating the obvious, Maxwell," she said dryly. "There are no suitors. Zero of them." She formed a small circle with her long fingers. "*Nulla. Aucun.*"

Another lady might have been in tears. Poppy, however, was all matter-of-fact about her circumstances.

"You're better off without them." Which were not simply words to make the lady feel better. Most lords of London were self-important, pompous bastards who'd never appreciate a spirited woman like Poppy Tidemore.

"Perhaps," she agreed. "But that does not take away from the fact that there are things a lady *requires* a husband for."

He dissolved into a fit.

"I meant freedom, Maxwell," she said, her tones rich with exasperation. "I meant my freedoms." She wrinkled her nose. "Is there anything you men think of other than sexual relations?"

Rarely. And as he couldn't sort out whether hers was a rhetorical question or one she expected an answer to, he swiftly diverted the topic along safer courses. "You'll find the right gentleman, Poppy."

Poppy folded her arms at her chest. "Will I, Tristan? *Will I?*" she repeated, placing a slight emphasis on those echoed syllables.

He opened his mouth to deliver the expected, and requisite, reply...and yet, the answer remained lodged there.

She sensed that hesitation. "And what of you?"

Tristan angled his head. "What about me?"

"Where's your bride?"

His brows went up. "Egads. I don't have a bride." He wasn't the marrying sort. Eventually he'd see to those responsibilities. Soon. One day.

"You're struggling, too, then."

"I'm not…struggling. Mine—"

"Is a choice?" she asked, without inflection.

Tristan searched for a slight tremble to her lips or tears in her eyes. Instead, there was only a curiosity in her clear gaze. "Because I, too, have not found the right person yet," he said smoothly. Nor was he in any manner of rush to do so.

Poppy sighed. "There's only one thing that makes sense." She gave him a look.

Something was expected of Tristan. And God help him, for all his effortless reads on discourse and women, any and every answer eluded him here. Tristan shook his head.

She nodded.

"Why are you nodding like that?" he asked, befuddled.

"A Marriage Pact, Tristan. A marriage pact."

He recoiled. "What in blazes is *that*?"

"A man and woman agree that should they not find a better match they shall settle on one another."

A laugh burst from him. "That sounds both positively horrific and pathetic all at the same time."

She glared at him, that look harder and sterner than that of any tutor or instructor he'd had in the whole of his life, and it effectively quelled his amusement.

"Very well, we agree…if I'm unwed by twenty-six, we shall marry one another."

At what point did the minx believe they'd come to that agreement? "Bah, when you're twenty-six, I'll be fast approaching forty."

"Not so much fast-approaching as gracefully sliding into it," she allowed, holding her index finger and thumb up a smidge.

And because he'd never forgive himself if he didn't hear the whole of this out, he asked, "And what are the terms of said arrangement?"

"You won't hunt."

He paused.

"I'll not agree otherwise, Maxwell."

He blinked slowly. "Uh…were you not convincing me of the terms?"

"Your word, Maxwell."

His lips twitched. "Very well. No hunting."

"If it is any consolation, you shall be nearly forty at the fateful date, and entirely too old for hunting anyway."

Another grin tugged at his lips; not the practiced one he'd affected for scandalous purposes. And how much better this smile felt...and was. "I thought I was sliding into my doddering years."

Then with a remarkable aplomb for a lady whose gown was damp from lemonade and waters—she gave a toss of her curls. "I was being polite."

He knew better than to point out that as long as he'd known her—now four years—the chit hadn't ever opted for politeness over honesty. He again perched himself on the edge of the work table. "Carry on."

"There'll be no mistresses, Maxwell."

He strangled on his cough.

Poppy sharpened her eyes on his face. "That fit had better not be because of an inability to commit to that vow."

"N-not at all," he managed to rasp between his great, heaving gasps for breath.

With a grunt, Poppy thumped him with an impressive strength between the shoulder blades.

And it occurred to him in that instant that had he provided a disagreeable answer, the minx would have happily left him choking. He didn't know whether to be impressed or terrified. "It occurs to me, Lady Poppy, that your list is comprised largely of things you do not want, and not that which you desire."

"Hmm." She nibbled at the tip of her finger. "I do believe you've a good idea there."

"Occasionally I manage that," he said dryly.

"I'm to have the largest space in the residence for an art room." There was a challenge in her eyes; one that indicated she expected him to rebuff that pretend clause.

She still sketched. The last time he'd seen her with a sketchpad in hand, she'd had a rough-looking outline of a dog on the page. "Any space you desire will be yours," he said with a flourish of his hand.

"I'll keep company with whomever I wish." Her fingers balled into fists at her sides. "None of this disapproval society is so famous for."

A little pang struck. The Tidemores had been riddled with scandal for more than a decade now. They'd been met with unkindness and disdain. It had become as casual a fact as the London streets fogged over. And yet…to her, to this young woman, it was her life. He bowed his head somberly. "You'll have no complaints from my future self on that score."

She nodded slowly, approvingly.

"Anything else, my lady?"

The lady settled into her seat, one wholly warming to her role of arbiter of her fate. "I'll wear what I wish, without being made to feel guilty for choosing whichever garment I choose."

"Absolutely," he said automatically. Unbidden, his gaze took in the heavily ruffled satin skirts. He repressed a shudder. Poppy caught him in the shins with her foot. "Oopmh." Scowling, he bent down and rubbed the wounded flesh. "What in blazes was that for?"

"For eyeing my skirts in that manner."

Tristan tossed his arms up. "You hate white." She'd said as much, no fewer than…well, at nearly every exchange they'd had.

Poppy gave another toss of her head. "That's entirely different."

"How so?" he asked, unable to help himself.

"I can be annoyed by my skirts. It's altogether different when other people express their opinions over what I'm wearing. Do you understand?"

Nothing much made sense whenever he was around or with Poppy Tidemore. "Completely," he lied.

"Now." She hopped up and drifted over until their knees brushed. Nearly five inches shorter than him, she had to tip her head back to meet his gaze. "What do you want?"

In any other woman, there would have been a veiled suggestiveness to those four words, an invitation that welcomed sin and seduction…and God help him for the scoundrel he was, his blood thickened at the slightly sultry quality of her contralto. He slipped his gaze lower…

And by the tangle of white ruffles, was hit with the reminder that: one, he was chatting with his best friend's sister-in-law, and two…the chit was…innocent. And three, being caught with her was no longer the same as it had been when she'd been a child of fifteen. Now, she'd be ruined, and he'd be trapped, and—

Poppy narrowed her eyes. "Are you going to go choking again?"

"Beg pardon?" he said hoarsely.

"Your face has gone all red and your voice is gruff."

God, the minx missed nothing. "I'll require help with the running of my household."

"Very well. What else?"

Did he imagine the faint moue of disappointment at that tedious and expected-by-a-gentleman requisite? And he allowed himself to consider the child's game she played, he caught his chin between his thumb and forefinger and rubbed it contemplatively. "Hmm... there is the matter of my dogs."

She perked up. "What about them?"

"I'd require someone to help me care after them and see to their daily walks."

Poppy nodded enthusiastically. "Of course."

"And then, fishing. I'd expect that we fish daily."

A smile curled her lips up. "In the winter, Maxwell?"

Tristan tapped his chin thoughtfully. "Very well, spring and summer months. In the winter, you'd be permitted your own time."

A shadow darkened her eyes; but was gone so quick it might as well have been a trick of the light. "Is there anything else you require?"

He shook his head. "I think that quite settles it."

Taking his hand in his, she shook it once. "It is settled."

With that, she spun on her heel, and rushed off.

Bemused, Tristan stared after the swift-retreating slip of a girl. There was only one certainty; whichever bounder found himself wed to the minx was going to find himself in deuced trouble.

V 1

London, England
1826

ᴇVERYTHING WAS A LIE.

All of it.

The fortunes. The landholdings. The title. The respectability.

And because of it, even Tristan Poplar, the Earl of Maxwell's honor was being called into question.

Which therefore meant...*everything* was gone.

Or that was what the man—nay, the investigator—seated across from Tristan expected him to believe.

It was also the moment where Tristan was to say...*something*.

He knew as much. He, ever effortless in discourse and conversations, so affable he'd earned a reputation for it and never missed a beat, knew this moment was his cue.

But he could manage...nothing.

His office crackled from the tension at the revelation which had been made...ten minutes? Ten hours? Ten lifetimes ago?

Only, if the investigator seated across from Tristan was to be trusted, this wasn't Tristan's office. According to the last utterance made, this space and everything in it belonged to another.

Or had it been, not an utterance, but rather an accusation? Mayhap it was both. It was all jumbled in his confused mind. After all, there was no certain protocol, no code of etiquette for how to respond to charges that the title one had inherited, in fact, belonged to…another.

The hearth crackled; the flames snapped and hissed angrily across the room.

He's burning…my God, he's on fire…do something, Tristan…

That haunting echo of those memories upon the battlefield that would never fade echoed in his mind, in a sobering reminder… that for everything that the stranger seated across from him had revealed, Tristan had faced down cannon fire and the bayonet of Boney's most ruthless soldiers with calm. With the smallest of garrisons, he'd faced down Napoleon's assault eighty guns strong. He'd not be reduced to silence by the stranger before him.

Steepling his fingers, Tristan rested them on his chest. "I beg your pardon?" he began in shockingly steady tones. "You are claiming I am not the rightful holder of the Maxwell title?" Somehow, giving those words life helped steady him. It was too fantastical to ever make any sense. It was a title he'd inherited less than ten years ago. "That the title, in fact, belongs to—"

"Another," the illustrious investigator Connor Steele put forward smoothly, for a second time. "Percival Northrop."

So the man had a name; the Northrops had been the family who'd died along with their staff and seen Tristan's father—and now Tristan—elevated to the rank of earl. And an obscenely wealthy one at that. He laughed, the mirthless rumbled in his chest.

Leaning forward, Steele set a thick leather folder down. "He now goes by the name of Malcolm North. He—"

"He can go by the name of Satan's Spawn for all it matters," he clipped out, as fury took the place of his earlier shock. "There were no living Northrops. The family, along with all their servants, had been wiped out by smallpox." That fateful event had seen Tristan's father named heir apparent. "There *are* no living Northrops," he corrected. With that, he shoved the folder back toward the other man.

Steele made no attempt to take it.

"That is what the world was expected to believe," Steele said cryptically. "There was a boy." The investigator paused. "Which makes him the rightful heir."

The rightful heir.

Tristan narrowed his eyes. "How fortuitous that the long-lost heir should come forward now. And this…Percival Northrop should just so happen to reemerge after—"This time, he reached for the file. Opening it, he skimmed the top sheet. "Twenty years." Tristan tossed it down and it landed with a thump. According to the paperwork before him, this brought the grasper, to… twenty-six, nearly twenty-seven years of age. He searched his mind in a bid to recall anything either his mother or late father had said about the Northrops. "Consider me cynical, but isn't it odd that the rightful heir, as you call him, should appear now?" Suddenly, after all these years? Shoving back his chair, Tristan stood, ending this meeting.

"He didn't come forward," Steele said quietly, remaining seated. "I located him."

That gave Tristan pause. The unease that had been churning through him the moment Connor Steele had stated, "The title Earl of Maxwell belongs to another," returned.

He reclaimed his seat. "I don't understand," he said in measured tones. "Smallpox wiped out not only the Northrop family but their staff along with it." All had perished. He'd been too young to remember, but knew the origins of the title that had passed to him. Or he'd believed so. Everything was dangerously close to being flipped upside down. "No one survived."

"Incorrect," Steele murmured. "Two people survived." The other man paused. "And it was scarlet fever, not smallpox." He nudged his chin at the folder. "It's in the file."

"Two people?" Tristan asked, ignoring that latter part of what the investigator had said.

"A maid on her deathbed, and a boy turned over to an orphanage, raging with fever."

Tristan sank back in his chair. "And just how do you come to know all this supposed information?"

A cool smile turned the other man's lips up in the corners. "It is my job to know everything."

Filled with the need to move…to think, free of this stranger who'd invaded his office and made threatening claims against the future he'd inherited, and now sustained his two unwed sisters and mother with, Tristan stood. He made his way to the sideboard. Grabbing the nearest bottle at hand, he poured himself a glass.

All the while, his skin prickled with the intensity of the gaze trained on him by the other man.

Refusing to give in to the panic raging through him, Tristan forced himself to face Steele. "I trust you understand why I'm... skeptical as to your claims? Claims brought forward by a..." Tristan's lips twisted in a cynical grin. "Malcolm North... What is his background?"

Steele frowned. "I've already—"

"Not that supposed one," he said with an impatient wave of his glass. "Where has he been these years?"

"In the streets of East London." The investigator offered nothing more than that.

"Well, then forgive me, but I'm hesitant to simply turn over my future"—and more importantly, the future of his siblings and mother—"because of the sudden appearance of a long-lost relative." Tristan swirled the contents of his drink and took a sip.

"The transaction...the *sale* of the child, it was marked with coin and a formal agreement."

Tristan stopped with his drink halfway to his lips. In writing, then. "Anything could be forged for the right amount of funds. Anything can be said or done when there is power and wealth at stake."

The investigator leveled a hard look at him. "And that is precisely what happened."

Ice trickled up his spine, and despite his bid for self-control in front of the man threatening to upend his future, Tristan tossed back a long, much needed drink of brandy.

"I trust this comes as something of a shock?" Steele said when Tristan held his tongue.

Only, there was a question there from the immobile stranger. Which implied he was also here to probe Tristan's role in the elaborate scheme he'd just laid out before him. Indignation swept him, an outrage that proved restorative.

He set the glass down hard. "I'm not some subject to play your word games with. What you are suggesting—?"

"I'm not suggesting anything, Lord Bolingbroke. I've done my research. I'm never wrong."

It didn't escape his notice that Steele had appropriated Lord Bolingbroke, that lesser title belonging to his late father before he'd become the Earl of Maxwell. "This time you are," he said flatly. The other man had to be. What was the alternative? That someone in his family had orchestrated the greatest theft? Harmed a child and stolen a lifestyle and wealth that had never rightfully belonged to them?

And worse…what would it mean for Tristan's mother and two unmarried sisters? What the other man proposed was a scandal that—if true—the Poplars would never recover from.

Taking another drink, Tristan steeled his jaw. "This time, you are wrong, Mr. Steele." What the other man spoke of was impossible. "We're officially done here." He stood, but once more Steele remained as tenacious as his name.

"Are you familiar with your family's circumstances prior to their great reversal of fortune?"

Impoverished.

The Poplars had been an impoverished lot with land that hadn't produced and crumbling properties that had been largely uninhabitable. There'd been frequent tears and fighting between his parents. And with the thick folder the investigator had amassed, Tristan would wager the title he now fought to cling to that those details were all neatly penned in the other man's hand.

He came round his desk and dropped his hip on the edge. "My family's previous circumstances prove nothing."

"They provide motive."

Motive.

One word that made the situation…more real. Nay, more foreboding.

As if he sensed that weakening, Steele pounced. "Your father had motives and was responsible for removing the rightful heir."

A chill scraped his spine. It was on the tip of his tongue to tell the overconfident investigator where he could go. And yet…to do so would be an impulsive act. One that wouldn't right this situation. And as he'd never been one to run from a battle, he forced himself to grab the folder and confront the ugliness that this man attempted to heap upon him and his late father—*and your sisters.* This file and this detective represented a peril to those dependent upon him. Coming to his feet, he presented his back to the investigator and skimmed the top page.

Percival Theodore Charles Northrop.

Aged: Twenty-Six.

Age at kidnapping: Six.

His stomach churning, Tristan flipped to the next page.

Accompanied to London by the only servant to survive the sickness. Child was sent to a foundling hospital. Sold at the age of six. In that time...

Skipping over those details, Tristan searched and searched.

And then found.

Payments made through the years, in the amount of one hundred pounds monthly, by the Baron Bolingbroke to maintain the silence of the former maid.

My father. That was who stood accused, and supposed monetary evidence inked on these pages, linking the late earl to...this.

Tristan snapped the folder closed. He held the thick stack out. "You are wrong."

This time there was no attempt to debate the veracity of the claims being made. And the now pitying glint in the other man's eyes sparked terror that not even the previous iciness had managed. "I trust you'll require time to consider...all of this and the ramifications." With that, Steele took his leave.

As soon he'd gone, Tristan carried the folder to his desk, and sat—just as the door exploded open. His mother burst inside.

Bloody hell. "Moth—"

"There you are," she exclaimed hurriedly, pushing the panel closed and joining him at his desk.

"Mother," he finished his earlier greeting, welcoming the distraction...even if it came from his mother and surely pertained to seeing his sisters properly married and finding himself a wife.

"What was he doing here?" she demanded, and before he could reply, she spoke on a rush. "That man cannot possibly have any dealings with us."

Dealings with *us*.

It was a...singularly minor detail to take note of. And yet... Tristan frowned. "Why do you assume Mr. Steele came on a matter affecting us?"

Angry color splotched her cheeks. "Any dealings he has with you affects all of us, Tristan. Unless I need to remind you, there are your two unwed sisters." His mother began to pace before his desk. "Marry for happiness, he said," she grumbled. "They'll find a husband in due time, he said."

Using her distracted, back and forth march before his desk, Tristan collected the heavy file, and deposited it into his top desk drawer. "Need I point out that Christina"—the eldest of his sisters—"is, in fact, happily married with two babies and another on the way?"

Not breaking her angry strides, she scoffed. "To a self-made man."

"He's gentry, Mother," he said in the same gentling tones he'd used when schooling his sisters on how to hunt.

"*Poor* gentry." She stopped abruptly. "And it is all because of you." She stabbed a finger in his direction.

As if there could be another "you" in question.

Tristan threw back a drink. "Wanting my sisters to marry happily. How positively barbaric of me," he said dryly.

"Shortsighted," his mother clipped out. She pressed her palms to her cheeks. "Oh, whyever did I not persist? Your sisters need…"

And while his mother dissolved into a lengthy cataloguing of what his sisters required, Steele's pronouncement whispered forward.

There was a boy… Which makes him the rightful heir…

Tristan's stomach turned. For though matches for wealth and power had been a luxury before, now the lack of them represented peril. Uncertainty. For his sisters. His mother. Even if…when… Tristan triumphed over some street tough scheming for his title, along the way his name and that of his sisters would be dragged across every gossip column.

"Are you listening to me?" his mother snapped. "This is a matter of the"—*uttermost importance*—"uttermost importance," she finished with her usual overdramatic detailing. Only…where it had once been an almost farcical reaction from his grasping mother, now there was an urgency that she didn't yet see.

"I'm listening." He usually lied. Now, he was. Now was different.

"There is also your need of a bride and an heir."

"In that order?" With the scandal set to hit London involving Tristan and his family, the prospects on that score were grim, indeed. Not that he'd any interest in marriage.

Her eyes flashed. "Of course in that…" She pursed her mouth. "This is not a time for your lighthearted teasing, Tristan."

There'd been no truer words ever to leave the hard-hearted

woman he called mother.

"As I was saying…that man—"

"Steele."

"Has no business here with our family." She thumped her hand on his desk once more. "None. I don't want you keeping company with him."

The countess' concerns, however, only stemmed from her desire for proper appearances. "Ah, of course. Poplars don't interact with those outside the peerage?" he delivered that familiar, gratingly arrogant mantra she'd been uttering since she'd gone from baroness to countess. "I assure you even with my *vaunted* station"—a station that, according to the previous visitor, was nothing more than stolen goods—"I'm not so arrogant that I'd turn away Mr. Steele." Steele had uncovered a ring of kidnappings that had been conducted on behalf of a London gang lord.

Of which, he'd suggest my family is part.

"You're not being reasonable, Tristan. He is…he is…"

"The son of an earl." Tristan had never moved in the same social circles but society well knew the history of Mr. Connor Steele.

"The *adopted* son from the streets," she said, not missing a beat.

"And therefore not to be trusted?" he drawled.

She gave an uncharacteristically enthusiastic nod. "You do understand."

"It was a question, not a statement, Mother," he said coolly.

His mother slammed her palm down twice on the surface of his desk. "That man is not to be trusted. Why, he was taken in by an earl. Named an adoptive son and how did he repay that warmth? By shedding the earl's name and marrying a common street rat."

Her rank as countess and their family's wealth had long mattered to her above all else—including her children's happiness. "Mother, I've more important business to attend than your…worry about Mr. Steele's birthright." What would she say if she knew how precarious their existence had become…? "Now, if you'll excuse me?" he asked for a second time. Taking one more much needed drink of his brandy, Tristan set the glass down—

When he registered his mother sweeping into the seat.

Bloody hell. Tristan swiped a hand over his face. He didn't have the time for this. Not now. Now, he had to try and sort out…what to do…how to proceed on the threat made by Steele. "What is it now, Mother?" he asked, making no attempt to conceal his impatience.

"What did he say?" Her query came faint and threadbare. This from the countess known as a dragon among all Polite Society for her fierceness and fearlessness.

And the previous bells that had pinged at the back of his mind chimed once more. Louder. More incessant. Tristan eyed her wan features. "What did who say?" he asked measuredly.

She dampened her lips. "Don't be coy and don't play games. What did he want?"

And for her earlier fury, now all that remained was a shaky fear.

The reason for the investigator's visit would shatter her, but the story would inevitably come to her. And it may as well be now.

Tristan glanced past her shoulder, and when he spoke, he did so in hushed tones. "I'm not sure how much you're aware of the manner of investigative work Mr. Steele has done these past years."

"I'm aware," she said immediately.

"He came because he…" God help him, he couldn't even get the damned words out. Untrue though they may be, once he uttered them, the impending scandal became real.

"What is it?" she whispered.

"He claims the previous Earl of Maxwell had a son, and that son did not perish."

Silence met that revelation. Punctuated only by the occasional snap and hiss of the fire in the hearth.

"I'm sure this comes as something of a shock," Tristan went on, when still she didn't speak.

And yet…his mother, given to histrionics when her morning gossip papers were set down on the wrong side of her breakfast plate, remained…motionless. Entirely too calm. Her features even. Her color…the same. There was no call for her smelling salts, or noisy waterworks that produced no water.

He narrowed his eyes. "Mother?" he quietly prodded.

The countess jumped. "Hmm? I…" She scrabbled at her throat. Her fingers frantically moved to her skirts. And then back again to her throat.

"What does he b-believe?" her voice cracked.

His stomach muscles knotted. "That father was responsible."

"Take a child and place him in some…some…foundling hospital?"—The earth stopped on its axis—"You shame your father's memory, Tristan. Shame him."

Oh, God. *No. No. No.* Tristan's stomach pitched. "I didn't say anything about a foundling hospital."

His mother pressed a palm to her mouth, and then abruptly let it fall. "Why…of course you didn't. I'm simply saying…I was merely hazarding what that…that Mr. Steele said to you."

A humming filled his ears. *It is true. It is true.* Everything Steele had uttered had been based on fact. "Stop."

"As if your father would ever do something so callous—"

"Stop," Tristan said through that distant tunneling of his hearing. "*So* heinous."

"I said 'stop'," he bellowed, exploding to his feet.

Gasping, his mother jumped back…and for the first time in the whole of his thirty-two years—she had no words.

His hands shaking, Tristan grabbed his half-empty snifter and downed the remaining contents; welcoming the burning trail it scorched down his throat. He set the glass down hard, and then looked to his mother. "I want the truth."

"Tristan," she began in those affronted tones she adopted with the damned servants.

"I want the truth." He bit out each syllable as he spoke.

"He did it for you," she said on a broken whisper.

Oh, God.

A piteous moan swelled in his throat, choking him with the perfidy that had been his existence. Nay, this…none of it had been his. He'd lived the life belonging to another. An exalted one of wealth and opulence…stolen for him by his parents.

A restless energy filled him. Tristan took a step. And then stopped.

He took another. He needed to flee. To think.

Only there was nowhere to go. And there was nothing that would make sense of…this. Of what his family had done. Of what he himself had unwittingly been part of. Tristan, who'd held his honor above all else: on the battlefield. In his family. In his every relationship. Should now find his fortunes and recent past and now present were a product of the greatest dishonor.

I am going to throw up.

"Don't look at me like that," she whispered, snapping him back. "And how am I looking at you, Mother?" he asked quietly. "As though, you and Father schemed to kidnap a child and divest him of his future? Stole from him so that we could have...this?"

She exploded to her feet. "Hush," she hissed, alternating a frantic glance from the door and back to Tristan. "It was your father. He convinced me there was no other way."

A half-mad laugh exploded from him, and at last, he managed to move.

No other way than to kidnap a child. To leave him for dead. To steal his title and his fortunes, and give them instead over to another family. An undeserving one. Tristan's family.

His mother touched his sleeve, and he startled. He whose hearing and senses had been so heightened that he'd saved himself with nothing more than the crack of a brush in Brussels. Everything had been muted. Distorted as his whole life had become.

"He was sick, Tristan," she cajoled. "He couldn't have survived."

And Tristan wanted to believe that. Only... His gaze fell to the drawer where that folder rested. "Mr. Steele has made a claim to the contrary." And Tristan had rebuffed it outright. He'd called Steele out for being wrong, and leveled accusations against the man whom Steele had titled the rightful heir. "He survived, Mother," he said flatly.

"Bah, what does this street rat turned investigator know? Why it's very likely a fellow street rat colluding with him to divest us of everything we have."

"The sickly maid hired to escort the boy to London has confirmed the history. There's a payment history made to this woman, confirming not only that Percival Northrop lived but that the maid who accompanied him was paid off for her silence."

His mother's legs weakened and she caught the top of the leather winged chair to keep from collapsing.

Oh, God. Tristan dragged a hand through his hair. "And you know it."

"He was on his death bed. *Feverish*. His lungs rattled. His throat swollen. What could be the harm?" The countess lifted her palms up in entreaty. No, not the countess. She was the baroness...his mother. Nay, he couldn't even think of her in that light. Not in this instance. "Surely you see?"

Did she try to reason with him? Or herself? Tristan wrenched away from her. "What could be the harm?" he croaked. "*What could be the harm*?" Another half-mad laugh rumbled in his chest and died in his mouth, choking him. He reached for his glass. Found it empty. And then grabbed his bottle. Bringing the decanter to his lips, he drank deep of the fine French spirits, spirits that belonged to another.

He slammed the bottle down so hard it splintered, cracked, and then rained down amber droplets upon the previously immaculate surface, marring the mahogany. "Tell me this, Mother?" he whispered. "If the boy was upon his deathbed and Father was so certain death was imminent...then why..." *I can't. I can't bring myself to utter that heinous phrase,* "...why...?" Why take him to a foundling hospital? Why steal security out from under a child?

"There were you and your sisters, Tristan. We struggled mightily. You don't recall. But I do." She pressed a hand to her chest. "I do."

"Our life was comfortable."

"You know nothing of it," she scoffed. "Your father would have ended in debtor's prison and we would have suffered."

Instead, another had suffered. The rightful heir. Tristan clenched and unclenched his fists. "But at least he would have had his honor."

"Bah, honor," she cried, her voice pealing around the room. She immediately went silent. Closing her eyes, his mother ran her hands over the front of her skirts. When she opened her eyes, her face assumed its usual unflinching mask. "When you have children of your own, then you can speak to me of honor, Tristan. Then you can tell me what you would have done or not done."

"Not this," he spat, cynicism dripping from those two words. He shook his head. "I would have never done this."

His mother gave him a small, hardened smile. "But because of what your father did, you'll never have to make those decisions."

Creasing his brow, he stared at her. What was she saying? And then the truth slammed into him—"You want me to fight him for his claim to the title."

"It can be dragged on for years and there's no solid proof." His mother gave him a pointed look. "Not truly."

And she was correct. It would. Such entanglements would be messy. It would drag on and on for years, unending. Mayhap forever. In that time, Tristan's sisters would live their comfortable lives...albeit still scorned for the scandal surrounding their family.

Valor nudged at his hand, the dog's cold, wet nose, burrowing against his palm, as the pup he'd once given comfort to became protector. Tristan automatically stroked the silky top of the dog's large head, and there was something steadying in the loyal creature's presence. "You were correct on one thing, Mother," he said quietly.

A shaky smile curled her lips up.

"Because of what my father did, I'll never have to make those decisions." He started around his desk. Valor immediately fell into step beside him. "Instead, I'll make others. Different ones." A previously slumbering Honor sprang to his feet and joined them. Tristan sat. Opening the desk drawer, he withdrew the folder left by Steele. Except, he didn't truly need the proof contained within the leather file. His mother had confirmed...everything. He yanked out a piece of parchment...and then reached for a pen.

"What are you saying?" his mother demanded sharply, her voice pitched with panic.

Head bent, he didn't bother to look at her when he spoke. "It is not what I am saying, Mother," he murmured, dipping his pen into the crystal inkwell. He tapped the excess ink on the edge, and began writing.

"And what are you doing?" When he still did not answer, she cried out. "I asked what you are doing."

This time, Tristan lifted his head very slowly. A muscle leapt in his jaw. "Why, I am at last making it right, Mother." And with that, he penned the remainder of words upon that page that would erase the comfortable, elevated existence he'd lived these past twenty years.

CHAPTER 2

Around that same time…
Mayfair, England

In every club throughout London, wagers had been placed not on "if" Lady Poppy Tidemore would be ruined…but rather "how"…and *when*.

The only club where there hadn't been a wager had been the Hell and Sin Club, and that was entirely because the lady's brother-in-law was, in fact, the notorious owner of that respective establishment.

Odds had been three to one that her downfall would occur in a garden with some equally scandalous man.

Two to one had placed her inside her brother-in-law's gaming hell, the Hell and Sin Club.

Many of the *gentlemen* betting hadn't expected Poppy to make it past her first Season.

Most had her falling sometime within her second.

Poppy took heart at having made it through two Seasons and a bit of her third before the inevitable had come.

In the end, it had, in fact, turned out a gentleman had ruined her…just not for the reasons scribbled down in those betting books throughout London.

Oh, Poppy had no complaints about how she'd been ruined. If a lady was to shred her reputation, it should always be in the name of art.

Alas, the same, however, could not be said for the opinions of the other members of her family.

Her now, still silent family.

She grimaced.

Silence was the most dangerous of the Tidemore responses. One should think that her eldest sisters, who'd all been recipients of like scandals, should be a bit more...commiserative. Why...they couldn't bring themselves to look at her: not her mother. Not her sister-in-law, Juliet. Nor any of her sisters. And certainly not her brother.

Her brother, reformed rogue and now proper brother, she could expect such a response from. Poppy, however, had far higher hopes for her brother-in-law.

Why, for all the saints under the sun, he owned a blasted gaming hell. Not even he could speak or meet her gaze.

No one could or did.

Poppy glanced down. And that included her dog, Sir Faithful. With his enormous head resting upon his equally enormous paws, he stared at Poppy with round, disappointed eyes.

Leaning down, Poppy stroked the dog at his side. "Et tu, Faithful?" she whispered, in a bid to break the endless quiet that had greeted this unhappy family gathering. "With your name, I expected better of you," she said in hushed tones. She softened that rebuke with another stroke, finding that spot. His leg twitched in reflexive pleasure, until his eyes closed, and he flipped onto his back—sated.

Poppy tamped down a sigh. If only one's family could be so easily appeased.

Yes, she quite expected this of most of them. But not her elder sister, Penelope. Penelope, who'd been caught in a compromising position with a stranger, should have offered far greater support than her silence.

The sisters' gazes caught across the room.

Poppy narrowed her eyes. "Disappointing," she mouthed.

"I'm sorry." Coming to her feet, Penelope claimed the seat next to Poppy.

"I feel I would be remiss if I didn't say that at least Lord Rochford wasn't *completely* naked," her favorite sister put in...unhelpfully.

Dropping an elbow on the arm of her King Louis XIV chair,

Poppy slapped a hand over her eyes.

Their mother's shuddery sob punctuated the end of Penelope's optimistic utterance, and her mother buried that sound unsuccessfully into her kerchief.

Poppy let her hand fall to her lap, so she could favor her favorite-until-now sister with a glare. "Really?" she mouthed.

"I tried," Penelope said from the corner of her mouth. "I was trying to help."

"You didn't," Poppy, Prudence, and Patrina muttered in unison.

As if to punctuate that very point, their mother let out another wail. "A *niiiiiiightmare.* What were you *thinking*, Poppy?"

Patrina, the eldest of their sisters, and also the first of the Tidemore sisters to be involved in a scandal, awkwardly patted the dowager countess' back. "It is going to be…all right," she finished weakly. "Why…why…it always works out."

Prudence flashed one of her bright-if-strained smiles. "Indeed. Patrina married Weston."

The towering marquess in question lifted his fingers.

"Weston didn't ruin her," Penelope reminded.

Weston let his arm fall.

Poppy shoved an elbow into her side, earning a grunt and glower. "What?" Penelope demanded. "I'm merely pointing out that she didn't marry the man who ruined her like I did."

Ryker scowled. "I didn't ruin you. You stumbled upon the place I'd been hiding."

His wife waggled an eyebrow. "And glad for it, you are."

He winked in response.

The Marquess of St. Cyr cleared his throat. "I'd like to point out, if I may, that I did not ruin Prudence."

As her family dissolved into a discussion of all past scandals and hers faded from the forefront, Poppy slipped to her feet, and started for the door. The key was to always know when to make one's retreat. It was an art, really. One that had unfortunately failed her with Rochford.

"Stop," Jonathan called out, freezing Poppy mid-stride. Sir Faithful knocked into the back of her legs, forcing her to complete that step. Blast and damn. She eyed that doorway to freedom. "Yes, you, Poppy."

Bloody hell. Drawing her shoulders back, Poppy faced the large gathering of Tidemores and their spouses and made the eternal march back to her previously abandoned seat.

"Now," Jonathan began as she'd taken her seat beside Penelope. He glanced around at the semi-circle of seating. "Obviously the Tidemores have faced far greater scandals—"

"Have we, Jonathan?" their mother cried. "Have we?"

"I am with Jonathan," Poppy slipped in. "I personally believe Patrina eloping was—" A single glare from her eldest sister effectively silenced the rest of that.

"All scandals inevitably…blow over." Her brother rested his folded hands on his belly. Her gaze went to his whitened knuckles, the telling tightness that belied all hint of his bid for calm.

"Blow over?" the dowager countess asked incredulously. She stole a horrified glance at the door and when she spoke, she did so in a furious whisper. "There is a house full of guests out there even now talking about…what has happened."

"Some greater one will come along, Mama," Patrina murmured, reaching for her mother's hand.

"That is your answer to…to…this?" Their white-faced mother slashed her spare palm in Poppy's direction.

This.

Yes, that is what she'd become. For even as the Dowager Countess of Sinclair loved her children…they were first and foremost their reputations.

"Mother," Patrina, the motherlike figure of the Tidemore sisters, chided.

Jonathan collected the untouched snifter of brandy at the arm table beside him. "That is my answer," he said tiredly. "What is the alternative?"

Their mother opened her mouth—

"Don't even finish it," he bit out through his teeth. "She's not marrying Rochford." He took a long swallow and then rested the drink on the arm of his chair. He glared at Poppy. "You are not marrying him."

Poppy inclined her head. "I assure you, I've no intention or desire to marry Rochford."

A swell of emotion flooded her chest. Jonathan had been both a father and brother. Any other gentleman would have demanded his sister or daughter marry to save her reputation. Not Jonathan.

He'd always loved them more than their rank.

A look passed between them.

"Thank you," she mouthed.

He discreetly waved off that silent expression of her gratitude. "Now," he continued. "As we've agreed that Poppy, under no circumstances is marrying the marquess—"

The dowager countess thumped the arm of her chair. "We most certainly did not agree to that." Angling her shoulder dismissively at her son, Poppy's mother stared directly at her. "You have no intention of allowing Lord Rochford to do right by you?"

Oh, blast and damn. Feeling very much the small girl she'd once been under those piercing stares, Poppy shifted in her chair. "He did not offer." Though in fairness, even if he had, she wouldn't take the bounder up on it.

"Your brother can change that."

And blast if Poppy didn't discover too late that she'd rather preferred her mother's tears and incoherent ramblings to this mercenary attempt to see her wed.

"Her brother has no intention—"

Poppy lifted up a hand staying the remainder of Jonathan's loyal showing of support. Appreciated though it was, she'd have no one—not even a beloved sibling—speak for her on the matter of her future.

"I'd rather he not." Poppy forced a smile. "I'm quite happy with my circumstances."

The dowager countess arched a single, dark brow. "And what circumstances are those?"

Ruined for marriage. Poppy, however, knew better than to say as much to the room before her. In the end she settled for vagueness. "My current ones."

"Ah, yes, while society is set ablaze by your actions, you give no thought to how any of this affects your siblings."

Guilt slipped in.

"Mother," Patrina scolded, and in a show of solidarity, her sister, heavy with child, quit her chair, ambled toward Poppy and struggled into the seat next to her.

Oh, bloody hell. Poppy squirmed.

"It is fine, Poppy," Prudence drifted to her feet and joined them at the already cramped sofa. "Move, I'm closer to Poppy."

"I resent that. It's the principal of what we're doing," Patrina whispered. "Not where we're sitting." Even so, she scooted over anyway.

A moment later, Poppy found herself sandwiched between all three of her sisters.

"How could you have not thought of Patrina in her delicate state? Why, why would you ever accompany a gentleman to Juliet's art room?"

Warning bells went off. Oh, blast. *This* was the resolute dowager countess. This was the unflappable version of her. And worse… this was the I'm-determined-to-marry-my-daughter-off-at-all-costs one. Poppy mustered a smile. "Why, I couldn't very well have painted him nude in Jonathan and Juliet's ballroom."

It was the wrong thing to say.

"P-Painted him…" Her mother strangled out, choking on the words, before attempting again. "Painted him…"

"N—" Poppy went to finish for her but Penelope shoved her knee against Poppy's leg, silencing her.

"Nude," Jonathan finished through his teeth.

The room erupted with chastisements and cries. With the exception of Ryker who, cracking his knuckles, looked ready for battle.

Oh, blast and damn. "It is going to be all right, Mother," she said soothingly, attempting those expert tones adopted by Juliet and Patrina.

Their mother sobbed all the harder. "Of course it is not going to be all *riiiiight.*"

Whimpering, Sir Faithful dragged himself under Poppy's chair.

Nay…at least, not in the way that would make it "all right" for the dowager countess: with her last unwed daughter, married to a proper, respectable gentleman. Had it been any other time, she'd have happily pointed out to her mother that she had no intention of wedding, either way, so all the hullabaloo over her reputation was really a bit much.

Damned Rochford for ruining her. If he'd been set on destroying her reputation, at least let her complete the painting she'd been intending to capture.

Juliet cleared her throat. All eyes swung to the current Countess of Sinclair. "Might I suggest, given the guests, that many of us return to the ballroom?" The former Tidemore governess, she could still command a room with the ease of Wellington himself.

Poppy's former governess held her gaze; the bond they shared as artists had only cemented their relationship through the years.

Alas, Juliet had taught Poppy and her sisters all too well about strength. "I'm not going anywhere," Prudence insisted.

"When Patrina was ruined, was I permitted to take part in that discussion?" Poppy asked the room at large, effectively silencing them. She turned to Prudence. "Or when your scandal hit, was I invited to take part on the discussion about your future with Christian?"

"It's not the same," Prudence muttered.

Poppy arched an eyebrow, until her elder sister dropped her gaze to her slippers. The only difference being that Poppy was the youngest of their clan of Tidemores and regardless of how old she might, in fact, be, she would forever, in their eyes, be the baby of the family. Sensing victory, she turned to Penelope. "And what of you, Penny? When you were caught in a compromising position with Ryker, where was I for that discussion that occurred between you and Jonathan and Mother?"

Penelope pressed her lips together, and mumbled something.

Poppy cupped a hand around her ear. "What was that?" she pressed. "I could not—"

"You were in the corridor…listening at the door."

Folding her arms, Poppy nodded slowly. "I was *outside* the room. Now, all of a sudden, there's some new code within the family that makes my public scandal a familial discussion?"

The dowager countess snorted. "All of a sudden you are concerned with your privacy?"

"Enough. Juliet is correct." Her brother caught his wife's fingers in his and Poppy lingered wistfully upon that small, but significant touch. One that spoke of devotion, a steadfast love and commitment to standing shoulder to shoulder beside her. *I wanted that…* She'd also given up on it. Her art was now enough…that decision went back far beyond the compromising situation she'd found herself in. "It would be wise if all of you return to the ballroom so that I can speak freely with Poppy about Rochford's actions."

Rochford's actions? "I'll not have anyone take ownership of my decisions or actions." She might be ruined, but she was the mistress of her own fate, and would own every last one of her mistakes. "I am the one responsible for my situation."

"Respectable gentleman do not sneak off with the intention of ruining a lady," Patrina quietly put forward, as she accepted her husband's hand and came to her feet "*Rochford* is the one to blame."

As if taking that cue, Prudence jumped up. "Who would have imagined Rochford? He's really not known for being a rogue or rake or cad."

Welcoming that slight diversion—even if it was on the character of the man who'd compromised her—she pounced. "I know," Poppy said on a rush. "He really seemed quite safe for my purposes."

"Your…purposes?" Their mother strangled and choked on those words.

Poppy sighed. "Painting, Mother. I've already told you…I sought to *paint* him." She hefted an imagined paintbrush and made several strokes through the air. He'd gotten no more than his jacket and shirt off and had been reaching for the waistband of his trousers before a collection of guests had come wandering in as if they'd been touring the Egyptian Rooms at the Royal Museum. "One should expect if I was to be ruined that I should at least have had the opportunity to see the gentleman in all his naked form."

Jonathan reached for his glass in one fluid motion and downed the contents of it.

"See him in his…in his…?" Her mother's eyes bulged from her face.

Poppy opened her mouth to reiterate the source of her discontent.

"Hold that thought if you're wise," Penelope whispered from the side of her mouth.

Poppy bristled. "It's tru—"

"A horrid idea, bringing that up," Penelope cut in. "Horrid."

"That will be all," Jonathan said tightly, as he set his glass down. Oh, thank God. She hopped up.

"*Not* you," her brother ordered, staying all hopes of Poppy's flight.

He glanced around the room, brimming with their siblings and spouses.

"I am not leaving," Penelope began. "I…" Her pronouncement faded as Poppy faced her.

"I'm fine, Penelope," she said quietly. For the whole of her life, well-meaning though their intentions may have been, her siblings had all sought to baby Poppy. "Go."

Penelope drew back as if she'd been gut-punched. A moment later, the large gathering stood, and filed from the room…each sister and her spouse unable to meet Poppy's gaze—until only Penelope and her husband remained.

God love Ryker for being the only one to look her in the eye. He leaned down. "I can always have him killed," he offered in his graveled faint Cockney; and but for the faintest glint in his eyes, anyone—Poppy herself included—would have believed his offer a true one.

Her lips twitched, and she repressed that smile. "I promise I shall think hard on it," she said with false somberness.

Leaning up on tiptoe, she kissed her brother-in-law on the cheek.

A moment later, only Jonathan and her mother remained.

Poppy glanced to her mother and found the dowager countess' displeased gaze could still raise abject terror in her breast. "There is no way I intend to leave this room."

And, in the course of her twenty-one years, Poppy had gleaned the important skill of selecting one's battles most carefully. Having dispelled with Jonathan's help a room full of distressed siblings, facing the pair before her could only ever be a victory.

"Well?" her mother snapped. "Do you have nothing to say?"

Anything more than had already been said? "As Prudence pointed out, Rochford's reputation as being a staid, proper gentleman quite precedes him." Of course, he'd not truly been a gentleman. He'd been some cad who'd had no intention of doing anything other than maneuvering her into a scandal and earning some sizeable wager he'd placed at White's. "How was I to know Rochford's intentions were anything but honorable?"

"Your clue was when he met you alone and offered to take his clothes off," Jonathan snapped. "*That* was the clue."

Poppy shifted on her seat. Yes, well, he quite had a point there. Still, it bore pointing out… "I asked him to."

Their mother dropped her head into her hands and shook it back and forth in a slow, agonized rhythm.

"You stepped into a trap," Jonathan said flatly, and the disappointment in his gaze cut sharp in ways that pierced far more painfully than any spoken word.

A trap is precisely what it had been. With the handful of exchanges they'd had with one another, he'd spoken of his appreciation of art. "I know that now." Unable to meet her brother's eyes, Poppy glanced down at her lap. With the knowledge he had aptly displayed, she'd taken him as more than one of those "nodders", as she'd come to think of the other gents in London. What an utter fool she'd been. Out of all this situation, what she regretted most was her failure to identify a bounder in her midst.

"This cannot be u–undone," their mother whispered, her voice cracking.

No, it couldn't. Alas, Poppy couldn't muster even a feigned amount of the expected tears ladies in her circumstances were supposed to muster. It was an unfair world that permitted men freedoms over any choice while women were to always conduct themselves one way. Annoyance brought her head up. "It was only art," Poppy said defensively. Albeit still unfinished art, as she didn't even have the benefit of her nude model.

"It was you alone with a partially naked man," Jonathan shot back, and their mother broke down crying again. He turned an impatient glare on the dowager countess. "As you've stated, there can be no changing what happened. Therefore, we need to determine what becomes of Poppy."

What becomes of Poppy…? Her fingers made automatic fists. There it was again, the expectation that others make determinations about her fate.

Two sets of eyes swung to Poppy.

"Well, that has a rather ominous ring to it," she said under her breath.

Her brother went on as though she hadn't spoken. "There are two options—"

Their mother brightened.

"Not marriage to Rochford," Poppy and Jonathan said in time, and the dowager countess instantly deflated.

"Poppy either retreats to the countryside with you, Patrina, and Weston until the scandal abates. Or she remains here in London to confront the storm."

She sat up straighter in her chair. "As I see it, there's really only one suitable option." And it certainly wasn't making herself the burdensome third wheel, accompanying one of her sisters during her confinement.

Jonathan stood. "Precisely," he agreed, gathering the decanter and the glass. With the articles in tow, he started for the sideboard. "It is settled. You'll go with Mother."

That had certainly not been the option she'd been thinking of. Poppy frowned. "I'm not Patrina." Her sister would be journeying to the country for her confinement. The last thing Poppy wanted or would ever allow herself to be was the underfoot, unmarried aunt. "I'll not be a burden on her at this time."

Their mother scoffed. "Now you'd express a concern over her delicate condition?"

Poppy's cheeks heated. It was a deserved criticism. And the fact that Jonathan made no rush to defend this time, indicated he quite agreed with their mother in this.

Jonathan started for his desk. "Then Juliet and I will accompany you to the country, until this blows over. We'll depart for Yorkshire on the morn." With that, he claimed a seat, removed several sheets of paper, and dipping a pen in the crystal inkwell, proceeded to write.

"Yorkshire?" she echoed dumbly. They'd leave London for Yorkshire, that far-flung property they rarely visited? *Of course…he's selected it because he'd have you in hiding.*

"It is decided then," their mother said, coming to her feet. "I'll see Poppy's belongings packed."

"I'm not joining *any* of you," she said simply.

That brought Jonathan's head up from whatever business he'd previously directed his attention to.

"What do you mean you're not joining any of us?" their mother demanded, and before Poppy could reply, the dowager countess quickly turned that question on her son. "What does she mean?"

"You are going, Poppy," he said through his teeth.

"I'm not. If I retreat, the world will take that as an admission of my guilt. I've no reason to hide, Jonathan." Her greatest mistake hadn't been in her decision to paint a naked man, but rather, the man she'd selected as her subject. She turned her palms up. "I concede to my mistakes, but I'll not allow any of you to go about hiding me like I am some dirty familial secret to be shamed for my actions." With that, she marched for the door.

"Get back here this instant," their mother cried. "You cannot be seen this evening. Or ever."

"Ever seems a tad too long for my *sins*." Poppy continued on her way.

"Poppy," the dowager countess bit out.

Poppy reached for the door handle, and drew it open.

Penelope fell into the room, effectively ruining Poppy's grand exit. With all the aplomb one who'd been caught shamelessly eavesdropping could manage, her elder sister rose.

"Really?" Poppy mouthed.

"You were listening in on my ruination discussion, too," her sister whispered.

Yes, well, she had a fair point there.

"What is it, Penelope?" Jonathan asked impatiently as Penelope closed the door behind her.

Lifting her palm she glanced about the room. "I could not help but hear the current...debate."

"Of course you couldn't help but hear, you had your ear pressed to the panel," Poppy drawled.

"And would like to put forward an...alternative solution to Poppy," her sister went on over her.

Poppy paused. lingering her focus on two words of distinction: to Poppy. Not "for" Poppy. In a world where everyone, her own kin included, was content to make decisions for her, with her opinion on it more an afterthought, Penelope would give her the gift of that control. "Go on," Poppy said solemnly.

"Prudence has all she can handle with three little ones about. As for Patrina, she will be focused on the delivery of her babe, and unless I'm mistaken in what I'd heard, Poppy has no wish to impose on that intimate time."

Poppy nodded. She'd been unfairly bothersome to her sister. She owed her a debt that could not be repaid.

"She should have thought of that before Rochford," their mother said, tears welling in her eyes yet again.

Jonathan came forward with a kerchief that the dowager countess promptly took, and dabbed at her eyes with.

"Yes, yes," Penelope said impatiently. "And Jonathan shouldn't have put an indecent offer to Juliet and Prudence shouldn't have made a deal with a rogue, and I shouldn't have been caught sneaking around the Duke and Duchess of Somerset's gardens. And yet, that happened, and it all worked out for the best...for all."

"It also resulted in each of you marrying," their mother's needless reminder was muted by the rumpled kerchief she held to her face.

Poppy stiffened. "Surely you are not suggesting that I marry him." She'd sooner meet the cad across the dueling field herself than to him for all time.

Penelope grimaced. "Egads, no. No. Never. *Ever.*" She slashed her palms back and forth for emphasis.

"What are you suggesting?" Jonathan demanded impatiently.

"I'm suggesting Poppy move in to the Paradise Hotel...with me and Ryker and Paisley. She'll be away from prying eyes, and yet, not run off in shame." Her elder sister glanced over. "And with the renovations underway, we would welcome help with the artistic design of the establishment."

Poppy's heart thumped in her chest. The loudest thing in a suddenly still room. What her sister presented...what she proposed represented not only an ability for Poppy to remain in London, not being run off like the Tidemores' latest scandal to be hidden, but seeing to the artistic design. There she'd select and set the aesthetic, influencing the artwork that would remain. A mark left by her.

In the end, it was Jonathan who broke the silence. "If Poppy would like—"

"Surely you are not seriously considering this as an option, Jonathan," their mother squawked.

"I would" Poppy said quickly. "I would like very much to join Penny."

Their mother slapped the kerchief down. "Absolutely not. Why... why...anything can go wrong with Poppy there, Jonathan." As if Poppy weren't present before them, the dowager countess lowered her voice to a scandalized whisper. "Anything."

Poppy bristled. "I resent that."

When her mother and brother glanced over with like expressions, she folded her arms defensively at her chest. "What?"

Clearing her throat, Penelope slid between Poppy and the two most disapproving of the Tidemore lot. "I personally vow that no scandal shall befall Poppy as long as she resides with me."

"No further scandal," Jonathan said tiredly, and then he leveled a sharp look at Poppy. "It is decided then. Poppy will reside at the Paradise."

Poppy repressed a smile.

Why, it would seem her ruination hadn't been so very terrible, after all.

CHAPTER 3

¶IN MAKING THE DECISION TO hand over the title of Earl of
Maxwell without a fight, and losing all the properties and wealth
that went with that respected title, Tristan Poplar, now the Baron
Bolingbroke, came to appreciate that his ruin had been far worse
than he'd anticipated.

Seated in the middle of the empty ballroom floor, with his
youngest sister in a like repose across from him, Tristan took
another long swig of brandy from his flask.

Except...

He lingered his gaze on the letters etched with the gleaming
silver. TP Earl of Maxwell.

Turning the article over in his hands, he studied it, the value
and quality previously unappreciated. Now, however, the silver
represented wealth and prestige. Was the damned thing even his?
Purchased with funds belonging to another man, the answer was
decidedly...no.

Tristan took another drink.

"It is not *all* bad," Claire murmured.

He quirked an eyebrow. "Oh?"

"Well...there is...or...and..."

As if on cue, a wail went up from somewhere outside the ballroom, followed by their mother's diatribe, which came muffled
and broken. "...you cannot...that does not belong to...put it in
the pile with the other..."

She released a sigh. "Yes, Yes. Well, it is certainly not good. I'll allow you that." Claire plucked the flask from his hand and took an impressive swallow.

Yes, it was dire indeed when not even his eternal optimist of a sister could find a single bit of light in the entirely dark situation. He narrowed his eyes. A sister who had entirely too much ease downing liquor. "Where did you learn to drink spirits?"

Claire wiped the back of her hand over her mouth, and then handed back Tristan's—nay, the new Lord Maxwell's—flask. "Oh, hush. I'm twenty-two, a woman grown. There are far greater things to worry about than my drinking habits."

And oddly, that proved *true*.

The Poplar name had been eviscerated and—with the late baron responsible for stealing not only a child but that boy's rightful place in the world—rightfully so.

The previously inherited Maxwell title that had brought greater riches than ten other titles of the peerage combined—had reverted back to its correct owner.

Tristan had instead taken over the title of Baron Bolingbroke; a more apt title for him, there wasn't. The reverted title that brought no wealth and, certainly now, no respect.

As such, there was only one thing a family could do when faced with such a change of circumstances and the destruction of one's previously respectable standing in society—flee.

Brightening, Claire picked her head up. "I've never been to the wilds of Devon. So, there is *that*."

"The optimist." Tristan leaned over and ruffled the top of her curls.

She swatted at his hand. "*You* are the one who's always been the optimist."

"Yes," he said wistfully. Even in Boney's war, he'd seen a way out. He'd clung to hope, and fought back the demons of war that haunted him still, with memories of the friendships he'd forged, and the soldiers who'd gone on to live happy lives because of his actions in battle. "You are correct on that score."

She winked. "I usually am."

Of course, all that optimism had come before. Before all had been lost and his honor left in tatters about him.

A delicate hand settled on his arm, bringing his attention over to his youngest sister. Her usually teasing features were set in a somber sketch better suited to a stranger, and the blade of guilt low in his stomach twisted all the more. "You've always spoken so fondly of the wilds of Dartmoor," she said almost hesitantly. "I thought it might be a grand adventure for all of us." Claire lowered her voice an octave and, as she spoke, gestured with her palms. "Hundreds upon hundreds of remote moorlands. Hills so high to climb one might almost touch the sky." She let her arms fall to her side. "Unless…all of that was a lie."

"It wasn't a lie," he said tiredly. The troubled glimmer in her eyes managed to break through his self-focus on their circumstances. "Thick layers of peat cover much of the land," he murmured. "It's topped with bright green moss. The bogs of Devon, they say, are a pixie's playground…" Claire's eyes went so wide, she was transformed in his mind to the small girl who'd sat in awed silence through his telling about Dartmoor. Only, she wasn't a child. She was an unmarried woman whose reputation was in tatters through no fault of her own.

Claire stared questioningly at him, and he forced himself to finish that whimsical telling.

"And when one walks the hills in dark, with the moon shining down, one could almost believe the legends that said those creatures do, in fact, dance throughout the land."

She sighed, and dropped her chin atop her knees. "It sounds magnificent."

"It is," he said automatically. It was. Or it would be…under other circumstances brought about than the Poplars running into hiding.

Claire brightened. "Then, it should be just fine. A grand adventure that we will all embark on together." Just like that, with her usual childlike enthusiasm restored, she spoke on in an excited rush. "I don't remember much of it. All my memories largely came from what you shared."

"Yes, well, you were young when the Maxwell title passed on to Father."

All the air was sucked from the ballroom.

Passed on.

Passed on suggested a rightful claim to holdings and title. Claims which the Poplars hadn't a right to.

Swiping the flask up from the spot beside him, he took another long drink of the fine French spirits.

Claire cleared her throat. "At the very least, I am elated at the prospect of rediscovering the land I was born to."

Their mother's cries spilled into the ballroom once more. "See that they a–are s–sent to D–D–*Dartmoooooor,*" she wailed.

Claire turned a tense-looking smile up. "Even if Mother is not excited."

No, their mother had always abhorred their ancestral holdings and craved an existence in the heart of London. Her wants, however, were secondary to the two younger sisters reliant upon Tristan. He ran a hand over his face. "I'm sorry, Claire." Sorry for so damned much. He should have seen her married. But there'd been no reason to rush her into any match. Or so he'd thought. "Oomph," Tristan grunted, and rubbed at his upper arm smarting from an unexpected punch. "What in blazes was that for?"

"For being so...so glum." She punched him again. "I'm not worried about my circumstances, Tristan."

Another shriek filled the corridors, and Tristan and Claire both winced. "You cannot simply...that is mine...do you hear me...?"

"I think they heard her all the way in Dartmoor," Tristan muttered.

"She is going to struggle mightily with this," his sister conceded, in more somber tones that he'd ever heard her use. "I for one don't much care if some proper lords and ladies give us the cut direct. If a gentleman doesn't wish to know me or marry me because of actions beyond my control? Well, then I'm quite better off without such a bounder in my life."

He smiled wistfully. "When did you grow up?"

"Years ago," she shot back, and then she scooted over so that they both faced the entrance of a ballroom that had once been filled with guests to greet them. No more. All that had come and now gone. "I'm fine and Faye will be fine and Mother, too."

Her promise was punctuated by another shriek. "Do not take that...I said..."

"In time, she'll be fine, then," Claire amended.

No. The baroness would not be. She'd forever mourn her lost title and connections and position as a leading society hostess. She'd weep over the matches her two unwed daughters would not make.

And one day, his romantic sisters, who'd been set on love matches, would turn cynical at finding there were no honorable gents to overlook the crimes of a family.

"Perhaps." He forced himself to concede that assurance his sister likely didn't even realize she sought.

A pair of footsteps echoed outside the ballroom.

They both looked up, as their butler—now Percival Northrop's butler—entered. "The Marquess of St. Cyr," the loyal servant, who looked one more utterance away from crying, announced Christian Villiers, one of Tristan's only two friends in the world.

"See, we haven't been shut out by *all* the peerage."

Tristan gave her a look.

Claire stuck her tongue out. "Boo, I despise this serious side of you." Hopping up, she went and greeted St. Cyr. "Christian."

"Lady Claire." The marquess dropped a deep bow.

"No need for formalities, Christian," Claire scolded, as she went on tiptoe and kissed the taller man's cheek.

"How is he?" Christian murmured.

"Quite dreary," Tristan's imp of a sister said on a less than discreet whisper. "Perhaps you can help."

"I hear you," Tristan snapped.

"See?" Claire continued in those exaggerated hushed tones. "You've been warned," she said as she departed; lifting her fingers in a waggle, she didn't even bother to glance back.

Without hesitation, St. Cyr came over and joined Tristan on the floor. But then, the both of them having slept on muddied battlefields with horse shite and soil their only mattress, they'd returned not much ones for formalities.

"How are they?" his friend asked without preamble.

"Claire and Faye are putting on a brave show," Tristan said, not pretending to misunderstand the other man's question. "And Mother…"

"You cannot take the silver," the baroness screeched. "That is *miiiiiine*. I brought that—"

St. Cyr's lips curved up in a wry grin.

"As one would expect," both men said together.

The brief moment of levity faded as quick as it had come. Tristan had gotten his fellow soldiers out of entrapments which by all rights should have seen them all dead. He'd survived countless frontal assaults in the head of battle.

But this…this was one situation he could not put to rights.

"Where are they going?"

"Off to Dartmoor," Tristan answered quietly. What was to have been a fortnight given to them had been snatched away. Tristan had just hours to empty out what did belong to him, and leave. To give his fingers something to do, he picked up his flask once more. It was the wrong thing to do. Those etched letters within gleamed back at him, taunting. Mocking.

"And what of you?"

"I cannot leave," Tristan replied. His friend would know him enough to gather what Tristan's own family had yet to realize—he wasn't going to Dartmoor. Not yet. Someday. Eventually. But not now. Now, there was too much to be done. Too much to set to rights. Or attempt to, anyway. "If I flee, it will only fuel the scandal and the world's perception of my guilt."

"Nor should you flee. It will, however, do well for your mother to escape some of the…" St. Cyr's face pulled. "Attention."

"Indeed," Tristan said dryly. Though, it was more likely that being relegated to the moors of Devon would only increase his mother's histrionics.

"And what is the plan, then?"

That was the rub of it. Tristan could look down a field of two hundred enemies, with only fifteen men at his side, and know the precise course of attack, but in this instance, it was all a murky haze of confusion still. "I don't know." He finally brought himself to make that humbling admission. "I, Tristan Poplar, have no bloody idea how to disentangle myself from this. A fortnight ago"— before the scandal had broken and been splashed across every last scandal sheet—"I could have made an advantageous match that would have helped my sisters. And now?" Lifting the stolen flask in a mock toast to his fallibility, Tristan allowed himself another drink, before passing it over to his friend. St. Cyr accepted the small silver scrap, and set it down without so much as a glance. "Now, my name isn't even good enough to secure membership to White's and Brooks's." His previous membership had been revoked. "Other gentlemen and ladies turned on their heels and marched to the opposite end of the street when I was near."

"You've never been one to care about society's opinion," his friend pointed out quietly.

"It is not the point," he gritted out, dragging a hand through his hair.

"Then what is the point?" St. Cyr put forward, with no recrimination to that question.

It was…a humbling experience for one who'd been the *ton's* previously beloved rogue. "Now, I cannot find a person to so much as look me in the eye."

His friend gave him a look.

"You and Blackthorne excluded," Tristan said gruffly of his two friends, who'd stuck beside him through hell on earth. Restless, Tristan jumped to his feet and began to pace. "How can I care for my sisters? I've a name that is blackened. I've barely two coins to rub together." He stopped abruptly, and when he spoke, did so on a whisper, lest his mother or sisters chose this moment to be marching by. "And a townhouse in London with damned holes in the roof and rotted floorboards and an infestation of rats." He could not allow his mother and sisters to remain or return to a place infested with rodents. "Rats, St. Cyr. Rats." Unable to meet the other man's eyes, Tristan turned and faced the dais where orchestras had once played and the marble floor where couples had once twirled throughout.

And they would again one day…just with another family residing here.

His senses heightened since his days at war, an inherited skill that would never leave him, he registered his friend coming over. "Here," St. Cyr said gruffly, handing over a folded sheet of paper.

Accepting the page, Tristan stared quizzically down at it. "What is this?" he asked, skimming the contents.

The Paradise Hotel…En suite…Duration of Stay—Indefinite.

Tristan whipped his head up. "I don't… What…?"

"My wife has spoken to her sister, Penelope; they want you to have this…for as long as you require it. Until you find your feet again."

Penelope, now the Viscountess Chatham, along with her husband, had allowed Tristan rooms at the viscount's latest properties. Emotion clogged his throat: shame, regret, and along with those emotions, appreciation. "I—"

"Do not say you cannot take it," his friend interrupted. "That is what we do...one helps where one is able."

Tristan's fingers curled reflexively around the corners of the page, and it crunched noisily in the expansive ballroom. "I don't know what to say," he said hoarsely.

St. Cyr slapped him hard on the back. "There's nothing you need to say. It will work out," he vowed, and started for the door. "Oh, there's but one more thing," he added; lifting a finger up, he turned back.

Tristan stared at his friend expectantly.

"My wife offered that on one condition..." Oh, bloody hell. What now? "She insists that you do not do anything so foolish as find yourself a wealthy heiress and marry for anything less than love."

And for the first time since his world had been turned, flipped upside down, Tristan managed a real laugh; until mirth shook his frame. "You may assure Lady Prudence that the last thing she need worry after is me making a match...with anyone."

St. Cyr clicked his heels together. "I'll be sure and relay that to my wife."

After he'd gone, Tristan focused on the gift his friend had given him.

A place to stay, payment free, with a pledge required of him.

It was, however, a pledge that had been all too easy to give...not because Tristan was too proud to make an advantageous match. Because he wasn't. Following his family's ignominious fall from grace, he would do anything to secure his sisters' future. The truth, however, remained that not a single lady in the whole of England would trade her family's fortune and respectability for a connection to Tristan's besmirched title.

The best he could hope for was that in the near future some other scandal replaced his.

Until then, his name was as good as ruined.

CHAPTER 4

ℐT COULD ALWAYS BE WORSE.

Not much worse, however.

Standing in one of the vacant rooms of the Paradise Hotel, Poppy, with her hands on her hips, assessed the spacious and very dreary chambers. From the Griffin mahogany secretary and matching carved folio stand to the Dutch Neoclassical carved cabinet, the rooms evinced opulence…at the cost of space.

"It is something, is it not?" Penelope piped in, pride brimming from her voice.

"Uh…it is…certainly *something*."

Either failing to hear or choosing to ignore the less than enthusiastic endorsement of the suite, Penelope skipped over to the four-poster bed. The massive piece had been draped and re-draped with heavy netting that gave it the look of some ancient medieval pyre. "We've spared no expenses, and Ryker's enlisted the aid of only the most sought after cabinet-makers," her sister was saying, her form now lost on the opposite end of that bed with drapery over it. "Of course, there is always room for improvement…"

With her sister prattling on, Poppy did another circle around the room—or as much as one could manage with the furniture claiming most of the available space at the center.

The brightest bit of color within the hotel rooms came from the silvery-grey muslin curtains.

Grey?

She repressed a shudder.

"This room is as of yet, unfinished," Penelope explained. "However, a…guest in in need of lodging…" That slight pause, stirred Poppy's curiosity. "And I was hoping you might…" Her sister popped out on the other side of the four-poster bed. "…add your 'Poppy touch'."

"You cannot allow anyone to remain in this room," Poppy blurted.

Penelope glanced around with befuddled eyes. "What is wrong with this room?"

"Nothing," Poppy said, earning a pleased nod from her elder sister. "There are any *number* of things wrong with this room."

Penelope drew her shoulders back. "I beg your pardon."

How was it possible, two sisters, so often of like opinions could be so very apart on basic aesthetics. The curtains and upholstery… that was the easiest place to start. "It is not *my* pardon you should seek, but rather that of the patron who will be inhabiting these rooms," she continued on over her sister's protestations. "Grey curtains. Grey velvet sofas." Poppy stalked over to the bed and lifted a pillow. "Grey." Tossing it aside, she lifted the edge of the coverlet. "Grey." She peeled the article back, and paused…

"White," Penelope said triumphantly, and with an arch look, she marched over. "Either way, I'll have you know, it's silver."

And apparently, Penny's eyes were off, too, which no doubt accounted for the current state of her hotels. "Grey."

Emitting a sound of frustration, Penelope set to work righting the sheets. "Furthermore, you're messing the room. I've asked you to help tidy it, not make it uninhabitable."

Poppy bit her tongue to keep from pointing out that the spacious suite had found itself in that state long before she had ruffled the bedding.

"You asked for my help, Penny," she reminded, as her sister set to work righting the sheets.

"I asked you to design a painting that would…make the room more cheerful."

More cheerful? As it was, the suite was at best dark. At worst… grim. She pitied the poor blighter who found himself calling this home. "A mural," Poppy corrected. "Have you forgotten every art lesson Juliet gave us?" And then the truth slammed into her with all the weight of a fast-moving carriage. She rocked back. "You gave me a pity assignment."

Head bent, Penelope devoted all her focus to straightening the coverlet. "I don't know what you're talking about."

Narrowing her eyes, Poppy came 'round the other side of her bed and shoved back the draping so she could face her sister. "Why, you don't actually *believe* your establishment requires improvements."

"Everything can be improved," Penelope defended, her tones as sheepish as her blush.

"You sought to give me a task."

"That is *preposterous*," Penelope said quickly. Too quickly. And by the deepening color that splotched her sister's cheeks, very much on the mark.

With a growl of frustration, Poppy let the fabric slip from her fingers, so her sister was lost to the other side of the four-poster bed. A pity assignment. That is what she'd been given. Nay, worse. Stalking around the mammoth piece of furniture, she faced her sister. She jabbed a finger at Penelope. "The only reason you invited me here was out of pity."

"Of course not," Penelope said tightly.

Her outrage burned sharper in her veins. "I expected society to see me as a poor, pathetic Tidemore, ruined by scandal. But you, Penelope?" Penelope who'd been ruined and had known just what it felt like to only be seen as that single event in her life. She leveled an accusatory stare at her favorite-until-now sibling. "*You?*" All the fight went out of her, as she sank onto the edge of the comfortable mattress.

Soft but firm.

It was something her sister and husband had gotten right in the design of the hotel room…and a nonsensical detail to note. And yet, safer than acknowledging that even among one's family, one found herself an object of pity.

With a sigh, Poppy tossed herself back and stared at the mahogany lattice overhead, the frame also draped in grey.

The mattress dipped as her sister joined her on the bed. Wordlessly, she lay down beside Poppy, so that they rested shoulder to shoulder.

In the end, Penelope broke the impasse. "I don't pity you, Poppy. I could never pity you."

Poppy angled her head and gave her sibling a pointed look.

"Oh, fine, by the very definition of pity, I am filled with regret."

Poppy made to shove herself up on her elbows, but her sister settled a firm hand on hers, staying her. "But not for the reasons you think, Poppy. I regret that some bounder sullied your name. And I'm sorry that too many will fail to see anything but that scandal when they see you." Penelope turned her head so she could look Poppy squarely in the eyes. "But I could never pity you. When I blubbered and sulked about my scandal, you've only held your head high and proud, and I could only wish to have your strength."

Poppy's lips pulled. "That is a perfectly splendid apology."

Her sister gave an awkward toss of her head, knocking her chignon loose. "Why, thank you." Penelope tempered her smile, and her features settled into a solemn mask. "I'd have you know, Poppy, I did invite you to stay with Ryker and I because I don't believe you should be run off, and I wanted you here."

"You just didn't believe your hotel required any true work," she said dryly.

Penelope stuck her tongue out. "I did think you might add paintings—"

"Murals."

"To the guest suites."

"Thank you," Poppy said dryly.

Her sister shoved an elbow lightly against her side. "And I did want you to add an additional touch to these rooms."

"Because the guest is so important?" She was expected to believe that, when her sister and brother-in-law, Ryker Black, as a rule didn't allow rank to matter in any way?

"Because it's Lord Maxwell, and Prudence mentioned he was decidedly glum and asked—"

Poppy sat up quickly. "Maxwell?" she echoed, her heart doing a little leap, just as it had when she'd been a girl.

"Yes, well, I suppose you're correct," Penelope pushed up onto her elbows. "He is no longer Lord Maxwell," she said, misunderstanding the reason for Poppy's shock.

Oh, her girlish fascination with the lord who loved dogs and her determination to bring the earl up to scratch had eventually faded…she'd too much pride to pine for or woo a man still gallivanting about town with his fancy pieces. And yet…he'd become more of a friend over the years, and she despised the idea of the once charming earl, reduced to a glum figure who needed cheering up.

"He'll occupy these rooms, and Pru thought you might add a touch of something different to make them more cheerful." Penelope thinned her eyes. "Not," her sister spoke on a rush, "because there is anything wrong with silver."

"Grey," Poppy said as an afterthought. She hopped up, and set across the room to where her art supplies had been set and since forgotten—until now. "When is he arriving?"

"Within the fortnight."

"*A fortnight?*" Muttering under her breath, Poppy hurriedly opened her art case and drew out her brushes and paints. "Why didn't you say something sooner?" And here she'd gone on and on debating the décor, losing all this time.

"I've seen you craft great masterpieces in far less time."

"That was different," she said distractedly. "They weren't…" For Tristan.

"For Maxwell?" her sister hazarded.

Sir Faithful awoke from his slumber. Scrambling to his feet, the dog gave a lusty bark of canine agreement.

Poppy briefly paused, and glanced over her shoulder. "Do not be silly. And he's not Maxwell, he's Tristan. Christian's best friend and—"

"A man you were smitten with—"

"When I was a girl," Poppy neatly slipped in. "You've nothing to worry about. Now…" Returning her attention to her work, Poppy gathered up her apron and tied it at the waist. "If you'll excuse me?" Surveying the walls for the ideal canvas for her subject—her still unknown subject—Poppy considered her options.

"I will leave you to your business, then."

Poppy dimly registered Penelope's words, and then reminded herself to lift a hand in farewell.

Something cheerful. And yet…somehow elegant, as Tristan would only occupy these rooms temporarily and then another guest would replace him. She bit at the end of her brush, thinking. Thinking.

"Oh, and Poppy?" her sister called her attention over once more. "I didn't say I was worried earlier about you and Tristan being near one another." She swept her lashes down until she stared at Poppy through imperceptible slits. "Should I be?"

Poppy rolled her eyes. "I've far greater judgment than to fall for Tristan Poplar." Even if he did have a way with dogs. And even if he did have a tangle of dark curls and—

Enough. You're no longer the young girl mooning over the dream of the charming rogue…

"Of course," Penelope said in serious tones. "Lord Rochford is proof and testament enough of—" She ducked as in one fluid motion, Poppy removed her slipper and tossed it across the room.

The moment the door was closed behind her, Poppy returned her work to walls. Her sister now gone, Poppy retrained all her energies on designing the mural for Tristan's room.

Tristan, who loved dogs…and fishing and…women. He loved those, as well. Scandalous ones, which, of course, had been what had settled it for her. Far too clever to be offended, even with all her efforts and the hope that he'd at last see her there, she had come to accept this truth—love and an awareness of another, was simply not something that could be forced. Nor should it be.

As such, she could not, nor would ever, hold a grudge against Tristan for his inability to see her as a woman. He would, however, remain…a friend.

"And a friend who is in surprisingly more dire straits than I am," she said into the quiet. Folding her arms, she tapped the brush in a distracted staccato against her shoulder.

Elegant enough to appeal to any future guest, but specific to apply to Tristan…

The clock atop the mantel ticked a gratingly impatient rhythm. *Tick-tock-tick-tock-tick.*

"That is really quite enough," she muttered. Stomping over to the bed, she gathered up two pillows. Poppy marched across the room and promptly buried that timepiece.

She'd always been rubbish at designing under pressure, and even more so when she was creating work for family—she grimaced—not that Tristan was family. He wasn't. He was like family. Not a brother, per se. A friend. He was a friend. As such, his opinion of her eventual creation mattered.

"Think," she whispered as she returned to the center of the room. The muffled beat of the clock echoed, oddly more incessant.

"Th—" Widening her eyes, Poppy tossed her brush down. "*Of course.*"

And with the first real enthusiasm for anything art-related since Lord Rochford had lured her away under false pretenses, Poppy gathered up a pencil and set to work outlining her design on the previously empty crisp, white plaster. Tireless, Poppy sketched until the afternoon light faded and ushered in the London night sky. Servants filtered in and then out, lighting candles, and fanning a fire, and through their noiseless entry and departure she attended her mural.

Nay, Poppy's shoulders ached and her muscles strained from the continuous efforts, but the exhilaration of creating something upon a previously blank canvas won out over her discomfort.

Setting her brush down, Poppy retreated several paces and angling her head, left and then right, she eyed her mural. She squinted in the dim lighting, attempting to bring the details into sharper focus.

The door opened. "I'm not hungry," she said for the sixth time since one of four maids had attempted to bring her food.

"Which is good, as I've not come with food," her sister drawled, sidling up beside her. "You've finished."

"Not quite." Poppy gestured with the end of her brush at her work. "I've only applied the first coat; as such, the colors are muted."

"It is late, Poppy."

"Bah, it is just…"

Together, her and her sister's gazes went to the clock—still buried under the pillows.

"Nearly midnight," her sister supplied, pointing to the timepiece affixed to the front of her gown.

"I'm hardly tired." There was too much to be done. "Furthermore, I just need to—"

Penelope rested her hands on Poppy's shoulders and lightly squeezed. "Rest."

"I will. Soon." Eventually.

"Now," her elder sister pressed, releasing her. "Poppy, you're not leaving any time soon. The hotel? You'll have endless hours to work here. As many as you desire, forever, until the end of time, if you so wish."

How was it possible for one phrase to elicit both joy and regret…

such contradictory emotions that seemingly had no place blending. And yet…staring blankly at her recently completed work, she acknowledged the truth: she didn't want to be the underfoot aunt.

"You're not *that*."

"What?" she asked, glancing over at her sister.

"The underfoot aunt."

She gave thanks for the shroud of darkness to conceal the color rushing to her cheeks. "I didn't say that," she said gruffly.

"You didn't need to. I know you," Penelope said simply. "Either way, Poppy, you are not that and you never will be." Her elder sister lifted her shoulders in a little shrug. "You're my friend."

Emotion she'd not allowed herself since a gathering of society's leading harpies had descended upon her and Rochford filled Poppy. Not for the loss of her reputation or the uncertainty of her future, but for the gift that was her family. She blinked back the sheen of tears. "I promise I'll see my rooms shortly," she promised.

"Oh, you're impossibly stubborn." Planting a kiss on her cheek, Penelope started for the door. She lingered at the entrance a moment. "You're certain there is nothing I can say to convince you to—?"

"Good night, Penelope."

"Fine. Fine."

As soon as she'd gone, Poppy shrugged out of the apron stained with various shades of paint, and carefully rested the stained article along the scroll back armchair.

"Now," she murmured, taking in the flower stand and cloak stand side by side near the middle of the room. "To fix this."

With determined steps, Poppy began with the furniture she could herself move.

A short while later, slightly out of breath, and her curls hanging down her back, Poppy shoved the mahogany cloak stand from the center of the room to a more proper position near the doorway— off to the side where it was not another ornate piece on display.

Sweat trickled down her brow, and she swiped at it with the back of her sleeve before turning her attention to the hideous drapery atop the four-poster bed.

Hopping up onto the mattress, Poppy stood, and balancing herself on tiptoe, she reached for the front grey draping…just as the door opened.

She didn't move. Oh, bloody hell. Of course, she'd not be rid of her sister that easily. Twenty years together should have aptly prepared her for that much. "I can explain," she called to Penelope. Not allowing her sister a word edgewise, she continued, "I'm merely going to lift the fabric…" Gathering the silk in her fingertips, she stretched higher for the frame overhead, "…and hang it like…"

Her gaze collided with an all too familiar pair of dark eyes.

Eyes that were certainly *not* her sister's.

In a face that was decidedly masculine.

And heavily amused.

She blinked. She was imagining him. It was late. Of course, she'd ceased conjuring the memory of him in her mind, long ago. And yet…

Poppy squeezed her eyes shut, and when she opened them, he remained there: Lord Tristan Poplar—or whatever blasted title he went by these days. "Lady Poppy," he drawled, that also very much real voice snapping her to the moment, startling her from her precarious position.

And with a stream of curses stringing from her lips, wound in that hideous grey satin, she came toppling down with a heavy thump.

CHAPTER 5

TRISTAN BLINKED QUICKLY SEVERAL TIMES.

Of course, she would be here.

Because…well, quite frankly, through the years, he'd run into Lady Poppy Tidemore any manner of places he shouldn't: in a tree, under a table at an obscure London modiste. In various hosts and hostesses' conservatories or gardens.

Yes, as such, he should have certainly expected that he would find her here…in his temporary rooms.

Except…it was late. As such, mayhap he'd merely imagined her.

After all, the lumpy pile of silk on the floor remained absolutely motionless.

Entering his new rooms, Tristan pushed the panel closed behind him. "Have I imagined you?"

There was a slight pause. And then, a faint rustle.

"If you were to imagine me, I should hope it would be kinder than suffocating within a swathe of unpardonably hideous grey fabric." The silver fabric muffled her response.

"Was I shown to the wrong suite?"

"No." There was a slight pause. "You have, however, arrived earlier than you were scheduled to," she said tartly.

He smiled. A real, honest grin of mirth, which the minx had always managed to ring from him since he'd nearly run her down in Hyde Park six years earlier.

"Are you laughing out there, Poplar?"

Either she knew him too well, or had developed an uncanny ability to peer through heavy silk fabrics. "I wouldn't dream of it."

She snorted. Then, with that article draped over her frame that gave her the look of that mythical creature of Dartmoor his sisters were all too hopeful about running into, Poppy struggled to her feet. "Now, *that* I don't believe."

Tristan did a sweep of his apartments. They were his, were they not? "Have I entered the wrong rooms?"

"You've not."

After seven muffled ticks of a clock from somewhere in the chambers, when it became apparent the lady had nothing more to say on it, he added, "Uh…is there a reason you are in here?"

"There is," she said simply, still hidden by her fabrics.

He crossed his arms, and waited. And waited.

Alas, she intended to make him ask for it. Which was, of course, the absolute last thing he should do. What he should do was send her on her way. If they were discovered here, alone, it would usher in a scandal that would see Poppy Tidemore ruined. In Tristan's case? Well, Tristan could not fall any further than his present level of descent. Proper gentleman that he still prided himself on being, he'd do well to send her quickly on her way…or take his leave.

Only, the rogue who'd missed what it felt like to laugh and enjoy himself these past weeks selfishly preferred her just where she was.

"Dare I even ask what you were doing?" he drawled, as she made no move to emerge from her makeshift cloak.

At last, she popped her head through an opening. "Oh, this?" She stretched her arms out, revealing that makeshift cloak. "This is quite innocent, I assure you."

An indirect nod to the fact that, with her feats, she could not always claim to be "quite innocent".

Setting his ancient infantry gear down near the door, he ventured over. "I'm intrigued."

"I like you, Poplar," she said matter-of-factly, her hands on her hips, displaying that silk like a cape.

"Oh?" At that abrupt shift, he blinked several times. "And here I thought I was more insufferable than your mother with a respectable match for her unwed daughter ripped asunder."

"You remember that?"

"An insult that likened me to your propriety-driven mama?" he returned dryly. "Indeed, I recall that." Along with any number of clever ones Poppy Tidemore had hurled his way through the years.

The young lady wrinkled her—he squinted, and peered hard—paint-smudged nose.

"If you expect an apology for that, Tristan, I shan't."

"Because apologies are hard to give?" he asked, surveying the tattered bedding behind her.

Good God, he couldn't even begin to fathom what the lady had been up to.

"Hardly, you've been insufferable more times than I can count." She gave a toss of her midnight curls, which hung in a tangle down her back. "However, it is entirely possible to be insufferable *some* moments, and redeem yourself in others."

Tristan should be thinking about his kin making the long trek to Dartmoor while he attempted to put his future in some way to rights. Only, he found himself hopelessly curious—as Poppy no doubt intended—by that idea.

Settling into his new residence, Tristan rested a hip on the ornate nightstand. "And just how have I redeemed myself?"

Poppy's features softened. "You didn't rush to help me," she said, with a wistful air to her words.

His eyebrows drew together. "I didn't…"

Sighing, the lady gave another shake of her head. "Help me like I'm some fragile flower to be protected."

He stared on a moment, measuring her sincerity. Alas, any other lady would have found fault in his not rushing over the moment she'd come crashing down. "I redeemed myself by not helping you?" he asked slowly.

Two dimples appeared in her cheeks. "Precisely."

With that, Poppy shrugged free of the silver silk, divesting herself of the elegant fabric. And as always, he'd been spun in circles by the spitfire.

"If only society were as forgiving," he muttered, loosening his cravat.

"They aren't," she informed him. Poppy wouldn't be content to allow him any self-pity about his circumstances. "They're cruel vipers who'd happily spin their offspring in a silken snare and feed on the gossip they could ring from their lifeless bodies, if they were so absent of a proper scandal."

"You speak as one who knows."

"*Of course* I know." Did he imagine the faint hint of pride underlining that pronouncement?

"Firsthand?" Tristan, however, may as well have spoken inside his head. The young lady had already climbed atop his bed and all thoughts fled, as Tristan became aware of a handful of details all at once:

One, attired in close-fitting breeches and a paint-stained lawn shirt that hugged her every curve, Poppy Tidemore was no longer the young girl he'd first met.

He swallowed painfully. And two…was there a two? As she stretched her arms up, the fabric pulled across her chest, and the garment strained, highlighting the dusky hue of her nipples. Lust bolted through him.

And what is more, she is in my chambers.

It was a detail previously noted but one that, with her body on display like a lithe Aphrodite, now took on a whole new meaning…and peril.

Only one course remained.

"You should leave," he blurted, his voice hoarse to his own ears. Nay, it was the wrong word choice. She needed to leave. Tristan opened his mouth to correct himself.

Poppy drew her attention away from whatever task so occupied her. "When did you become stuffy, Poplar?" Her plump lips formed a perfect Cupid's bow, and the desire winding its way through his veins blazed all the hotter, and made a mockery of that very charge she now leveled at his roguish being. And pointedly rejecting his suggestion that she leave, Poppy resumed…

He cocked his head. "What are you doing?"

"Decorating."

"Decorating," he repeated.

"Hmm. Mmm." Catching one corner of the silver fabric in her teeth, Poppy stretched the other out until it was drawn straight, and then lifting up on tiptoes, wound one corner around one of the bedposts.

"And…uh…does your sister know you are *re*-decorating her suites?"

There was another of those "Poppy Pauses", as he'd come to think of them. Her tell. It was one of her only ones. Having played games of whist and hazard with the lady at various points over the last six years, he'd come to know as much. "Poppy?" he prodded.

She jumped. "She...knows. Enough."

"And your mother."

"Is probably trying not to think about what I might be up to," she said with her usual candidness...and accuracy.

He felt another grin form on his lips; pulling his facial muscles up. "Yes, I suspect that much is true."

"Will you hand me that?" She jabbed a finger toward the floor. Tristan looked around.

"The silver bed curtains?"

"No, the Aubusson carpet, Tristan," she said drolly. "*Yes!* I mean the bed curtains." Poppy sank down on her heels. "And I'll have you know, they're grey."

Feeling like he'd stepped upon a Drury Lane stage and was the only one without the benefit of his lines, Tristan slowly picked up the bed curtains.

"Splendid. Now, if you'll walk that to the end of the frame. No, no, the other way," she chided when he took several steps toward her. "I already have one end of it so how would that even work? You're not very good at this, are you?"

As he didn't have a damned inkling what "this" in fact was, he did the only thing that made sense—he followed her directives.

And here, he'd believed earlier that morn he found himself headed to the unlikeliest of places...only to find himself there now...on a bed with his best friend in the world's sister-in-law... hanging bed curtains. Poppy continued twining the netting until it spiraled along the front poster.

Retreating to the middle of the bed—his bed—she dropped her stained palms on her waist, bringing his gaze inadvertently lower to her rounded hips. Hips that begged a man to sink his fingertips into them. Only, they weren't simply a woman's hips. They were *this* woman's hips. Poppy. Poppy Tidemore. St. Cyr's sister-in-law.

That enumeration of all the reasons it was only caddish to ogle her figure didn't help. He gulped.

It was simply that she was in pants that clung to her person when he'd never before seen a lady in such a state. That was all that compelled his attention. *Liar...*

"They're lovely, are they not?"

He strangled on a cough, choking. "Th-they?" he managed to gasp out.

Poppy gave him a peculiar look. "The…bed curtains."

The bed curtains? He swiftly jerked his gaze up and made a show of considering her work.

"It is marginally better; would you not say?"

Gone. He needed her gone. *Now.* "Absolutely," he said quickly.

In the end, intervention came with a slight scratch upon the heavy oak panel.

Oh, bloody hell. Pulse hammering, Tristan dropped to the floor. He caught himself on his palms. Pain radiated from his wrists up his arms from the force of that fall.

Pain that would be a minor sting compared to the beating the lady's brother-in-law would dole out were she to be discovered.

Another muffled scratch split the quiet, followed by the slight squeak of the mattress as Poppy climbed off…and…

What in hell?

Peeking over the top, he batted at the bed curtains, and stared across the opening made by Poppy's work.

Poppy, who was even now striding purposefully across the room—toward the door.

His stomach muscles clenched. Dead. His fall from societal grace would be a polite stroll through Hyde Park compared with what would follow if she opened that door. "Poppy," he whispered furiously. "Poppy," he repeated, his hushed voice slightly pitched.

The minx glanced back; her high brow wrinkled in consternation.

He gave his head a shake, and then tapped a finger against his mouth. "No," he mouthed.

It was the absolute wrong word ever to utter in any form to Poppy Tidemore.

The young lady resumed her previous course.

He dove back down and, lying on his back, he edged himself under the mahogany bedframe. The door opened and Tristan lay motionless. His pulse hammering in his ears, he stared up at the wood slats.

In the course of his roguish existence, he'd found himself in this situation any number of times, always when a tryst had been untimely interrupted by interlopers. Never had he been caught with an innocent lady, because no matter the reputation he'd earned himself, Tristan hadn't been one to dally with debutantes.

The irony, that he would now be facing pistols at dawn for a misunderstanding…with his best friend's sister-in-law, was not lost on him.

Except…he strained his ears for some hint of discourse.

A faint staccato *click-clack* reached him.

What…?

Tristan turned his head, and peered at the light filtering under his hiding place, just as a large canine head ducked under the bed-frame.

Thumping his paws playfully on the gleaming hardwood floor, Sir Faithful panted wildly; calling forth a painful reminder of Tristan's own dogs.

Tristan had lost everything.

And as such, he should certainly be mourning the luxurious townhouse he'd forfeited or the sprawling country properties he'd thrilled in visiting each summer. Or the endless supply of fine French spirits.

As it turned out, as he let himself in his new—and temporary—chambers, chambers given him solely as an act of charity, he found himself missing his dogs.

The pair of hounds, Valor and Honor, now in a carriage bound for Dartmoor with his likely still sobbing mother.

As if sensing that melancholy, Sir Faithful whined and proceeded to inch his way closer. When the dog was within reach, Tristan stroked that place between Sir Faithful's eyes, and the creature's tongue lolled out the side of his mouth.

He sighed.

Yes, he missed his dogs.

Dreadfully.

"I assure you, it is safe to come out," Poppy teased, her voice heavy with her amusement. "Sir Faithful won't harm you."

"Minx," he muttered. He grunted as the mattress dipped, the article hitting him in the nose.

"I heard that, Poplar."

How did she always do that? Tristan gave the enormous dog one more pat before inching his larger frame out from under the bedframe. His gaze promptly collided with Poppy's, which stared down at him. "I swear you are part owl, Poppy Tidemore."

A faint scowl marred her heart-shaped face. "I'll have you know my ears aren't crooked."

As if to accentuate that very point, Poppy pushed her midnight curls back, revealing perfectly delicate shells.

"What are you talking about?"

"You likened me to an owl. The entire reason they hear as well as they do is because one is positioned at the front of their head and the other higher up."

He stared bemusedly up. "How do you know that?"

"I've observed them in the country so that I might sketch them."

He chuckled. When other ladies were painting floral arrangements, she'd gone off into the woods of her family's properties to paint something different. "Is there anything you do not know?"

"Actually, there is." Leaning further down, she peered under the bed.

He opened his mouth to ask again what she was doing now.

And then, promptly closed it. Having known Poppy Tidemore since she'd been a girl, he knew enough to know when not to prod her. "Hmm." Then with an uncharacteristic restraint, she let the remainder of that statement go unfinished. Leaving her meaning veiled, and his intrigue redoubled.

Poppy started across the room, to where containers of paints and stained brushes lay out, items he'd failed to note until now.

Drawn to the brightly painted mural, he joined her. "Did you do this?" he asked; awe coated his question.

"I did," she said matter-of-factly, as she wiped the tip of a brush upon a multi-colored stained rag.

That was it: "I did." When any other woman would have used the opportunity to search for compliments and talk about her work.

Moving closer, he stood shoulder to shoulder beside her, and continued his perusal up close. "Are you an artist?" she asked, interrupting his examination.

"An—?"

Poppy eyed him with a newfound interest in her expressive gaze. "Your hair is long. You've scruff on your cheeks"—she brushed her knuckles over his in a touch that was more clinical than caressing—"and you're rumpled."

"Alas, I fear that is where any similarities between me and an artist ends."

"Ah." She eyed him with such abject disappointment that left him feeling wanting, an increasingly familiar and quite despised sentiment. "Well, then you shouldn't go about looking so rumpled. Artists are rumpled with scruff on their cheeks."

"Duly noted, my lady," he said drolly. With her dismissive pronouncement, Poppy began cleaning her brushes.

Tristan examined her work once more.

His heart slowed.

A pair of hunting dogs remained poised for all time, reaching for the hawk mid-flight. That creature forever from their eager reach. From the arch of their wide stances to the upturned positioning of their noses, Poppy had masterfully captured the pair of dogs' excitement.

Only, they weren't just...any dogs.

Tristan leaned close, and his chest constricted with the weight of emotion.

"They are my dogs," he whispered.

Not pausing, she continued to tidy her workstation. "Yes."

She'd painted Valor and Honor, as Tristan had always enjoyed their company most—on the hunt. She'd captured the lush green grass of his Kent estates...beloved grounds that had gone and passed to another. And now Valor and Honor would explore anew, elsewhere.

He glanced over at her. "You despise hunting," he murmured, as he was swept by a genuine curiosity to make sense of her subject.

"Yes, but not everyone does. Some love it."

He loved it.

"It is a compromise." Poppy shrugged. "I've created something that anyone might appreciate. The hint of a hunt, with a bird taking its flight to freedom. Anyone might enjoy it, that way."

With that she closed up her neat leather case.

Tristan glanced over at Poppy. "What are you doing?"

"Cleaning up."

"But..." Tristan returned his attention forward. "You've not even signed it."

At her silence, he looked back. A blush stained her cheeks. "I'm not."

"Whyever not? It is your painting." Hers was magnificent work.

"It shouldn't be anonymous. The world should know it is yours, Poppy."

"It is enough that *I* know it is mine, Tristan," she said softly.

He scoffed. "You've created something that will be remembered through time and you'd leave everyone who stepped inside this room to wonder at the artist's identity?"

"Yes," she said simply.

Did she realize that she was afraid to reveal her talent to the world? "I'm disappointed, Poppy…"

He let that hang on the air; knowing she would not be able to let it remain in silence for long. "About what?" she asked defensively.

"You, who'd thumb her nose up at society, would hold yourself back from sharing your art." It fit not at all with the woman he knew her to be. But then, each person had their vulnerabilities.

"I don't hold myself back," she said impatiently. "I've created it. As I said, art is to be enjoyed. People will enter this room and do precisely that."

"And the artist should be honored," he persisted.

"I'm not signing it, Tristan." He opened his mouth to continue debating the point, but she glowered him into silence. "Enough about what I should or should not do with my work." Poppy bent down and rummaged through a basket. For several moments, she fished around and then drew out several of the sketchpads there. She proceeded to flip through book after book, discarding them for the next. "Full," she murmured, dropping the journal in exchange for another. "Nearly full."

He craned his neck. "What are you doing?"

Ignoring his question, Poppy turned through the pages of another. "*Perfect.*" Book in hand, she stood. "Here."

Tristan grunted as she pressed the heavy volume hard against his chest. A question in his eyes, he glanced between her and the sketchpad. "What is this for?"

"Go ahead," she urged him. "Have a look."

Tristan hesitated before taking the thick sketchpad. He flipped it open. "My God," he whispered, to himself. The Kent lake where they'd fished so many times. He turned to the next. A young girl on a riding path in Hyde Park. How expertly, how perfectly she'd captured every detail. Tristan looked up. "You truly are nothing short of remarkable, Poppy Tidemore." And yet, she couldn't bring herself to memorialize her name.

Another one of those pretty pink blushes stained her cheeks. "Uh...yes...well, thank you, but that is not what I'm showing you," she mumbled, endearingly discomfited by his praise. Ripping her pad from his fingers, she flipped through, and held the sketchpad out so it faced Tristan.

He stared perplexed. "They're empty."

She nodded.

"I'm...confused," he admitted. But then, the minx had always had that effect on him.

Poppy lowered the book. "You need to find yourself, Tristan."

Find himself...

Two words which suggested he was lost. Which was perhaps the most accurate way with which to describe who and what he'd become. He'd been a rogue. A soldier. A war-hero. None of what he'd been or done helped him from his current circumstances. "I'm no artist," he said gruffly. With that, he closed the book, and made to hand it over.

She lifted her palms and refused his rejection. "It is a journal, Tristan. Let the pages guide you."

"I can't take your book, Poppy."

"I have plenty more." Filling her arms with the remainder of her art supplies, Poppy started for the front of the room.

Tristan sprang into movement. His longer-legged stride surpassed her shorter one, and reaching for the handle, he opened the door. Ducking his head out, he did a sweep of the corridors, and then motioned for her.

With impressively noiseless footfalls, Poppy slipped from the room. The quiet, however, was broken by the enormous dog trotting at her side.

Tristan followed her retreating frame several moments.

"Poppy," he called after her on a whisper.

She paused, glancing back.

"Thank you."

With a smile, Poppy bowed her head, and then rushed off.

He stared after her until she'd gone, and then closed the door. Leaning against the panel, he glanced around the fine hotel rooms. With Poppy and her dog and her teasing gone, the melancholy returned.

This was...*home*.

CHAPTER 6

Most people despised rising early.

Poppy had never been one of those people. In the early morn hours, when most of the world slept on, one was permitted the freedom to do what one wished, without those prying eyes about.

There was a difference, however, between early…and ungodly.

Quarter to four in the morning fell firmly into the latter column.

She raised her arms filled with art supplies, to stifle yet another yawn.

Tristan.

He'd always lived life his own way.

Arriving early and upending her schedule was on point for the earl.

Nay, he went not by the title Earl of Maxwell now. But, rather, baron.

It was a foreign concept to try and wrap her mind around, still. What must it be…for Tristan? To have lost everything familiar? And his entire circumstances—the very name he'd gone by these past years—ripped away.

And yet, he'd not descended into some surly, dark scoundrel. He'd retained that ability to tease and be teased. That had been one of the reasons she had been so enamored of the gentleman. That and, of course, his appreciation for dogs.

Only, now there were no dogs; the pair of hounds that had followed him for his morning rides in Hyde Park. Or who'd risen with the sun to join him as he'd fished at the estates of his best friend, Poppy's brother-in-law.

Sadness filled her.

Yes, Poppy's mother might believe there could be no greater tragedy than the loss of Poppy's reputation at the hands of some cad, but she was so very wrong in that self-centered opinion.

Poppy reached Tristan's apartments. Balancing her work supplies in one arm, she inserted the universal key given her by her sister, and let herself in. The well-oiled hinges made not so much as a creak of protest as she entered and closed the door behind her.

The grey curtains drawn and the fire at the hearth having long since died, but for a lone candle flickering from a sconce near her mural, the room had since been pitched into darkness. Blinking to help adjust to the dim space, Poppy slipped inside, and then carefully pressed the panel closed behind her.

From behind the thick bed-curtains, a shuddery snore penetrated the quiet.

He snored.

It was not a new detail. Poppy had gathered Tristan's slumbering habits when she'd come upon him hiding in a copse at Christian's summer house party nearly three years ago. Finding him with his back pressed against a majestic oak, and his hat bent low over his eyes, had been endearing. There was, however, a deeper intimacy to this moment, with Tristan on the other side of a curtain, sleeping in his bed.

He emitted another snort, and Poppy gave her head a disgusted shake.

Do not be a silly nitwit. She'd ceased waxing on about Tristan Poplar in her mind some years ago. Well, two years to be precise. Regardless of whether she'd set aside her infatuation with the charmer, was neither here nor there.

The work she'd been brought in by her sister to do, however, was what mattered.

Carefully making her way across the room, Poppy took the path over the plush carpeting. As she set down her art supplies, she inspected her work from the previous evening. Setting down her case, she touched the tip of her smallest nail against the paint, and gave a pleased smile.

Dry—

Click.

Poppy went absolutely motionless.

"Not another movement."

And despite knowing Tristan Poplar, she'd never heard this side of him; the steely baritones, that even laced with sleep, contained a sharpness and threat within them.

Her heart thudded in her chest, and she angled a glance to where Tristan slept—or had slept.

The head of a pistol glinted in the dark…that weapon pointed directly at her breast.

"And here I thought you'd been more appreciative of my work," she said, her voice emerging faintly threadbare.

The gun disappeared, to be replaced by Tristan ducking his head out between the bed curtains, and she breathed more easily. *"Poppy?"*

It was not that she'd thought he'd kill her—not intentionally, anyway. But one never knew what another person might do when startled from slumber. "Who do you *think* it would be, Tristan?"

"I don't know. I'm living in a hotel after my father coordinated the kidnapping of a nobleman and rightful heir…who's since become a lord of the underworld. I can hardly imagine the reason for my paranoia."

"Truly?" She tipped her head. "Because you've quite laid out—"

"Not truly, Poppy." All vestige of sleep had vanished from his voice. With a long stream of curses, Tristan let the bed-curtains flutter shut. "I was being sarcastic," he snapped.

"Sarcasm doesn't suit you," she took delight in informing him, as she fished her brushes from her apron. In a small jar, Poppy added yellow, orange, blue, and red and then blended the colors together until they'd formed the rich auburn of Tristan's hunting dogs. Raising her brush, she made to touch it to the mural—

When she registered the utter still in the rooms.

Lowering her brush to the jar, she glanced back. "You're not sleeping."

There was a pause.

And then… "I might have been."

Her lips twitched. Alas, he'd never been able to stop himself from rising to her baiting. As he was awake, she pushed the heavy curtains open. The glow from the moon sent light spilling into the room. "No one falls asleep that quickly," she pointed out as she returned to her task.

"I do."

That was a detail she'd not gleaned about Tristan Poplar; it highlighted, despite the connection she'd imagined between them, how little she truly knew about him. Just like the fact that he slept with a pistol. "Perhaps you do," she conceded. "But you were not snoring enough to wake the person in the other rooms."

"I...I most certainly do *not* snore," he stammered.

A snort escaped her. "With all the mistresses you've kept these years, not one of them had the forthrightness to share that you snore worse than an overweight pug running too fast in the heart of summer?"

"I...I..." He strangled on his words.

Well, if that wasn't certainly a first in all the years she'd known Tristan Poplar, effortless conversationalist. Her lips twitched up in a smile. "I'm personally of an opinion I would prefer to have a lover who was *truthful* with me about my habits."

"You are not taking a lover," he barked from the other side of the bed curtains, and Poppy *might* almost be endeared by the idea that he cared...if he didn't have the indignant tones to match her overprotective brother.

"No," she conceded. She counted several beats of silence. "At least not at this precise moment, anyway, as you are the only gentleman ab—"

The heavy netting around his bed did little to conceal the animalistic growl emanating from the gentleman tucked away there. "You are most certainly not taking any lover. *Ev—ah—*"

A heavy thump followed by a grunt filled the rooms as Tristan hit the floor hard.

Oh, this was entirely too much fun. Fighting to control the mirth shaking her frame, Poppy devoted all her focus to her mural. "Worry not," she said with a false somberness to her tones. After Tristan's reputation and the death of Poppy's girlish dreams, coupled with Rochford's treachery, the *last* thing she desired was a lover. "I've no intention of taking a lover. At least, not..." She cast a flippant glance back, "...soon—" Her words withered and died on a high-pitched squeak, as her gaze took in Tristan desperately clinging to a sheet around his waist.

Good God... It would appear there was one bit of information she'd not been privy to all these years—Tristan slept in the nude. Information, that would have been decidedly more helpful... before she'd gone and enlisted Rochford's assistance. "You're... naked," she whispered. Her heart threatened to pound outside of her chest.

Clutching the sheet close to his body with his spare hand, Tristan slapped a hand over his eyes. "Why aren't you closing your eyes?" he croaked.

He was *magnificent*. A towering, chiseled wall of muscular perfection. Flat of belly, narrow of hips, a light dusting of dark curls upon a sculpted chest...he epitomized the male form. That figure artists since the beginning of time had sought to forever memorialize.

Say something. Say anything. Be breezy. He'd of course be accustomed to breezy females.

"I believe the better question, Tristan, is why are you closing *yours*?" Except, for all her attempts at control of the situation... and her body's awareness, her words emerged breathless. Faint and awestruck to her own virginal ears.

And embarrassment that weakness for him was ultimately what brought her eyes quickly closed. She pressed a palm over them for good measure, and promptly mourned the sight of him before her.

Tristan groaned. "Close your eyes."

"They are. If yours were open, you'd know as much," she said from around her hand. Even with that assurance, she slid her index finger and middle finger apart the minutest fraction.

Clutching at the satin sheet wrapped about his waist, Tristan jumped to his feet with an impressive agility. That slight movement sent the muscles of his flat stomach rippling.

Of their own volition, Poppy's fingers slid apart a fraction more.

She needed a canvas. Immediately. And charcoal. As she committed the planes of his physique to memory, she catalogued the paints she'd require.

"Good God, are you *peeking* at me?" he choked out, tripping over himself as he rushed to the opposite side of the bed.

"No," she lied, sliding her fingers tightly into place. In fairness, she'd been more openly staring.

There was the whispery rustle of silk indicating he'd let the sheet fall from his fingers.

And this time she let her arms fall to her sides. She scowled at those grey bed-curtains that obscured Tristan, and hated those dark articles all over again, and for very different reasons than their design.

"Why aren't you sleeping, Poppy?" There was the sharp slap of fabric.

A moment later, Tristan emerged from the other side of the bed—bare-chested. Barefoot.

Bare for *everything*, except the tan trousers he'd donned. Her mouth went dry once more. *Words. Speak words.* Poppy mustered a smile. "I've never been one to rise late."

"No, you haven't," he muttered, scouring the room. "Don't you have an early morning ride to see to? A suitor to prepare to greet?"

Poppy retrieved the white lawn shirt near her feet, and held it up. "There's hardly a rush of suitors now."

Tristan sprinted over and tugged the garment from her fingers. "Not now, per se. But soon." He drew the article overhead, and stuffed his arms into the sleeves.

She scowled. "Oh, come, you know there's no suitors waiting." And she'd never known Tristan to be deliberately mocking.

Teasing? Yes. Hurtful, no.

He dropped his hands on hips. "And whyever not?"

Such a rich indignation pulled that response from him and sent warmth filling her chest.

And then it occurred to her.

"You...don't know." It was a statement that left her on a slow exhalation.

Tristan shook his head. "Don't know what?"

When everyone in London knew of and whispered about her scandal with Rochford, there remained one who hadn't—Tristan. And there was something so very...refreshing in his not bothering with that gossip.

He closed the handful of steps between them, so just a hands-breadth separated them. She tilted her head back to meet his dark gaze.

"Know what, Poppy?" he clipped out slowly.

She smiled. "Why, I was ruined."

CHAPTER 7

MAYHAP HE'D MISHEARD HER.

After all, she'd delivered those words conversationally with her usual smile in place. The one that dimpled both her cheeks, and lit her gaze.

Only, searching his tangled mind, he couldn't bring together a single word that rhymed with those to explain any misunderstanding on his part.

Nonetheless, it bore confirming. "You were ruined?"

Poppy nodded once.

He shook his head.

She nodded a second time. "Ruined…as in one with a shattered reputation. A scandalous lady. A—"

"I know what ruined means," he said tightly. "What I intended to ask was…" He slashed a hand at the air, and the lady ducked out of the way to avoid his gesticulations. "Was…was…?"

"What happened?" she hazarded.

Who. Tristan's fingers curled into reflexive fists, as a blinding haze of red-hot rage dulled his vision. It was a name he sought. The blackguard who'd succeeded in destroying Poppy Tidemore's name and reputation. The "what happened", however, would do…for now. "We'll begin there," he said, in the calmest tones he could manage.

Poppy wandered over to her box of art supplies, and proceeded to unpack the remainder of its contents. "I went off with someone

I had no business going off with, and we were discovered."

An image flickered forward…of Poppy, with her gown shoved up around her hips, while some rogue guided her down the path of ruin. Rage sizzled in his veins. Biting. Sharp. Red-hot. "You. Went. Off…" A primal growl climbed his throat. *Dead*. Once he had a name, Tristan would kill the bastard with his bare hands in a death that would be as slow as it was brutal.

Setting down the brush she'd been holding, Poppy faced him. Her eyes formed perfect circles. "Are you thinking…never tell me you believe I…" A laugh burst from her lips.

And just like that, the tension went out of him. In her usual Poppy fashion, she'd been teasing him. And he didn't know if he wanted to shake her or breathe a sigh of relief. Either way, her amusement, combined with his own, proved contagious. "You didn't—?"

"Good God, *no!*"

His shoulders trembled, and he dusted his hands briefly over his face. "I thought—"

Laughing, Poppy slashed her palms at the air. "Absolutely not. I've no interest in a liaison with some faithless bounder."

Oh, thank God. Because the idea of her, Poppy, wrapped in the arms of any man sent something dark and insidious rolling through him. Some emotion he didn't care to examine or name. It was enough that Tristan needn't worry about that image as a reality. Only…

His amusement ebbed. "If you weren't…" *I cannot even say it.*

"Having sexual congress?" she supplied, the innocence of her tone belied by the sparkle in her mischievous eyes.

The minx. Only Poppy Tidemore would have devilish fun while discussing how her ruin came to be. Nonetheless, he was determined to have the whole story in the lady's own words. Except… His brows came together. "Were you ruined because you accompanied a gentleman…somewhere?"

"One might say that," she said, as she applied another frantic flurry of brushstrokes to her mural. Resting her brush in a jar dirtied with water, Poppy reached for another. Tristan slid into her path, intercepting her efforts.

"One did say that. *I did.*" He folded his arms, and when she made no move to speak, impatience swirled. "Well?"

"I was merely enlisting the gentleman's help with my current art project." He caught the crimson color now staining her cheeks.

Tristan narrowed his eyes. There was more there. More specifically, there was a reason for the blush. The dark niggling was back; pulsing at the back of his head. "And society was scandalized because you were discovered alone together?" It would be reason enough that a lady was ruined.

Knowing Poppy Tidemore, however, it could only be something more...

She paused. "And he may have beenpartiallynak—"

Even as close as he stood to the lady, his ears strained to make sense of those muffled words she rolled together. "I'm sorry? It sounded as though you said 'he may have been partially...'" He tried to get the word out. For, it had sounded a good deal like she'd said...

Darting out from behind him, Poppy slipped away, moving to the opposite end of her mural. "Naked, Tristan. He was partially naked," she enunciated like instructing someone who'd never before heard the words.

And damn if it did not feel that very way. Because in this instance, he tried to talk. He tried to order his thoughts. Both efforts failed. That same red-hot sentiment of before returned; dangerously deep that commanded him to hunt the bastard and kill him dead.

"Again, I have to say I am very disappointed in you."

Because she directed that utterance to the likeness of Tristan's dogs, it took a moment to register that she, in fact, spoke to Tristan. "You're disappointed with *me*?"

"That you should be so prudish about me seeing a naked man." She glanced pointedly at his shirtsleeves. "And this from a gentleman who"—he sprinted over to the minx—"sleeps in the nuph—" He caught the remainder of those words with his palm.

"Do not." Reflexively he darted his gaze around the room, more than half-fearing the lady's brother-in-law would spring forward and cut Tristan down...which Tristan would rightly deserve. It was in bad form enough that he'd been in a state of dishabille around the lady. It was an altogether different matter to continue speaking on it.

Over his hand, Poppy withered him with a glare.

"Furthermore," he went on, "we were discussing you and your

naked gentle—ah!'"Tristan yanked his injured hand back and stared at the imprint of her teeth upon his skin. "Good God, you're savage," he said on a breath, and it was admiration that drew that exclamation from him—smarting flesh and all.

Poppy gave a toss of her plaited hair. "Thank you." She made to add another stroke to her artwork, but he caught the brush and held it out of her reach.

"The story, Poppy," he gritted between clenched teeth.

Going up on tiptoes, she plucked the article from his hand, and proceeded to blend several paints together. "I don't answer to demands, Tristan." Then in a wholly dismissive gesture, she proceeded to re-paint the auburn patches upon Valor or Honor's fur.

There wasn't a prouder woman than Poppy. Even as a girl of fifteen who'd been adamant that her elder sister not marry some bounder who'd tricked her. In the end, her sister had married Tristan's friend, anyway, but through it, Poppy had been the lady, outraged and stubborn in the face of her sister's tears. That remembrance of the girl she'd been, and the woman she'd become, stayed with him now. He rested a light touch upon her shoulder. "*Please*, tell me the rest." And when Tristan had that information, the cad would pay a price.

With an uncharacteristic display of vulnerability, Poppy studied the tip of her brush. "There's nothing more to say, Tristan. He accompanied me to Juliet's art rooms, and we were discovered."

She'd accompanied some man to her sister's art rooms… Equal parts rage and pain swirled inside him; in a contradictory melding that left an ache in his chest. None of her telling, or the state of her reputation, should come as any kind of surprise. After all, the last unwed Tidemore girl was the most frequent wager laid down at the betting books from White's on down to the Devil's Den. And yet, it was a bet Tristan himself had never, nor would have ever made…not against any lady's reputation.

But certainly not this woman.

He cut through his fury to find a proper response. "I'm sorry, Poppy," he said quietly.

Her head came flying up, and gone was the wounded expression she'd briefly worn, replaced by a palpable fire that set her hazel eyes aglow.

The air flow in his lungs froze, leaving him breathless.

"Don't you do that, Tristan," she demanded, magnificent in her fury. "I'm not injured and I'm certainly not dead." She jabbed her brush against his chest, splattering paint upon his linen shirt. He grunted, as she advanced toward him, backing him up until his legs knocked against the mattress. "I'm very much alive, and I won't be pitied because of what happened." She stuck him with her brush-turned-makeshift-weapon once more. Then the fight seemed to go out of her. Poppy sank onto the edge of his bed. "And certainly not by you…" Her voice faded to a whisper. "I expected more from you than to care about my scandal."

And the disappointment there—for him—not because of *his* scandal but because of how he'd failed her in this instance, left him gutted. When he'd come upon her in his hotel rooms yesterday evening, he'd welcomed the freedom with which she'd spoken to him. For in their exchange, she hadn't seen the man whose scandal filled the gossip columns and drawing rooms. Rather, she'd spoken to him as she always had—and he'd failed her.

Tristan shoved open the bed-curtains.

Poppy stiffened as he claimed the spot alongside her. But still said nothing, that silence so un-Poppy-like, so all that he wanted was to restore her to the previously fiery warrioress about ready to take his head off for his affront.

He weighed his words a long while, measuring each one before speaking. "Of course I care about your scandal, Poppy."

Her back went up.

"But only because I care about you," he said softly. He always had. From the moment she'd chased her troublesome dog into his riding path and he'd nearly trampled her, he'd come to care about the spirited girl. "And so, what you did or did not do, matters not one whit to me…except in how you're hurt because of it." Tristan shoved a hand through his badly mussed hair. God, mayhap it was the early morn hour that was causing him to make an absolute blunder of this. "What I'm attempting to say and doing a splendid poor job of is that—"

Poppy rested her spare hand on his knee.

He glanced from that delicate touch, to her face. "Thank you," she said softly. Then with a sigh, Poppy stuffed her brush into her apron pocket and flung herself backwards on his bed. "It was a foolish decision, though. I'll concede that to you and not anyone else. And if you tell anyone I said as much, I'll meet you with pistols at dawn."

Tristan joined her, lying down so they lay shoulder to shoulder, hip to hip. "I wouldn't dream of it."

She angled her face toward his. "Telling anyone? Or meeting me with pistols at dawn?"

"Either," he said, with a wink.

They shared a smile before simultaneously glancing overhead at the curtains. There'd always been an ease around Poppy. With her, he could always be assured that she'd never fawn or simper. Rather, she was always her teasing, blunt-speaking self. This time, however, tension thrummed within his frame.

"Who was the bounder?" he forced in casual tones, determined to have the name of the bastard who'd sullied her reputation.

"Lord Rochford."

Lord…? He rolled onto his side. "The Marquess of Rochford?" he asked incredulously. "Staid. Proper. Unnaturally tall."

"The very same." Her face scrunched up. "Except, given that he ruined my reputation on a wager, he's a good deal less staid or proper than credited. Though, in fairness"—she rolled over so she could face him—"he's not unnaturally tall."

Tristan narrowed his eyes. "Oh?"

"He's quite pleasing."

Quite pleasing.

Tristan stiffened. "You'd defend the bastard who ruined you?" That went against everything he knew of the fiercely proud, indomitable young woman.

She lifted her shoulders in an awkward shrug. "I can separate what he did from what he looks like. And"—she touched a fingertip to the corner of her eye—"he is appealing to the eye." With that far too casual utterance, she sprang from her reclining position, and found her way over to her mural.

And then removing her brush from her apron, she dipped it into a small glass jar…and proceeded to paint.

As though she'd not just lauded Lord Rochford's form. Or spoken about her admiration for the bounder. The same bounder whom she'd been discovered with.

A muscle leapt in his jaw. Did she care about the blackguard? And why did that idea rankle as much as it did?

It is only because she is St. Cyr's sister-in-law. As such, through that relationship, Poppy by default was more of a de facto sister to *Tristan.* Why, he'd fished and raced with the lady. By God, he'd chatted about the breeding times of his dogs with the girl. *Of course* he'd worry about her as he would…any of his sisters. Tristan stood. "And that mattered to you?" he forced casualness, even as a dangerous energy hummed in his veins. "That Rochford was, how did you phrase it?" He knew precisely how she'd phrased it. "Hmm? Pleasing to the eye?"

Poppy added another stroke to her painting. "For the purpose it served."

Despite her earlier assurances, all manner of unwanted images flitted past: of Poppy alone with the too tall Rochford—the too tall, partially *naked* Rochford. Rage clouded his vision, and he registered her words coming through the blood pounding at his temples.

"His physique is quite proportional," she said, so conversational as she alternated her brush for a medium sized one, and added to the faux finish. Popping out light areas, as she captured his former Kent estate.

"*Proportional?*"

Her fingers flew quickly, as she dabbed at several errant spaces upon the mural that came together as the summer sky through those trees. "Proportional. That is a term used in art. It generally refers to the relative size of parts of a whole."

"The whole in this case being Rochford?"

She angled a winning smile back like he'd solved the question of man's existence. "Precisely," she lauded, and went back to her work. "Did you know?" she asked, this time without so much a glance for him. "The *proportions* within the body are based on an ancient Greek mathematical system which is meant to define perfection in the human body."

"I…I…" That penetrated his jealousy, and he found himself not for the first time completely befuddled by Poppy Tidemore. "That is a rather clinical description of the gentleman." And that managed to ease some of the tautness in Tristan's frame.

With the back of her spare hand, Poppy brushed a curl behind the perfect shell of her ear. "That is all one requires when painting a subject."

Painting. Understanding dawned, as at last it made sense. Why... why... "You met him alone so that you might paint him." Tristan was unable to keep the relief from his voice. That was all it had been. Not some girlish infatuation with...with... His mind balked at even completing the earlier thoughts that had haunted him.

"Sketch," she corrected. "I was going to paint him later." Poppy let her brush fall to her side, as she looked at him once more. Through the blanket of her thick black lashes, wariness spilled from her gaze. "I'm sure you have something to say on it."

Because no doubt her family, along with every member of Polite Society and then some, as the lady succinctly put it, had something to say.

"Do you truly expect me to pass judgment on you?" They'd known one another for more than six years now.

"Everyone else has."

"I'm not everyone else," he said instantly.

Poppy's eyes went soft, and lips parted—ever so slightly with such adoration that should have terrified the hell out of him. Only, his gaze slid of its own volition, to that mouth he'd not allowed himself to think about...that he'd forced himself to not think about. Lush crimson flesh, Poppy's, that begged to be kissed...and more.

Choking, he wrenched his gaze over her head to the mural taking shape.

Hell. I am going to hell.

CHAPTER 8

FOR THE FLICKER OF A moment, Poppy had believed Tristan was going to kiss her.

Which was as ludicrous as it was preposterous. As a girl of fifteen, she'd *yearned* for that moment. Why, she'd even practiced it. That was, within the confines of her rooms upon a pillow.

But practice her first kiss, she had.

Only to find herself twenty-one, and in possession of still wholly virginal lips—and wholly unfair given her now scandalous reputation.

Poppy stole another sideways peek at the man standing beside her.

No, his gaze was firmly fixed on her mural; if there had been any doubt that his attention had been on her, then it had only been a trick of that girlish part of her deeply buried that had always hoped for his attentions.

Tristan leaned in; his nose nearly brushed the painted brush the pheasant took flight from. "It is as though if I look close, I can almost see the River Grom," he murmured, as one lost in thought.

Since Juliet had opened Poppy's eyes to the wonderment of art in all its forms, Poppy had found herself in a like state. Never had Tristan, nay anyone she'd known, fallen into that deep, reverent introspection. And certainly not as a result of anything Poppy had created.

It was as heady as the thought of the kiss she'd once imagined from this man.

"It is," she said softly, moving to stand beside him. With the tip of her brush, she gestured to the hint of blue-grey water taking shape, of that river she'd once swum in, attired in nothing more than her undergarments. "I wanted to capture the memory of it." Of those beautiful lands he'd since lost. "To memorialize the river here." Forever. For selfish reasons, as much as for Tristan.

And as the silence stretched on, she curled her toes into her boots. This sharing of her work was foreign, and she'd been so excited by Penelope's offer to transform the walls of the Paradise Hotel, that Poppy had not properly thought about how...*exposed* she would be. Her work would be on display, as it now was before not just any patron, but Tristan. Poppy forced herself to look over.

Tristan's eyes were riveted upon that painted river, and in his gaze, there was a sadness, so haunting, his pain so palpable that her heart spasmed. Teasing one another as they'd been, it had been all too easy to forget that they'd been brought together in her sister's hotel because of their own scandals. His, however, was the far more devastating.

"But do you know the thing about the mural, Tristan?" she asked quietly. Not waiting for a reply, she shifted closer so that their arms brushed. "The River Grom is an afterthought to the focus of the image. Going on the hunt with Valor and Honor? Be it in the country or here in London, they're with you still." An awkward pall fell over the room.

For his dogs weren't with him. "Well, they are not with you here, per se." Dogs were not permitted in the hotel and the only exception made had been for Poppy. "I'm sorry, Tristan."

"Poppy, it is fine," he said softly.

Only, it wasn't. "I didn't mean to add further upset."

"You didn't."

Another horrifying prospect slid in. She pressed a palm to her chest. "You've not had to give away your dogs?" she whispered.

"God, no," he exclaimed. "That I would have actually fought Northrop on." Tristan paused. "Maxwell," he quietly corrected.

Maxwell. How both singularly odd and wrong it was to hear Tristan speak of another in a title that he'd worn so well.

"They're with my sisters in the country." No doubt, the only happy pair of that group in Devon.

"I can paint over it," she was already stepping back to reanalyze her mural. Chewing at the wood tip of her brush, she contemplated the wall. "It will be nothing to—"

"No."

"Do away with the river. I can add brush—"

"Poppy," he said with a greater insistence. Resting a hand on her arm, he silenced her. His gaze worked over her face; filling her with a warmth as real as a physical touch. "I wouldn't have you change a single aspect of it," he murmured. "It is…perfect."

Perfect. Her heart fluttered, and blast and damn if she didn't fall in love with Tristan Poplar once more in her life. Only for reasons that had nothing to do with a girlish infatuation or his love of dogs and his scandalous reputation. He appreciated her work. Even if he appreciated it, however, she'd not have the subject of his room focus on a painful memory in his life. She wetted her lips. "You're certain? Because I—"

"I'm certain, Poppy," he said, giving a light squeeze; his grip, contradictorily gentle, and yet, firm, sent heat tingling from the place he touched.

Her mouth went dry.

Stop. You've made peace long ago with your purely platonic relationship with Tristan Poplar.

Telling herself as much did little to stifle the butterflies dancing in her belly.

He released her and Poppy remembered how to breathe once more. Clasping his hands behind him, he resumed his study. "When did you discover a love for art then?" he murmured in reverent tones.

"My sister-in-law, Juliet, came to serve as our governess." The scandal of Jonathan marrying the family governess had shocked society, and earned them countless whispers and stares. This man, however, gave no outward reaction. She may as well have stated the color of the sky overhead. "Until her, I'd only seen…art in one way. But then, she encouraged me to look and see the world around me and sketch that which is in here," She pressed her brush to her chest. Tristan's gaze followed her gesture, and then he slowly lifted his eyes back to her own. Her fingers trembled under the intensity of his stare. For in this moment, he didn't stare back at her as though she were troublesome Poppy Tidemore, but rather with the wicked glimmer reserved for those scandalous ladies his name had been linked to through the years.

"You enjoy it."

She shook her head. "I love it," she corrected. There was a distinct difference. Letting her arm fall, Poppy cleared her throat. "When I create something, nothing matters: not my mother's hopes for me, not my reputation, or name. Nothing. All that matters is that I'm leaving a mark that hadn't been there before."

As the strident emotion in her voice pitched around the room, heat went rushing up her neck.

A sad smile transformed Tristan's mouth from its usual carefree grin. "One's mark."

And there it was—that indirect reminder and…mention of his lost title.

A somber quiet descended upon the room, an altogether unfamiliar state for her and Tristan. Whenever they'd been together, there'd always been teasing, and never a shortage of words.

Tristan continued that contemplative stroll down the length of her mural.

She mourned the loss of the affable gentleman who'd entranced her once impressionable self.

Poppy joined him at the mural; forcing him to stop his pacing. "A title does not a legacy make, Tristan," she said gently.

He whipped around to face her. "In our society, it does, though, Poppy." There was a faint pleading there.

"No." She shook her head. "That is what our society thinks a legacy is. They're wrong."

A pained chuckle rumbled from his chest and spilled from his lips. "God love you, Poppy, you're the only one who could so convincingly call out the way our world, in fact, is."

Her heart did a somersault. His was the singular greatest compliment anyone had ever paid her. Even as she'd wager the fingers she used for sketching, he didn't intend it that way. She smiled. Poppy slipped a hand into his and squeezed. "Finding our own way and our own happiness and leaving our own marks? Those are the only legacies that matter, Tristan."

They looked as one to their interlocked fingers, and something shifted in his gaze. He made no immediate move to disentangle his hand from hers. The air crackled around them like the still before a lightning storm. His hand still in hers, Tristan slowly, inch by slow inch, lifted his gaze to her mouth…and the heat within his eyes stroked her like a physical caress.

Since she'd been a girl she'd despised her mouth. Her full lips were at best too big for her face. And yet, Tristan's eyes darkened, filling with an intensity that robbed her of breath. For in this moment, she felt nothing at all wrong with her mouth.

Nothing wrong, at all.

Tristan could not look away from her. Nor did he want to.

Time had lost all meaning.

Logic meant nothing.

He saw only Poppy Tidemore. Which was faulty and preposterous because of who he was. Because of who *she* was.

A battle raged within him: to claim her lush lips, slightly parted. Or to leave.

"You are looking at me oddly," she whispered, her voice a husky enticement that beckoned. Hers were the sultry bedroom tones that didn't fit with the young girl he'd only allowed himself to see.

Or tried to. At various times—fleeting ones—over the years, he'd taken note of her in ways he shouldn't: the deep, enthralling shade of her eyes; a honeyed hazel, that was flecked with gold. The curve of her hips and legs when she donned breeches.

Along the way, he'd done a convincing job of forgetting those details or excusing away his notice—until now. Now there could be no escaping this enigmatic pull she held over him in this moment. What was the last thing she'd said? His mind moved like mud.

Words, Tristan. Form words. Flippant ones. "Am I, Poppy?" Except, that question came out graveled and tortured. "Looking at you oddly?"

Poppy nodded slowly, sending a lone curl bouncing at her shoulder, drawing his gaze lower. "*Differently.*" Her chest rose and fell with quicker intakes, in an age-old hint of desire he was all too familiar with.

Only not from this woman.

Tristan closed his eyes. "And how am I looking at you?" His was a dangerous query. For he already knew the answer, and even in her innocence, she'd somehow gleaned it, too.

The floorboards groaned as she shifted, standing before him. "Well, in this instance," she said hesitantly. "You aren't looking at me, at all." The hint of mint and chocolate wafted from her mouth and filled his senses.

Tristan forced his eyes open.

Poppy's lips formed a moue. "Oh," she breathed.

Desire burgeoned, dangerous and potent—because of who she was. Because of who he was. And yet, in this moment, he was powerless. "What?" That lone syllable emerged hoarse.

"You look as though…" Her lashes fluttered closed, and she tilted her head back as if to claim his mouth, "…you wish to kiss me."

His eyes slid closed. "Poppy." Her name was an entreaty. A plea for her to restore order to the world when the thin thread of control he held over his desire was frayed, and the slightest move away from breaking.

"And do you know something, Tristan?" The conversational shift of her tones managed to bring his eyes open once more.

"What?"

It was of course the wrong question for this woman.

Deviltry and desire danced in her eyes. "I want you t—"

I am lost. With a groan, Tristan cupped Poppy by the nape, and with that managed the seemingly impossible—he silenced Poppy Tidemore. Shifting his body toward hers, he availed himself of her mouth as he'd ached to since he'd discovered her in his bed. Nay, that wasn't altogether true. He'd secretly—selfishly—shamefully—craved a taste of her these past years.

Poppy went absolutely motionless and then, moaning against him, she wound her fingers in the fabric of his shirt and pressed herself close to him.

She kissed as she lived life: with abandon and so full of blazing enthusiasm it consumed him in an inferno he was all too eager to give himself over to. Fire…it scorched and seared him and he slanted his mouth over hers again and again. With each meeting, he explored the contours of her lips, learning their feel, reveling in the silken softness of the plump flesh.

Poppy crept her hands up, and ran them through his hair.

"This is wrong," he rasped against her mouth. Even knowing that, he cupped the gentle swells of her buttocks and drew her to the V between his legs.

"How can it be wrong when it feels right?" she returned with a like breathlessness that stoked his masculine pride.

"That is what makes it wrong, Poppy," he managed between each meeting of their lips.

And ultimately she proved the stronger of the two of them, as she drew back, breaking their embrace.

His body went cold at the loss of her.

Poppy, however, remained in his arms, working her desire-laden gaze over his face. "That doesn't make any sense." She caught him by the shirt once more and dragged him close. "You are awfully terrible at this roguish business."

With a half laugh, half groan, he again kissed her, and this time abandoned the earlier restraint. Later, he'd allow room for regrets and guilt and shame. For now, he only knew he needed to taste more of her. To lose himself in Poppy Tidemore. Catching her by her trim waist, he lifted her. Poppy instantly wrapped her legs around him. "*Breeches*," he moaned.

As she spoke, her words came breathless. "I quite like them." She angled her head so he could place a trail of kisses along her neck. "Do you n—"

"I adore them."

She was the first woman he'd ever known to wear the garment, and there was something so erotic in the movement it allowed them both. Gathering her wrists in his hand, he raised them above her head, so the fabric stretched tight over her shirt. The dusky hue of her dark nipples teased and tempted and he released her wrists. "Beautiful," he rasped, palming one of her breasts. "So perfect," he marveled, the swell made for his palm.

Moaning, Poppy closed her eyes and thrust her hips, in that silent aching plea for fulfillment. Tristan reclaimed her mouth; urging her lips apart, he slipped his tongue inside.

She touched hers experimentally to him, and then they dueled with their mouths. Thrusting and parrying in an erotic play that tunneled his thoughts into nothing but pure feeling.

Setting her on her feet, Tristan worked his hands down her waist, sinking his fingers into the curve of her hips.

Poppy whimpered; that little hum of vibration maddening and blissful, all at the same time.

She let her head fall back, and he swooped in, pushing a tangle of curls aside so that he could avail himself of the long curve of her neck.

"Tristan," she moaned, his name a husky entreaty that fueled his ardor.

He pressed his lips to the place where her pulse pounded hard; lightly nipping and sucking at the flesh. Her legs went out from under her but he caught her. Never breaking contact with her mouth, he swept her into his arms and carried her to the bed. He lay her down, knowing he should retreat. Knowing he should end this. But he was entirely powerless to stop.

Tristan came down beside her, and bracing his weight on one elbow, he used his opposite hand to continue his exploration. Through the thin fabric of her lawn shirt, he teased one breast, capturing the erect tip between his thumb and forefinger until it pebbled all the more with her desire.

"Mmm." Her incoherent pleading coaxed a low groan from him. "Mayhap you are...more accomplished at this rogue's business than I'd credited."

"Minx," he whispered, kissing her again.

Poppy's fingers came up and twined about his nape as she kissed him back with a like desire.

Who she was, her surname, her family connections. Her reputation, God forgive him, none of it mattered. Only this. Only his need for this moment to stretch on.

It would take a bolt of lightning to free Tristan from the web of desire the lady had spun around him.

Scratch-Scratch-Scratch.

In the end there was no thunderous boom or crack of lightning. It was a faint scratch.

A frantic scratching at the hotel door penetrated the blanket of desire that had stolen his control...and good judgment.

Gasping, Tristan released Poppy. She lay there: flushed, thoroughly kissed, and her eyes glazed.

Oh, God in heaven. *I kissed her.* Nay, he'd done far more than kiss her. He'd molded every delicate curve of her in his hands. His stomach churned.

Poppy grabbed him by his shirtfront.

"Wh-what in blazes are you doing?" he choked, batting at her palms.

Her eyes twinkled. "Kissing you," she said on a breath.

Blanching, he evaded her lips. "The door—"

Scratch-Scratch-Scratch.

"It is just Sir Faithful," she vowed.

With a restraint Atlas himself couldn't have managed, Tristan caught Poppy's very determined fingers and removed them from his person.

"I am most certainly not kissing you."

"No." She beamed. "Not in this instant. Before you were and it was quite…splendid."

Tristan tripped over himself in his haste to put space between them.

"Certainly the best kiss I've yet to receive."

He scowled, as a dark, insidious jealousy jolted him from his previous horror. "Who in blazes have you—?"

Her eyes danced.

She was incorrigible. "You're teasing."

"Indeed." She hopped down from the bed.

"Stop!" he commanded, his voice faintly pitched and God love her for choosing to obey an order for once in her life.

He proceeded to pace.

I kissed her. I kissed Poppy Tidemore. Poppy Tidemore who was—

Marching for the door.

Oh, thank God. She was leaving. That was safe.

Poppy let Sir Faithful in and then closed the door behind them.

He recoiled. "You have no intention of leaving."

She eyed him like he'd sprang two heads. "Why should I? I—?"

Tristan was upon her in three long strides. He took her by the elbows and steered her toward the door. "Out."

"Tristan, what are you—?"

"You have to go. Now," he gave her a slight shove, all but dragging her.

And her emptyheaded dog seemed to believe he'd stumbled upon some new game involving his mistress and proceeded to run in excited little circles about them, yapping.

"My mural, Tristan."

"Can be finished later." When he was dressed and far from this room…and her. His gaze slipped downward to the neckline of her shirt, accentuated by the paint-smattered apron she donned. "That shouldn't have happened."

"My mural? I believed you said it was splendid?" she asked with stricken eyes.

"No. No. The mural *is* splendid. I was referring to—"

Poppy's lips trembled with a smile.

He narrowed his gaze. Why, the minx was teasing him…again. Only, this teasing was entirely different. It wasn't about his snoring—which he did not do—or his reputation as a rogue or the way he cast his fishing line. This was about—The Kiss. Their kiss.

The one that should have never happened. "You have to leave," he repeated.

This time, as they reached the front of the room, she did not fight him. Poppy sighed. "Very well." She lifted a single finger, the tip red from her forgotten paints. "I will say this: I prefer the roguish charming side of you, Tristan Poplar."

That was the side of him he should have never allowed her to see. "Goodbye, Poppy."

"Goodbye, Tristan." She clasped the door handle.

"Poppy?" He cleared his throat. "You've been a friend to me over the years." Guilt assailed him. Nay, not just a friend. "You've been like a sister to me." That reminder was as much for him, as the lady herself.

"A sister?" she echoed.

He lowered his brow to hers. "Yes, Poppy. A sister. As such, what just happened?" He shook his head. "It shouldn't have." Even though he could acknowledge to himself in this moment, he'd longed for it. Even though he ached to have her in his arms, still.

"I…see."

Did she? Either way, what she saw or thought she did, or had misconstrued, mattered not. What mattered was the embrace that had taken place in his bed could not happen again—ever.

Pulling her shoulders back, Poppy leveled him with a single look. "I'll say just one thing before I go, Tristan. You might *say* I'm like a sister, but I have a brother, and Jonathan has *never* kissed me like that."

And on that note, she left. He hurriedly closed the door behind her and her oft-underfoot dog.

Stifling a groan, Tristan began to pace. Why, he was no better than Rochford. His honor had been shredded by the scandal over the Maxwell title. But that scandal? Tristan increased his strides, whipping around, and marching the same path again. What had happened to the Maxwell title had been a product of Tristan's father's treachery. What had transpired in this room? All responsibility for those dishonorable actions resided squarely at Tristan's own feet. Bounder that he was, he'd kissed his best friend's sister-in-law.

Tristan stopped abruptly, and inhaled deeply.

He'd lost his wealth, title, and respectability, and now he'd nearly cast away his honor, too.

When his honor was all he had left, and his familial honor, what he sought to restore.

Shame swelled in his gut.

It was one kiss.

A kiss that would never happen again. That act needn't define him or alter in any way his relationship with Poppy...or St. Cyr. Or St. Cyr's family. Or...anything, really.

Except, as he returned to her mural, the memory of Poppy's soft, seeking mouth under his, haunted him still.

CHAPTER 9

TWO DAYS LATER, POPPY FOUND herself making the final strokes of another mural her sister had commissioned in another empty hotel room.

Tristan's suite since completed, she'd moved on to the neighboring ones in his corridor.

And since their embrace, she'd not caught another glimpse of the gentleman. It was as though...he was avoiding her.

Or mayhap it wasn't that he was avoiding her.

Mayhap it was just that their relationship had resumed the course it always had: friendly when they were together, without any expectation when they were apart.

They were, and had been, as he'd pointed out—friends.

Poppy added a stroke to the nocturnal landscape she'd added to the wall. Friends.

Nay, a friend was not all he'd considered her...

A *sister*. Poppy snorted. He'd dared likening kissing her to kissing a sister. She had a brother, and could say with certainty enough to stake her life on it that there'd been nothing fraternal in her and Tristan's embrace earlier that morn.

For someone with the reputation of being a rogue, he was deucedly awful about all that went with it. A gentleman did not liken a woman he'd just thoroughly kissed to a sibling. One...just didn't do it. He didn't.

Well, Tristan had.

She sighed.

Her toes curled tight into her arches at the taunting voice, needling away as it had done since he'd all but physically tossed her from his rooms. As though he'd not scorched her from the inside out with his kiss.

But then, perhaps that is why he'd earned a rogue's reputation. The gentleman could simply kiss, and move on.

Which was fine. Poppy was capable of viewing an embrace in a coolly methodical way as well. Desire was merely a bodily response. What needled still were those three damning words…

"Like a sister," she muttered.

"What is wrong with a sister?"

With a shriek, Poppy spun around. The small jar of paint slipped from her fingers, and her stomach plummeting, she made a swift dive, catching the glass before it hit the floor.

Even with her efforts, paint went splashing over the side; splattering her face, and apron, and marring the floor.

Oh, bloody hell. This is what Tristan had turned her into. A woebegone miss that her sister was able to sneak up on.

Penelope clapped her hands. "Splendid catch!" she praised.

Poppy managed a painful laugh. "You're the only proprietress in England who'd praise a catch and not lament the condition of your floors." As if to accentuate that very ridiculousness, a glob of orange paint dripped from the tip of her nose, and fell to the floor.

The maids at work on the bed curtains scrambled to set down the expensive articles. "No, thank you! I have it." The last thing the rooms required were stained fabrics.

With a curse, Poppy returned the brush to her work-station, and hurried to gather up several rags.

Her elder sister blinked slowly, and then glanced down at her floor. "Oh, dear," she blurted. "You've quite…stained it."

The pair of maids finished their drapery work.

"Brandy, if you would," Poppy called, blotting at the mess she'd made. Anabelle and Aster scurried from the rooms.

Penelope dropped to a knee beside her. "I'll have you know, this is hardly the time for a drink, Poppy."

"Pfft, this is the perfect time for a brandy, I'd say." She nudged an elbow into her sister's side, earning a grunt. "*Of course* it is not for drinking. It's to be sure I don't leave any remnants of paint. Here," she tossed a cloth at Penelope and her sister caught it against her stomach. "Wet this."

Penelope rushed over to the wash basin, and as she dunked the rag, Poppy fumed.

Distracted.

This is what he'd made her.

Nay, this is what she'd made herself. She, Poppy Tidemore had allowed herself to go starry-eyed for Tristan Poplar. Damn him and the effect he'd always had upon her. Jamming the green rag into the pocket of her apron, she reached for the clean one and wiped at the nearly immaculate floor.

"Woah," Penelope soothed, resting a hand on hers. "You're going to take the finish off my flooring."

Poppy immediately stopped, and fell back on her haunches. "I'm sorry."

"That is, if you haven't already done so." A teasing twinkle danced in her sister's eyes.

Poppy sighed, and gathered up the other cloth.

Her sister's face took on a serious air. "I was teasing, Poppy."

"I know," she hurried to assure. She sighed.

"I know what this is about."

Her mind went blank.

"You…do?"

Penelope nodded slowly. "I do."

Oh, bloody hell. This was bad. Poppy briefly considered the distance between her sister and the doorway. She'd been transparent. She always had where Tristan Poplar was concerned. It had been mentioning his dogs years earlier and his love of them and… she may have even mentioned a thing here or there about one day wedding him and, of course, her sister would never abandon memory of—

"Poppy?" her sister prodded, giving her a suspicious look.

Poppy jumped. "Yes?" she squeaked.

"It is about Rochford."

Who? "Rochford?" And then at the confused glint in her sister's eyes, Poppy continued on a rush. "*Rochford! Of course,* it is Rochford and the scandal. Of course it's that. Whyever, would it be anything other than—" *Stop. Talking.* Poppy bent her head and stroked her rag over the remaining paint.

Penelope settled onto the floor, directly across from Poppy. She drew her legs up close to her chest much the way she had when she'd been a child. "I have to admit, Poppy," she began softly, and Poppy slowed her frantic back-and-forth scrubbing, "when you moved in, I was excited at the prospect of seeing you."

Poppy glanced over and her sister held her gaze. "Part of the reason I'd invited you is because…well, I miss you," she said simply. "I was…*am*," she hurriedly corrected, "excited about the idea of us being together again." A sad smile formed on Penelope's lips. "And yet, you've been here several days and I've not seen you but once. Well, now twice, if one considers this. Day in and day out you work-work-work. You don't even join Ryker and I for meals."

Guilt took root. "I'm—"

Penelope wagged a finger. "Hush and let me finish. What I was going to say, is that you were correct."

"Oh?" After all, this would be the first time in the whole of her life that her sister had made that concession.

"I did offer you the role of overseeing the décor in this corridor out of pity."

She stiffened. Of course, she'd known as much. But there was something that stuck in her chest at having it confirmed. Penelope shot a leg out, and with the tip of her boot, she caught Poppy in the shins.

She grunted. "What in blazes was that for?" After all, if either of them was deserving of a good kick just then, it was her faithless sister.

"Because you didn't let me finish. I want you to oversee the redecoration of the entire hotel."

Poppy didn't move for several moments. She couldn't manage to blink or breathe. And then all at once, the blood whooshed through her ears and her heart pounded. Surely she'd misheard her. "What?" her voice came muffled to her own ears.

Penelope smiled widely and nodded.

Poppy shook her head. "You want me to redecorate your hotel?" she whispered, at last managing words.

"We do, Poppy." Her sister gathered up her hands. "Ryker and I."

Elation lifted her, buoyant and wonderful…and then she fell promptly back to earth. "I don't want your pity," she said, coming to her feet. "I appreciate that you've allowed me to make some minor changes—"

"They weren't minor and it isn't pity." Penelope's brow creased. "Well, before it was pity but then Ryker and I saw the rooms, Poppy…Maxwell's"—her sister grimaced—"I mean, Tristan's, and we spoke about your work."

They'd spoken about the changes she'd had made to his rooms? "You did?" she asked, her work briefly forgotten. She flew back over to her sister. "He was? You spoke to him about m—" Her cheeks went hot. "M…my work," she managed to correct. What had he thought about the final changes she'd made? And more, why did his opinion matter so much?

"Of course I saw him, Poppy." Her sister flashed her a peculiar look. "He's Christian's best friend. Do you think I wouldn't ask his opinion or speak to him simply because he is a guest here?"

"I…I…" That was what her sister believed was the reason for Poppy's questioning. Any other time she would be offended that her sister would believe her capable of snobbery. Now, she welcomed the easy inhalation of relief. "And what did Tristan have to say?" she asked flippantly.

"He was quite complimentary."

Her heart thudded. "He was?"

Penelope looped her arm through Poppy's and urged her on a turn around the room. "In fact, after you'd completed your work and he found his way to his apartments, he was certain he'd entered altogether different rooms. He said they were…" Her sister paused alongside the partially completed mural.

"Yes," Poppy urged, giving Penelope's arm an impatient tug.

"I'm trying to recall how he said it. It was really quite poetic."

He'd been…poetic in describing her work? "*Penelope.*"

Her sister's eyebrows went up. "I have it. He said: it is an oasis in a world where he'd begun to believe there was none for him."

Poppy fell back on her heels. An oasis. Emotion suffused her breast: pain for what Tristan had lost, and along with it…an unfettered lightness that he'd found some peace in those rooms she'd created for him. "He said that?" And she'd given him that. Annoyance that he'd avoided her—or worse—forgotten her these past days aside, he'd been correct—he would always be her friend, and she only wished for his happiness.

Penelope nodded, and glanced about the room as if she feared even now someone was listening in on their exchange about the scandal-ridden baron. "I don't believe he intended for Ryker or I to hear that latter part," she said in hushed tones. "It was more spoken to himself."

Poppy's heart tugged. There was something even more aching in that admission from her sister.

"And so, as a result, of what Max—Tristan shared, Ryker and I were forced to consider not only our recent design of the hotel but also…your role in it."

At that abrupt shift away from mention of Tristan, Poppy worked at following. "What are you saying?"

Pointing her eyes to the ceiling, Penelope gathered Poppy's hands in her own. "We want you to make the changes you see necessary for the aesthetic design of the hotel."

Poppy's lips parted. Her sister—nay, not just her sister—Ryker Black, Penelope's intractable husband, who'd completed construction on the establishment, sought to turn that responsibility over to Poppy? It was unfathomable. "But you just completed the construction."

Releasing Poppy's hands, Penelope shrugged. "What is the good of having a completed project if it is less than majestic? You've made the rooms you've overseen special, Poppy. We want you to do that to all the hotel, now."

We want you to do all that, now. Breathless, Poppy took a step away from her sister. Stopped. And then started forward again. She swept her gaze over the latest rooms she'd completed, each transformation thrilling. Each mark she made, something tangible in a world where women weren't permitted tangible—not for themselves, anyway. Here, she'd left her mark: a hint of her artistry, and love of design that would live on. And now, her sister and brother-in-law would allow Poppy to have an imprint upon the entire establishment. There had to be more to this gift. She spun around. "But… all the money you've invested."

Penelope leaned a shoulder entirely too close to Poppy's recently completed mural. "Lah, Poppy, if you continue like this, I'd think you're trying to haggle a higher rate from me. Of course, you'd have to reside here indefinitely until the project is completed."

Tears formed a sheen over her eyes and she blinked back those bothersome drops. Her sister made a gentle sound of protest. "I'm not going to cry," Poppy vowed, brushing at her cheeks.

Her sister looped an arm around her shoulder. "Good, because that will make me weepy and I do despise crying." Penelope's lower lip trembled. "Well, what do you say? Will you do it?"

Poppy smiled. "I would be honored."

CHAPTER 10

SINCE HE'D MADE THE MISTAKE of kissing Poppy, Tristan had gone out of his way to avoid her. The memory of their embrace, however, had haunted him.

As such, he welcomed the diversion presented by his man-of-affairs, particularly as the man was here with a way out of his circumstances.

Seated in the smoke room of the hotel with Sanders opposite him, Tristan drummed his fingertips on the arms of the chair.

The man was a miracle-maker. Years ago, upon learning the man could squeeze sovereigns from tea leaves, he'd hired him out from his employer. And now, more than ever, Tristan needed those skills. "I can't go on like this, Sanders," he said through the wizened man's typical ritual of organizing his materials and notes. "I cannot stay here."

"It seems a nice enough place, my lord," Sanders murmured, his head still bent over his files.

Tristan gritted his teeth. "It isn't about whether it is nice or not. It is about my accepting…charity." He stumbled over the word. Every last shred of honor he possessed chafed at living as he was: off the generosity of his best friend's in-laws, while his own family remained shuttered in the far-flung corners of England. Oh, it wasn't that he was ungrateful. Far from it. It was, however, humbling in ways he'd never been humbled. "Get on with it," he urged, impatient as he'd never been before with any servant.

As Sanders ordered his papers upon the table as if it were some private work station, Tristan felt something stir to life—hope. God love Sanders. The loyal man-of-affairs he'd hired on had turned Tristan's fortune into wealth enough to last ten generations of Poplars. Granted, all those monies had since reverted to the rightful holder of the Maxwell title. That, however, was neither here, nor there. In war, Tristan had been left with several key takeaways: one, survive at all costs. And two, the only path to focus on was a path forward.

Sanders, with his acumen and uncanny business ventures, represented that path. "Well, out with it."

The white-haired servant briefly paused in ordering his already tidy stacks. "There is nothing."

Tristan frowned. There *was* nothing. There *is* nothing. "I know that." It was not a new sentiment. "Everyone knows that," he muttered.

With that announcement, the older man returned to shuffling through the stack of papers on the table. Just as he'd been rustling for the better part of seven minutes now. "No. No. I'm afraid it is more dire than that." At last, Sanders stopped his infernal shuffling, and settled on a single ivory page. He slid a paper across the table.

"What is this?" Tristan asked, already with the official-looking document in hand.

"You've made sizeable investments through the years, my lord. Wise ones."

"Yes," he said impatiently. Despite his mother's lamentations, Tristan had taken pride in expanding his ventures to include speculative properties and industries. Many of which had proven lucrative. He glanced up. "According to your review of my books, those ventures are the reasons my family is not in dun territory."

"Precisely." There was a pause. Tristan heard it. "That is the problem."

Tristan lowered the page. "That is the problem."

It was a statement more than a question, and yet, Sanders nodded, anyway.

"I do not follow."

His man-of-affairs reached within his leather folder once more and withdrew another sheet.

Tristan took the page from him. "I'm sorry. Did you say, this is a problem?" Granted the sum he'd earned from his investments was not an amount to see his family and future ancestors secure, but it was enough to at least see they were comfortable...until Tristan put his life to rights. "We'd determined that shuttering the town-house and having my family reside in the country, foregoing the Season and expenditures, would stretch the amount."

"We did and it will." Directing his bespectacled gaze down, Sanders fumbled with a latch on the inside of the leather bag on his lap.

Tristan had never truly appreciated a solidly direct gaze, until his fall from society's grace. In that time, he'd been greeted with averted eyes, downcast ones. In his mother's case, tear-filled ones. Invariably, none of those stares met his, at least not for long. They were all avoidant.

That list of those unable to look him in the eye it would now seem extended to his man-of-affairs.

When it became apparent that his man-of-affairs intended to say nothing else, Tristan leaned forward. "Then how is that a prob-lem?"

"The funds came from your investments made with the Max-well title."

Warning bells clamored at the back of his brain. And he knew. Knew before the other man had even finished that thought.

"As such, all profits earned revert to the current title holder, the new Lord Maxwell." Sanders swallowed loudly. "Or the prior Lord Maxwell." His man-of-affairs had the look of one ready to burst into tears. "Given that he was the original Earl of Maxwell, before you."

"I'm well aware of the circumstances surrounding the title," he said sardonically, that cynical bid at humor the only thing that kept him from turning himself over to the panic knocking around his chest. Those funds had represented all he had left to get his life in order. And now, even that had been snatched away. Tristan dragged a shaky hand through his hair.

"I am sorry, my lord," Sanders whispered.

"It is fine," he said quietly, turning to the next page, to give his fingers something to do. Still seeking that great distraction...only this time, not one because of Poppy Tidemore, but from the hell that his life had become. Tristan drew in a breath. This wouldn't

crumple him. "We'll sort this out. There's a way on from this."
He'd found his way with ten men out of a standoff with one hundred of Boney's men. He could figure this out. "It just requires a
bit more thinking on our part."

Sanders's lips quivered, and a glassy sheen formed over his man-
of-affair's eyes. "There cannot be...an 'our part'."

And then it registered. Tristan glanced around the smoke room,
the gentlemen seated at the surrounding tables. Why... "You
brought me here to break it off?" After his scandal had come to
light, Tristan's mistress had been the first to end it, followed by
the proprietors of every club he'd held membership to. His sisters'
companions. But this was rich. He'd been tossed over by his loyal
man-of-affairs. A laugh rumbled up from his chest at the absolute
ludicrousness of it all. "Et tu, Sanders?"

"Please understand," the older man implored, dragging his seat
closer. "I've gone through all the calculations." All business once
more, his former man-of-affairs withdrew another handful of pages.
"There are no funds for you to employ my services"—Tristan
accepted the latest sheet and did a cursory search of it—"and
therefore, it would be fair to neither of us to continue on this way."

He'd paid the servant well. Greater than most men offered their
solicitors and man-of-affairs combined. Funds enough to see the
man and his family comfortable for the remainder of his years, and
yet, he'd not beg anyone to stay on. But then, Sanders had been
all too easily swayed out from Cartwright's employ. "Who is he?"

"I don't under..." The old servant dropped his head. "The Earl
of Mph..."

Tristan cupped a hand around his ear. "I'm sorry. It sounded as
though you said..."

"The Earl of Maxwell. He sought my services, my lord."

The Earl of Maxwell. The rightful heir. Who appeared all too
eager to exact his revenge, after all. In fairness, the gentleman was
entitled to any hatred and rage he might carry.

Sanders cleared his throat. "I believe you'll be fine, my lord.
You're very resourceful."

Tristan gave him a droll look. "Thank you for your faith in my
abilities. You may go." He'd not even finished speaking and his
former man-of-affairs was already on his feet, with an agility better suited a man forty years his junior. Stacking his notes into two

piles, Sanders returned one to his leather bag and the other he pushed across the table.

Tristan drew the file open and scanned the pages. "What is this?" he asked incredulously, passing a questioning look between the papers and Sanders.

"That contains the items you must liquidate in order to pay the debt you incurred while...while...Lord Maxwell was *missing*."

Missing. So that was the more polite explanation they would go with. "Items I must liquidate?" All his earlier attempts at drollness snapped. "Debt I *incurred*?" he barked. "I left the man a damned fortune. One far greater than he would have otherwise known."

The other patrons glanced over.

Red-faced, Sanders adjusted his already immaculate cravat. "Yes. Yes. That may be true."

"It *is* true."

"But you still borrowed against ventures, and so there is interest that had to be calculated for those loans you took."

"Loans. I. Took," he clipped. By God, this mercenary tactic had Sanders all over it. And what had once been a source of admiration for his brilliant acumen, now marked the remainder of his demise. "Get out, Sanders," he warned on a steely whisper.

Sanders jumped. "Yes. Yes. I-I w-will," the man stammered, grabbing his back. He lifted a finger. "If I might suggest, before I go, that we work out a timeframe of when you'll pay b—"

"Get out," he thundered, and whispers went up around the staff and patrons.

"I'll send a general timeline along then." This time, his man-of-affairs had the wherewithal to hightail it to the exit.

After he'd gone, Tristan sat there motionless, his life falling apart yet again. There was little left to give, and yet, more the Earl of Maxwell intended to take. Tristan reached for one of those scraps of tobacco he so despised.

What in God's name was he to do? With fingers that shook, he attempted to light the lone cheroot that had sat untouched upon his table. To no avail.

A flint-and-steel striker appeared under his nose. "You look as though you require help."

He stiffened.

A small flame appeared, and Poppy touched it to the edge of

his cheroot. Poised directly at his table with an enormous basket in hand, she put him in mind of the Belgian village girls who'd wandered the fields proffering drinks to soldiers after battle. "You shouldn't be here, Poppy," he said tiredly. Reasons that moments ago would have had everything to do with the fact that he'd nearly taken her in the very bed her sister had given him free use of. But now, had only to do with the fact that after Sanders' revelation, Tristan wasn't fit for company.

"And whyever not?"

"It's not respectable." He paused to glower at the three strangers watching them. The men immediately dropped their eyes. "Furthermore, people will talk."

Poppy snorted. "When did you ever care about people talking?" Setting her basket down on the floor, she settled into the seat across from him, picked up his cheroot and smoked it with far greater ease than he'd managed these past days. Exhaling a perfectly formed round ring, Poppy puffed it toward him.

"Poppy," he said warningly. Leaning across the table, he made to pluck the cheroot from her fingers, but she shifted it out of his reach, and he was left grappling with the air. "We aren't in Kent. You're not a child," he spoke in hushed tones, mindful of the other patrons. "Things are…"

"Different?" she supplied.

He nodded. "Different." Different when it shouldn't be. Different when he didn't wish it to be.

Tristan had managed the impossible—he'd silenced her.

Poppy sat there contemplatively puffing on his cheroot.

Tristan swatted at the little cloud. "I trust your family is aware of your habits."

"Actually they're not. But even if they were?" She lifted her shoulders in a shrug. "I wouldn't care, Tristan." He'd have to be deaf to fail to hear the pointed criticism.

"I don't have that luxury anymore, Poppy," he said quietly. "Not since my reputation was destroyed and I've been left trying to rebuild it." His gaze fell to the damning pages before him.

Poppy stretched the cheroot across the table, and he took that offering. Raising the small scrap to his lips, he inhaled deep. The pungent smoke filled his lungs, and exhaling a small plume, he grimaced. It was a habit that hadn't gotten any more pleasurable.

But it did prove briefly distracting. "Since when have you begun taking up in The Gentleman's Smoke Room, anyway?"

Poppy pointed to that oddly shaped basket. Brushes jutted out from a crack in the top.

"You're painting this room, too." Of course she was. There would be no sanctuary in even this area reserved for gentleman.

"You needn't sound so pleased about it," she muttered. "Goodness, and here I thought you appreciated the work I'd done in your rooms."

Did he imagine the lady's faintly hurt expression? "I do." That mural of his dogs had alternately filled him with an ache of loneliness and a light happiness at the memory of them. He noted the twinkle in her eyes. "You're teasing."

"I was," she confided on a whisper. "My sister and brother-in-law have entrusted the interior decorating of the hotel over to my care."

He sat upright. "Poppy," he exclaimed. "That is wonderful." And it was. He found something calming in knowing that something had at least gone right for her.

A pretty blush filled her cheeks, that deep crimson color the same she'd worn when he'd had her in his bed, trapped under his body. "Yes, well, your words to Ryker and Penny played a part in their decision and for that, I'm grateful."

"I want you to sign this one, Poppy."

Her brow creased.

"When you complete this one, leave your name upon it, so everyone will now for all time that you were its creator."

She dropped an elbow on the table and leaned forward. "Why is it so important for you that my work is recognized as mine?"

"Why is it so important to you that it's not?" he countered. Tristan rested a hand on hers. "Leave your mark, Poppy, and do it without apology."

Poppy turned her palm up, so theirs met.

His gaze, of its own volition, slid lower to where they touched.

He went absolutely motionless. It was the most innocent of touches, and yet, it scorched and seared and whispered of an intimacy far more perilous than mere lust.

"Tristan," she whispered, her fingers curving slightly, so that their fingers locked.

He should pull away. Touching her was wrong in every way. Doing so where strangers might see them was the height of folly that would see him leveled at dawn. And yet, God help him…he couldn't. Their palms joined together felt oddly…right. And he could not, even for the remainder of his monies and lands, draw away.

Beyond her shoulder, his gaze snagged on another pair of gentlemen just entering the smoke room.

A very familiar pair.

Tristan yanked his hands back. "*Bloody hell.*"

"Tristan?" Poppy ventured.

This day had gone from dire to he-was-better-off-on-another-Continent bad. St. Cyr and Blackthorne. Their friendship had been formed when they'd been boys and then forged through the hells of warfare but there were certain things no gent would tolerate—Tristan's newly formed relationship with Poppy being one of them. "You have to go," he said with greater urgency, when she made no attempt to rise. Due to the Duke of Blackthorne's limp, the pair moved along slowly. "*Now.*"

"What is the matter with you?" she muttered, climbing to her feet. She followed his gaze. "Oh," she said happily. "It is Christian."

"You should go now," he said, not moving his lips as he spoke.

She scoffed. "Never tell me you're worried about what Christian would say about us being together?"

"I am." Among other things.

"You and I have been together before countless times."

His jaw worked. Yes, that much was true. But that had also been before The Kiss.

The lady dug her heels in, waiting until her brother-in-law and Blackthorne, Tristan's other only friend in the world, arrived.

"Poppy!" St Cyr greeted warmly when he reached their side.

She went up on tiptoe and kissed St. Cyr on the cheek. "Christian. I trust you've come to spy on me and provide a report to Prudence?"

The marquess' eyes twinkled. "Alas, you're not the subject of my spying today."

As one, brother-in-law and sister-in-law looked to Tristan. "Oh, stuff it," he muttered.

"Don't mind him. He's in a foul mood." Turning, Poppy greeted

Blackthorne. "Hello, Your Grace." She flashed the duke a blinding smile. With half of his face burned in battle, and sporting a patch where an eye had once been, nearly everyone averted their gazes to avoid looking at the once great soldier. Poppy proved to have more strength and character than most of Polite Society combined. And Tristan's appreciation came at a time when the last thing he could afford where the lady was concerned was that esteem, or any other sentiment of admiration.

"A pleasure as always," Blackthorne returned in his graveled voice.

"Dare I ask what you're doing in a smoking room, Poppy?" St. Cyr folded his arms at his chest.

"You should know the answer to that by now, Christian." She winked.

Winging his lone eyebrow up, Blackthorne shifted his weight over the head of his cane. "May we join you? Or are we…interrupting?"

St. Cyr puzzled his brow. "Interrupting what?"

Oh, bloody hell.

Poppy laughed. "Of course you may join him," she answered for Tristan. "Even if he isn't appreciative of company today," she tacked on. Blackthorne sharpened a gaze on Tristan, who in a bid to act casual under that scrutiny gathered another cheroot and that flint Poppy had previously used. "Now, I'll leave you gentlemen to one another's company." Touching a hand to St. Cyr's shoulder, she leaned in. "Have a care with that one," she said in a loud whisper. "He's not fit for company today."

St. Cyr's eyes twinkled. "Duly noted. We'll proceed with care."

With a curtsy and a wave, Poppy hurried off.

"What was that about?" St. Cyr mused, taking a seat.

"Do not ask," he muttered. All the while silently pleading with a God that hopefully existed that his friend didn't.

"Since when did you take up smoking?" St. Cyr asked.

In answer to that, Tristan inhaled deep of the pungent scrap. "It is a newly discovered habit," he muttered. And cheaper than brandy; the last of his bottles of which sat in his rent-free rooms. Tristan took another long pull.

St. Cyr and Blackthorne shared a less than subtle look with one another.

"We're worried about you," St. Cyr said quietly.

And who in hell would have figured that Tristan's dire circumstances should prove a welcome discussion. All previous thoughts of Poppy Tidemore fled. At least his friends would not dance about it.

"I am fine," Tristan clipped out.

A servant came forward with a bottle of brandy and three glasses.

When the young man had gone, Blackthorne poured drinks. "What do you require?" he pushed a glass over to Tristan.

My reputation back. My honor and title and wealth restored.

Alas, all that remained was his pride and he could not shred that, too. Not even to his friends. For all they'd shared. For all they'd endured together...he could not speak to them about this. "I thank you for your offer of support, but there is nothing I require." Even if he accepted the funds they'd likely give, those monies would soon be gone and then he'd be precisely where he was now—lost.

"I don't believe that," Blackthorne said with his usual bluntness.

And with good reason; Tristan lied through his damned teeth.

St. Cyr gave their friend another look. "What Blackthorne intended to say—"

"No, I said precisely what I intended."

"Is that we are here to help as you need. Or simply listen. That is…" As St. Cyr continued on, Tristan's gaze wandered back to the solitary person whom he'd found himself able to speak to.

You've shared freely with Poppy.

Poppy applied another stroke to the mural. At some point, Penelope had joined her. Whatever she said to her younger sister earned a laugh; bright and clear, it rang like bells and emanated pure light. Hers wasn't the practiced husky expressions of restrained mirth adopted by the women he'd always kept company with. Poppy's was as unfettered and bold as the lady herself, and sucked under her spell, he found himself briefly closing his eyes, allowing that joy to wash over him. It was a laugh that could drag a man from darkness. Help him find himself…

You need to find yourself…

He sat up slowly.

"What is it?" St. Cyr asked.

And despite the immediate rejection of his friends' offer of help, there was…one possibility he'd not considered.

Until now.

"There is something I would ask your assistance with?"

"Anything," Blackthorne said gruffly.

"I'm in need of funds." Even as a lifetime of friendship with the men before him allowed him to make that humbling announcement, shame still stung like vinegar on an open wound.

"Name the amount," St. Cyr said unflinchingly, in a testament to that friendship.

And mayhap if Tristan were another man he would have taken that offer. But that had been before his father and mother had done away with the rightful Maxwell heir and laid command to that fortune. "No...not funds, per se. Employment."

St. Cyr's mouth moved but no words come out.

"I've lost the ability to request favors," Tristan explained. "I'd ask whether either of you might speak to someone in the Home Office, regarding employment."

It was what made sense. How had he failed to see it now? The military had been the one aspect of his life where he'd been skilled. And the one area of his life where he might earn a salary and work at restoring his honor.

"You want to reenlist in the military," Blackthorne said flatly; a haunted glint lit the duke's lone eye, a tortured gaze that remained firmly entrenched in the past.

"I'd...inquire as to whether it is a possibility."

"I'll of course make inquiries," St. Cyr said quietly. "If that is what you wish?"

There was a question there. "It is."

St. Cyr took a drink, and then pushed the barely touched snifter away. "If you'll excuse me? Despite my assurances to the contrary earlier, I promised my wife before I'd return, I'd collect a report on Poppy." He waved both men off when they made to rise.

Neither Tristan nor Blackthorne spoke as St. Cyr made his way through the restaurant; winding his way between tables of guests. He stopped beside Poppy and Penelope, and said something in greeting that earned another one of Poppy's laughs.

Tristan let the lightness that sound always elicited, wash over him.

"Poplar?"

He glanced over at his other friend. Blackthorne gave a nearly imperceptible tip of his head in Poppy's direction. "Careful there."

Another damned guilty flush splotched Tristan's cheeks. "I've neither said, nor done anything." *Liar.* He'd crossed all manner of lines.

Blackthorne eyed him for a moment, and then nodded slowly. "Be sure you keep it that way." He paused, winging an eyebrow up. "Unless your intentions are…honorable?"

Intentions? Nay, his friend spoke more specifically of honorable intentions.

Toward a lady? Not just any lady.

Poppy?

Not only was she, well, Poppy. But even if he had honorable intentions to the lady, which he decidedly did not, he had nothing to offer her. Tristan shot his palms up. "You've entirely misread…" *The situation.* Tristan cut himself off from saying as much. To refer to it as a "situation" only implied there *was one* between Tristan and his friend's sister-in-law.

Just then, another of Poppy's fulsome laughs went up, filtering over, and compelled Tristan's gaze toward her.

Leaning around her brother-in-law's shoulder, Poppy looked in Tristan's direction and gave a roll of her eyes. Despite the room of patrons, Tristan found himself grinning back.

"*Have I* misread the situation?" Blackthorne drawled. "I may have lost one eye but I'm not entirely blind."

Tristan shot a frantic glance around at the other patrons. Even largely isolated as Tristan and Blackthorne were from those tables, when he again spoke, he did so in a quieter voice. "You have my word, nothing untoward has happened. We're merely friendly toward one another."

Just as they'd always been. Nothing had changed. They still teased one another. Baited the other. The only difference being, with his rogue's eye, he'd at last noted that with her rounded hips and generous buttocks, the lady had grown up along the way.

Quite normal stuff, that.

Blackthorne pressed his palms on the tabletop and leaned forward. "If you value your friendship with St. Cyr, I suggest you keep your distance from the lady."

It was an easy directive. Or it should be.

And yet, long after his friends had gone, Tristan sat there drinking that bottle of brandy, trying to make himself believe the lie he'd given to Blackthorne.

CHAPTER 11

LYING IN HER BED, HER palms resting on her stomach, Poppy drummed her fingertips…and waited for the commotion outside her rooms to fade.

There was the periodic thump, followed by a grunt.

Poppy had long found the idea of living in a hotel quite thrilling. It was a rather Continental idea.

What she'd not expected, however, was the annoyances that also came in sharing a residence with inconsiderate strangers.

It would stop.

"Oomph."

Because there was no way Ryker Black or his staff would tolerate a patron stumbling noisily around his halls at—

Poppy glanced to the porcelain clock at her bedside table.

Two in the morning.

"Ah."

With a soft growl, Sir Faithful abandoned the comfortable place he'd made at Poppy's side, and rushed for the door. Whining, he scratched against the panel. Periodically casting pleading looks back Poppy's way. "He'll be gone soon," she promised.

As if to make a liar out of her before her dog, those uneven footsteps grew closer. "Damn it."

Poppy didn't blink for several moments as the noisy guest's voice reached her. What in blazes? Swinging her legs over the side of the bed, she bolted across the room. She paused, gathered up her wrapper, and donned it as she went. "Shoo," she whispered to Sir Faithful, as she belted her wrapper at the waist.

Opening the door a smidge, she ducked her head out into the hall.

The gentleman passing by had made it no further than three paces, and even with his back presented to her as it was, she recognized the broad width of his shoulders, his narrow waist. The muscular thighs.

"Tristan?" she whispered.

On slightly unsteady feet, he wheeled around. "Poppy," he greeted loudly.

Oh, bloody hell.

Racing from her rooms, with Sir Faithful hot at her heels, she rushed to Tristan's side—his unstable side, that was. "Woahhh," she muttered quietly, catching him by the forearm.

He was going to get himself thrown out. Ryker had been generous to allow Tristan a payment-free residence in the unfinished portions of his rooms, but Poppy would wager every last sketchpad that such patience ended when the gentleman made a disturbance for other guests.

"Are you escorting me to myyyy rooms, lovvve?" Tristan asked on a loud whisper.

Love. "Ever a flirt, even when drunk," she said dryly, as she guided him purposefully down the end of the corridor in the direction of the vacant halls.

"I'llll have you know. Ahm nah drinking."

Poppy grunted, stumbled, and then kept her feet. "No, I suspect you rather drank all there was to drink already."

They reached the end of the wing. Tristan made to take a left down the vacant hall under construction.

"Wrong way," she muttered, steering him in the opposite direction.

She breathed easier when they'd escaped the hall where other guests now slumbered.

"Quite impressive with directions, you've always been, Poppyyy."

"Have I?" she asked dryly, her breath coming slightly heavy from the way he leaned against her. "I'd greatly love to hear your remembrances."

"There wasss the rainstorm in Kent where weee couldn't see

two feet in front of us. You were sooo sure, even with a downed limb that hadn't been there before, that wass the way."

Poppy's steps slowed, and she came to a complete halt. And Tristan was forced to a stop beside her.

"Thought I forgot that, loove?" A half grin curled his lips, doing wicked things to her heart.

We're going to die out here… And all the world will be left wondering what in blazes my roguish self was doing alone with you, Poppy Tidemore…

That teasing bellow, which he'd shouted into the storm, echoed around her mind; clear all these years later. "I…" Because she'd simply come to accept that he hadn't remembered those moments which had meant so much to her. That all of those memories had been one-sided, held tight by a hopeless girl, for an unaffected rogue. "Come," she said gruffly. "You need your rooms."

Fortunately, he didn't say another word the rest of the way, and she was left trying to get her heart to settle into a normal cadence.

It was just one memory he'd had of her. Of them, together. She'd be a fool to make anything more out of it than there was. She'd spent the prior six years doing that.

"Here," she said when they reached his rooms.

Tristan fell into the wall; catching himself with his shoulder. "Myy apologies that you'd see me thisss way."

"You're not the first man I've seen with too many drinks in him, Tristan."

He narrowed his eyes. "Is there someone ahh will need to call out?"

A smile tugged at her lips. That had become the protectiveness she'd grown used to: a slightly brotherly caring. "Only if you're intending to off my brother."

"Pass. Ahv never had a problem with yourrr brother. Quite an upstanding fellow."

"Then you haven't spent enough time with him," she said dryly.

Tristan cupped a hand around his ear. "What was thatttt?" he asked, entirely too loud, his voice carrying.

Poppy slapped a hand over his mouth, silencing any further words. "Hush, unless you wish for us to be caught."

He snorted. "Someexplainingdo," She made out most of that muffled reply.

"Where is your key?"

Again, he said something into her hand, and then lifted his shoulders in a clear message: he didn't know.

Sighing, Poppy released her hold on his mouth, and reaching inside his jacket, she felt around for the tiny article.

"Whyy, Poppy," he whispered devilishly. "IIII never knew you felt that way."

Of course he hadn't. That had always been the problem between them. "Hush." Her fingers brushed over a thick packet of notes, and she paused. What in blazes?

"Have we lost it?" he asked again, entirely too loud.

Poppy jumped and resumed her search...at last finding it. "Here," she exclaimed triumphantly. Inserting the key, she opened the door. "Now, in you go."

Mistaking that cue, or mayhap simply doing as he wished, Sir Faithful bounded forward.

"Whyy, thank you. Myyy knight in shiny armor."

"It's shining," Poppy whispered. "Now, go." It was one thing to casually converse openly in the smoke room or restaurant as they'd done today. There'd been nothing clandestine in those public encounters. They'd simply been two friends meeting. Being alone in his rooms, at this hour, in her night shift? That was altogether different.

"Verrra well. I bid you..." Tristan swept his hand in an elaborate flourish as he sketched a low bow—and promptly fell on his face. "Oomph."

Poppy pressed her hands briefly to her face and shook her head. "You are hopeless."

"No truer words have been spoke," he replied, his mouth buried in the carpet.

Her chest tightened. As charming and teasing as he'd been these past days, it had been too easy to dismiss the real threat Tristan faced. With their every exchange, he'd seemed...unchanged. Or mayhap it was simply she'd been too much of a coward and hadn't wanted to fully confront the perilousness of his scandal. "Here," she said, this time more gently. "We need to get you inside." Offering him a hand, Poppy helped him struggle to his feet. She staggered under his added weight, as she led him inside his rooms. Kicking the door closed with her heel, she urged Tristan forward. Gasping lightly from her exertions, she steered him to the bed.

He fell onto the edge; the mattress dipped under his weight.

Falling to a knee, she proceeded to tug at his boot.

"Used to have a valet, youuuu know."

"I do." Poppy didn't lift her head from her efforts to remove his footwear. "He knotted your cravats too tightly," she said, battling the slightly scuffed boot. And here she'd spent her life admiring the ease and functionality of a man's attire. Straddling his leg, she set to work on easing the stubborn article off.

"Did youuu think so about my valet? Always thought ahh was quite presentable."

"Oh, you were. Just presentable in a 'his-cravat-is-too-tight' sort of way." At last, the boot gave way and she went sprawling on her buttocks. She grunted as pain radiated up her tailbone. "I will say, I have new appreciation for the work they do," she muttered, rubbing at her injured flesh as she made to relieve Tristan of the other article.

"You'd say I'm better off without immm then? Because I lost himmm. Lost all of them."

There it was again. The reminder of his circumstances. They were no doubt the reason he now found himself three sheets to the wind.

"It might help to talk about it," she offered as she divested him of his next boot. This time, when it loosened, she braced herself, and kept upright.

"Nothing willl help," he said matter-of-factly, even in his drunkenness. He battled with the task of removing his jacket. "And yet, just beinnng around you had always brought some peace."

Her heart did a series of wild leaps in her breast. Which was the height of foolishness. Tristan merely spoke from a place of too many spirits.

Tristan managed to wrest himself free of his jacket. "Always so easssy talking to you."

That she could understand. It had always been that way with him, too.

Poppy sat beside him, and waited.

"I have nothing," he said hoarsely. "Along with the title ahhhve lost and the properties and fortune, I'm being expected to pay for debts incurred in making the fortunes that now belong to another."

She puzzled her brow. "Well, that doesn't make any sense."

He released a tired sigh. "And yet, it does. I borrowed monies that weren't mine to make investments that also weren't mine."

"Which you were, at the time, unaware of."

Tristan dug around his jacket and withdrew a cheroot. "How confident you are in my honor. When all of society believes myyy hands are fully in Percival Northrop's kidnapping." There it was: the first time he'd uttered aloud before Poppy the ugliest parts of his own scandal.

"Here," she said softly. Taking his cheroot, she lit it on the candlestick at his bedside and handed it over.

"Mannny thanks," he said, with the scrap of tobacco stuck between his teeth.

"I know you. Furthermore," she went on. "Even if I wasn't certain in your character, you would have been a mere child yourself at the time the boy went missing."

He stared wistfully at her. "If onllly society were as logical in their reasoning." Taking a long pull of his cheroot, he exhaled slowly. "Either way, I'm now left with two unmarried sisters and a mother to care for. Yet all of it belongs to him." *All of it.* "And there is no way out."

"Of course there is," she said.

"Thatttt speaks to the contrary," he drawled, his slurred words rolling together. He pointed his cheroot and Poppy searched around for the "that" in question.

"Your jacket?"

He chuckled. "Annnnd even when my life is in the gutter, you manage to make me smile." His laughter abated, and even in his inebriated state, he held her gaze with clarity and focus and seriousness.

Those butterflies danced in her belly.

She made herself reach for the rumpled garment, and fished inside. She withdrew the stack of notes. "This?

"Preccciisely."

Assuming permission to read had been granted when he'd motioned to the packet on the floor, Poppy unfolded the ivory sheets, and began to read.

She paused mid-sentence. "Tristan," she exclaimed.

"Precisssely. Again." He fell back on the mattress and lay there silent, puffing away at his cheroot. Occasionally stubbing the ashes onto the crystal tray beside his bed. More often than not, missing.

Poppy resumed her reading.

Lord Bolingbroke,

Per our most recent discussion, you are well aware of the circumstances in which you now find yourself. Lord Maxwell is determined to see that you pay your—

"Debts," she whispered into the quiet.

I am in the process of compiling a list of the outstanding debt owed to the current Lord Maxwell.

"Your faithful servant?" she squawked.

"Ahm not the only one who found that closing a bit in irony?" Tristan called with that scrap of tobacco still clenched between his teeth.

She slapped the pages closed. "What a *bootlicker.*" It was one thing to take up employment elsewhere, but to do so with the current earl? "You've a problem with servants and loyalty."

"Hadd," he mumbled, as he exhaled a perfect smoke ring. "Past tense. I don't have any servants."

Poppy hopped up, and removed the cheroot from his fingers. "All right," she said determinedly, stamping out his smoke on the crystal dish. "You must address that unfair debt." And care for his sisters and mother. "What is the amount?"

He shrugged. "Sanders is sending that 'round soon. Though in truth, I sussspect he had the information when he was here but was scared to mention it with me seated before him."

"There's always a way out."

Tristan edged himself higher on the bed, toward the pillow. "That is what IIII said. And never tell me, you have the answer because you always have the answerrrs." He chuckled. "To questions I didn't even know most times I had."

Actually, she didn't. Not this time. Not any time, really. If she did, she'd have known how to get herself unscathed from her own scandal.

She froze. Then her mind picked up speed as the plan took root and grew. Of course. It was the answer. For both of them. In fact, she was really quite disappointed in herself for not thinking of it earlier. In a way, she already had. The contract.

"That is it," she whispered. Tristan's situation was dire and Poppy had already given up on marriage, and that had been before she'd gone and been ruined.

"What is it?" he asked, half-asleep.

Climbing onto the bed, Poppy waved the damning packet sent by his feckless former man-of-affairs. "Why, we need to marry, of course."

Tristan opened and closed his mouth continuously like the bass he'd plucked from the river the last time they'd gone fishing. Struggling up onto his elbows, he managed to get himself upright. "I beg your pardon. I know I've had sahm drinks. Did you just...?"

"Propose marriage?" She nodded. "I do believe I did. Though, in fairness, it's not quite me proposing to you but rather us entering into that agreement we reached."

"We did?"

She nodded.

"You and I?" he repeated.

"Which is really just another way of saying 'we', Tristan."

He collapsed back into the pillows. "When in God's name did we do anything like that?"

A pang struck, even though it shouldn't. Even though she should be very well accustomed to his not recalling that particular day. There had been all number of "particular days" he'd forgotten. This one, however, had been different.

"Our Marriage Pact." That paper she'd meticulously written down following Lord Smith's ball...and saved all these years.

"Our Marriage Pact." His mouth moved, but his words came out inaudibly. "Doesn soun' familiar."

"It really is the answer. We're both trapped here, mired in scandal, wanting out of our circumstances."

"Shh," he whispered, stealing a glance about.

Poppy rolled her eyes. "First, we're alone in your rooms. Secondly, I'm not making you an indecent offer."

"No, you're offering me marriage," he said on a frantic whisper. "Which is realllly just the same thing."

She bristled. "Actually it is quite the opposite."

"Not when a lady does it."

Poppy pinched his arm. He grunted. "Careful, Poplar. It is not too late for me to renege on the agreement. Who says a lady cannot propose to a gentleman?"

"*What agreement?*" he sounded so pained she almost took pity on him. Almost.

"If we were unmarried, we'd both be one another's plus one in life. Lord Smith's? Is that familiar?" He shook his head. "My lemonade stained dress?"

Understanding at last sparked in his gaze, and then… His eyes bulged. "Surely you were not *seriousss?*"

"I was." Poppy thinned her eyes on his face. "Deadly."

Tristan sighed, that faintly condescending whisper of air that sent her fingers darting out once more. "Oomph. Would you please *stop* pinching me?"

"I will when you cease patronizing me."

"I'm not." Color splotched his cheeks. "At least, I wasn't intentionally doing so. Poppy," he began again, and this time had the speed and sense to draw his arm out of reach. "You were involved in a scandallll, Poppy," he said placatingly. "One that will eventually be forgotten, and then there will be some gentleman there who'll make you a proper husbannnd."

"What exactly is a proper husband?" This she'd dearly love to hear from Tristan Poplar.

And even for as drunk as he was, there was a clarity in the gaze that met hers. "One who will love you and make you happy, in a marriage that didn't begin as a business arrangement. I want more for you than that, Poppy."

Warmth tingled in her heart. In Tristan Poplar, the world saw a detached rogue, but heartless rogues didn't speak of love and they certainly didn't put a young lady's happiness before their own need for self-preservation. "And I want a husband who doesn't get to decide what I want."

He folded his arms across his broad chest, and waved his fingers, urging her on. "I'm listening. I'm not saying I'm going to agree to this madnesss, but tell me what would you possibly gain from marriage to me?"

A man who was honorable. A man who loved his sisters and mother enough to worry about their happiness and futures before his own. Her heart fluttered, that butterfly effect he'd always had upon her senses. He'd never gathered that she'd carried a *tendre* for him as a young girl. Which was all the better, as they'd likely never have entered into the pact they had. "We've already gone through that, Tristan."

"Ahm afraid you'll have to refresh my memory."

Two and a half years. It had been two years since she and Tristan had agreed to be one another's spouse if—or as the case turned out—when they proved unsuccessful in finding one. He had no recollection of that night. It shouldn't matter. It was a chance meeting they'd had long ago. Only, Poppy recalled every detail of that night, and he should remember…none of it. Poppy proceeded to recite the familiar lines, memorized long ago. "If either Tristan Poplar or Poppy Tidemore fail to wed when I, Poppy Tidemore, reach the age of—"

"Verrry formal language you've adopted."

"—twenty-six, then we shall marry one another."

"Twenty-six!"

Poppy cocked her head.

"The contract would only take effect if you were unwed at twenty-six, which you are not." With that, he fell back on the mattress and reached for a pillow. As he dragged the article over his face, there was a finality to that gesture. "There was a reason we said twenty-six because at twenty, you're still young and deserving of hope and love." The pillow garbled those words, and yet, nonetheless, the meaning was clear.

Poppy frowned at the veiled undertones of what he truly implied: she was a girl, still. She yanked the pillow from his eyes and tossed it aside. "I'm twenty-one."

He grabbed his pillow back. "Fine. Then, in five years, if I'm not out of this mess and you're unwed and still desiring marriage, then we can speeeeak."

And then, he proceeded to snore.

The great lummox.

Poppy shoved his shoulder until he grunted himself awake.

"Whaat? What?"

"Age is arbitrary, Tristan. It was the significance of the terms and what I desire that mattered most in that pact."

Tristan slowly removed the pillow. His gaze roved over her face, touching on each place with such an intensity it scorched, as if he could see inside and pluck out the lifetime of secrets she carried. "And what was that?"

"A say over my own fate." Poppy turned her palms up, willing him to see."To marry a man who'll not stifle my artistic endeavors but who'll instead allow me the freedom to create what I wish and how I wish." She looked at him for a long moment."Would you? Seek to prevent me from undertaking any artistic endeavor?"

"Of course nooot," he said with such conviction, she feared the weakening of her heart.

"Then we will still do quite nicely, Tristan."

"You never wished to marry for looove?"

I wished to marry you for love…

She stilled, stricken by that reminder. Because it had no bearing on any of this. Poppy was a woman grown now, with a mind for what she wanted, and also a mind for what she'd already accepted would never be.

Tristan offered another sad little smile."I'm grateful for the offfer, but I cannot allow either of us to do this. At least, not until another five and a half years." With a teasing wink, he flipped onto his side.

Teasing. He'd always been teasing.

Poppy scrambled around the other side of the bed so that they lay close, facing one another."What of your sisters and mother?"

That brought his eyes flying open.

Her heart thudded hard in her chest. Was it her body's awareness of him? Or the proposition she awaited an answer on? Or both?

"I am grateful to you for the offfer. But I cannot, Poppy. Not for you. Not even for my family."

"Can't you?" she whispered. "Your sisters would have entry to Polite Society once more." Some emotion flickered in his eyes. He wanted to say "yes" in that instant. She saw in the silver flecks that glinted. "I have—"

He blanched. "Please, don't say it."

Her stomach muscles twisted. Countless English lords had married because of their need for funds. Prudence's husband had been a fortune hunter. Why, even Ryker had married Penny to save his club after he'd been discovered in a compromising position with Penny.

And here was Tristan. So proud, refusing to enter into an arrangement that would see him as a fortune hunter.

Drawing in a deep breath, he flung his legs over the side of his bed and sat there a moment. Then coming to his feet, he padded across the room, to the double doors that emptied out onto the balcony. A wave of cool night air spilled into the room.

Poppy stared at him a long moment, uncertain. And then drawing her wrapper close to ward off the chill, she joined him.

Breathing deep of the night air, Tristan rested his palms on the smooth stone surface and stared out.

She matched his stance, and followed his gaze to the reflecting pool her brother-in-law had constructed at Penny's request. With the breeze dusting ripples upon the surface and the overflowing gardens that bloomed with flowers, one could almost believe they were the teasing pair at her family's summer picnics.

"You would regrettt it," he said quietly, not taking his eyes from a pair of white swans that glided over the surface.

It did not, however, escape her notice that he'd not outright rejected her offer.

"Why?" She glanced up at him. "Because I'm young and don't know my own mind?"

"Because you are young and will one day cooome to regret that you don't have what your siblings share with their spouses."

How very…easily he assumed they'd never have that. And for the first time since she'd put forward their marriage pact as the answer to both their situations, reservations crept in.

Could she spend a lifetime with Tristan Poplar and not fall hopelessly under his spell?

Poppy drew herself up onto the ledge, and perched herself there. "We like one another. We get on well. We're honest. We've laid out very clearly our expectations of one another. I say we'd be better off than most married couples."

A grin tugged his lips up into that rogue's half smile that never ceased to play with her heart.

A moment later, the sharp planes of his face returned to their earlier, more serious mask. He caught her wrist in a grip that was an enthrallingly, contradictory mix of steel and softness. He guided her hand to his lips. "Tell me your expectations."

"I-I have our list saved."

"Uh-uh." He guided her off the ledge, and anchored her there between the small stone wall and his chest. "I want the words from your lips, not ones written in a child's hand long ago."

Two years wasn't so very long ago. She intended to say as much but he lowered his mouth; his breath tickled her skin, sending shivers radiating along her arm. Her breath caught.

And then he kissed her.

"Tell me, Poppy," he whispered into her mouth. Tristan brushed the pad of his thumb along the inseam of her wrist, in a distracted back and forth caress. Her lashes fluttered under the deliciousness of that warmth. "Tell me what you want."

You. I want you...

"I'm to have the largest space in the residence for an art room," she managed to get out that first ask she'd put to him at Lord Smith's.

"I've two properties. A crumbling estate in Dartmoor and a London townhouse, falling down. All the rooms are yours and you should use them as a great, big exhibit for all your art work." He flung his arms wide. "All of it and signed, tooooo."

Her lips twitched. "Great and big are redundant."

"You're trryying to change the topic."

"A bit, I am," she conceded.

"Have I mentioned I've a rat infestation?"

"You've not, Tristan." She made a mental note of that detail. "We'll require cats, then. Sir Faithful won't be pleased, of course, but he should also dislike the alternative."

A pained laugh escaped him. "Poppy, I've no words. What else would you request?"

"I'll keep company with whomever I wish."

He shifted his hip onto the edge of the balustrade. "Would that list include Rochford?"

Poppy lifted her chin. "And if it did?"

"I'd trust you to choose your friendships assss you would."

It was the answer she should prefer. The one she should want. An absolute trust in her judgment and freedom to choose. And yet, perversely, she wished he might care enough to not want her anywhere near the bastard Rochford. "There'll be no hunting," she quickly added, lest he detect that inexplicable disappointment she couldn't herself understand.

"This is becoming decidedly more real," he muttered.

Yes, for the both of them. The significance of what she'd suggested and what they now spoke of, hit her like the weight of a fast-moving carriage...she and Tristan joined forevermore in a marriage of convenience.

As if he'd followed the uneasy path her thoughts had swerved, Tristan palmed her cheek, his caress gentle and hypnotic. "You see it," he said quietly.

"See what?" she whispered.

"That you want more." Tristan lowered his hand to the rail, and she bit the inside of her cheek at the loss of his touch. "That you *deserve* more, Poppy."

It was then that she knew definitively with all reservations lifted: she was going to marry Tristan Poplar. Her decision wasn't born of a young girl's flight of fancy. Or a young woman's secret yearning. Nay, it came from a place of knowing that if she could not have love in her life, she would have a man of honor, who put her happiness before that of his own. Poppy smoothed her palms over her skirts. "There is the matter of my garments, Tristan. I'd wear—"

"Whatever you wished." He held his palms aloft. "I assure you, I am in no way attacking your white garments. I wellll understand you are free to be annoyed by your skirts; however, it is an altogether different matter for others to express an opinion as to what you're wearing."

Her heart skipped several beats. Those words, a near verbatim echo of her warning to him, tugged forth that long ago night. That night, which despite his protestations he recalled. Oh, he might *say* he had no recollection of their exchange in Lord Smith's conservatory, but he'd just proven otherwise. Something told her that if she asserted that point, this increasingly "more real" discussion would be at an end, and so too would their pact. Poppy came 'round to face Tristan, effectively trapping him upon the perch he'd made. "There are two more matters to address," she said, tipping her head back.

His gaze slid to her mouth. Heat filled his eyes. "Yes?" he asked hoarsely.

He wants to kiss me. And I want that kiss. She wanted all of him and a lifetime of exploring the desire he'd awakened in her just days ago.

Then drawing her shoulders back, she put that last, and most important demand to him. "There's to be no mistresses." She'd have his loyalty. "Ever," she added. "No opera singers, actresses, widows, serving girls. And…and…any other type of woman I might be missing." Whether they never moved beyond anything more than friendship—which, given that was the state they'd found themselves in these past six years, was increasingly likely—she'd know she at least had his loyalty.

"There'll be no mistresses, Poppy," he murmured.

How effortlessly he made that pledge.

She darted her tongue out, tracing the seam of her lips. Could she finish the remainder of that request, one she'd been too innocent and even shy to present two years earlier but now could not have a marriage without a commitment from him? "There is one more…"

"And what is that, Poppy?" Tristan ran the pad of his thumb along the same path her tongue had traveled. She shivered, as a streak of heat went through her. His eyes darkened, reflecting back the very desire that now throbbed within her.

"I won't have a marriage in name only, Tristan."

"Say what you would have, Poppy," he urged in a husked voice, just as he'd urged in Lord Smith's conservatory. Only then there'd been teasing. Now, there was only his passion-laden command that liquified her. "Tell me what it is you want." Tristan shifted his teasing caress lower, along the line of her jaw, and lower to the small teardrop-shaped birthmark upon her neck; he lightly touched it, as if discovering that mark she'd hated as a girl and sought to conceal as a young woman. But with his ministrations, somehow felt like a thing of beauty.

Her pulse thundered in her ears, and as she spoke, her voice came thickly. "I would have you…" Poppy tried again, her voice breathless, "…share my bed."

A smile ghosted his lips; this was the smile she'd never had turned on her. Not from this man. Not from any man. This was the rogue's grin more potent than the apple that had tempted Eve into sinning, and every fallen lady thereafter, into willingly—happily—shedding her virtue—for the promises contained within that smile. "I assure you, Poppy, ours would never be a marriage in name only."

His veiled promise said everything and nothing all at the same time, weighted her eyes closed.

Tristan lowered his head, so their breaths mingled. "Very well, Poppy." As he spoke, their lips brushed in fleeting, all too brief kisses. "I'll marry you."

CHAPTER 12

TRISTAN HAD DONE MANY OUTLANDISH things while drunk.
There'd been the time, on a wager, he'd raced shirtless astride his
mount in the dead of winter. A wager he'd won. Or the time,
fresh out of university, when he'd broken into a tavern ditty at
Almack's. An invitation that had been rescinded and then again
only extended after his return from Waterloo.

Never before, however, had he proposed marriage.

Had he proposed marriage? Even drunk as he'd been, he would
wager the rest of his holdings that it had been Poppy Tidemore
who'd put the offer to him.

He, however, had been the one who'd accepted.

In the light of a new day, with his head throbbing to beat the
Devil, and being escorted through the halls of the Earl of Sinclair's
townhouse, Tristan conceded that he may have made a mistake.

And a terrible one at that.

It had been one thing to lose his fortunes and his title. There'd
still been the possibility of Tristan restoring his wealth and eventually redeeming his name.

It was an altogether different matter forfeiting his life, which
was certainly what he was doing, coming here to ask Poppy
Tidemore's, loving, overprotective brother for the lady's hand in
marriage. After all, there could be no going back from being mur-
dered dead.

In fact, had he not given the lady his word, he might actually have changed his mind altogether.

Nay, that wasn't altogether true.

The memory of her, on that terrace outside his rooms, with the scent of crimson roses thick in the air, and the crisp hint of citrus clinging to her skin, whispered forward as it had since their meeting. He'd wanted her in that moment. And he'd been spellbound with the possibility of knowing her—in every way.

"Here we are, my lord," Lord Sinclair's butler murmured, and he stifled the urge to groan as that slight sound sent another round of throbbing to his temples. The servant rapped once on Sinclair's door.

Dying.

I am dying.

His stomach pitched, and he gave brief thanks when the knocking stopped and the door opened.

That relief was short-lived, however, as the reality of what he intended replaced that previous misery.

The brother.

The offer of marriage.

Or hell, he wasn't ready for marriage in and of itself.

And certainly not to Poppy. He'd only hurt her. There could be no other outcome. She was young. Innocent. At some point, she'd convinced herself that she cared more for him than she did. More than he was worth.

"Baron Bolingbroke," the servant announced, and Tristan flinched as his head again screamed in protest.

He tried to make his legs move.

Who would have imagined that running to face a French soldier's bayonet should prove easier than entering Lord Sinclair's offices and putting an offer of marriage before him.

The butler coughed into his hand.

"Bolingbroke," Sinclair called from the middle of that room. "Have you found yourself at the wrong residence? Is it my brother-in-law whom you seek?"

With that, the other man unknowingly offered Tristan an out. Tristan could very well claim to have been seeking St. Cyr on a matter of importance.

Only…

He could not. Not for Poppy whom he'd entered into an agreement with. And not for the sisters who depended upon him. That compelled Tristan forward.

He entered. "No, my lord," he said, even the sound of his own voice excruciating. The servant bowed and took his leave, closing the door behind Tristan, and sealing off that path of escape. Uninvited, Tristan came forward, joining the earl in the middle of his Aubusson carpet. "I wished to speak with you."

The other man's eyebrows came together ever so slightly. "Oh?" There was a warning there, one that suggested he knew, which was both improbable and impossible. Tristan himself hadn't known until just last evening that there would be anything between him and Poppy. The earl crossed to his sideboard and made himself a brandy.

It didn't escape his notice that Poppy's brother offered neither a seat, nor drink. Which was all well and good. After the bottle he'd consumed last evening, he never intended to touch a drink again.

Tristan tugged off his gloves, and beat them together in a nervous rhythm before catching Sinclair's focus on that distracted movement. Tristan hurriedly stuffed the articles inside the front of his jacket, and clasped his hands behind him.

"I must admit," Sinclair said, as he carried that drink over… and then promptly bypassed Tristan, for the sofa. "When I was informed you were here to meet with me, I wondered: what business we could possibly have with one another," the earl went on, as he settled himself into the leather wingback chair at the hearth. "Because we've never had any business together that should merit a sudden visit." Over the rim of his drink, Sinclair arched a single, dark, menacing brow. "Am I correct?"

So it was to be that manner of meeting.

"May I?" Tristan asked, looking to the seating.

Wordlessly, the earl waved his spare hand.

Tristan joined Poppy's brother. Stopped. Considered the available seating, before ultimately opting for the matching wingback chair furthest from the earl…with a rose-inlaid table between them. Directness was always the best way. "I'm here to ask for your sister's hand."

The Earl of Sinclair went absolutely motionless; his untouched drink dangled from his fingers. And then…Poppy's brother downed the contents in one long, slow swallow, his throat muscles frantically working. When he'd finished, his face twisted in a grimace. "I'm sorry," he said darkly. "It had sounded as though you said…"

"I want to marry your sister."

"My sister."

"Poppy." When the other man's face remained peculiarly static, Tristan clarified. "Your sole remaining unwed sister."

The earl opened his mouth. And closed it. He opened it again. Then, lifting a finger, he stalked over to the sideboard. He returned a moment later with the same bottle of French spirits. Pouring himself another drink, Poppy's brother set the decanter and snifter down before him. "You want to marry Poppy."

All things considered, even with the repeating echo of Tristan's every word, the earl was handling this a good deal better than he'd expected. "I do."

"No."

Tristan frowned. "I—"

"Beg my pardon? As you should."

"I was going to say 'I don't understand'," Tristan drawled.

Ignoring that bid for levity between them, Sinclair rested his palms on his knees, and leaned forward. "You asked for my permission, and the answer is 'no'."

He resisted the urge to rub at his aching temples. "I was being polite."

"Pooolite? Polite. *Polite.*"

Perhaps at another time, Tristan would have been singularly impressed at the earl's ability to transform the same word into three different meanings: incredulity. Shock. And fury. Now, his patience was really wearing thin. "That is correc—"

"Ah-ah," the earl cut him off before he'd finished. Poppy's brother wagged a finger at him like he was a troublesome child. "Polite is not entering my household and stating a desire to marry my youngest sister." Sinclair's voice grew increasingly strident. "My sister whom you know, not at all, Maxwell."

"Bolingbroke," he felt inclined to point out. Errors in names and forms of address were a good deal safer than the other man's volatile rage simmering and about ready to boil over. "And you were correct, I misspoke."

Some of the tension eased from the earl's shoulders. "Indeed."

"Poppy and I wish to marry one another." His earlier tolerance gave way to annoyance. Tristan knew how to make her smile and what she found joy in. He knew those interests that mattered most to her. And now, he knew the taste and feel of her, too… "And we know one another quite well, in fact."

The earl's face went red.

"Not in that way," Tristan rushed to reassure. At least, not in ways he'd ever admit. Not if he still wished to remain breathing.

"Not. In. What. Way," Sinclair's whisper was lined in steel.

Tristan wrestled with his cravat. "Ah, intimately that is. Not yet. Not until we marry, that is." *Stop talking.*

There was a beat of silence, and then—the earl roared. "Get out."

He swallowed a groan. *Ill. I'm going to be ill.* The agony beating around in his skull was going to make him vomit right on Sinclair's office floor, in the middle of a proposal. In a bid for calm he didn't feel, Tristan looped his knee across his opposite leg in response. "I am afraid that is not going to make the situation go away. I'm here asking to marry your sister. Your sister who wishes to marry me." The sister who, in fact, was the creator of their marriage pact, and the one who'd proposed.

"Absolutely not."

Gathering up his glass and decanter, the earl started for his sideboard. He returned the bottle to the row of other fine spirits, and then took a more casual sip, before returning to his desk. Setting his drink aside for the open ledger atop the mahogany piece, the earl proceeded to dismiss him.

Very well, directness had not worked. Tristan employed another tactic with the gentleman. "In fairness, we are not unalike, you and I." Even the sound of his own voice made him want to cast up his stomach.

Sinclair leveled him with a flinty stare. "We are nothing alike."

"We both have sisters whom we care deeply for," Tristan pointed out.

That effectively silenced the earl. The other man did tip his chin reluctantly to the vacant chairs, and Tristan took heart.

"We have mothers who greatly value their station in society, and the family reputation."

"We do at that," Sinclair muttered, making that surprising concession of a shared connection.

"And, of course, we are both rogues."

That was the moment he lost Poppy's brother.

Sinclair jabbed his pen toward Tristan, splattering ink upon the previously immaculate surface of his desk. "That is where we are different. I *was* a rogue. Now, I'm a married, boring lord with a passel of babes and children. You, however, are still a rogue." With that, he lowered his focus once more to the book before him.

Undeterred, Tristan remained seated. "Your wife reformed you."

"I'm not looking to have my sister *reform* any man."

Tristan scoffed. "Well, that's hardly fair given you yourself must credit your wife."

"The man Poppy marries will be worthy of her from the moment they meet."

"As in, he'll not, say, put an indecent offer to her," Tristan said dryly. Unlike the rumors which had circulated surrounding the earl's ignoble beginnings with his wife.

The Earl of Sinclair's pen snapped from the tension of his grip; the article fell in two useless pieces. And Tristan braced for another thunderous explosion. That didn't come... Sinclair steepled his fingers "Why do you want to marry Poppy?"

Why? His mind went blank. He'd not lie to the other man with false promises of love for the lady. He cared about her. But theirs was a business arrangement. To say as much would end Sinclair's discussion quicker than it had begun. "We share similar interests. We fish. We... like dogs," he finished lamely.

"You like...?" A pained laugh burst from Sinclair, and the other man slapped a hand over his eyes. "Do you know that is the first thing she mentioned to me when you nearly trampled her as a child. That you both liked dogs."

Despite the volatile exchange with the earl, Tristan found himself smiling wistfully. "I recall that day," he murmured. She'd been a bright-eyed girl, chattering on quicker than he could formulate an answer to her many questions about his dogs.

Sinclair sighed. "Good God." It was a prayer that Tristan would have made had he found a bounder like himself seated opposite him asking for any one of his sisters' hands. "Bolingbroke, you are in dun territory. You've been stripped of a title, mired in scandal, and you've lost the wealth you once possessed." Ice glazed the other man's eyes. "Do you truly expect me to believe that doesn't have anything to do with this sudden offer?"

Tristan fell silent. He'd not outright lie to the man.

"I thought so." Sinclair seethed.

"You are correct. I would not want my sister to marry one such as me, either. And yet, Poppy wishes to wed me." In a decision she'd only been logical about. As such, there were no worries about an emotional entanglement. *Or are you merely trying to convince yourself of that…?*

"Poppy doesn't know what she wants," Sinclair exclaimed.

"She is not a girl anymore." Tristan held the other man's gaze. "She is a woman. A woman capable of knowing her own mind and heart." A muscle leapt in Sinclair's jaw. Tristan sat forward in his seat. "Sinclair, I understand what it is to marry off a sister. I understand it is an impossible moment, accepting one's sister is no longer a child, and hoping that the man she will spend the rest of her life with is one deserving of her."

"I assure you, the man Poppy weds *will be* deserving of her." And no doubt, if Tristan accepted the other man's rejection of his suit, Poppy would, in fact, do just that. He was unprepared for the hot rush of jealousy that whipped through him. "She is not for you." Sinclair pulled open his desk drawer and drew out another pen. "Now, if you'll excuse me?"

The last vestige of his patience fled. "I'm marrying Poppy, Sinclair. If you wish to keep her dowry or we agree that it remains in a trust for her and our future children, then that is fine." Tristan came to his feet and, laying his palms on the desk, leaned halfway across until his gaze met Poppy's brother. "But this *will* happen."

They remained locked in a tense primal battle, one that Tristan had no intention of losing.

The earl glared blackly at him. "Are you suggesting you would take her on to Gretna Green?"

Oh, bloody hell.

The other family scandal.

"There won't be a need for that." Just a special license. Would Poppy truly marry with her family refusing to support the union?

The earl curved his lips up in a smile that didn't meet the frost in his eyes. "Make no mistake, you will never marry Poppy."

Given that Tristan had himself felt every last reservation the other man had hurled at him, he should take his leave and accept that this was not to be. That Tristan's initial response to the idea of marriage with Poppy was, in fact, the correct one.

He smiled coldly. "We shall see about that, Sinclair." Poppy would be his bride. They would have the exact arrangement the lady had put before him last evening.

And her brother could go hang.

With that, he turned on his heel and quit the earl's offices…and found his way a short while later to the one person who couldn't go hang.

Shown to St. Cyr's offices, Tristan waited for the other man to arrive.

And all the while, through the haze left by too much drink, plotted and planned what in hell to say to his best friend.

Funny thing…I've accepted an offer of marriage from your sister-in-law.

Or mayhap he'd be wise to go with…

I know this will come as a surprise to the both of us…

Tristan eyed his friend's sideboard. He'd been wrong earlier in Sinclair's offices: he could use a drink, after all.

"Bolingbroke!" his friend called, strolling in. That booming echo of St. Cyr's jovial greeting seemed a fitting kind of punishment for the information he was about to impart. "An unexpected pleasure. May I offer you a drink—?"

"No," Tristan said quickly, his stomach in full revolt.

The marquess shifted course, and found the place behind his desk. "Ahh," he said with a casual knowing, after he'd settled into his seat. "I know that look."

Precisely what was the look the other man thought he saw: *I accepted an offer of a marriage of convenience from your sister-in-law, and brought the wrath of your brother-in-law's fury down?* "Uh—" Tristan loosened his cravat; it didn't help. He was being choked off by his own mistakes.

St. Cyr winked. "The look of one who's consumed too many spirits."

"Ah, yes." Well, that was certainly a segue he might use: *You see, in the midst of a drunken stupor Poppy Tidemore proposed and I accepted.* Tristan thrust aside the horrid idea.

In the end, he opted for blunt honesty. "I thought I should mention, prior to my…" St. Cyr was opening his desk drawer. Tristan stiffened. Mayhap his lifelong friend intended to shoot him on the spot. "Uh…that is…prior to my coming here…" St. Cyr withdrew an official-looking note, stamped with a gold seal.

"Perhaps I should speak first?"

No, Tristan would rather have this said. "I asked Sinclair for Poppy's hand in marriage," he blurted.

Tick-tock-tick-tock.

The marquess sat there dumbly, that official-looking note dangling in his fingers.

"I know this must come as a…surprise," Tristan brought himself to say. "And I wished for you to be the first to know." He grimaced. "After Lord Sinclair, that is."

"*What?*"

"I asked Sinclair for Poppy's hand in marriage. He declined that offer, but I…" *intend to marry her anyway.*

St. Cyr's eyes formed threatening slits of rage. "But. You. *What?*"

"I'm going to marry her, anyway." Because he'd given his word. And more…because he had no choice. That pronouncement ushered in another round of heavy tension.

"Why?"

It was ironically the first time he'd been asked that by either Sinclair or St. Cyr. And it was the absolute best question that should have been put to him. Only, it was the one that would never be suitable.

St. Cyr slammed the page in his fingers down on the immaculate desk. "I asked 'why?'"

"Given our…like circumstances—"

"Oh, Christ," St. Cyr whispered, sliding his eyes closed.

"We saw the mutual benefits of—"

"A marriage of convenience?"

Yes…well, when put in those terms, that was precisely what Tristan and Poppy had worked out.

"You had one bloody rule to obey," St. Cyr thundered, and then blanched. His gaze went to the doorway. When he looked back to Tristan, and again spoke, he did so in hushed words that couldn't be caught by any potential passersby. "One rule.

"I know."

"And you gave me your word."

"I understand that. But I'd have you know I didn't intend—"

"What? To offer her marriage?" And then St. Cyr stilled, his eyes widened with a slow understanding that could only come from two men who'd been closer than brothers. "You didn't offer for her."

Heat tripped up his neck. "I made the offer to Sinclair."

"That is not what I said," the other man shot back. "Poppy proposed to you, didn't she?"

He'd not lie to the other man but neither would Tristan reveal that intimate secret—not even to his best friend in the world.

Or mayhap his former best friend in the world?

"I'm aware you are likely displeased by this turn of events."

"Displeased? *Displeased?*" A cold, harsh mirthless laugh spilled from his friend's lips. Coming out of his chair with jerky movements, he stalked over to the sideboard grabbed a bottle and a single glass. He poured himself a whiskey and then downed it. "That is all you'll say?" St. Cyr demanded, slamming the glass down hard enough to shatter it. "What do you expect me to tell my wife about this?" His friend didn't await a response and with every accusation a well-placed lash, his guilt swelled. "What assurances will I be able to make her about her sister's future and happiness…?" St. Cyr dragged a hand through his hair. "*Nothing.* There is nothing I can say that she will understand. Unless…" Hope flared in his eyes.

Tristan shook his head.

"Do you love her?"

Did he love her…? It was a query that gave him absolute pause. He cared about Poppy. Very much. He always had. They enjoyed one another's company. But love? "I…"

St. Cyr dropped his head into his hands, and sighed. "Your silence was your answer."

"I care about her," he said, the reassurance lame to his own ears.

"You care about her?" Another jaded chuckled shook St. Cyr's frame. "How…*reassuring.*"

And for the first time since he'd faced the criticisms of both Poppy's brother and brother-in-law, annoyance stirred. "I'm so unsuitable, am I, that you'd have this reaction?"

"Don't you do that." St. Cyr slammed a fist down, and the bottle and glass both jumped under the weight of his fury. "You don't get to play the wounded party. This has nothing to do with your circumstances, and you know it. This has *everything* to do with Poppy and her happiness." His friend drew in a slow breath, and when he again spoke he did so in calmer tones. "If you told me you loved her, I'd go to battle side by side against my damned brother-in-law for you. But you can't tell me that. You can only speak of a formal arrangement." All the fight went out of St. Cyr and he fell back in his seat.

"I am sorry," Tristan said somberly. "We've come to an arrangement suitable to both of us. I'll not renege on the word I gave her. I merely came to ask that you stand beside me."

St. Cyr's brows went arching up. "That is why you came? That is the sole reason?"

"And to apologize." How lame that sounded to his own ears.

Fury burning from his gaze, St. Cyr grabbed a thick packet he'd been holding earlier and tossed it across the desk.

Tristan caught it against his chest. "What is this?" he asked, already opening the pages. He stilled.

"There were several non-purchase vacancies as part of a new regiment created. It took some...convincing, given the scandal surrounding your name. However, I managed to secure the rank of lieutenant with the cavalry."

Shock. Relief. Excitement. All emotions he'd given up hope on ever again feeling since Northrop's reemergence swarmed him. His service in the military had been the only area in which he'd excelled. Where his efforts had made a difference. And the commission alone, when eventually sold, would go towards settling the debt Northrop—Maxwell—insisted he pay. When he spoke, emotion hoarsened his voice. "I don't know what to—"

Except, that expression of gratitude went unfinished, as reality took root. "*Poppy.*" The air trapped in his lungs. Bloody hell.

"Don't know what to say?" St. Cyr finished for him. "Are you referring to me? Or your...betrothed. My sister-in-law."

Oh, bloody hell. His palms slicked with moisture. "Christ," he whispered.

"I trust if you intend to move forward with this, you're going to need the Lord's help in dealing with your bride-to-be."

He didn't blink for several moments. "If I move forward with it?" Tristan scanned the official document. "There's no other alternative *except* me fulfilling the commission." To sell it outright or fail to honor the commission would only be looked at for the dishonor it was.

"I know," St. Cyr snapped. "And what of my sister-in-law? Do you still intend to see this through?"

Did he...? That question hovered on the air. Filled with a restiveness, Tristan came to his feet, and wandered a back and forth path before his best friend's desk. The promise he'd made Poppy had come in the heat of the moment, with him three sheets to the wind. It had been met with disapproval by...*all* members of her family, and Tristan's own best friend included. As such, there were numerous ways in which to disentangle himself from this. Poppy would be fine. In fact, she would be better off without him. As he'd reminded the lady, she'd be free to marry a gentleman whom she loved.

Jealousy wound its way through his veins; pumping fire, and spreading rage.

His nape prickled with the intensity of St. Cyr's focus.

"I...gave her my word. I cannot renege on that pledge." *Is it really about your honor this time? Or is it about more? Is it about a visceral hatred for any man who might win her affections?* Thrusting aside that silent jeering, he faced St. Cyr. "Poppy knows her own mind. This"—he lifted the commission—"it changes nothing."

St. Cyr flashed a sad smile. "Are you trying to convince me of that, Bolingbroke? Or yourself?"

Perhaps a bit of both. "I am sorry I've betrayed your trust—"

"Not sorry enough to do anything differently, however."

Touché. What was there to say to that? Tristan turned to go when his friend called out.

"I'd tell you not to hurt her, and yet, I know that there is no other possible outcome of this."

And with that ominous prediction lingering, Tristan took his leave.

CHAPTER 13

HE'D BEEN GONE FOR THE better part of the morn. Poppy knew because she'd waited for a glimpse of him leaving the hotel. Partly out of uncertainty in the light of a new day that Tristan had, in fact, changed his mind. Partly because of the need to see him.

That perilous, inexplicable desire that had plagued her as a girl, and did so all these years later.

Adding a second coat to the wall in her brother-in-law's hotel smoke room, Poppy stole yet another glance at the doors that led out to the patio.

He'd said yes.

Oh, that "*yes*" had come with a good deal of convincing. But in the end, when he'd accepted her terms, there had been a heat in his gaze that had touched her to the core. That primitive glimmer that could not be feigned, and proved that at somewhere along the way, despite his words to the contrary, he'd ceased to see her as "younger sister" or "little friend".

I assure you, Poppy, ours will never be a marriage in name only…

She made herself draw a slow, even breath.

"I felt a dark brown would…" her sister was saying.

"Mmm." Poppy had simply assumed that Tristan would see them live together as friends, friends who happened to be joined in a marriage of convenience.

"…with tinges of olive green and mustard yellow."

But he hadn't expected theirs to be a formal arrangement devoid of intimacy. He—

Wait… Poppy blinked slowly. "Olive green and mustard?" What in blazes was her sister asking for? "I swear every art lesson Juliet gave you was in vain. Surely you aren't asking me to paint…"

Penelope's eyes twinkled.

"Oh."

Penelope pushed aside Poppy's sketch for the smoke room redesign and drew herself up onto the work table cluttered with paints, brushes. "You seem distracted."

"Why do you say that?" She bristled defensively. She was not some kind of silly ninny to be woolgathering about Tristan and his kiss and…well, anything. *Liar. You've been thinking of him and only him since you parted ways on the patio outside his room early this morning.*

Penelope leaned in. "Because you've had the brush poised at the wall for nearly two minutes now and haven't made a single stroke with it since," she whispered. Her sister gave a pointed look at Poppy's fingers, and she followed her stare.

Poppy blinked. "Oh." She added a belated swipe to the wall, covering a place where a grotesque pair of horns sprang from a cherub's tousled golden curls. "Quite hideous, really," she said lamely. "A devilish cherub."

"The artist intended for the room and mural to represent a contradiction."

"What does that even mean?"

Penelope lifted her shoulders in a shrug. "It sounded perfectly reasonable when he explained it. Just as it sounds as though you are attempting to distract me now."

Poppy tamped down a sigh. The problem with sisters is they saw all; there were no secrets. Not well-guarded ones, anyway.

"What is it, Poppy?" Penelope asked softly, shifting closer.

What could Poppy say? She had to tell her something. Nay, she had to tell her the truth. Why, at this very instant, Tristan was either speaking to or had already spoken to Jonathan. Her sister would find out, and Poppy would rather she was the one in control of that narrative. For she'd done nothing wrong. She was no different than her sisters who'd taken control of their own fates. "Penelope—" she began.

In the end, she was interrupted from sharing by a thunderous bellow.

Both women jumped.

Next came the slam of doors, and the frantic shouts of hotel staff.

Horror creeping in, Poppy looked to the glass doors of the empty smoke room. "Oh, bloody hell," she whispered.

After all, she well knew that voice. Rarely had it been raised, and when it had? Never had it been raised at her or her sisters. Nay, this was bad.

"Not now, Black," her brother shouted from somewhere outside the smoke room. Jonathan's shouting grew increasingly close in frequency. "I'll deal with you later." And then he was there, outside the double doors, with a gaggle of hotel staff at his back and Ryker at his side. "Where in holy hell is my—" His gaze slashed through the crystal panels. Poppy dropped to the floor.

"I saw you." Jonathan exploded into the room.

"Sinclair, you are bad for my business," Ryker bit out, closing the glass doors behind them.

"I don't give ten bloody damns on Sunday about your business."

Poppy remained pressed to the floor. Oh, hell. It was a dire day indeed when not even Ryker Black could quell his brother-in-law into silence.

"Get up, Poppy," her brother ordered. "I see your legs sticking out."

Poppy glanced down at her damning boots.

"I take it this is the reason for your previous distraction?" Penelope whispered.

"Of a sort," she prevaricated.

"*And* I hear you," Jonathan snapped.

At least he was no longer yelling or slamming things. It was little consolation. Gathering what Joan of Arc must have felt on that fateful day she'd met her maker, Poppy climbed reluctantly to her feet.

His cheeks splotched red, his eyes brimming with rage, and his chest heaving. Whether it was from his ride here or fury, she knew not, and cared not to speculate.

Except, when the storm came, it wasn't with a thunderous bellow, but on a whisper.

"No."

Penelope looked between brother and sister, perplexed. "No?"

Poppy gave a slight shake.

Jonathan's lips curved into an ice-cold smile she'd never before seen on him. That was, not turned on her, anyway. "Will you care to tell her? Or should I?"

"Tell me what?"

"I'm not having this as a public discussion," she said tightly, ignoring her sister's query.

"Tell me 'what'?" Penelope pressed, with a greater urgency. "Furthermore, this is not a 'public' discussion. It is merely Ryker and I."

"This is all your fault." Jonathan turned his rage on the elder of his sisters present. "Both of you," he shot over his shoulder at Ryker, who'd set himself up as a sentry of sorts at the doorway.

"My fault?" Penny squawked. "What in blazes have I done?" Not allowing a beat for an answer, she spun to Poppy. "What have you done?'

"Have you watched her?" Jonathan demanded.

Penelope and Ryker exchanged a look.

Oh, Poppy had quite enough of all this. "I am not a dog."

Sir Faithful hopped up and barked angrily.

The Tidemores spoke in unison. "Quiet."

With a soft whine, the dog sank to his belly and buried his face in his paws.

Jonathan stalked across the room, and Poppy's earlier bravado flagged. "Have you seen how she spent her days?"

Penelope slid herself between Poppy and their fuming brother. "She has painted, Jonathan. Painted." She enunciated each syllable, while jabbing at the canvas behind her. "And I'll not make apologies for that."

Emotion clogged Poppy's throat at her sister's impassioned defense. But then, that was the bond they'd always had: steadfast. Unwavering.

"And I trust you gave her free rein of the entire hotel." Jonathan tossed a furious glance over at his brother-in-law. "Both of you?"

Still silent, his arms folded at his broad chest, Ryker's dark brows came together.

Penelope paused. "I…" Her cheeks went grey.

"Which included, no doubt, rooms generally reserved for gentleman patrons?"

Penelope's mouth dropped, and exhaling a noisy hiss through

her teeth, she grabbed Poppy tightly by the arm. "What have you done?"

So much for unwavering sisterly loyalty. "I've not *done* anything," she said indignantly.

"And did the rooms you provided her access to include Tristan Poplar's?"

That seemed to penetrate her brother-in-law's previously unflappable repose. His body went whipcord straight.

"She painted a mural and redesigned his rooms, but—" Penelope gasped, her grip going slack on Poppy. And with that, her loyal sister stepped out of the way and allowed Jonathan a direct path over.

Poppy hurried to put several safe steps between them. "Nothing improper occurred." Not that she'd ever dare admit what happened to a single Tidemore. Not if she wished to have a living, breathing bridegroom.

"Did you paint him…naked?" Penelope asked on an outrageously loud and horrified whisper.

"The bastard," Ryker hissed. "Oi'll kill him and then throw 'im out on 'is bloody arse."

"You'll do no such thing," Poppy ordered, stabbing a finger in her brother-in-law's direction, before facing Penelope. "I didn't paint him." Though, in fairness, she would *like* to paint Tristan naked. His form needed to be preserved on canvas.

"No," Jonathan gritted out between clenched teeth. "It is worse. She proposed to him."

Penelope slapped hands over her mouth. "You…?"

"She. Asked. Him. To. Marry. Her."

And at last…there was silence.

Which was a rather impressive feat; few were able to quiet Penelope, the most garrulous of the Tidemore sisters. As such, Poppy should be contented. As long as no one was talking, there was no fury to counter or outrageous shows of temper.

And yet…

"Is that what Tristan said?" Poppy exclaimed, indignation pulling that question from her. Oh, the lummox would be lucky if she didn't end it before it began. Unless, that was what he'd hoped. Or intended. "It wasn't really me offering marriage." She chewed at her fingernail. Though the idea squarely rested with her.

"I *knewwww* it," Jonathan exclaimed; sticking a finger in her direction, he waved it about. "You *did* propose."

Poppy winced. And here, she'd let Jonathan trip her up into revealing the truth.

Her brother began to pace frantically before them. "The moment you mentioned his dogs six years ago, I should have called him out."

Her lips twitched, and she fought to conceal that smile. "He didn't do anything then, Jonathan, and he didn't do anything now," she continued over his interruption. "I want this arrangement."

And all the fight seemed to go out of Jonathan. His shoulders slumped, and misery marched across his features.

"Poppy," Penelope started in with a gentleness in her eyes. "You don't need to make a match. Not as I or Patrina or Prudence once had to. And certainly not because of a bounder like Rochford. You'll find the man worthy of you."

She already had. In fact, entering into a marriage with Tristan, she already had far more than her sisters had previously known with men who'd been strangers to them. She had a friendship.

"I don't need to make a match," Poppy agreed. She touched her gaze on her family present. "I want to."

Her sister stared back with stricken eyes.

Poppy gathered her hands and squeezed them. "I know what I am doing." And what she wished for.

"May I speak alone with Poppy?" Jonathan asked quietly, with complete restraint and entirely different than the man who'd stormed the hotel.

Penelope looked to her, the meaning clear in her Tidemore eyes: if Poppy wished for her to remain, she would.

Poppy gave a slight nod. "I'm fine," she promised softy, and with reluctant steps, her sister joined her husband. Ryker slid his fingers into Penelope's and raised them to his lips for a brief kiss, before taking their leave.

Poppy stared after them wistfully.

"You see that," Jonathan quietly noted, without judgment.

"See…?"

"That tenderness. That partnership. That is what your sisters have with their husbands. That is what I have with Juliet. And that is what I want for you, Poppy," he finished quietly.

A sound of impatience escaped her. "You do not get to decide what is best for me. You don't get to decide what I should want or have, nor not want nor never have." Having been the youngest of the Tidemores, she'd long been the one they sought to protect. An eternal baby of their family that they were determined to relegate to the role of un-aging child whom they would keep with them always. "I want to marry him, Jonathan."

Sadness flickered in her brother's eyes. "I know," he said softly, his words barely reaching Poppy's ears, "and I think that is what concerns me most."

"He spoke to you."

"He stated his intent." Her heart thumped against her ribs. "And I informed him that I'd not be accepting that offer."

Poppy curled her hands into fists. "I am a woman, capable of making up my own mind."

"Funny, Bolingbroke said that very thing."

Her heart fluttered. "And that makes him someone I wish to wed. Someone who trusts my judgment and allows me a freedom of choice."

Her brother jerked as if she'd slapped him. His features twisted in such a mask of sadness, her heart spasmed. "Ah, Poppy, but that is the thing: I do. I recall the moments I first held you or wiped your tears or made you laugh. I don't get to erase that because you're grown. We protect the ones we love."

She strode over to her brother. "Preventing me from making my own decisions, Jonathan, is not protecting me. It is controlling me."

Jonathan dragged a hand through his unfashionably long hair. "Very well, if you wish to marry him, you may."

Poppy sprang forward, and then suspicion immediately sank her movements. "What is the catch?" she asked, eyeing him carefully.

"Wait until Patrina delivers her babe and Mother returns. If you still feel the same way, I shall not object."

"That is arbitrary, Jonathan," she snapped. It was him simply fishing for time in the hopes that she...or Tristan would change their minds.

Poppy placed her hands on her hips. "I don't require your permission, Jonathan. Not truly." Spinning on her heel, she marched past him.

She made it no further than four steps. "Poppy," he implored. "Only you could take every single one of your sister's scandals, make them all yours and add your own damned scandal to the mix."

It was hard in his beleaguered tones to determine whether he was on the cusp of crying or laughing.

Poppy took another step, and then stopped. A memory traipsed in: her earliest one of Jonathan hefting her upon his shoulders and racing around the nursery. Poppy returned to her brother's side. "Do you recall Chase the Monster?"

A smile ghosted his lips. "Chase, both a name and the game. Clever, you were."

She nudged him in the side.

"Clever, you are," he corrected. "It was your favorite game." His gaze took on a far-off quality as it shifted over the top of her head. "You always loved hiding from pretend monsters."

"Do you remember the time we were running in frantic circles, and it all became too real for me?"

The slight knob in his throat moved. "You buried your head against my chest and cried."

Until her chest had ached from the force of her tears. "You promised you'd protect me always from anything and everything. Real and pretend." And he had. He'd been the father she'd never known, and the elder brother a lady could only dare dream to have. That was why she hadn't been able to simply walk out on him. Not without making him understand and offer his support.

"If I let you do this now, Poppy, then I f-fail." His voice broke.

"Oh, Jonathan," she whispered. "There is no failure in allowing me to make my own decisions. You empowered me to be a woman who could have my own mind and take control of my own life, and because of that, you've only done right by me."

His face contorted. "Ah, God, Poppy."

Stepping into his arms, she hugged him.

He stood there, stiff, before folding his arms around her.

Neither spoke for several moments. "I'm marrying him, Jonathan."

Her eldest sibling sighed. "I know. I suspect I always did."

"You believed Patrina's decision to wed Weston was the wrong one," she reminded.

"It was," he muttered. "At the time…"

Her lips curved in a smile.

"And you had reservations about Christian," she pointed out.

"Any brother would."

"And you also were violently opposed to a match between Ryker and Penelope."

"Fair point." A scowl lit his features. "She was, however, nearly killed because of him."

Stepping out of his arms, she gathered his hands and squeezed. "I'm going to be happy, Jonathan," she vowed. "You will see."

This time, there was no echo of agreement.

"You don't know that," he said sadly. "What I do know, is if you marry without love, then you will *never* be happy."

And despite her resolve up to this moment, it wavered and doubt crept in, iced with fear. "Who is to say I won't come to love him?"

He took her by the arms and lightly squeezed. "It is not that I believe you won't come to love Bolingbroke." But rather, that Tristan would never come to love her.

Could it be enough? Nay, would it be enough? Or was she merely attempting to convince herself as much?

CHAPTER 14

THE MOMENT TRISTAN ENTERED THROUGH the double doors of the Paradise and found his trunks and valises stacked at the center of the rooms, several facts became clear on sight: Poppy's brother-in-law had gathered Tristan's intentions to marry Poppy. Two, Black was throwing him out on his arse for that offense, and three, with the proprietor standing there in wait, a menacing glower affixed to his scarred face, he intended to beat Tristan to a pulp before he did.

As if in confirmation of that fact, Ryker Black cracked his knuckles. "Bolingbroke," he greeted in graveled tones.

God rot this day.

But then, what did you expect? Despite Tristan's scandal and circumstances and dire financial straits, Poppy's family had opened their business to him, free of charge, and he'd repaid that.

By what? Offering to marry the lady. Nay, as he'd said to Poppy's brother, Tristan couldn't very well blame them. What respectable family—any family, for that matter—would want a beloved sister or daughter or sister-in-law to wed him?

A small servant came rushing over. "Mr. Black, Oi've 'ad the carriage brought 'round," the boy whispered, adjusting his cap.

"Thank you, Oliver. That will be all."

The small child shuffled off, but not before he flashed Tristan a faintly pitying look.

"Oi'm not pleased with you," the proprietor growled, after the boy had gone. Was the gentleman's movement from proper King's English to Cockney intentional? Meant to intimidate and terrify? And then, as if in answer to that silent wondering, Black shoved his jacket back to reveal the dagger there. "Not pleased, at all."

Tristan flashed a bored glance at the less than subtle threat. "I'd gathered as much." Perhaps had Tristan been another man, that tactic would have roused sufficient terror. Tristan's having survived five years at war, there was little Tristan hadn't himself seen…or done. "I was rather able to tell as much by my belongings being all lined up," he said dryly.

Fire flashed in those near obsidian eyes. Assessing his current nemesis, Tristan contemplated the same strategies he had when dealing with Sinclair, before settling for direct honesty. Tristan marched the remaining distance to Poppy's brother-in-law. Of a like height, he met the equally tall gentleman's gaze. "Have I crossed some line with the Tidemores and Blacks? I'm certain you see it that way," Tristan said in hushed tones that could not be overheard by the servants and patrons milling in the lobby. "Does Poppy deserve more than m—?"

"Yes," Black said flatly.

"Me?" he finished. "Yes. The lady certainly deserves far greater than a worthless rogue such as myself." And she would have had so much more, and had the expectations for it…had it not been for some ruthless cad, who'd taken advantage of her trust. Except, there never would have been a marriage with her, which even with the suddenness of the idea of a lifetime with Poppy left him oddly…bereft.

Chatham narrowed his eyes into menacing slits. "Wot are you saying?"

"I am saying what Poppy wants is what matters most and no one: not you, not her brother, not any one of her sisters gets to determine her fate."

Black looked him up and down, with that eerily menacing stare. "Ya got a lot of nerve," Poppy's brother-in-law began his stingingly inventive diatribe.

At his back, Tristan faintly registered the tinkling of the door as the butler admitted another patron. A moment later, out of the corner of his eye, he caught a patron stalking with bold strides through the hall.

"Oi let ya into my home and this is wot—"

Tristan narrowed his eyes, as the gentleman pulled into focus. Nay, the man wasn't a patron. The tall, very proportional, and pleasing marquess started through the lobby. What in blazes?

Rochford?

The bastard dared to show his face here, of all places?

I can separate what he did from what he looks like. And…he is appealing to the eye…

"Appealing to the eye," he muttered to himself. And jealousy reared itself once more, a green-eyed monster that raged all the more at the gentleman's approach.

"Are ya cracked in the skull?" Poppy's brother-in-law snapped. "I ask ya why ya want to marry her and ya say because she's—"

He ignored Chatham; all his focus tunneled on the Marquess of Rochford.

Rochford should dare show his face here, so casually? And carrying a damned hothouse bouquet, for there could be no doubting just what the reason was for his visit, and for that bouquet. As if flowers or what else he surely intended made up for what he had done.

A primitive growl climbed his throat, as he surged forward.

"…ya'll be lucky if Oi don't cut yar—"

Tristan was already charging past Chatham.

"Bolingbroke," Poppy's brother-in-law thundered after him.

Ignoring him, Tristan raced forward, fury pumping through him, hatred lengthening his strides. Blood rushed through his ears as he was transformed once more into a soldier charging into battle.

He caught Rochford by the back of his cloak, and spun the man around.

"Hey, now!" Rochford cried. Confusion glazed the taller man's eyes. "Bolingbroke? What is the meaning of—*ahh*," he cried out as Tristan connected a flawless right hook square with his nose. The marquess' legs crumpled, but Tristan had a hand at his cloak, keeping him up, so he could deliver another cuff to his left cheek.

This time, he let the bastard fall. Rochford collapsed, dazed, on his back.

"You bastard," Tristan hissed, towering over him. His chest rose and fell hard and quick as the same primal energy that had pumped through his veins in the midst of battle, raged within him now. In his mind's eye, there was Poppy with a sketchpad in hand and a smile on her lips and—

Black settled a hand on his arm, catching the blow before it landed. As Rochford got to his feet, Tristan shrugged off Poppy's brother-in-law. "I should kill you, Rochford." He took an unholy glee in the way all the blood drained from the marquess' cheeks. "You dared ruin her. You dared hurt her and made a mockery of her love of art."

"I'm sorr—"

A flash of fury blinded him once more, and he slammed a fist into Rochford's stomach, killing that useless apology as all the air hissed between the marquess' clenched teeth.

Pleasing form, my arse.

"Bolingbroke," Chatham barked behind him. "That is enough." Tristan threw off Poppy's brother-in-law and the man hit the floor hard.

For, it wasn't enough. A quick beating would never be sufficient retribution for the man who'd deceived Poppy. "I'm merely doing what you and St. Cyr and Sinclair and every last damned male relative Poppy has should have done," he bellowed. Tristan caught the marquess by his cloak front.

"I want to do right by her," Rochford cried, blood streaming down his ashen cheeks.

Shock knocked into him, and his grip slackened.

Do right by her...

Which implied marriage.

"I came to offer marriage," the marquess croaked, as if he'd followed Tristan's thoughts.

"Marriage," Tristan repeated, struck dumb.

Rochford managed a jerky nod.

An image flashed behind his mind's eye: Poppy wed to the bounder at his feet. Poppy in his bed, twining her long limbs about his neck, and kissing him with the same enthusiasm she'd made love to Tristan's mouth with.

Growling, Tristan punched Rochford in the opposite cheek.

"Bolingbroke," Black bellowed.

Rochford again hit the floor, and Tristan became the beast of war he had been, so that all he was, all he saw, breathed, and felt, was the heart of battle.

Poppy's brother-in-law attempted to separate him from the cad who'd ruined Poppy. Tristan effortlessly shrugged him off.

"Please, don't," the marquess cried out. Like a wounded animal, he scurried on his back to put some distance between them. Rochford fished a white kerchief from his cloak and pressed it to his nose. A crimson splotch immediately stained the fabric.

Tristan growled. "I'm going to happily kill you." He reached for the marquess once more.

"Tristan, stop."

In the end, it wasn't the heavy hand of Ryker Black, Viscount Chatham, or the burly servants hovering in a circle around him just waiting for the call from their employer that stopped him.

The click of booted footfalls striking the marble floor faintly reached him.

Poppy broke through the throng of observers. She staggered to a stop beside him.

The haze of violence lifted from his vision, and reality slid in— she slid in. "Poppy," he said flatly.

Wide-eyed, her cheeks wan, Poppy stared at him as if they'd never before met one another. As if he were a monster.

Which is what he'd been in war. That viciousness had earned the accolades of every military man who'd ever fought with him in battle, or learned of his pursuits. It was not, however, a side a single member of Polite Society had borne witness to. Over the years, Tristan had taken great care to control that part of himself. Until now. Now, he'd laid the warrior who'd killed more men than he could count, and remembered little of it, open before society.

Tristan had to say something.

A pin falling could be heard in the lobby.

"Poppy," He lifted his palms up.

She gasped.

Tristan blankly followed her eyes to the blood staining his knuckles.

The remaining color leeched from her cheeks.

Oh, God. He'd lost control. The walls of the hotel lobby were closing in, and he whipped his gaze around at the sea of observers staring on. Among them Sinclair, Black, and Poppy's sister, Lady Penelope. None of her kin mattered in this moment.

God help him. Tristan couldn't even meet her eyes. "I trust if there'd been even a spot of hope that your family would approve of a marriage between us, that is officially at an end." He attempted humor, but it came out regretful to his own ears.

"Hush." She caught him by the wrist, and tugged him from the circle of on-lookers. He braced for the hue and cry of her family to go up…that shockingly didn't come.

But then, she could bend the sun to her will, if she so wished it.

Poppy didn't stop until they reached an elegantly furnished room, and she closed the door behind them.

And alone, away from the prying eyes, and his heart having since resumed a normal cadence and the bloodlust lifted, reality sank in.

She watched him through hopelessly round eyes and sat silent. Silent when Poppy had only ever been garrulous, and his chest constricted.

"Poppy," he began hoarsely. "I am sorry you witnessed—"

Going up on tiptoe she pressed herself against him, and claimed his mouth, a spark of heat and warmth that erased the ugliness he'd turned himself over to moments ago.

He kissed her, finding an oasis. A sanctuary. Taking when he had no right. Wanting when, with her brother's refusal, it was only wrong.

She sank back on her heels.

"Poppy," he tried again.

Poppy kissed him, and this time, he slipped his tongue inside the warm, moist cavern of her mouth. Heat raced through him as he tangled with her tongue.

It took a herculean effort, but he managed to pull away.

"I am so sorry," he said hoarsely, gathering a dark ringlet between his thumb and forefinger; he caressed the silken tendril, before tucking it behind her ear.

"Because you kissed me?" Her lips, swollen and red from their kiss, tipped down in a frown.

And for the first time since he'd left her brother's with a "no" to his proposal and then beat up Rochford, he found himself smiling. "Never that, love." Which only confirmed what her family had already believed—he was a scoundrel, unworthy of her.

"Why, then?" she asked with her usual Poppy-like curiosity.

"Because you saw… *that.*" Unable to meet her piercing stare, Tristan slid his gaze to the painting behind a broad mahogany desk. He wandered over to that painting.

There was the faint rustle of satin, indicating Poppy had moved. She drifted over, and slipped between him and the wall, all space gone between them. "I saw you defend my honor."

"You saw me bloody Rochford to a pulp," he said bluntly.

"Yes." Clasping her hands behind her, she leaned against the wall, and arched her neck back so she could better meet his gaze. "You challenged him when, as you indicated, my own family did not."

"They did not because they didn't want him making an offer for you."

"And why did you beat him then?" she asked softly.

"Because he'd wronged you. Because he violated your trust. Because he sullied your name." He swept his gaze over her slightly flushed face, and lowered his mouth close to hers and confessed the whole truth. "And like your family, I didn't want him to marry you, either."

Her chest heaved. "Why?"

"Because I despised the idea of you being with him," he whispered. Falling as fast as Adam, Tristan touched his lips to her neck, and thrilled at the rapid acceleration of her pulse. "Because even as I was denied your hand, even as you won't be my wife, I'd sooner kill Rochford than see you with him." He needed to taste her once more. Tristan lowered his mouth, but Poppy brought her hands up between them, and pressed them against his chest, halting his kiss.

"There is…just one thing."

He forced himself to focus on those words and not the raging hunger to take her in his arms. "What is that?"

"We are to be married. My brother relented."

That knocked him firmly back to earth.

"What?" He searched her face. Sinclair had been adamant. Not even God himself could have changed the earl's mind.

She smiled. "I was able to make him see reason."

Make him see reason. Of course she had. But then, that was part of Poppy's magic. She could convince a saint to sin. They would marry. It had been the goal that had sent him to Sinclair's that morn, and when met with rejection, he'd been left hollow. So there should be greater relief. Only, panic reigned.

Her smile slipped. "You're…not pleased."

"No. I am. I'm…" *Terrified out of my mind.* For with her revelation, what they'd agreed to—what this represented—had suddenly become all too real again. "…pleased," he settled for; the word lame to his rogue's ears. "Very pleased," he added, grimacing.

And yet, as she raised her mouth to his, he could not help the niggling that he was going to make a blunder of all this.

CHAPTER 15

IN THE END, POPPY HAD managed the same feat as her sisters before: a rushed wedding.

Granted, an entirely different scandal had brought her to this point, but a scandal, nonetheless.

In the end, her mother had come. No doubt fetched by Jonathan in the hope that she might make Poppy see reason.

Either way, one would expect the dowager countess would be grinning. As it was, she'd been grim since the moment she'd descended from the carriage, weary from the pace set so she might attend Poppy's wedding…so she might then return for Patrina's confinement.

"At least it is to be a real wedding," Penelope chimed happily as Prudence chased her toddling daughter about the room.

"Seraphina, come away from there now," Pru scolded, scooping the unsteady babe up as she wandered close to the hearth.

All the while, Mother remained silent as Poppy was prepared in her wedding attire. Did the dowager countess hear Penny's falsity ring? Or was it only Poppy who knew her sister so very well that she picked up on the sadness, anxiousness, and disappointment?

Regardless, at least, she was trying…which was a good deal more than she could say for her Mother. The pair of them, who stood with arms folded, wearing like expressions of disapproval.

"If it were a real wedding, we would be waiting until Patrina delivered her babe," their mother said in arch tones.

Touché.

Poppy had never known or appreciated until her scandal, her mother's ability to sting.

Penelope's daughter clapped her hands excitedly, and shimmying down from her mother's lap, Paisley toddled over to Poppy.

"Weddy—Weddy."

Poppy scooped up the babe. "At least someone is excited about Aunt Poppy's wedding," she said, nuzzling the little girl's neck folds.

Paisley giggled uncontrollably, flailing her arms in the air and a squealing Seraphina immediately made a beeline for the excitement.

"And tell me why should we be excited?" the dowager countess snapped, and Pru's daughter toppled over.

The girl promptly began to cry.

"Mother," Prudence chided, gathering up her babe. With a look to the nursemaid, she handed her daughter off. "Will you bring Lady Seraphina below stairs to join her brothers and my husband?"

"As you wish, my lady," the young woman murmured, keeping her eyes downcast.

The moment the maid had gone, their mother turned her outrage on her daughters. "What do you expect?" she asked in strident tones. "Am I to be happy that my last remaining daughter fulfilled all of society's expectations and brought a scandal down upon her name?"

Poppy's smile fled as she held her niece closer. "That wasn't my fault."

"And whyever not?" their mother scoffed. "Because you should be able to act any way you wish, and do whatever you wish without consequences."

Paisley squirmed in her arms and, studiously avoiding the gaze of both her mother and sister, Penelope rushed over and rescued her babe.

"I've handled my situation," Poppy said tersely.

"Bah, you've handled your situation. By proposing marriage to a man who is only marrying you because of his dire circumstances?"

That all too accurate charge struck like a well-placed arrow to her breast. And with that, unease roiled in her belly. She battled back that disquiet, the one that whispered that her offer might have been for reasons more than she could ever admit to anyone—

herself included.

"I've had more than two Seasons," she said calmly. "What do you expect, that there is some other respectable gentleman we've yet to meet who will come along and be both the proper husband you sought for me and—?

"Yes," her mother said bluntly. "That is precisely what I had hoped."

With a sound of impatience, Poppy angled her shoulder dismissively and trained her gaze on the mirror.

Except, her mother slid into the glass panel so that their gazes locked. So that there was no escaping this discussion she didn't wish to have. "I had hoped that you would marry for love because that is what you deserve. And at the very least, I'd have you marry a man who could provide a secure future for you."

"I have a sizeable dowry," she gritted out.

"Oh, and is that what you wished for yourself? To marry a fortune hunter?"

Tension crackled around the room. Her patience snapped and Poppy spun and faced her mother. "He is not marrying me for my dowry." How many men in the financial state Tristan had suddenly found himself, would have insisted that the contracts be drafted where she was responsible for all her funds? That the only assurances he'd sought were for his sisters' Seasons? "He is marrying me because it is mutually beneficial for the both of us." Even as that pathetic defense left her lips, she winced at the emptiness of it.

And what was worse, in the eyes of all the Tidemores gathered, she saw pity in their expressions.

"Fayfe," Paisley jabbered happily once more, in her innocence so wholly unaffected by the tense exchange. Now seated on her mother's lap, the little girl patted the adoring dog.

Their mother's face buckled. "I just want you to be happy." She buried a sob in her fist.

Prudence rushed over with a kerchief, which their mother took. She dabbed at the corners of her eyes.

Poppy considered her weeping mother a long while before speaking. "You say you want me to be happy, and yet, you had no qualms about marrying me off to Rochford."

"Because he can offer you security, Poppy," the dowager countess cried. "The shameful legacy that clings to Tristan's family—"

"Which is through no fault of Tristan's," Poppy bit out.

"And yet, that doesn't matter, Poppy," her mother spoke in entreating tones. "That legacy will only hurt you and your children and I w-won't have that. I can't," her mother's words dissolved into a whisper.

And just like that the fury Poppy had carried eased. Just like all of Poppy's siblings, her mother sought to protect her. To keep her safe. To keep Poppy's someday children safe. "Mama," she said gently, and when the dowager countess finally met her gaze, she continued, "You've confused security and happiness. They are not the same. I *am* happy," she said simply. And…she was. Yes, as a girl, she'd been enamored of Tristan. But over the years, she'd come to accept that there wouldn't be more between them. He would always be her friend… And that would be enough…

Will it, though?

Her mother sighed. "I *do* like Tristan," her mother gruffly conceded, giving another sniffle.

Poppy's lips twitched. It was a generous concession for the dowager countess to make about anyone.

"And it was not so very rushed," Prudence pointed out.

"And it was not so very rushed," their mother repeated.

A knock sounded at the door, and all the Tidemore ladies gathered looked to the entrance of the room.

"Enter," the dowager countess called.

Jonathan ducked his head inside. "Have you changed your mind?" he asked without preamble.

Poppy rolled her eyes. "No. I've not."

He sighed. "The guests have assembled. It is time."

It is time.

Her heart fluttered wildly, and at last, some small part of herself acknowledged the truth she'd been so adamant to keep at bay: she wanted this marriage to Tristan. She wanted it for reasons that didn't have solely to do with the business arrangement she'd laid out before him.

Standing at the front of one of the Viscount and Viscountess of Chatham's many parlors in the hotel, Tristan had never felt more alone…and with a sea of glaring Tidemores at his back. Though, in fairness, they weren't *all* glowering. There was a sea of Tidemore babes and children giggling and cooing and happily prattling on with one another.

To give his hands something to do, Tristan reached for his time-piece.

His fingers collided with nothingness.

Of course, it had been repossessed by the current Earl of Max-well. Tristan stole a glance at the ormolu clock across the room.

Seven minutes.

She was seven minutes late.

The florid vicar, just two paces away, made a show of studying his bible, frantically whipping through pages.

From the corner of his eye, he caught St. Cyr turning his two sons over to the Countess of Sinclair's care.

A moment later, his friend came to join him.

Tristan whipped his gaze over.

"Of course, I'd be here," St. Cyr said grudgingly, his eyes forward. Tensely silent and unsmiling as he'd been since Tristan had taken his leave of his residence to share his plans for marriage. Which was no less than Tristan deserved. And yet, for the other man's dis-appointment, he stood beside Tristan anyway. But then, he'd always been a better friend.

"Thank you," Tristan said quietly.

His friend gave him a sharp look. "I don't want nor need your thanks. I need your promise that you won't hurt her."

"I will do everything in my power to never bring pain to Poppy."

"The commission with the hussars," St. Cyr said from the side of his mouth. "Have you spoken with her?"

"She'll understand." Wouldn't she? Of course she would. They'd come to a formal agreement; their match was one they were entering into for mutually beneficial goals. "We each shared our expectations of the union and Poppy's requirements all pertained to her autonomy and freedom." Tristan's being in the military cer-tainly provided her that freedom.

St. Cyr slid his eyes closed. "Christ." It was a prayer.

Even so, the vicar scowled darkly at that blasphemy.

Muttering his apologies to the man of the cloth, St. Cyr turned to Tristan. "Answer me this, then. If you were *so* certain she would understand, then why didn't you tell her when I presented you with the commission?"

"I…" Tristan's chest tightened.

Because he'd been afraid she'd renege on their arrangement. That she would somehow decide she wanted more, and a future with him was not it. And it was terrifying, inexplicable madness that he could not make head or tails of.

Tristan sensed Poppy before he saw her.

His gaze slid to the entrance of the parlor.

And he forgot to breathe. As guilt and worry for the future melted away, and all that he was capable of seeing…was her.

She was a vision.

An ethereal vision, not in white, but for the first time in all the years he'd known her, attired in something different than those whites and ivories which had failed to do her any justice. She wore a shimmery silk, a masterpiece that didn't know whether it wished to be blue or purple, and yet, had somehow perfectly blended into one distinctly new hue.

He devoured the sight of her in that creation. The silken white sash wrapped about her trim waist the single nod to the girl she'd been. That girl was gone, replaced instead with womanly perfection.

If she'd made her Come Out in that glorious shade of blue silk, that clung to her every curve, they wouldn't be here even now. She'd have been snatched up by some other. And selfish once more, Tristan was so very glad she hadn't been.

From across the length of the makeshift aisle formed by the guest's seating, Poppy smiled. It dimpled her cheek and lit her eyes and—

He grunted as St. Cyr sent an elbow sliding into his side.

Tristan blinked several times to dispel the spell she'd cast.

"Close your mouth," St. Cyr suggested, smiling for the first time since Tristan had shared his plans to wed his sister-in-law. "Sinclair looks about ready to remove your head from your person."

Sure enough, Lord Sinclair scowled blackly at Tristan.

His cheeks fired hot, and he gave his head a slight, clearing shake. "Fair enough," he muttered. "But he's worn that same look for the better part of…" He searched his mind. Well, hell. "All the years I've known him."

St. Cyr sighed. "The same holds true for me." He paused. "Be good to her." And with that, his more-loyal-than-Tristan-deserved friend returned to his family...and Poppy reached Tristan's side.

"DEARLY *beloved, we are gathered together here in the sight of God to join together this Man and this Woman in holy Matrimony; which is an honorable estate, instituted of God in the time of man's innocency, signifying unto us the mystical union that is betwixt Christ and his Church; which holy estate Christ adorned and beautified with his presence...*"

As the vicar droned on, Tristan angled his head down. "Have you changed your mind?"

"I have," she whispered. "It was all an elaborate scheme on my part. Replace my scandal with Rochford with an altogether different, and slightly less scandalous one."

"A wise plan," he said, keeping his features deliberately masked in seriousness. "The only thing that might scandalize them more should be if you were to attempt to paint me naked here in front of—"

Poppy laughed, and the vicar stopped mid-sentence, pausing to glare at her.

Poppy feigned a cough.

"You are incorrigible," she said in barely there tones.

"Unapologetically so."

They shared one more private smile, before falling silent for the recitation of the vows.

"*First, It was ordained for the procreation of children, to be brought up in the fear and nurture of the Lord, and to the praise of his holy Name...*"
Children.

Poppy had been adamant that they'd not have a marriage in name only, and as he'd assured the lady, he was not so very honorable that he would ever enter into such an arrangement with her. As she'd insisted on those terms, Tristan had thought of the feel of her under him. Over him. Crying out her release, as he buried himself inside her.

However, he'd not allowed himself to think about...children with her.

His gaze went to the curly-haired babe perched on Lady Penelope's lap. A babe with dark curls who was the image of Poppy.

And an image slipped in...of a different babe, this one with Poppy's dimpled smile, a little girl with her mother's spirit.

And perhaps he was becoming melancholy with the passage of time, but that musing enticed.

"Have you changed your mind, after all?" Poppy whispered.

Tristan didn't blink for several moments, and then as he looked into Poppy's twinkling gaze, he registered the flurry of whispers that went up behind them.

The vicar cleared his throat.

"You missed your vow."

"Did I?"

"You did," Sinclair snapped from the front row. "The part about having this woman, to live together after God's ordinance. *Loving* her. Comforting her. *Honoring* her. Keeping her in sickness and health, *forsaking* all others—"

"I will," Tristan pledged, directing that oath to Poppy.

"Are we entirely certain it counts as a complete vow given you don't know what exactly you've agreed to?" Poppy teased, enjoying the moment far too much.

They glanced to the vicar. "May I proceed?" he asked in his nasally tones, impatience snapping in his gaze, and Poppy and Tristan redirected their focus to the ceremony.

The remainder of the day continued in a blur; beginning with a noisy, surprisingly jubilant celebration hosted by Poppy's sister and brother-in-law. With toasts made by each of her siblings present, and their children, along with Tristan's friends Blackthorne and St. Cyr, one might almost believe his and Poppy's wedding was, in fact, a real one.

Seated beside a laughing, bright-eyed Poppy, regaling the gathering with a tale of her and her sisters driving off their first governess, Tristan stared on, a silent observer.

They were married.

He had married Poppy Tidemore.

Little Poppy who'd fished and raced him astride her mount whenever he visited her family's annual summer picnic.

And what's worse? I'd tell you not to hurt her, and yet, I know that there is no other possible outcome of this...

St. Cyr's warning pinged around the chambers of his mind. Tristan wiped his suddenly damp palms along his trousers. It had been so easy to become swept up in...Poppy, and the out she'd offered him so that he might care for his sisters that, just as St. Cyr had accused, he'd not truly given thought to the fact that this was Poppy. Poppy, whom he could barely support, whose dowry was all that would see her comfortable.

Poppy leaned over. "You look like you ate a plate of rancid kippers," she whispered.

He forced a smile, even as his gut churned. "I know better than to touch the kippers." Gathering her fingers, he raised Poppy's knuckles to his mouth and brushed a kiss against them.

The slightly adoring look there in her eyes redoubled the unease that had followed him since St. Cyr's warnings. "It is nearly over," she assured, mistaking the reason for his unrest.

Nay, it was just beginning.

As if on cue, a servant hurried through the dining rooms, and stopped before Lady Penelope. The viscountess nodded once, and then said something to her husband, who stood. Raising his glass in a final toast, he hefted it toward Poppy. "To Poppy and Bolingbroke." He thinned his eyes on Tristan. "Don't muck it up," he warned. "Your carriages are readied."

Carriages were readied?

Whose carriages?

It was certainly not Tristan's as he'd only two; one here in London but the other at Dartmoor with his mother.

And furthermore, where in blazes would he be going? There weren't funds for a honeymoon. His stomach clenched.

Except, a servant drew back Poppy's chair, and as she sailed to her feet it became clear—Black had been speaking to them.

Tristan jumped up and before Poppy could join her sisters, he took her by the arm, and steered her to the corner of the room. She stared at him, a question in her eyes.

"What is going on?" he asked, surveying the remaining guests as they climbed systematically to their feet, and proceeded to take their leave.

Poppy angled her head. "The breakfast is over, Tristan. We're going home."

With that she took him by the hand and tugged him toward the entrance of the room. Digging his heels in, he forced Poppy to stop.

"Home?" he repeated. "You're returning with your family?"

She laughed, and then that clear, bell-like expression of her mirth faded and her eyes went wide. "Of course not." She started toward her sisters once again, and he caught her, loosely about the forearm, bringing her back around to face him.

"Then where are we going?"

"Your townhouse."

"My townhouse."

She nodded, even as his hadn't been a question but rather a puzzle he'd sought to work through.

"I don't have a townhouse."

Not anymore. He had neither servants nor silver, nor even the most basic furnishings that made a townhouse…well, a townhouse. Why, he barely had a roof. Not one that worked, anyway.

"Yes, we do."

We do.

Not "you" do.

And then it hit him.

"You intend for us to live at my townhouse." It was an impossibility. He'd not bring her there. Ever.

"We're going, Tristan."

Ignoring the blatant stares her family had on their exchange, Tristan retained his grip on her arm. "My residence isn't habitable."

She scoffed. "I'm certain—"

"No, Poppy," he interrupted. "It is quite dire. Quite dire, indeed." He couldn't live with her there. As ashamed as he was to accept the charity from her family, neither could he allow his wife to reside in a townhouse falling down around him.

"Surely you didn't expect that we'd remain here?"

"Why…" He had. He stopped himself from making that humbling admission. Releasing her quickly, Tristan curled his fists tight at his side. Never more had he resented and regretted the new state of his affairs. He'd taken a battlefield-like planning to the decision that had brought him to this point. Only to find himself responsible for another person…whom he was wholly unable to care for.

Poppy moved so close the tips of their shoes brushed. "We're not staying here, Tristan," she said quietly. "This isn't our home."

This isn't our home.

Ours.

Only he'd nothing to offer.

Not truly.

Tristan briefly closed his eyes. He couldn't bring her there. He opened his eyes, and tried again. "Poppy," he implored.

And when presented with begging more charity from her already more-generous-than-he-deserved family or giving in to his wife's insistence, Tristan knew there was no countering Poppy on this, either.

CHAPTER 16

THE REMAINDER OF POPPY'S DAY continued in a whir.

With the aid of her lady's maid, and the elderly housekeeper and butler, Poppy had swept the dirt from her floors, beat the more than faintly musty coverlet and draperies until they'd been cleared of dust. Most dust, anyways. Her garments had been properly stored and tucked away.

Until she stood there…

"Oi never thought it could be done," Mrs. Florence whispered.

Poppy looked around the room, pride filling her at the transformation that had overtaken the previously dusty, cluttered space. The furniture was still absent of a proper coat of wax and missing a shine, but despite Tristan's glum prediction of the place where they'd reside, it was anything but uninhabitable.

At least, this room, anyway.

A faint squeaking split the quiet, and Poppy followed the frantic path a lone mouse took across the floor. Barking wildly, Sir Faithful charged hot on the rodent's heels.

"There's a lot more to be done than this," Mr. Florence muttered.

His wife jammed an elbow into his side.

"Oomph."

"Wot?" he shot back defensively. "There is."

"Her Ladyship's done a fine job."

While the couple proceeded to bicker themselves right out of the room, Lucy hurried to close the door behind them. "They're a peculiar lot, my lady," the girl was saying as soon as they'd gone.

Yes, garrulous and bluntly rude even, the older pair of servants—the only hires in her husband's employ—were certainly unlike any Poppy's family had ever employed. In truth, however, she found them refreshingly honest and real.

"Is there anything else you require, my lady?"

From across the room, Poppy caught a glimpse of herself in the cracked bevel mirror; the intricate arrangement Lucy had created of Poppy's hair for the wedding was long gone. Her hair having since been plaited. Several curls had popped free and now lay in a sad tangle about her face. And of course, there was the matter of her dusty garments. "A bath. I'll require a bath."

Lucy dipped a curtsy. "As you wish."

The moment she'd gone, Poppy found herself *alone*.

Busy tidying her rooms as she'd been, she'd waited for Tristan to join her. Only realizing now—Tristan had no intention of doing so.

The memory of his face upon their arrival came back to haunt her; the resignation in his gaze. A gaze that could not meet her own. The regret.

He hated this.

He hated everything about his situation. Any other gentlemen would have welcomed the marriage to an heiress which would see them freed from their circumstances. Tristan, however, had ceded all of Poppy's dowry over to her, the only sum set aside a small one dedicated to his sisters', so that they might have another Season.

Her gaze snagged upon her sad visage in the mirror of the mahogany dressing table.

And what was more, she hated this for him. Tristan was so much more than what he'd lost and what he didn't have. He, however, was too proud to see that.

Was that why he even now avoided her? Or did he do so out of regrets about their marriage?

Stop it.

"You stay here," she urged Sir Faithful.

He let out a little whimper, and scratched at her skirts.

Poppy ruffled his ears affectionately. "Ah, you know there is too much work to be done here. There's mice for you to chase." His dark eyes were filled with canine disapproval. "I could always add several cats?" she suggested.

Sir Faithful promptly sprinted off in the opposite direction.

Abandoning her plans for a bath, she drew the door closed behind her, and went in search of her husband. After all, a bride couldn't just spend her wedding night…alone. There were certainly rules against it.

Her husband.

Butterflies fluttered in her belly.

I am married.

Nay, not just married. Married to Tristan Poplar. Poppy wound her way through the dark, cold townhouse. The first whispering of uncertainty stirred. It danced low in her belly, a reminder of what this night would entail.

Oh, she'd dreamed of kissing Tristan, and had even done so… but what would happen this night, what her sisters had spoken of candidly, if in slightly veiled terms and descriptions, would be real, and for the sliver of a moment, she eyed the path behind her that she'd traveled, and considered returning to her rooms…

The faint flicker of a candle's glow penetrated the otherwise dark corridors. Feeling very much like that proverbial moth to the flame, Poppy drifted forward—and then stopped.

She'd found him.

Lingering outside the open doorway, the oak slab ajar, Poppy peered inside.

Tristan sat behind a George III sideboard. The narrow piece of furniture, a makeshift desk, overflowed with a stack so high of ledgers and books they nearly met Tristan's eyes. It was not a book that held his attention, however…but an official-looking letter.

The harshly beautiful planes of his face were a study of intensity.

Whatever words were written there, were ones of import.

Tristan stiffened, and then, as if he felt her presence, he looked up.

"Poppy." He hastily came to his feet. "Forgive me," he said, swiftly folding the letter along a crease. "I did not hear you enter."

"No. No. It is fine," she assured, hovering at the entrance; waiting for him to mention whatever it was that had held him so engrossed. She was awash with disappointment as he tucked that note in his desk drawer, and said…nothing. Her own siblings and their spouses all belonged to marriages that were equal partnerships, where secrets didn't exist. *But then, your marriage began as an arrangement in business.* As such, what expectation was there in Poppy and Tristan sharing those worries and concerns with one another. None. *There is none.*

And in this instance, there was not even an invitation extended for her to join him. "May I...come in?" she ventured hesitantly.

"Certainly," he said quickly, coming around the desk. He drew out a chair, and a cloud of dust danced from the slight movement, little flecks dancing on the air.

As she settled into her seat and that awkward silence stretched on, Poppy used the opportunity to study his offices, which may as well have been a window into another time. The gilt furniture, dusty from neglect put the items from at least a century ago. And while society preferred new commissioned mahogany pieces, Poppy found herself admiring the originality of her—their—new residence.

"You are...well?" he asked after he returned to his seat; that query came...awkwardly.

When had she ever known Tristan to be...awkward? Or for that matter, formal?

She preferred them as they'd been. Wanted to go back to the effortless teasing, instead of this new stiltedness that had come with their marriage. "Very."

Did he know her enough to know that she lied to him, even now?

They sat there with more uncomfortable silence, and Poppy glanced around once more. For, now that she was here, she didn't quite know what to say. After all, a young lady didn't go about asking her husband to come to her chambers and...get on with the wedding night. Did she?

She flickered her gaze over Tristan's desk, and then she froze, her gaze caught on a familiar book, lying open. "My sketchpad," she blurted.

Tristan followed her stare.

"You've been studying my work."

An endearing blush stained his cheeks. "Yes."

And just like that, the tension was snapped. Poppy hopped up and came around the desk to join him. "You weren't supposed to be admiring my work," she chided, as she gathered up the sketch-pad.

His lips turned up in an involuntary grin. "Were you any other woman, I'd believe you were courting compliments."

She snorted. "I've no interest in compliments—false or other-wise sincere." Poppy waved the book at him.

Clasping his hands over his head, he spun in a peculiar swivel seat so that he faced her. The faded leather crackled from the movement. "On the contrary. Over the years, I've employed no fewer than five art instructors to deliver lessons to my sisters. As such, there've been any number of times my three sisters have had sketchpads in hand, or some floral or fruit arrangement displayed upon a canvas."

"And you...disapproved of their subjects?" she ventured.

"I remained unmoved by *any* artwork..." He paused, "...until yours."

Until yours...

Her family had viewed Poppy's fascination with the arts as a hobby, at most. As such, they'd been complimentary of the work she'd sometimes displayed in their home, but never had they truly celebrated those works, either. Heat blossomed in her chest.

Letting his arms fall, he swiveled his chair forward. "I now know how greatly I underestimated—and failed to appreciate—all that went into those works. Even more..."

She looked at him, with a question in her eyes.

"I attempted my hand at sketching," he confided, almost hesi-tantly.

Poppy's brother, Jonathan, had never had much use for the arts... until he'd fallen in love with his wife. Even after his marriage had wrought about the complete reformation of the rogue, he'd sup-ported Juliet, but never truly taken part.

Nay, unlike Poppy's sister Prudence, who shared with her hus-band a mutual love and admiration for art.

"May I?"

He nodded toward the notebook. "Of course."

Secretly, Poppy had craved that bond Prudence had shared with Christian. Only, as a woman grown, she conceded, that there was something equally—mayhap more fulfilling—in not necessarily having the same interests as Tristan, but exploring and sharing one's interests with one another. It required that one cared enough to invest any time in learning about those pursuits.

And yet, as he'd said…he'd attempted his hand at it. How easy would it have been for him to politely tuck that gift away, and not again think about it? But he hadn't. He'd not been deprecating about what Poppy did, or condescending. He'd tried something, at her urging.

Perching her hip on the edge of his sideboard-desk, she fanned through the pages of her book, until she'd found one of the pieces in his own hand: an indecipherable image he'd captured in pencil. She angled her head. There was something mystical about the abstract rendering. Entrancing.

"I'm rot at it," he conceded with a small grin.

"I find it intriguing."

He snorted, and plucked the book from her fingers. "Like you, I'm not one for false compliments," he said, turning her own words back at her. "I'm merely acknowledging that I attempted… and failed."

Hopping down from her ledge, Poppy shifted around his shoulder, and leaning down, she placed her lips near his ear. "Like you, I'm not one to simply hand out words of praise unless I mean them, Tristan Poplar."

He angled his head, inadvertently setting the chair to a light swivel. Molten heat spilled past Tristan's thick, dark lashes.

Lashes, that when she'd made her Come Out, she would have traded her left littlest finger for on the hope that she might flutter them for this very man before her. *Breathe, Poppy. Breathe.*

"I also attempted poetry," he murmured.

"D-Did you?" An image tempted the edges of her musings; Tristan stringing together a stream of words lauding her. As a girl she'd dreamed to hear such words dripping from his lips. Which was foolish. She was a woman grown, entered into nothing more than a business arrangement with a man who'd become a friend.

"I was rot at that, too."

Too.

"Art isn't supposed to be clear, Tristan. It isn't always perfectly rendered captures of life's moments," she said softly.

He caught one of her curls and twisted it about his finger. "Isn't that precisely what art is, Poppy?"

It was a caress that didn't so much as brush against her skin, and yet, she felt it within her like the burn of a thousand suns. She drew in a shallow breath. "N-not at all." Her fingers trembling, Poppy plucked the book from his fingers, and returned that aged volume to his desk.

"Come with me."

Not waiting for his response, she hopped up. Collecting the candlestick, she started for the front of the room.

Together, she and Tristan wound their ways through the lengthy corridors. The floors, bare of carpets, creaked and groaned, echoing behind them as they went.

They reached the ballroom, and Poppy entered ahead of him.

"Are we waltzing, lady wife?" he called, his deep baritone soaring around the expansive room. "If so, we should remove the coverings on the flooring."

He'd always been her favorite dance partner; he moved with an effortless grace. His name on her dance card, however, had always been a polite courtesy he'd paid her brother-in-law. And how much, as a girl, and then as a young woman, she'd wanted it to be more. "No." Carrying her candle around the room, Poppy proceeded to touch it to the other wicks. "We are not dancing."

"How very mysterious my wife is," Tristan teased.

Poppy continued to light the other candles until a bright glow fell over the room. She faced her husband, and wavered. Forgetting the candle she held. Forgetting what she was to do with it. Forgetting to breathe.

With his shoulder propped against a Doric column, Tristan managed both regal elegance and effortless ease; her fingers ached to see him free of his garments so she might commit all his masculine form to paper.

A lazy grin pulled at Tristan's lips, and wrought havoc on her heart. A smile that said he knew precisely the effect he was having on her. And was thrilling in it.

The rogue.

Tristan wandered to meet her—stopping when a handful of steps separated them.

All the while, he surveyed the room, touching his gaze on the empty white walls and the worktables littered with brushes, paints, and jars. "Very well. I'll admit. You have me intrigued."

Poppy hurried over to fetch an apron. Pulling it on, she tied it at the waist. "Remove your jacket."

Tristan flashed a wolfish smile.

She felt her cheeks burning. "For shame, Tristan Poplar. One would think I asked you to remove your trousers." She dipped her gaze to the fitted pants that clung to his muscular limbs, and all her amusement fled. Her breath quickened and her fingers twitched. Both with an awareness of him as a man...and as a subject. She chewed at her lower lip. Why...she had wasted her time with Rochford. Tristan, however...she'd not considered him because—

"Poppy," he said hoarsely, his features strained. His voice faintly pleading.

And then it hit her...

In this instance, he didn't tease. In this instance, the emotion burning from his eyes was, in fact, real desire—for her.

Emboldened, she nodded for him disrobe.

"I've no idea why you're nodding at me in that way."

She motioned to his still fully clad frame. "Your jacket. Remove it."

Tristan pressed his palms to his lapels and glanced down, and then up at Poppy once more. "I..." She gave him a look, and his hands went to the buttons of his jacket. "Only one thing can come from this," he said hoarsely.

He tossed the garment aside and it fell with a noisy flutter.

His muscles strained the lawn fabric of his shirt. Tightly corded biceps more fitting of a man accustomed to work and so very different than the lean, wiry swains who padded their shirts and jackets.

Her mouth dried, and she, who'd initiated this exchange, fought to remember the purpose of why she'd brought him here. "Your boots...please."

That arrogant glint was back in his eyes, and he winked. "Well, only because you said, 'please'." Tristan shook his head, and a dark strand tumbled over his eye, giving him a rakish air. "If you were any other woman, I'd say you were attempting to seduce me," he murmured, as he balanced on one leg, and proceeded to tug at the gleaming black Hessian. At last free of the article, he tossed it aside where it landed with a thump. "That is if I had a title or fortune for a lady to trap."

Poppy went and gathered that discarded shoe. "Come now," she scolded as she neatly lined it up alongside his jacket. "I'll not have you be the self-pitying sort." Loyal and loving as he was to his family, and champion that he'd always been to the Tidemores, even without his fortunes, he was of greater worth than any other lord.

"I'm not being self-pitying," he said matter-of-factly, as he went on to battle his other boot. "I'm being truth—" His boot went flying from his grip, and thumped her in the back, before falling to the floor.

His shoulders shook. Why…why… "Are you laughing?"

"I wouldn't dream of it."

She narrowed her eyes on the smile ghosting his lips.

"Now what, my lady?" he urged, splaying his arms open. "Does my shirt come next? Or my trousers?"

"Don't be silly. Although…" Poppy chewed at the tip of her index finger. The plans she'd abandoned—been forced to abandon—because of Rochford presented themselves once more.

Tristan folded his arms, almost protectively at his chest. "Get that look off your face, Poppy Poplar."

She scowled. "What look?"

"The one that says you might very well be considering it."

How in blazes did he know her so very well? How, when she'd believed herself to be invisible to him? "You're the one who suggested—"

"I was teasing," he cut in.

She stuck her tongue out. "You are not the fun rogue the world proclaims you to be."

"*Proclaimed.* I'm now the dark, wicked scoundrel who'd steal the king's crown if presented with the opportunity."

There was nothing dark about him. Charming still, with his life in shambles, he was the same affable, kind-hearted, clever-witted gentleman who'd made her heart race at their every encounter over the years. "A razor and hair trim would help with that."

He dusted a hand over his eyes, and his shoulders shook. "You are…something, Poppy."

Something.

Which was more than "nothing" but so vague as to leave her with boundless questions. Taking him by the hand, Poppy tugged him forward, and he went unquestioningly. She released him and fetched one of her aprons. Donning it, she fumbled with tying it. "We are taught to believe life is a certain way. That art is a certain way. One uses simple, geometric, and linear shapes and from that comes a distinct symbolic or decorative purpose." Dipping a brush into a jar of green paint, Poppy hurriedly crafted an evergreen on the wall.

"It is lovely," he murmured, leaning in to observe the final, hurried, but complete project.

Heat blossomed in her cheeks at that admiration and she forced herself to focus on the lesson. "You are failing to see the point."

He puzzled his brow. "And what is the point."

Poppy returned her brush to the table. "It is lovely because you recognize it and have connections to it. It makes you think. But in thinking, sometimes we overthink." Picking up a clean brush and a jar of blue paint, Poppy soaked her bristles and then whipping her arm she flung paint at the wall. It splattered upon the previously white plaster; leaving a trail of dripping dots and lines.

Tristan stumbled back a step. "What are you...?"

"Several years ago, I was attending an art exhibit at the London Museum. There was one area no passersby bothered visiting. An antechamber filled with the works of Buddhist painters." The same wonderment of stepping into that room flared fresh as it had been when she'd first entered. Wonder at the puzzling pieces affixed to the walls. "I could not understand how the world had simply hidden those great works, as if they were somehow inferior...because of their subject. Because of the artists responsible for creating them. Until one day, I began to experiment with paint in that same way."

"You've gone and marred your magnificent tree," he said, his voice pained.

She smiled. Poor Tristan. Polite Society...his friends, the world on the whole may have taken Tristan for a carefree sort. Yet, with him pacing alongside her, unease emanating from his frame, he proved constrained in ways that only hurt him now. "Stop thinking, Tristan." Poppy soaked her brush and let it fly again, filling empty portions of the wide wall.

He winced.

"Overthinking strips one of the ability to search inside for what is inside one. It does not for analysis or head based questions."

Poppy grabbed another brush and held it out.

He stared at it like he'd never before seen a brush. "What is that?"

Poppy shook it. "It's for you. Dip it in paint." When he made no move to take it, she sighed, and carried the brush over to the row of jars. Poppy dunked the bristles in green and carried it back, dripping remnants on the covering over the floor. "Here."

A question in his eyes, Tristan took it. "Now paint," she urged.

"I don't—"

"Then feel," she whispered. "Close your eyes." And for the first time since she'd begun her lesson, he complied. "Now, open them. Paint," she said once more.

He took a step closer and made an experimental stroke.

She tunneled her focus and energy and every thought upon the blossoming color before her. Until she registered Tristan at her side, flinging green splatters of paint upon the wall, their colors melded together.

And then they stopped.

As if attuned in this most special of ways.

"It is magnificent," he said in reverent tones. He touched his gaze on every detail, and warmth filtered to every corner of her person. For this was not Tristan the rogue with all the right words on his lips. His palpable appreciation of their work was real, and so very beautiful for it. "Do you know, Poppy? I can't name anything that has made me feel that way."

She remained silent, waiting for him continue. *Wanting* for him to continue. All these years she'd known him, and yet…at the same time she hadn't. She knew his likes and where and how he found his pleasures…but those were surface-level joys. They said nothing about who he was as a man.

Her chest still rising and falling, she kept her eyes upon that abstract rendering. "Whether it is or isn't wasn't the intended outcome," she quietly explained. "All that mattered was what I felt in here." Raising her brush, she pressed it to her heart. "It clears the mind and cleanses the soul and brings clarity into who we are."

He glanced down at her, and the emotion that spilled from their depths robbed her lungs of breath. "And who are you, Poppy Poplar?" he asked in hushed tones, gathering the ends of her plaited hair, and teasing it in his fingers. His actions an afterthought, and quixotic for it.

Poppy raised her gaze to his. "I know who I am, Tristan," she whispered. She touched a hand to his chest. "It is a matter of you determining who you are." Under her touch, his heart thumped wildly. Her gaze heavy, she glanced to the place her fingers rested. Reflexively, she curled them, crushing the fabric of his lawn shirt.

CHAPTER 17

OVER THE YEARS, TRISTAN HAD fought the pull of desire for the woman before him.

He had lied to himself. Had done such a good job of convincing himself that he'd come to believe the moments of awareness between he and Poppy were fleeting moments of madness.

Until now.

With a handsbreadth between them, and their chests rising and falling in a like frantic rhythm, he no longer had to lie to himself—he wanted her.

"Are you going to kiss me?" she breathed, her husky curiosity temptation itself.

"Would you like that, Poppy?" he whispered, running a palm down her cheek; thrilling as her eyes fluttered shut. For despite the terms she'd put to him, he would still have her know that he'd cede control to her in this decision—always.

"If you cannot tell, I f-fear you're not as roguish as p-purported."

"Oh, I can tell," he said softly. "By the faint part of your lips." He brushed his mouth over hers in a fleeting kiss that earned a little moan.

Poppy angled her head, pleading without words, and only actions for another.

"I can tell by the way your pulse pounds here." He touched his lips to that throbbing beat, and lingered his attentions there. He lightly nipped and sucked until Poppy melted into him.

Looping an arm around her waist, he steadied her, and continued his tutorial on seduction.

"And here, I can tell by how hard your breaths come, Poppy," he explained, in husky tones, as he the seducer became sucked under a spell that had him powerless to anything but his want, need, and awareness of this woman. Tristan tugged loose the strings of her paint-spattered apron, and drew the garment overhead. Letting it fall at their feet, he swept a hand along the bodice of her dress.

Her breath caught.

"There," he murmured. "Right here." With a deliberate, infinite slowness, he lowered his head, and then brushed his lips along the lace trim. He flicked his tongue over the soft, hot skin there, and then lightly blew.

Poppy bit her enticingly full lower lip, muting that whimper. "I...I may have been w-wrong, after all," she conceded in agonized tones.

"Oh?" Tristan shoved aside the tangle of black curls and buried his face in her neck. "How so, love?" He kept his lips close, deliberately withholding that kiss.

"Tristan," she panted, curling her fingers in his hair, wordlessly urging him to continue.

"Yes." He flicked his tongue out.

"Y-You are s-skilled, after *alllll.*" Her admission ended on a long moan, as he dragged the bodice of her dress down, and kissed along the sensitive spot at her shoulder, working his lips on a path, lower. He brought his mouth close to one of the swells of her breast shielded by her chemise, and then through that thin fabric, he kissed her.

Poppy's head fell back, and an endless groan spilled past her lips. He lightly suckled the already pebbled tip.

"Please," Poppy rasped.

"Tell me what you want," he urged, running his thumb over the erect peak.

"You."

Another wave of desire pumped through him as his shaft swelled to a painful hardness. Tristan made quick work of the row of buttons down the back of her gown, and shoved it low over her hips.

Panting, Poppy stepped out of it and kicked the garment aside. She hesitated.

Tristan reached slowly for the hem of her chemise and slid it up, over her hips, higher, and then he removed it. Her drawers followed.

And then, she stood there, before him, splendorous in her nudity. He paused to work an admiring gaze down every swathe of exposed olive-hued skin. Where English ladies were pale and cream white, Poppy's skin, a sun-kissed shade, spoke to Roman roots. Tristan stretched both palms up to cradle the gentle swells of her breasts.

Her breath rasped loudly in his ears. Or was that his own? It was all jumbled in his mind. "So beautiful," he whispered, and lowered his head.

He caught one of the pink tips in his mouth and suckled, ringing a cry from Poppy. She clutched his head close to her chest, as if to entrap him in the only place he yearned to be. He flicked his tongue back and forth over the peak, alternately laving and sucking. Until Poppy's hips were undulating wildly.

"I want to feel you, too," she panted, breathtaking in her lack of restraint and honesty. Her determined fingers were already dragging his shirt up from his trousers. Her movements frantic, firing his hunger. Together, they divested Tristan of his lawn shirt.

With jerky movements that fit not at all with the restraint he'd managed over the years, he raced to be free of his trousers, pushing them down, struggling out of them. He kicked them aside until he was naked before her. He reached for her, but Poppy darted out of his arms.

He silently cried out at the loss and fought to retain some control over his passion.

Poppy's gaze drifted over him, before ultimately settling on the hard flesh jutting toward her.

"Oh," she breathed, and with the boldness he'd always admired in her, touched him.

Tristan groaned, the sound low, primitive, and hungry, lodging in his throat, and emerging strangled from his lips. His manhood jumped in her hand, as she worked her exploring fingers over him. He closed his eyes and gave himself over to the sensation of her hand on him.

"Does it hurt?" she murmured, lightly squeezing.

Tristan moaned. He'd never survive this. Not without embarrassing himself with his lack of control.

"I'm sorry." Poppy made to draw her fingers back but he shot a hand out, holding her there.

"Only the most wonderful kind of hurt," he managed to rasp out, his voice hoarse as Poppy resumed her exploration. She stroked his length, teased a single finger around the plum-headed tip, coaxing a bead of fluid.

"Amazing," she marveled in awe-struck tones.

Tristan squeezed his eyes shut and selfishly took for himself the aching pleasure of her touch. He rolled his hips, reflexively. Wanting to turn himself over to the mindless bliss that she tempted. With a pained groan, he removed her fingers from his person.

Poppy looked up; a question in her desire-heavy gaze.

Catching her in his arms, Tristan kissed her. Her mouth was already open and he was tasting her; stroking her, and being seared by every bold lash of her tongue against his.

She tasted of chocolate and honey, sweeter than any dessert that he'd ever tasted.

Poppy sighed and he swallowed that breathless whisper of her desire.

For Tristan, through the years, sex had become an emotionless, physical act, one that he'd welcomed for the brief, explosiveness that came in reaching that peak of gratification. With the passage of time, with every bored widow or discontented wife he'd bedded, an ennui had eventually set in. Only to now find himself wholly alive and aware, drunken off the intoxicating magic of Poppy's innocence.

Tristan guided her down to the blanket made by their garments. Not breaking contact with her mouth, he devoured her, drinking of her innocence before shifting his focus to the line of her jaw.

Poppy's heavy lashes drifted up. "I-I've dreamed of this," she rasped, turning her head slightly so he could worship her delicate collarbone. "The kiss. M-Making love."

His breath rasped in time to hers. "Never tell me with the pleasing Rochford." His teasing coaxed a laugh from her.

"You are...inco—" The air hissed between her teeth as he worked a hand between them, and slipped his fingers in the soft curls between her legs.

Poppy stiffened, and then with an incoherent word that emerged garbled from her swollen lips, she let her legs fall open.

"What was that?" he asked. He slid a single finger within her sodden channel. Heat. Molten heat that he'd gladly let consume him.

She tossed her head back and forth wildly. Her hips bucked as she arched toward his touch. Tristan continued to stroke her. In. And out. Until she was fire in his arms.

And then she opened her eyes. "Incredible," she whispered, working her gaze over his face; the depth of emotion there in her eyes burning with trust, and something more. Something he couldn't identify. Something he didn't want to identify. For that unacknowledged emotion in her crystalline gaze sent terror stabbing through him. Because of what it signified…that emotions were involved and always would be with Poppy. And he forced it back. Forced himself to hold on to this moment with her.

Tristan kissed her, reveling in her fingers stroking his back, the light drag of her nails as she marked him.

He lay between her legs. Tristan moved slowly, easing himself into her.

Each of those slight movements sent a painful throbbing to his shaft. An ache for him to complete the act that would join him and Poppy.

"Tristan," Poppy moaned into his mouth.

Sweat slid from his brow, those drops slid down his cheek. This need. This hungering… *It has never been like this.* Where logic melted away, and he was reduced to an almost painful thrum of desire. Not with any woman before her.

Poppy opened her eyes once more, still heavy with desire, but soft.

Panting, Tristan dropped his brow against hers. "You are perfection, Poppy Poplar." And then he claimed the pebbled tip of her right breast between his lips and sucked deeply.

Poppy arched her hips, and he thrust deep.

She stiffened in his arms, and he braced for her cry of pain as he tore through that barrier.

Except, her breathing increased its rapidity, and a slightly pained smile hovered on her lips. "I preferred the before," she whispered, her voice ragged.

Tristan brushed his lips against her temple; that kiss brought her eyes open. "Wait until the 'after', love," he vowed, and slowly withdrew. Lowering his head, he swept his mouth over the crest of her right breast. He worshipped it with his lips, laving, sucking, until Poppy was incoherent once more, lifting her hips to meet each thrust of his. *Slowly*. And then increasing in frenzy until Poppy's quiet cries were spilling from her lips and pinging around the empty ballroom, a symphonic medley that drove him faster.

They arched against one another. Their bodies straining.

Poppy arched her back, tossing her head, those shimmering black curls a beautiful cascade about her.

He stared, riveted by the pleasure contorting her features.

Never had it been like this. Not with any woman.

Where her fulfillment was all that mattered, where his passion was fueled by the flush of pleasure upon her skin.

"Come for me, Poppy," he urged. Tristan stroked deep.

She went absolutely motionless in his arms. Her entire body stiffened. And then Poppy came undone.

She screamed her release to the rafters, and he thrust once more, joining her over that precipice with a guttural shout, just one word: "Poppy."

Their voices blended, as they found their surcease, together.

The life drained from him and he collapsed over her, catching himself by the elbows. He could hear nothing beyond the solid, thundering beat of his own heart. When their chests slowed, he rolled onto his back, and brought her atop his chest.

"Mmm," she murmured, her eyes closed, a sated smile on her lips. "You are correct."

"And there were words I never thought to hear from you, lady wife." He buried his lips against the sensitive skin of her collarbone, earning a laugh. "On what have I proven right?"

Poppy opened her eyes; and an impish sparkle glowed in their depths. "The 'after' is far better."

Tristan's shoulders shook as he joined in the tinkling sound of amusement that spilled from her lips, until she rested her cheek against his chest…and went silent. She stroked her fingers at his shoulder. His skin jumped at the butterfly-soft caress. "I didn't notice these the first time I saw you shirtless." And then she abruptly stopped. "What happened?"

He dipped his chin at an awkward angle to see the spot she

spoke of.

The white flesh puckered and scarred. "Luck," he murmured.

She glanced up questioningly.

"I ducked out of the way of a Frenchmen's bayonet, and missed the bullet another soldier had intended for me," he explained.

On your feet, Poplar. They're charging…

He briefly closed his eyes. Through the years, he'd become a master of controlling the memories. He'd shaped the narrative in his mind, and kept it all locked away. Compartmentalizing those years as he did, kept them…safe. Moments that belonged to another. But occasionally…they trickled in. It had been so long…

"You nearly died," Poppy whispered. Her eyes darkened, and she brushed her fingertips lightly over the mark.

Tristan caught her hand and raised it to his lips. "Ah, but I didn't and that therefore makes me lucky."

Instead of those assurances deterring her from further talk about his years as a soldier, Poppy sat up. Her breasts bobbed slightly with that movement, before her cascade of black curls fell about her shoulders, shielding those soft mounds. She proceeded to run her gaze over his person, touching her gaze…and fingers to the marks left by bullets and blades.

Over the years, the women he'd bedded had shown almost a sick fascination with his scars. As if there was something dangerous about Tristan and because of that, thrilling to bed. For the first time since the mad frenzy to disrobe and make love to Poppy, however, he considered how he must look…to *her*. Poppy with her eye for artistic perfection had desired to paint one such as Rochford. And then there was Tristan…in his own flawed form. He shifted, and reached under him.

"What are you doing?" Poppy asked as he grabbed his lawn shirt.

"Dressing." Protecting her.

Or are you protecting yourself?

Poppy caught the garment, and tugged it from his fingers. "You're hiding." There was an accusatory edge to her tone.

"I'm protecting you."

It was the wrong thing to say.

Poppy's eyes narrowed into thin slits of fury. Pressing her hands hard against his shoulders, she shoved him back. Tristan grunted as he hit the floor. "You think me so weak that I'm somehow horrified by your scars?"

"I saw your eyes, Poppy," he said softly. "You wear your every emotion in them." Every emotion.

Poppy's scowl deepened. "You're correct. I *was* horrified." The fight seemed to go out of her, and she sank back on her haunches. "At the idea of you hurt, T-Tristan." Her voice broke.

"Poppy," he said softly, reaching for her.

She swatted off his touch. "Don't patronize me. I—"

Cupping a hand around her, he guided her down, and then kissed her.

She stiffened, and then with a sigh, melted into his embrace.

"You're trying to distract me," she murmured, when they broke apart.

"I wouldn't dare. It would be futile. You cannot be distracted, Poppy Poplar."

Poppy picked her head up, resting her chin on his chest.

A smile teased her lips. "Poppy Poplar sounds atrocious."

"Yes," he conceded. But it felt right. "It is, however, far preferable to Lady Poppy Flowers." Even in jest, the tendrils of jealousy wrapped about him, and he wanted to beat Lord Rochford all over again.

Poppy propped her chin on his chest so she could look him in the eye. "Oh, there's something poetic in Poppy Flow—"

He rolled her under him so quick, he rang a startled laugh from her. "Minx," he growled.

"S-stop," she howled, breathlessly, as he nuzzled that sensitive spot at her neck. "I was t...teasing."

"No regrets that you are not, in fact, Poppy Flowers, Lady Rochford."

Snorting and gasping, she thrashed her head back and forth. "Y-You must c-concede that all together, i-it is a v-very g-garden inspired—ahhh." Tears streamed down her cheeks, as he raised her barefoot and glided his fingers over the sensitive arch. "I-I concede."

Tristan relented and while she regained control of her mirth, he studied her. Her cheeks flushed. Her eyes sparkling. She was temptation personified.

And had it not been for that bounder Rochford, she and Tristan even now would have never been wed. Why did the idea leave him bereft? Why should it when they'd entered into a marriage of convenience?

Because you lied to yourself. It was always going to be more with her... And there was a certainty: Tristan would have despised any man who'd lured her into her sister-in-law's paint room.

"You've gone all serious," Poppy murmured.

He lifted his head. "Have I?" Tristan stroked his palm along the soft curve of her back, alternating an up and down stroke with his fingers along her spine. How...right this moment felt. With Poppy in his arms. Not even a week ago, the idea would have been laughable for the inconceivability of it; because of who she was. Because of who he was. And yet, she belonged here.

She ran a finger along his lips. "Here. You become all tense." She lightly touched his brow. "And you've three creases here that draw up. What are you thinking about?" Poppy murmured.

"Rochford."

Of all the reasons for her husband's sudden seriousness, mention of Rochford would have been the last reason she expected. "Rochford? Never tell me, you've thought of painting him, too," she teased.

A half grin formed on Tristan's lips; the tension there, however, belied any hint of his earlier levity. He drifted his fingers through her thick, dark curls, brushing them back, and she luxuriated in the tingling along her scalp that his touch roused. "Why Rochford?"

She wrinkled her brow. "I already told you he—"

"Was pleasing to the eye and proportional. Yes. Yes, I know all that. But why?"

He had been the first to ask that question. In the immediacy of her fall, Poppy's family had been so caught up in the scandal that such a question would have never occurred to them. And then, even after...they wouldn't have bothered to ask. Rochford had nearly been naked and she'd been determined to paint him and no other details than that had mattered to them. Nor would they ever.

"Because I wanted to paint a male subject nude," she said matter-of-factly. "And he was the only one who seemed a possibility." Because he'd been the only gentlemen who'd come 'round. The only gentlemen who'd expressed an interest in art. Those humiliating details, however, she could not bring herself to share or admit...especially with Tristan Poplar, the Baron Bolingbroke. Poppy rested her cheek on the light silken mat of curls on his chest, and savored the steady beat of his heart under her ear... when he again spoke.

"And is that something you still want to do?"

She glanced up, donning a pensive expression. "Paint Rochford nude—" He growled again. "I'm teasing." She laughed as he tickled her right side. When her hilarity abated, she shimmied up his chest so that she could better hold his gaze. "I want to paint everything, Tristan. Everything."

"For what purpose?"

For what purpose? It was an...odd question. "I enjoy painting," she said simply. Since Juliet had opened her eyes to the thrill in that pursuit, Poppy had found joy in simply creating things.

"But you wish to...what? Have your paintings hanging in your home? And the homes of your siblings? And beyond that?"

Beyond that? "I'd...never given much thought to beyond." Poppy lifted her shoulders in an uneven shrug, sending her hair cascading over her husband's face. "Some people just paint, Tristan."

"Yes," he agreed, stroking those curls back, behind her ears. "Artists paint. You never struck me as the manner of woman who'd reduce a passion to a pastime." His words were coupled with a look in his eyes, a look that felt very much like...disappointment.

She bristled. "You're implying that my enjoying my work is not enough."

"I didn't imply that. You said that."

Her mouth parted, but it took several tries to get words out. "Me?"

"You," he confirmed with a nod.

"If it was just a pastime, Poppy, you'd be happily sketching fruit bowls and floral arrangements like most every other lady in Polite Society. You wouldn't have taken on the responsibility of redecorating your sister's hotel."

Poppy lay her cheek back on the muscular wall of his chest once more.

And this time, they went silent, and there were no more words spoken between them. Poppy remained wide-awake, long after

Tristan's breath had settled into an even cadence, indicating he slept. Slumber, however, proved elusive as his admonishments lingered in her mind.

Had they been admonishments, though? Or had he simply challenged her to think about why she did the work she did? She chewed at her lower lip. In that questioning, he'd been no different than she had been earlier that night, telling him that he needed to find himself.

The difference was…Poppy had believed herself found. She'd been so very confident, in having a sketchpad in hand and creating paintings and sketches, that she knew her interests and that which brought her joy.

What he suggested, what Tristan had all but said without saying the actual words was that her enjoyment was just a hobby.

The thing of it was, Poppy hadn't really considered much beyond her enjoyment of art. She found pleasure in what she did. But doing anything else with it? Well, such an idea hadn't entered her head.

It was enough that it was enough for her.

Wasn't it?

A quiet snore spilled from Tristan's lips, breaking into her own distracted musings.

She used that moment to study him. His features were so softened in sleep, so at peace and unguarded. His dark locks tousled like a fallen angel who'd lost his halo. How very different this relaxed version was from the troubled man he'd become.

A memory slid in of when she'd found him in his offices, wholly absorbed on those pages he'd hastily tucked away. What had he been looking at when she'd arrived? She was his wife, and as such, she was surely permitted to know…whatever had been responsible for his disquiet. Nor would she ever be the manner of wife who was content to allow her husband to worry while she remained oblivious to their circumstances.

Tristan emitted a bleating snore, and then his breathing settled into a quieter, more even cadence.

Curled against her husband, Poppy stared at the mural she and Tristan together had painted.

Her family would, of course, say whatever Tristan had been reading wasn't her business. But neither would her siblings have secrets from or with their spouses. She warred with herself through thirty long ticks of the clock, before sliding out of her husband's arms.

Tristan snorted in his sleep, and then rolled onto his stomach. Rescuing her dress, Poppy struggled into the garment. She fetched a candle, and then tiptoed her way across the ballroom.

The moment she'd closed the door behind her, Poppy released a breath, and then took off quickly down the hall, her bare feet cold upon the hardwood floors.

"You are not doing anything wrong," she muttered under breath. *Except, if you aren't, why are you sneaking?*

Poppy thrust aside that taunting voice. Her husband shouldered so many burdens. Burdens no person should have to face alone. Tristan was her friend—nay, not just her friend, but also her husband. As such, she'd never be able to blithely ignore the troubles that tormented him. With a clearer conscience, Poppy held her candle aloft, and found her way below stairs. She didn't stop until she'd reached Tristan's office. The door stood ajar from when she'd led him through that threshold—two hours? Two years? A lifetime ago?

So much had changed in their relationship. There could be no doubting that the illusion of a fraternal relationship was just that— an illusion. Despite the chill hovering in the drafty townhouse, a blush heated her body.

Poppy stepped inside.

All the flames snuffed and the curtains drawn, but for the lone candle in her hand, the room remained pitched in darkness. She blinked several times in a bid to adjust to the dim lighting, and then entered Tristan's office. Poppy set the candle in an empty sconce, and then made her way over to his desk. "Get in and then get gone," she whispered, reaching for the drawer, and then she froze.

Her gaze went to the book resting atop the row of ledgers.

Stealing a glance at the door, Poppy found herself picking up her sketchpad. She fanned through the familiar pages.

Emotion swelled in her chest, as she brushed her fingertips over the telling little crease. "He dog-eared it," she whispered.

The drawing was a rudimentary sketch. One of her earlier ones, and as such missing the detail and skill that she'd improved upon over the years. But so very special because of when she'd drawn it and because of what it represented.

Her cheeky grin, as she stood conversing with the tall gentleman. Sir Faithful stood between them, looking adoringly up at the man who patted his head.

He'd marked the page.

Poppy sank onto the edge of the swivel chair and it rotated slightly under her added weight. She turned the pages until she reached another one marked by Tristan.

This sketch, a self-portrait of her fishing at Prudence and Christian's summer estate. A pair of legs stretched out from behind a tree; but the trunk obscured his identity. Had Tristan remembered that moment as well?

Why…*why* had he marked them?

And why are you making more of it than is there?

Poppy forced herself to close the book and set it aside. *Enough.* She'd come for a purpose: to find out what had so occupied her husband's attention and then leave.

Except, as she reached for the gold ring in the middle of the drawer, guilt needled its way back in. Because if she truly wished to know, couldn't she simply ask him?

Her stomach muscles clenched. *Stop.*

Poppy grabbed the drawer, and yanked it open. Picking up the ivory velum, she unfolded it, and proceeded to read.

Lord Bolingbroke,

Per our most recent discussion, you are well aware of the circumstances in which you now find yourself. After careful calculations, Lord Maxwell is determined to see that you pay your—

"Debts," she whispered into the quiet. Poppy resumed the lengthy details marked in ink, and flipped to the next page, and the next. And with each sum listed, she mentally tabulated all until she at last reached the end of the ruthless note.

This is what had so troubled him earlier. What a bloody fool she'd been to make it something in her mind, when all the while Tristan had been dealing with this—on his own.

He was expected to turn over a fortune, and if he did not?

A chill scraped her spine, and Poppy's fingers curved reflexively upon the pages, wrinkling their corners.

Grabbing her discarded sketchpad, Poppy turned to the first blank page, and sifting around the cluttered contents of the drawer, she found a small nub of pencil.

Poppy noted each number, marking them upon the empty sheet. Row after row after row of all the expenses and payments the current Earl of Maxwell expected Tristan to pay. She worked until the muscles in her neck strained from the position. Until she at last reached the end of the ruthless notes. She let her pencil fly over the page as she did a swift calculation, adding those numbers…

Her heart sank.

Bloody, bloody hell.

Poppy tossed the pencil down, and rubbing her neck, she examined the exorbitant sum. The current Earl of Maxwell and his man-of-affairs expected everything paid back, and that with interest, too: the salaries for governesses, art instructors, French tutors, dance teachers. Gowns and garments for all the years that the man had been missing. Tristan's stables. Tristan's…

"D-Dogs," her voice broke. She gave her head a shake, and thrust aside those useless, weak sentiments. That would fix nothing.

Fifty-five thousand pounds, however, was what would.

It was a fortune.

And Tristan had no hope of paying that debt.

Her jaw went slack as the truth slammed into her. Why, the current Earl of Maxwell didn't expect to receive that payment. The funds had less to do with him adding to his already no-doubt outrageous fortunes, but exacting revenge on those who'd stolen from him.

Poppy tossed her pencil down, and pressed her fingertips to her suddenly throbbing temples. Blast her husband. Why hadn't he confided in her?

I'll not touch your dowry…I'd ask for one thing, however…

Her heart froze in her chest.

"He knew," she whispered. It was one of the reasons he'd allowed Poppy control of her dowry when any other gentleman in England would have taken that fortune gladly and paid off his debts. But Tristan, the great lummox, in all his honor, had wanted to ensure his sisters were cared for, and hadn't mentioned at all the possibility of debtors' prison. Poppy grabbed the last page of Sanders' note to Tristan.

Lord Maxwell trusts you know there will be consequences should you fail to make repayments on the attached items…

"The bastard," she gritted out, refolding those pages from Sanders. Poppy returned them to the desk drawer when another note caught her eye.

The creation of a...

Poppy grabbed the packet and frantically scanned the page.

...new battalion has resulted in numerous vacancies. Among which, the rank of Captain in the 15ᵗʰ Hussars is being...

"What?" she whispered, re-reading the sentences in her brother-in-law's hand.

What was this?

Except, reading them again and again, with nothing changing, she knew.

"What are you doing?" a voice snarled from the doorway.

She cried out. And her stomach flipped over itself as she stared blankly at the towering, shirtless, barefoot gentleman filling the doorway.

"Tristan," she said weakly, as the packet slipped from her fingers, and landed with a decisive *thwack*, a damning *thwack* atop her husband's cluttered desk.

As one, she and Tristan looked to the pages from Sanders.

Oh, bloody hell. This is bad.

What was she doing?

Even in the dark, with more than ten paces dividing Tristan from his wife, he caught the telltale guilt in her expression. The color had drained from her cheeks.

His heart thumped loudly and he forced his feet forward. "Were you spying on me?" he gritted out.

"Yes. No."

"Which is it, lady wife?" he snapped.

Poppy held the pages she'd been reading aloft. "What is this?"

It had been inevitable. The moment he'd asked St. Cyr to speak on his behalf, and then his friend had secured that vacant commission, Tristan had been committed to that path. Just as it had been inevitable that Poppy would find out. "It is a commission."

"A commission," she repeated, like she'd never heard the word before. Like she didn't understand it. When Poppy understood all.

He would hand it to her; for one who'd been snooping on him and going through his papers, she was remarkably unapologetic.

"It is an assignment with the Home Office," he clarified, reaching for his paperwork.

Poppy wetted her lips and then reluctantly held it out. "You are…taking on work with the Home Office, then?" she repeated, in a second echo.

"I… It was something I'd pursued prior to your offer."

She flinched.

Bloody hell. He'd not feel bad. Even as he told himself that, his chest squeezed. "Our pact, that is. Before we'd agreed to the pact."

"I…see," she said quietly, hovering behind a desk that wasn't a desk, in a reminder of his financial state. He felt her eyes on him as he began stacking the paperwork. "And what will your assignment with the Home Office entail." It entailed him leaving. "Will you keep offices there?"

He stiffened. Oh, hell.

"Not that I have a problem with you working daily," Poppy said hurriedly. "I don't. I've my work at Penelope and Ryker's, in addition to seeing to our home."

This was a discussion they had to have. Mayhap one he'd owed her before they'd exchanged vows. And yet, based on the terms she'd set forth, a marriage of convenience to benefit the both of them, his work with the Home Office shouldn't have mattered.

And yet, low in his gut, he knew that would never be the case with Poppy. That in lying to her, he'd always been lying to himself.

"I owe Maxwell," How singularly odd speaking of another with the name Tristan himself had gone by for so long that everything else felt unnatural. "Fifty-five thousand pounds. Securing this commission, Poppy," he went on, willing her to understand. Needing her to understand. "It will work toward restoring my name," In the only thing he'd ever been any good at. "And eventually paying off those debts." And then…he'd be free. Free of the crimes committed by his family. Free of society's scorn.

Poppy approached, taking hesitant steps, when she'd only ever been bold in her every movement. "This…assignment is not at the Home Office, is it?" she asked in achingly soft tones.

He dusted a hand down the side of his stubbled cheek. "Poppy," he entreated; needing her to understand. Because the arrangement they'd spoken of on the balcony of his hotel suite had been one where this, his temporarily leaving, shouldn't matter. Not truly. Only, it would have always mattered to Poppy. He'd simply convinced himself otherwise.

She stopped; and toyed with the scalloped back of his desk–seat. "I…see." Poppy tipped her chin up.

"The King's hussars was expanded. It created a non-purchase vacancy. However," He was rambling to his own ears, and yet, he could not stop because then there would be more questions and a hurt Poppy when there was never supposed to have been a hurt Poppy. Only a Poppy content with a mutually beneficial union. "Generally an officer who succeeded to a non-purchase vacancy cannot sell one's commission for at least several years."

"Several years?" she echoed dumbly. "You'll work in the Home Office, then, for several years and—"

"No. I'd be employed through the Home Office."

Her eyes sparkled with confusion. "Where will you go then?"

"Ireland." She revealed no outward reaction to that announcement. "The Royal Barracks. It is not so very far," he said lamely. "Cork."

Several beats of silence passed. "That is Irish Nationalist country." His wife would be so attuned to all that she'd know that about British politics, too. She backed away a step. "You'd go and put yourself at risk, serving in a place where we have no right to be."

A muscle in his jaw jumped. "Such talk is dangerous."

"Dangerous?" Her voice pitched. "Are you threatening me?"

"No," he exclaimed. "Of course not." God, he was blundering this badly. Tristan scraped a hand through his hair. "I'm merely pointing out that you should have a care."

"A care?" she cried, throwing her arms up. "You tell me to have a care? You are marked with the scars left by bullets and bayonets. You escaped Boney's forces with your life and now you'd risk all by serving in a place where the English are not wanted?" Her words came in a frenzy, picking up a dizzying speed. "And furthermore, who are you worried about hearing us? There's two servants and my lady's maid, and soon, there won't even be you." Her strident voice echoed off the walls, hammering home her hurt, and it threatened to cleave him in two.

He took a step toward her, but Poppy presented him her back;

in a cut that may as well have been a physical one for the intensity of it. "Poppy," he began quietly, resting his palms on her shoulders. "What we agreed to—"

She shrugged him off in a complete rejection that left him empty. "I know what we agreed to," she said tiredly, and then with her usual spirit restored she spun, determination lit her eyes. "Why didn't you tell me about this?"

Tristan attempted to make her understand. "I...believed that you wished for autonomy." *Or is it that you're trying to ease your own deserved guilt.* "This commission, it did not interfere with the freedoms you sought, and so it did not seem to alter the terms we'd discussed."

Poppy flinched. "The *terms*," she echoed." His wife brought her chin up. "I had a right to know, Tristan."

He drew in a shaky breath. "You are correct, Poppy. I...owed you that. And I was...wrong to withhold this," he finished lamely. He'd married her, consummated their union, and all the while, he'd withheld a crucial piece about their future together. Now he could confront the truth of his own treachery. He'd not told her for one simple reason: he'd been afraid she'd break it off. It had been the ultimate act of selfishness borne of a fear that she'd break off their arrangement.

Poppy hugged her arms to her chest. "You don't have to go. I have money, Tristan. You don't need to take employment."

He jerked, feeling much the way he had when a bayonet's blade had lanced his side. "Is that what you believe I sought? Your fortune?" he asked tersely.

"Of course not, Tristan. You rejected my dowry."

Not entirely.

"That money is reserved for you and our children." A babe she might even be carrying now. And a hungering so fierce, so keen, left him breathless at the thought of it. A tiny girl with her mother's dark curls and spirit and—

"One has to have a marriage to have children," she said, with a bitterness he'd never before heard from her.

A piece of his heart cracked off.

I'd tell you not to hurt her, but that is inevitable...

In the moment, St. Cyr's warning mocked him with its truth. *But then, you always knew that.* In his desire for her, he'd refused to acknowledge that, and instead opted to believe the lie before him.

"There is a marriage, Poppy," he whispered, looping an arm around her waist, and as he ran his lips down the length of her neck, she melted against him. "This is not forever. There'll be a marriage when I return." Her breath caught as he trailed another path of kisses along the trim of her neckline.

"Tristan," she moaned.

It was a plea. For more? To stay with her always. For him to stop. *Please, do not let it be that.*

"Tell me what you want, Poppy," he begged, handing her control, even as her rejection would kill him.

Her smoky lashes fluttered open. "You, Tristan," she whispered. "It has always been you."

And terrified by the depth of emotion there and the meaning behind those seven words, he swept his mouth over hers.

There was nothing gentle in their meeting. Their kiss was violent and desperate. He slid his tongue over her lips, in a bid to memorize the lush, silken contours. Poppy nipped at him, a primitive mate, marking her right. Her place.

Tristan tugged her hem, lifting her dress, so that her long legs were exposed, and he guided her so that she was perched on the edge of his desk.

"Tristan," she rasped, as he fell to his knees before her. Catching her delicate foot, he angled her leg and brought her arch close to his mouth. He kissed the instep, reveling in the thready moan of her desire. He journeyed higher, pressing his lips to every bit of exposed flesh. "I love your legs, so firm from riding," he praised, caressing his mouth higher still. "And the smell of you, Poppy. All musky heat and womanly desire," he whispered, and she collapsed back on her elbows, sending all the books and ledgers toppling and tumbling to the floor in a discordant symphony, as he brought his mouth closer. Closer still to that apex. He teased a kiss along her inner thigh.

The breath hissed between Poppy's teeth. "What…oh, goodness…please…" All her speech dissolved.

And then he dropped a kiss atop her damp curls.

She cried out; as her limbs quivered; she let them splay wider.

"You are so wet," he praised. "I want to taste you."

"Yes," she hissed. "I-I want that."

He slid his tongue inside, stroking her; alternately toying with the sensitive nub. Suckling that flesh until Poppy was undulating. She bucked underneath him. Cursing and crying out. And even through the lust that cloaked his senses, he smiled at the colorful expletives falling from her lips.

"Don't stop," she ordered between great gasping breaths. "Don't ever stop."

"Do you mean like this?" He ceased his ministrations, teasing her to a fever pitch, angling away from the thrust of her hips.

She whimpered.

Taking no mercy, he breathed lightly at her heated flesh. "Tell me what you want," he coaxed, glancing up. "Let me hear you say it."

Her eyes heavy, her thick black lashes swept low, she managed just one sentence: "I want your mouth on me." Tangling her fingers in his hair, she guided him back to her center; so unabashedly free in her quest for pleasure; his shaft throbbed with the need to plunge deep inside all that molten heat. To only take, but he made himself give.

Tristan darted his tongue over her slit. Lapping her until he felt her trembling under him. Until her cries reached a fever pitch, and then she came. Poppy arched and lunged and twisted, her thighs closing tight around his head to hold him close, as she came loudly and wildly.

Growling, he climbed to his feet, and catching her by the hips, he thrust deep. She cried out, another peal of further pleasure he'd coaxed from her just-sated body.

"Wrap your legs around me," he ordered sharply, as he came down over her. He rocked into her. Deeper and deeper. Stretching her. Filling her. Until sweat fell from his brow, and her cries of desire mingled with his own. The force of his thrusts sent the desk rocking back and forth on its narrow legs.

And then she came again, screaming and screeching his name, and he was joining her over that glorious precipice, somewhere between here and heaven. He shuddered from the force of his release, and then collapsed.

They lay there, with only the sharp draws of their breaths to break the silence as they found their way back to earth.

But Tristan didn't want to climb down from this moment. He

didn't want reality to rear itself and return to the place they'd been before this, of Poppy's hurt and his inability to spare her from it. Mindful that she was stretched awkwardly out upon the hard surface of the desk, Tristan forced himself to straighten and right his garments. Coming around the desk, he retrieved a kerchief from one of the sideboard drawers, and returning to his wife, he gently wiped the remnants of his seed from her person.

"You are leaving," she said quietly, as if these past moments where their bodies had moved in exquisite harmony had never happened, and they'd simply resumed that tense exchange before it.

"I am." He had to.

"There's…nothing that can make you stay."

Her. He wanted to stay for her. He knew that now. Somewhere along the way, Poppy had become more than just a friend. She'd become someone he needed. Nay, the woman he wanted in his life…now and for always. And because of that, she was also the reason he had to leave. Straightening, Tristan hopped onto the edge of the sideboard so he and Poppy sat shoulder to shoulder. "This isn't solely about money, Poppy." For as she'd pointed out, she had money enough for the both of them.

"Then what is it?" she asked; her fingers shook as she struggled to straighten her dress.

"Here," he murmured, guiding her hands down, as he saw to the task himself. When her garments were righted, he stroked her jaw. "This is about your name and your reputation."

"I don't care about my reputation."

And he rather believed that. It was just one of the things he'd come to admire about Poppy over the years. "There will be our children. And even as you think you might not care in this moment, when you have a son or daughter"—or both—"you'll want to do anything to protect them from hurt." And he'd not be able to live in a world where Poppy grew to resent him, where he came to resent himself for not restoring their name.

Sadness spilled from her eyes. "I will want to protect them at all costs, but do you know, Tristan? I'll also know that as long as they are loved, nothing matters more."

"Perhaps."

Poppy climbed down from the desk and her skirts fluttered

about her legs. "When do you leave?"

His stomach muscles contracted. "A fortnight."

"A fortnight?"

And just like that, the shock and hurt of before blazed to life. "You've known this." A bitter laugh gurgled in her throat. "At what point did you intend to tell me? Or did you simply intend to leave?"

It had happened. St. Cyr's prediction had proven correct—Tristan was responsible for Poppy's misery. Just as he'd been unable to see his sisters happy, so too was he now failing his wife. "Of course I wouldn't just leave." Frustration with himself and his inability to make anything right brought his words out more sharp than he intended.

Poppy raked a pitying stare over him. "Your pride will be your ruin, Tristan Poplar." And her words, along with that condescending expression, grated.

He chuckled. "I was ruined when Northrop reentered. But at least now I will have my honor."

"Pfft, *honor*," she scoffed. "You equate your honor with how the world views you and not with how you live your own life."

Tristan stormed around the side of the desk so that only the swivel chair divided them. "How I live my life? And what of *you*?" Fury and hot emotion were calling forth every word.

"What of me?" she demanded, folding her arms defensively at her middle.

Soon he'd be gone, and he needed to know when he left, she'd have her work but that she wouldn't shutter herself away with it. He needed to know that she wouldn't trap herself indoors, hiding the one thing that brought her joy. "You, who paint your sister's hotel and your own walls—"

Poppy sputtered. Poppy, his always in command and in control wife, at a loss because of him, and through the swirl of emotion, he could not, nor would he call back a single word.

Then she found her legs in their battle. "You'd speak of it as though what I do is somehow bad."

"I speak as though what you do is *safe*," he said solemnly. "You'd call me out, and yet, bold and spirited and proud as you are, you've hidden yourself away. In your sister's hotel, away from Polite Society. On your sketchpad. Unable to so much as sign your name to what you create and own what you've done." He slashed a hand angrily at that book she'd gifted him.

She gasped, and like a mother protecting her babe, grabbed that book up. Clutching it close, a gift he did not deserve. Just as he'd not deserved her. "You're wrong. My work at Penny and Ryker's *is* there for the world to see."

"Just not as yours. Your refusing to claim ownership of your art allows you to go through life never truly having your pieces judged." Had his wife even realized she'd put those defenses up?

Anger rolled off her in waves. "How dare you?" she seethed.

"I dare because I might have been banished by society, but I've fought at every turn, and you? You speak of me, but you've done something far worse. You've hidden yourself…not because of Rochford but long before him, because you're too afraid of what the world might actually say about your talents. A coward in the face of—"

Poppy shot a hand out; the sharp crack of her palm connecting with his cheek echoed in the sudden quiet.

Their chests rose and fell furiously, their breath coming in fast, angry spurts as they locked in silence.

Then horror paraded over Poppy's features and she jerked her hand close to her skirts. "I'm… I… I didn't…"

"It is fine," he said tiredly. He'd deserved her fury and her blow, but for reasons long before this one.

"Why are you doing this?" she implored. "Make me understand?"

"I'm trying to make more of myself."

Poppy gripped him by the shirt and shook him lightly. "*You* are enough. Why can't this be enough?" *Why can't we be enough?* It hovered as real as if she'd uttered the question aloud.

"Because this cannot be enough," he said gently. "And someday you'll see that, Poppy Tidemore."

She reeled as if he'd struck her.

"Poplar," she whispered. The evidence of her hurt struck like a gut punch that had been landed by an iron fist.

He stared at her in confusion.

"I'm no longer Tidemore, just as you're no longer able to simply consider leaving without…without…"

"Without what?" he demanded.

"Telling me," she cried out, slashing a hand angrily at the air. "Or asking me." She forced herself to draw a calming breath. "You told me that Northrop was collecting a debt, not that he'd enumerated precisely every expenditure and the amount owed."

"It was all the same." Whatever the amount would have been, would have been too much. Expenses he couldn't afford.

"I was wrong. This will never be enough." She started for the door. And with every step that carried her away, there was a finality…to this moment. To them. Her strides widening the gap. "I'd ask that you say goodbye to me when I leave, and that you'd consider writing?" In requesting as much, his leaving became real in ways that it hadn't been. Being parted from her took on a realness that he'd not previously felt because he'd not allowed himself to.

Poppy stopped; her fingers on the door. "You want me to play the soldier's dutiful wife and happily send you on your way, waving with my kerchief, while you put yourself willingly in harm's way?" She shook her head. "I'm sorry, Tristan. I can't do that."

This time, as she left, he let her go.

And staring after her, long after the quiet echo of her footfalls had faded, he'd never felt more miserable.

CHAPTER 18

When she'd been a girl of fifteen, Poppy had secretly dreamed of a life as Poppy Poplar, the Countess of Maxwell.

Of course, it hadn't been the title which had mattered to her. It had been him: the charming gentleman with a love of dogs and an appreciation for horses.

As such, married a fortnight now, one might say Poppy had everything she'd dreamed of.

Except she didn't.

In the two weeks since they'd been wed, they'd been precisely as they'd been: teasing friends. Albeit teasing friends who made love to one another each evening. But during the day, they lived their own separate lives.

Which was fine.

Which was what she had essentially agreed to.

So why was she so bloody miserable?

On the heel of that was the rush of an answer: it wasn't enough. Selfishly, she wanted more. Nay, she wanted more with him.

Adding another stroke to the mural Penelope had commissioned for her daughter's nursery, Poppy stole another glance out of the corner of her eye at her elder sister and husband, the blissfully happy couple, crawling on all fours, chasing the squealing little girl around the room.

And there proved to be something inherently bad and wicked in Poppy, for she was awash with an envy that crippled her from making so much as another stroke.

That was what a marriage was.

Mayhap not to Polite Society and mayhap not for the world on a whole, but that relationship was all the Tidemores had ever witnessed or had for themselves. Until Poppy. Oh, she'd been the one to reassure Jonathan with the reminder that ultimately all the Tidemore women found love…even in the unlikeliest and formal matches they'd entered into.

But after fourteen days as Lady Poppy Poplar, the Baroness Bolingbroke, she conceded one very distinct difference that she'd failed to note…until now—Poppy had known her husband for more than six years. First as a girl on the cusp of womanhood, and then as a young woman, and now, simply, a woman. They were not strangers to one another. And as such there was affection, but what had never blossomed between them—was love.

"Da-Da," Paisley cried happily, and toddled away from the growling Ryker Black.

Her niece ran into Poppy's skirts, knocking Poppy slightly off-balance.

"Havn," the little girl happily crowed the safe word.

Breathless from the game of chase, Penelope fell back on her heels. "Aunt Poppy cannot be your haven. Aunt Poppy is painting."

Abandoning what had become a futile attempt at her work, Poppy set aside her brush, and scooped up her niece. "Don't you listen to your silly mum," she assured in sing-song tones. "Aunt Poppy always has time." She blew on the ticklish spot at the back of the little girl's neck until great big giggles spilled from her lips. Taking mercy, she dropped a kiss atop Paisley's black curls, and then set her on her feet. "Run," she whispered.

With another loud squeal, the girl went toddling off.

Poppy watched on wistfully as parents and child played, feeling like an interloper on that special family time they shared.

And that was what Poppy was missing in her own life: time that she and Tristan shared. Oh, they made love every night, but during the day, Poppy worked on the redesign of her sister's hotel, and in the early evening she returned and put the same efforts into her new residence. All the while, he remained either shut away in his offices or…elsewhere… "Sorting out his affairs", as he'd come to say.

His affairs.

Not theirs.

As though they were separate still.

But then, wasn't that precisely what they were? She made an angry swipe of her brush.

"Are you all right?"

Poppy started.

Concern filled her elder sister's eyes.

"I'm fine," she assured, making another stroke on the menagerie she painted on her niece's wall.

Penelope gave Ryker a look, and just like that, with no words, and some unspoken communication only they two understood, he scooped Paisley into his arms, and left the Tidemore sisters alone.

"You shouldn't be here," her sister said without preamble.

Poppy set her jaw. "You asked that I see to the redesign of your hotel. Where else should I be?"

"At home, Poppy," she said softly, resting an elbow against the wall. "Making your goodbyes…which is what a wife would do."

"A wife," she spat. She wasn't a wife. Not in the ways that mattered. Such, however, had not been the way of her new marriage. Collecting Penelope's arm, she moved her away from the fresh paint.

"You will regret not going," her sister persisted.

She shrugged. "He *chose* to leave." He'd chosen his commission and his honor over a future with her. And in fairness, she could not resent him for that decision. He'd only ever been honest in what he was able to offer, and she'd not asked him for more. In that, she'd lied…to the both of them—Tristan and herself. Nay, she'd not resent the future he craved. She would only ever regret that she hadn't been enough for him. But because of that, she could not go and simply blow a kiss to his departing carriage.

His departing carriage.

Oh, God. Her shoulders slumped. She could not take this.

Penelope slipped the brush from Poppy's loose grip. "Would you care to know what I suspect?"

"No," she whispered. She wanted to work on her mural and pretend this day was any other day of painting in her sister's hotel.

Why do you paint…?

Which had always been enough. Until Tristan had made her

question why she painted and she was still left these fourteen days later trying to determine an answer to that.

"That you are hiding away here during the day because you didn't quite think out this thing with Tristan."

Drawing in a shuddery breath, Poppy sank to the floor, and drew her knees close.

"I know what this is like. Precisely." Doing a sweep of the nursery, Penelope grabbed the child's rocker, and perched herself in front of Poppy, forcing her sister to meet her eyes.

"It is not the same." Poppy bit the inside of her cheek. Even though they were both sisters who'd married for convenience, it wasn't at all the same: Penelope's marriage was now filled with love…and a babe. And Poppy had a husband who didn't even know how to share his worries with her. "We fought about his leaving." *By God, it wasn't your place to go through my things, Poppy…* "On our wedding night, no less. A rather ignominious start, no?"

"And you've not talked since?"

"Oh, no…we…have. Well, mayhap not talking-talking, per se. But uh…some talk and then, other *things*…" she finished lamely. Her cheeks pinkened.

Understanding filled Penelope's eyes. "Ahh." She dusted a hand over her mouth, ineffectually hiding a smile.

"What was your argument about?"

Poppy recalled that disastrous night. The panic in his eyes. And desperation. And worse, the anger. "I went through his things and learned of the commission." But his outrage had seemed to come more from what she'd discovered. Tristan, in all his honor and pride, had chafed at her knowing the exact state he found himself in. "I implored him to stay. I offered him my dowry."

Penelope winced. "Husbands tend to not like that. In fairness, neither men nor women would."

Poppy picked her head up. "Do you know something of it?"

"Of course. I uncovered secrets my husband didn't wish for me to know."

And in the end, despite that, her sister and Ryker had worked through that. Poppy lay her cheek along her skirts.

"You have always been one to take charge of your circumstances, Poppy. Why should this moment be any different?"

Penelope's marriage had been one of convenience, too, but her

husband had also been there for them to try and build a future…
which they had. Poppy and Tristan? They couldn't very well have
anything if they were worlds apart. She toyed with her apron
pocket. "He's gone," she whispered. "There is nothing to take
charge of," she said, borrowing her sister's phrase. There could be
no "taking" when there was "nothing".

"No," Penelope concurred. "He's not gone. He's *leaving*." She
glanced pointedly at the long-case clock. "Unless he's left early.
Then, he's already gone. In which case, all I know is that if it were
my husband, regardless of the details of how we came to be married, I'd want to say goodbye."

Tears pricked Poppy's lashes, and she blinked them back. "I can't."

"We have no promise for the future. Will you be all right living
the rest of your life having sent Tristan on his way without even
a parting?"

A single tear slid down her cheek, and she swiped angrily at the
moisture. "I-I managed to c-convince myself that it w-was not
r-really happening. Th-that he wasn't leaving."

"He is leaving, Poppy," Penelope spoke the words aloud, saying
them when Poppy had prevented herself from doing so.

"I-I know." Poppy found the clock.

Forty minutes. He was to leave in forty minutes and then she'd
not see him again.

An agonizing pressure squeezed at her chest. Of course she
needed to say goodbye to him. She'd never forgive herself if he
left without at least a goodbye.

Poppy struggled to her feet. "I have to go," she rasped, and set
off running.

"I know," Penelope called after her. "The carriage has been sitting out front all morn."

Of course her sister would have had the foresight to prepare
that. Shouting her thanks, Poppy continued sprinting through the
hotel, and didn't break stride until the front doors of the lobby
were thrown open by the pair of butlers there.

Tripping at the top step, Poppy grabbed the rail and kept herself upright, before rushing on to the carriage. "M-my home," she
rasped. "Quickly, please."

A moment later the door was shut behind her. The carriage
dipped as the driver climbed atop his perch, and then they were

moving through the streets of London—the crowded streets.

Restless, Poppy whipped the gold velvet curtain back and stared out at the clogged streets. "Hurry," she whispered.

Only, the conveyance moved with an infernal, agonizing slowness.

Tristan was leaving.

In fact, he should have left ten, nearly eleven, minutes ago. The carriage was readied. His trunks and military satchel had all long been loaded.

And yet, Tristan hadn't been able to bring himself to go.

Not yet. Soon, he would.

Shortly.

He paced the marble foyer, no longer dusty, and the white stone shining since the touch left by Poppy.

She'd not come. Of course, that fact shouldn't have come as any form of surprise. Poppy had only ever been honest; and in a world where nearly all the women he'd had dealings with—his own mother, included—prevaricated or lied, Tristan had never ceased to be refreshed and in awe of her candor.

She'd disapproved of his leaving, and as a result, had insisted that she'd not give him that goodbye he'd sought.

Though in fairness, did she disapprove of his leaving…or his reasons for doing so…?

He ignored that jeering voice.

For ultimately, it didn't matter. He'd been unable to make her see reason, that this commission, to restore the Poplar name was now no longer just about him. That it was, as much for her and their someday babes.

A babe she might even now be carrying.

He briefly closed his eyes, that intangible imagining so very real he could almost touch it. And if there was a son or daughter, they'd be sullied by the legacy of crimes and sin left by their late grandfather.

At least when he departed, Tristan would know that the roof had been repaired and the rodent problem handled, leaving the residence habitable for Poppy and any babe that might have been conceived. *Both situations addressed through your wife's funds.*

It was all the reminder he needed of why he'd set the course he had.

Tristan abruptly ceased pacing. It was time.

St. Cyr and his wife, Poppy's sister, hovered at the bottom stair rail, along with Blackthorne and his wife, Lily, and their two children.

The group who'd come to bid him goodbye had been silent, until now. "I'm certain she wanted to be here," Lady Prudence murmured, the first to speak. "I suspect she must have been... caught up in whatever renovations Penny and Ryker were having her see to today."

"Of course," he said automatically, unable to meet the pitying expressions of his friends and their wives. Tristan tugged on his crisp white gloves, a flawless match to the immaculate trousers.

"Can we go play now?" Krisander whispered to his parents.

St. Cyr gave his son a look.

"What?" the boy mumbled.

Tristan had delayed long enough.

The marquess came forward and stuck a hand out.

Tristan clasped his friend's palm, and shook. "Thank you."

"That is what friends do."

Joining them, Blackthorne limped over. Using the head of his cane to balance his weight, he freed his right hand, and shook Tristan's. "Don't get killed," he said flatly, with a command only a duke could manage.

"It is my intention to return." Tristan glanced between his friends. How similar this moment was to one years earlier, back when they'd been young boys, resplendent in their military apparel. Then, as they'd prepared to head off and face Boney, they'd had stars in their eyes and excitement in their hearts about what was to come.

Only...everything had also changed. Now, Tristan was the only one riding out, while his friends remained behind with wives who loved them and children. There was no longer a thrill. There was no war. It should be the greatest of consolations, a commissioned captainship in the middle of peace time.

And yet...Tristan was hollow inside, gaping from the loss of... something he'd never truly had. But something he'd *almost* had.

Mindful of Poppy's sister, and Blackthorne's wife, who hovered in the background with their children and nursemaids close, Tristan spoke in a hushed tone reserved for his friends' ears. "I'd ask if something *were* to happen to me that you look after Poppy."

"Of course," St. Cyr and Blackthorne spoke in unison.

"She would require some guidance in navigating the mess left by my finances. And if you could see that there are no 'Rochfords' who'd impugn her honor."

St. Cyr clasped his shoulder. "You needn't worry. You'll return, but even if the worst were to happen, Blackthorne and I, along with every other sibling or in-law that Poppy has, will see she's cared for."

And it was a certainty; there was a sea of Tidemores who'd be there in the event she required it. Tristan balled his hands into reflexive fists. For he didn't want her to fall to others as a responsibility.

He wanted to stay here with her. Because…

His mind shied away from the "because"…

Nothing good could come from analyzing what was or what might have been. Not until he returned, and in that time, his scandal would have faded and his name and honor hopefully restored.

That would have to be enough.

It had to be.

Bringing his shoulders back, Tristan dropped a bow. "Thank you," he directed that appreciation at his friends who'd come.

St. Cyr's son Krisander skipped over. "Are you going to fight a war?" he asked, excitement in his eyes. His younger brother joined them.

"What is war?" Charlie piped in.

"I…no," Tristan said with a forced grin, ignoring the latter question, leaving it for the boy's father to one day answer. Even so, this leaving Poppy felt far worse than any battle he'd fought.

Krisander's shoulders sagged with disappointment. "Oh."

"I heard that." Blackthorne's young daughter, Grace, stomped over. "War isn't a good thing, Krisander," the little girl chided.

"I think it sounds like great fun." The boy held his arms aloft like he wielded a bayonet and bolted down the nearest corridor. Calling to him, Grace followed along. Charlie struggled to keep up with the pair.

"I'll see to them," the Duchess of Blackthorne assured, and handing the babe in her arms over to her waiting nursemaid, Her Grace set out after the quarreling children.

Tristan's sister-in-law came forward with her daughter in her arms. Prudence leaned up and placed a kiss on his cheek. "Be safe." Emotion filled her eyes. "And please come home to Poppy."

Unable to squeeze a suitable word out, he glanced down…and his gaze landed on the small girl she held. A babe smiling up at him. An impish Tidemore grin that was so very much his wife's. It was too much. Tristan forced his gaze away from a glimpse of the future he wanted. "You have my word," he made himself promise, and then headed for the door.

Florence, also cleaned up since Poppy's influence on the town-house, drew the door open. "Yar Lordship," he said, clicking his heels together.

"Florence."

Hurrying down the steps, Tristan started for the carriage. With one leg inside the carriage, Tristan paused and did a sweep of the bustling streets.

And then he heard it. "*Trissstan!*"

So faint, so distant, he might have imagined it.

"*Tristan!*"

There it was again.

Stepping down, he doffed his hat, and used the article to shield his eyes from the bright afternoon sun.

Then he spied her.

Weaving and racing down the pavement, she might have been confused for a fleet-of-foot pickpocket…if it hadn't been for the paint-splattered apron and muslin skirts whipping at her ankles.

His heart lifted.

She'd come.

Tristan hurried to meet her, quickening his strides, lengthening them, until he and Poppy skidded to a halt before one another.

Gasping and out of breath, his wife leaned forward and rested her hands on her knees. "Th-there was traffic."

All around them passersby streamed.

"I thought you weren't coming," he said hoarsely, his voice rag-ged.

His wife straightened, her narrow shoulders coming back, elongating her spine, and marking her the queen she was. "I almost didn't." She sailed over, so that the tips of their boots brushed. "But then, I knew if I didn't come"—her eyes held his—"I would regret it, and I'm not so proud that I'd put my pride before all."

And he was not so obtuse that he didn't know precisely what she was saying.

Tristan palmed her cheek. "I am so very glad you came." In the past, he'd earned himself a reputation as a consummate charmer only to find himself so inept with the one woman who mattered.

Poppy's throat bobbed up and down and that display of her hurt was enough to rip a hole inside his heart. "But not glad enough to stay."

"Poppy," he whispered, dropping his brow to hers. *I want a life with you. I want our future together.* And yet, he wanted it to be a future she was deserving of...a man who deserved her. Tristan brushed the pad of his thumb along her cheekbone. Before he left, however, he'd say what he meant to say to her in his offices; before he'd made an absolute mess of it all. "Regarding our... argument—"

"It is fine," she said quickly.

"It is not, though," he insisted, needing her to understand. "I spoke in anger but my words, what I intended to convey is true. I'd have you know, your talent, the art you create...it is a thing of beauty and wonder. Don't hide that. Not anymore. Let the world see..." Her lips parted. Uncaring about the crowd that watched, he leaned down and brushed his mouth over hers, in a kiss that would never be enough. He forced himself to draw back, and when her eyes fluttered open, he held her gaze once more. "Let the world see *all* of you."

"Tristan," she whispered. "I..."

Tristan strained, waited for the remainder of that.

She smoothed her palms along the lapels of his cloak. "Be well."

And as she rushed off to join her sister's side, Tristan had never wanted more in his life to choose a path of dishonor so that he could remain here with Poppy.

CHAPTER 19

Dearest Tristan,

I never noted how quiet London can be. Even…lonely. Or perhaps it is simply that I've never lived alone before. Mayhap having only known a noisy household filled with my mother and siblings, this is all just foreign. It reminds me, even more, with your being gone, how little I've seen of the world. Or experienced. I wonder what it must be like where you are. And I hope your days are full.

Ever Yours,

Poppy

UNTIL TRISTAN'S CARRIAGE HAD PULLED away and disappeared completely from sight, Poppy had convinced herself he'd return.

Nay, she'd convinced herself he wouldn't leave.

And that evening, when she'd been, for the first time in the whole of her twenty-one years, alone, she'd filled her new town-house with the sounds of her agonized tears. And she'd cried those same tears since he'd gone. The only thing that brought a surcease from those pathetic drops was her steady stream of visitors since Tristan's departure a week earlier—from Jonathan and Juliet to Christian and Prudence. Why hell, even her brother-in-law Ryker had abandoned his establishment during the busy daytime hours to accompany Penelope.

No one spoke of Tristan or her marriage. But what was worse was…how they looked at her.

Precisely how Prudence was staring at her even now. Within a few short days of his leaving, Poppy had found herself something she'd never wished to be—something no person ever wished to be—an object of pity.

Drawing back the red velvet curtain draped over the carriage window, Poppy made a show of studying the passing scenery.

"Stop," she gritted out.

Her sister's carriage lurched and swayed along the quiet London roads. "I've not said anything," Prudence said defensively.

"You didn't need to. I feel you staring."

"I'm not *staring*, per se. I…" When Poppy released the curtain, and glanced pointedly at her, Prudence sighed. "Very well, I was staring. But only because I'm worried about you."

She stiffened, willing her not to say it. "Please don't say," she pleaded.

Her sister's brow dipped. "Say what?"

"That you told me so." That Prudence, along with every last Tidemore, had both warned and predicted that the only thing awaiting Poppy at the end of the marital aisle with Tristan was, in fact, heartbreak.

Her sister slapped a hand to her chest. "I wouldn't say that," she said, affronted. "I mean, even if it is tr—" Prudence wisely let the rest of that go unfinished. She coughed into her gloved fist before continuing. "Either way, what has happened is water under the dam."

"That is not it. It is 'over the dam' or 'under…'" Poppy caught the twinkle glimmering in her sister's pretty eyes. "You're trying to distract me."

"Undoubtedly. Is it working?"

"Not a bit," she lied, adding a teasing smile in return.

"There," Prudence said, clapping her hands. "That is far better. I'll not have my sister sit around her townhouse crying all day."

"I don't cry all the day," she grumbled, shifting on the bench. In fairness, when they did come to visit, Poppy had greeted her kin with eyes still red from tears that she surely had to be nearly empty of.

"Very well, most of the day," Prudence conceded. "But sitting around and waiting for Tristan's mother to journey from Dartmoor?" She shook her head so hard, her straw bonnet fell back.

"No. No. No. That woman is atrocious and if you thought Tristan being gone was reason for tears, wait until you share a roof with your mother-in-law. Horrid woman. Horrid. Horrid. Horrid." Prudence slammed her bonnet back into place, and readjusted the dark sapphire ribbons.

At a loss as to whether to laugh or cry, Poppy buried her head in her hands and opted for the former.

"Never tell me you've gone and begun crying again," Prudence said, sounding so put-out that Poppy's shoulders shook all the harder.

And this time, when she picked up her head, Poppy dashed tears of mirth from her eyes. "I love you, Pru."

Prudence's lips formed a tremulous smile.

"Everything I ever said about Penelope being my favorite is slightly less tru—oopph," she grunted as Prudence's boot connected squarely with her shin. "I was *teasing.*"

"Which I'll allow is better than your crying."

Poppy laughed once more. When she was with Pru, she could almost forget that Tristan had gone. "Oomph." Bending down, she rubbed at her injured shin. "What in blazes was that one for?"

"You've got your teary-eyed Tristan look, and I'll not allow it. As it is, I feel in large part to blame."

"You're to blame for me marrying Tristan?"

"Indirectly, one might say. I'm to blame for your meeting him. Because of my husband and their friendship, that is."

"Ah, of course," she said with mock solemnity. God love Pru and her inability to detect proper sarcasm.

"As such, it is my responsibility to see that you're not sitting around pining." Pru's gaze sparkled with resolve. "Tidemore women do not pine."

"Actually, you pined a good deal."

"That was different." Prudence made a show of adjusting her bonnet strings.

"Oh?" She arched a brow. "And how so?"

"Because you're my sister." Her elder sister slid onto the bench beside Poppy. "I will see you smile again."

"It has been a week," she whispered; resting her head on Pru's shoulder. A week of her heart breaking and tears falling and missing him. There was that, too.

"I'm so angry with him, Poppy," Pru whispered. Stroking the top of her head the way she had when Poppy had burnt her favorite doll while having it pretend to smoke one of their brother's cheroots.

"Don't be."

Her sister briefly stilled her fingers. "You'd excuse it?"

"I'd understand it," she said wearily. Oh, upon learning what he'd intended and then in the immediacy of his departure, she'd railed at Tristan and his decision all over again.

"How?"

"Because at night when I've been unable to sleep, when I think of Tristan and…everything that's come to pass, I understand that he made me no promises. I asked him to marry me." Like Prudence had put an offer to her own husband. "Knowing I loved him. Knowing it would never be enough." And worse…expecting that he would come to love her. She could admit to that, too. "And in that, I deceived him," she finished on a faint whisper. Tears sprang again from those never-ending wells.

"Come now," Pru gently chided, resuming her distracted stroking of Poppy's head. "None of that. Today is a day where we shan't think of husbands or marriage proposals or any of it."

"We don't have to do this," she pleaded, not for the first time since her sister had arrived unexpectedly and announced her plans to bring Poppy to the Summer Exhibition.

"Oh, pooh. Of course we do. We always attend."

Held at the Royal Academy, the summer-long event in Burlington House featured paintings, prints, drawings, sculptures and, for that, had become one of Poppy's favorite times of the year.

In the end, the carriage rocked to a halt in Piccadilly, stealing the decision for her. "Here," Pru shoved Poppy's sketchpad into her arms, and then reached for her own supplies. "This shall be fun. You'll see," she promised, as the driver drew the door open and held a gloved palm inside.

"Pru?" Poppy said quietly; calling her from leaving. "Thank you."

"I love you," Pru said simply and then hopped down.

Mustering as much enthusiasm as she could, Poppy gathered up her reticule and hurried to join her sister, and the waiting lady's maid who'd accompanied them. They walked along the cobbled stones; where throngs of patrons were streaming through the three doorways leading to the exhibition.

And for all the ways in which her heart had ached these past days, as she swept inside the arched entryway, the same exhilaration she'd always found from the arts swept through her.

"That is better," Pru praised, her eyes already devouring the portraits and paintings that ran from the floor to the ceiling. Every last spare corner of the academy occupied by some piece of artwork. "Where are you going?" she called belatedly.

Lifting a hand in parting, Poppy didn't look back. "To explore."

And as Poppy wound her way through the crowd, the people around her remained wholly absorbed not in her or her scandal or her hasty marriage and then husband's subsequent departure, but rather the work on display. And here, she could simply become… lost.

Her sketchpad resting against her shoulder, she studied the exhibits, a blend of pieces that harkened back to the Greek and Roman classics, to the English landscape…when from across the room, a framed painting caught her eye. Cutting a swathe through the crowd, she found her way to the exhibit.

An oil on canvas, the artist had also captured a landscape, and yet…

Poppy angled her head; studying the piece at various angles.

There was a rawness to the land; a wildness at odds with the tame English countryside. Both beautiful and haunting, bare trees and hollowed-out trunks sprang around a lake in a haunting juxtaposition of death springing from that water.

"You have a problem with it?"

It took a moment to register that the owner of that rude query had, in fact, directed it to Poppy. She blinked several times and stiffened as she registered the gentleman standing just beyond her shoulder. Close enough to annoy but not close enough to be considered rude.

"I beg your pardon?" she asked when he still made no move to abandon his spot. Dismissing him, she directed her gaze forward.

"Been staring at it for the better part of fifteen minutes."

He'd go away.

But there were two certainties: one, she'd no intention of giving up her spot to some pompous gentleman who no doubt took exception to a woman being here. And two, she'd no intention of paying him any further note. "Have I? As a rule, I generally find it crass to spend one's time at museums consulting a timepiece."

The right corner of his mouth quirked. "Crass?" He spoke with an unfamiliar accent; it contained the traces of a crisp English but tended more toward the flat tones of an American.

"Rude," she supplanted, even as she well knew it wasn't a definition he sought. "Either way, I'm here admiring the painting." And there was an entire exhibit he could occupy himself at until she'd moved on. And petulant as it may be, as all the visitors began filing to the front of the room for the upcoming lecture, Poppy dug her heels in and prepared to stay all the longer for spite alone.

"You're admiring it, then?" Alas, it appeared the oddly dressed stranger had no intention of leaving.

"Well, not necessarily admiring."

"Judging, then." She was going to correct that erroneous supposition but he cut her off. "And what gives you the right to judge anything hanging in here, princess?"

"Two eyes. That is what gives me the right." The blighter. Just another gentleman who thought a lady had no right to analyze artwork, or have a meaningful opinion on it. Unlike Tristan. Tristan had only ever insisted she own her appreciation of artwork. He'd never questioned either her opinions or her right to them.

At the dais, the President of the Royal Academy stepped to the forefront. "I welcome you all to the Summer Exhibition. Each year, we are brought together…"

"Do you wonder why they refer to it as a summer exhibition when it's held in spring?"

"Hush," she said from the corner of her mouth, willing the boorish stranger gone so she could resume her study.

"…The first exhibition was held now some fifty-six years ago…"

There was a smattering of applause at that announcement from the speaker.

"I mean, it would be as arbitrary as calling it a Winter Festival and hosting it in April," he went on.

Poppy gnashed her teeth while the president of the Royal Academy spoke of the longstanding history of the exhibition and the distinguished artist who'd be honored that year.

"I'll go," the stranger vowed.

Thank goodness.

"After you tell me why you don't like it."

"I never said I didn't like it."

"...Largely self-taught, Mr. Caleb Gray relied upon books to develop his study of art."

Poppy straightened, and the stranger forgotten, she focused on that introduction of the exhibition artist. Ladies in Polite Society were expected to have art lessons, and yet, they were prohibited from attending classes or lectures given at museums. As such, she'd simply accepted that her artwork would always be considered inferior for that reason. Only to find—

"So which was it? Admiring or judging?" the stranger interrupted her musings. "You've been frowning at it for the better part of twenty minutes."

Which implied that not only had he been studying her but had been doing so for some time.

"Don't inflate your ego, princess. Has nothing to do with you."

Poppy sputtered, "I did not say anything," she said loudly, attracting stares from the sea of patrons who turned in unison, before looking back to the monotone president droning on. "You are uncouth," she muttered.

He winked. "Uncouth is a requisite of being American."

Why was he still here? And more, why was she still here? Adjusting the small burden in her arms, she started around the stranger.

He neatly slid into her path, that movement so slight as to not be noticeable and raise attention. "Isn't the purpose of attending an art exhibit to discuss art?"

"Yes. Just not with strangers." Poppy did a search for Pru, and found her near the front of the auditorium, speaking with Lady Diana Marksman, the daughter of a duchess, who'd married the head guard of the Hell and Sin Club.

Pain: vicious, biting pain clutched at her chest as the pair was joined by Diana's husband. A husband who accompanied his wife throughout London and all over Europe in her love of art. *That was what I wanted. With Tristan.*

"Doesn't seem like you English ladies are gonna learn much if you're just talking to each other."

It took a moment for the boorish stranger's criticism to penetrate her own miserable reverie. "I beg your pardon?"

A handful of inches shy of seven feet, the man was a veritable giant, and he lifted his broad shoulders in a shrug. "Sitting around, sipping tea, comfortable in your homes as you create art that no one will ever see."

She gasped as fury whipped through her. And yet…something held her stinging reply back.

I dare because I might have been banished by society, but I've fought at every turn, and you? You speak of me, but you've done something far worse. You've hidden yourself…not because of Rochford but long before him, because you're too afraid of what the world might actually say about your talents. Coward…

The stranger was such an aching echo of Tristan's own challenge, that emotion swarmed her.

And accepting that the tenacious bounder wasn't going to leave her unless she answered, Poppy relented. "The painting does not know what it wishes to be…it doesn't know whether it wishes to represent life…or death and so a person cannot sort out that which he sought to convey."

"Why can't it be both?"

She paused, as the first words this man had uttered to her made sense. "I…it can," she at last conceded. *It is why the imagery evokes both a sadness and light.*

"Exactly."

She started, failing to realize she'd spoken aloud.

"Do you sketch, princess?"

Poppy followed his gaze to the sketchpad she still clutched. "Don't call me princess."

"I wouldn't…if I had a name." He winked.

And it occurred to her…the bounder was trying to learn her name.

"Fine, princess it is, then. May I?"

Except, there was nothing even remotely improper in his eyes; instead, he again gestured for her sketchpad…

I speak as though what you do is safe. You'd call me out, and yet, bold and spirited and proud as you are, you've hidden yourself away. In empty rooms of your sister's hotel, away from Polite Society. On your sketchpad… Where no one will ever see your work or know what you do…

Her husband…he'd been correct about so much. It was why even now she found herself handing over her work to the unlikeliest of people: the rude stranger before her.

He flipped through quickly, with a methodical turn of the pages, not so much as pausing as he turned. Snapping the book closed, he held it over.

And said nothing.

Which was fine. His opinion didn't matter. He was a boorish, strangish man.

It was also why, as he turned to leave, she should be nothing but relieved. "Well?" she called after him. For his opinion did matter. She did wish to know what the world believed of her work, even as nausea roiled in her belly at the same time for fear of it.

"It's all safe."

There it was again. That word.

Poppy's toes curled in her boots, digging into the leather soles. "You barely looked."

And the nameless stranger took that as invitation to return... which may have been what he'd intended.

"Your skies are all perfectly blue. They conjure summer. The grass is crisp, a sharp emerald that depicts that same season. There's no contrast. There's no thought in it."

There's no... And Tristan proved correct once more...she had been hiding herself away. From this. From this criticism that shouldn't matter because it came from a stranger, and yet, was all the more agonizing, because it did. "Oh," she said, deflated because she had to say something. She'd not let herself say nothing.

"Not all of them."

Poppy lifted her chin at a defiant angle. "I'm not looking for false compliments."

"Pfft, princess, I don't hand out any compliments, false or otherwise. Tenth page." His was a dare.

Hefting her book open, Poppy licked the tip of her index finger and flipped through the sketchpad—and stopped.

Her eyes slid closed.

The sketch she'd created for Tristan's mural.

"Those dogs, poised to strike, the birds in flight; you've captured your loathing for hunting, and yet, also the excitement men find in the sport."

He'd seen that. Speechless, Poppy hugged her book protectively close.

"I saw that. Whatever emotion compelled you to create that,

princess? Find it again."

"…and introducing Mr. Caleb Gray."

"Excuse me, princess," he drawled.

And with a slow-growing horror, Poppy followed his march, praying, pleading…*please don't let it be*—the gentleman approached the dais and was met with another series of applause as Caleb Gray took up a spot at the front, and looking out through the crowd, his gaze found her.

"Bloody hell," she whispered.

He winked. It was him. The lead artist whose work was on display. And she'd stood there beside him, the whole while rude and—

"You were speaking to Mr. Gray!"

Poppy gasped. "Pru, you startled me," she said lamely.

"What did he say to you?" her sister demanded, catching her by the shoulder. "Or dear God"—horror stamped her features—"what did *you* say to *him*?"

"I…nothing," she lied as mortification crept up several degrees. After all, her sister suspected that Poppy had insulted the gentleman…which she had. She'd only questioned his painting and skill. "He…looked at my work."

Prudence's eyes threatened to bulge from her face. "And what did he say?"

"He was…unimpressed." Not wholly. There'd been one work he'd seen promise in.

"Unimpressed." A scowl replaced her sister's earlier reverence, as they looked to the front where Caleb Gray was just making remarks to the crowd. Brief remarks. No more than a handful of curt sentences, without so much as a "thank you" for his work being displayed, and then he was striding swiftly from the dais. "The boor," Pru muttered. "Your work is magnificent."

Yes, Poppy had been of a like mindset until the gentleman had rightly called her out for it. Safe. Tristan and Gray were both correct. For all the ways Poppy had believed herself bold and adventurous, in her work and in her life, she'd never challenged herself to see more…nay, to want more and expect it of the world. "He wasn't wrong, Pru." He was…

Cutting a path through the crowd, pointedly ignoring the men and women attempting to gain his attention.

"He knows nothing."

While her sister let off on an impressive tirade about artists with inflated opinions of themselves and their works, Poppy followed Mr. Gray's purposeful strides. Her stomach sank as the path he'd set became clear. *Oh, drat.*

"Stop, Pru," Poppy warned between compressed lips. "He—"

"I will not stop. I'll not let an uncouth American, or any man for that matter, diminish your skill."

"In fairness, one could make the argument I'm only slightly uncouth, as my parents were English born."

Pru ceased mid-sentence, her mouth agape. All the color leeched from her already pale cheeks. "Is he here?" she mouthed.

Poppy managed her first real smile since Tristan's leaving. "I fear so," she returned on a whisper that brought her sister's eyes sliding closed.

"Oh, God in heaven." Then with her usual Tidemore spirit, Prudence brought her shoulders back and squarely faced the artist. "I am sorry you heard all that but I should say, it is unpardonably rude to eavesdrop." Never mind that the Tidemores had perfected and used that skill since they were old enough to toddle.

His heavy features, slightly too broad to ever paint him as handsome, perfectly conveyed his boredom.

Warming to her argument, Prudence's nostrils flared. "Furthermore, I'll have you know Poppy is the most skilled artist of all those in our family."

Stifling a groan, Poppy slapped a hand over her eyes, but it was too late; she'd already caught the flash of Mr. Gray's cynical half smile.

"And I'll not have you or anyone else disparage her so." With that curt diatribe, Pru marched off.

"Rather impressive defense," the artist drawled after Prudence had gone.

"Yes," she muttered. "All except the part where she forgot me here with you."

He laughed, the sound emerging rusty and slightly graveled.

So very different from Tristan's laugh, which came easily and had always made her heart accelerate several beats.

"She's wrong, you know," Mr. Gray said after his amusement died down.

"About my skill? Oh, I know that, now."

His lips quirked in that jaded grin. "All it took was me insulting your work for you to see the light."

"No," she said slowly. "It was a matter of setting aside my pride to see that you were correct."

Did she imagine the spark of approval that glinted in his dark gaze? Either way... Poppy cleared her throat. "I thank you for considering my work and offering your opinion."

He lifted his chin in an acknowledgement that bordered on rude.

But then, she suspected rude was as much a part of his skin as the furrowed lines of his deep brow.

Poppy dipped a curtsy and started to leave.

"I'm disappointed in you, princess."

She froze and forced herself back. "I beg your pardon."

"I expected you'd ask for lessons. Want to hire me."

"Are you for hire?" she asked curiously.

He snorted. "No."

She shrugged. "I suspected as much."

"I don't get paid for lessons. I don't even give them."

Poppy leaned in and whispered, "Then, it is a good thing I didn't waste my time asking." Once more, she made to go.

"I'm making an exception. I'm giving you lessons, princess."

He was...

Poppy wheeled back. "I don't... Are you jesting..."

"No. But don't ask me why or I'll change my mind."

She opened her mouth and closed it several times. "Very well."

"I'm going to need a name, princess."

"Lady Poppy Tide..." No, that was no longer correct. "Poppy Poplar," she softly corrected. "Lady Bolingbroke."

Another bark of laughter escaped him. "Good God. I hope that's not a married name."

"It is," she said defensively. Even as she herself had lamented the ridiculous pairing of Poppy and Poplar since she'd dreamed of marriage to Tristan as a girl.

"You should have picked a husband with a different name."

Giving him a look, Poppy snapped her skirts, and swept off.

"We start tomorrow, Poppy Poplar," he called after her.

CHAPTER 20

Three Months later
London, England
Dearest Tristan,
I've greatly come to appreciate each of your sisters. The question remains: how have we not been friends before this? As for your mother…as I have vowed to speak with candor in all, I shall merely say, I hope you are endlessly well.
Yours,
Poppy

¶IT WAS A UNIVERSAL TRUTH long accepted by Polite Society that married ladies were permitted endless freedoms.

Poppy's mother-in-law, however, appeared to be the one woman in all of England wholly unfamiliar with the rules surrounding marriage.

Sir Faithful and Tristan's two dogs, Valor and Honor, bounded ahead, noisily announcing Poppy's arrival in the breakfast room. "Good morning," she called, plastering on her widest, most cheerful smile for the other occupants.

Head buried in the morning gossip column, the dowager baroness peeked over the top, and glanced down her aristocratic nose before reverting her attention back to her paper. Soon after her husband's departure for Ireland, when she hadn't been weeping copiously at his absence, she'd been cursing him for saddling her with the shrewish dowager baroness. And for everything that had changed in his absence, that annoyance with his mother had held steadfast. "Breeches," she spat like the vilest epithet. Though in fairness, to the ever proper matron, it no doubt was.

"Actually…" Claire, who'd become Poppy's greatest champion to the dowager baroness, smoothed butter on a piece of crusted bread. "They are trousers. Breeches would fall just below Poppy's knee." She paused mid-smear, and considered Poppy over at the buffet. "Though I do believe Poppy would look smashing with her legs exposed."

"Her legs? Her *legs*?" Over the top of the squawking dowager baroness, Poppy held her sister-in-law's gaze. "Thank you," she mouthed.

Claire winked once, and then discreetly dropped a sausage link over the side of her chair and the three dogs abandoned Poppy at the sideboard and raced over.

Faye, the more reserved, and sadly downtrodden of Tristan's sisters might have smiled. All hint, however, was effectively hidden behind the rim of her teacup.

"…Absolutely unseemly it is, prancing about as you are…" Her mother-in-law turned a page in the scandal sheet hard enough to tear the corner. "A public spectacle is what she is." She directed that criticism to her morning reading.

In the two months since she'd come to reside with Poppy, not a day had passed that she hadn't wanted to toss the miserable harpy out on her arse…and, in fact, respect for one's in-laws be-damned, she would have done that very thing if it hadn't been for her pity for Tristan's sisters.

"Might I point out—" Claire, Tristan's youngest sister piped in.

"No, you may not, Claire."

"That Poppy has not worn them in public." She fed a portion of her bread to Valor. "Only here."

"And at that hotel she is—"

"Decorating," Poppy supplied, carrying her plate of eggs and bread closest to Claire.

"Nor does she prance. She paints." Though, in fairness, it wasn't solely pity. Poppy genuinely liked the two women; near in age to her own sisters, and delightfully spirited, they'd become much needed friends in Tristan's absence.

"With that...with that...?"

"Artist?" Poppy dryly supplied, taking a bite of eggs.

"American." The dowager baroness slammed her paper down and exchanged it for her cup of coffee. "Americans are not artists. They are provincial. They are common."

"I'd hardly call Mr. Gray common," Claire said with a gleeful relish in her smile.

"Mr. Gray. Bah. Mr. Gray." Grimacing, Poppy's mother-in-law took a drink of that bitter tasting brew perfectly suited for her.

"His reputation quite precedes him," Poppy intoned. Although she appreciated her sister-in-law's defense of the famed artist, neither could she sit silent while he, or anyone, was disparaged by the shrew across from her. "His work is being praised throughout Europe for its originality of design and the manner in which it provokes thought."

"Art isn't supposed to provoke thought, dear." The other woman stretched out that chastisement with such patronization that Poppy gritted her teeth. "It is intended to be a thing of beauty. Like a woman."

Oh, good God.

Poppy shoveled in another mouthful of eggs to keep from saying something she'd regret. And the only reason she'd regret it was because she was forced to abide under the same roof until either the end of the Season or until her sisters-in-law made matches.

All these years Poppy had lamented having a mother who was so painfully staid and proper.

Only to find out how unfairly she'd judged the Dowager Countess of Sinclair.

Tristan's mother made Poppy's look like a tamer Elizabeth Chudleigh. Yes, Poppy's mother had sought matches for her children, but she'd always supported them and their choice in spouses: be it a former governess or widower with a past or, in Penelope's case, a gaming hell owner.

Whereas the dowager countess? The woman had a mercenary ruthlessness that terrified even Poppy. How could her husband have thought to take any blame or responsibility for the machinations surrounding the Maxwell title? There could be no doubting that the key orchestrator of that crime sipped on her coffee at that very moment.

"Poppy," the dowager baroness began, employing that affected tone she adopted when she sought to sway Poppy. "I know several perfectly acceptable French tutors who might provide you art lessons. Why, Claire's previous tutor, I've heard, even this late in the Season is accepting students."

"Because no one wants his services," Claire muttered, earning a sharp scowl from her mother.

Poppy took a sip of tea to keep from smiling. "Although I am grateful for that generous offer, I'm quite content with how my lessons are proceeding with Mr. Gray." Gathering up the remainder of her bread, Poppy hopped up. "Now, if you'll excuse me?" She started from the room, having learned early on the art of a swift exit where her mother-in-law was concerned.

She was halfway to the ballroom when the quick footfalls sounded behind her, along with the noisy parade of dogs following after. "Poppy!"

Poppy slowed her steps and waited until Claire had reached her side. The three dogs kept close, as the young woman had become a sort of defacto mother to the group.

Poppy stared wistfully at Sir Faithful, who could not go without being with the other woman.

Claire stopped before her, and thumped her side once. All the dogs, now trained in whatever skilled language the young lady had managed to speak to them, promptly sat in a line. "I wanted to—"

"Don't." She already anticipated the familiar exchange.

"Apologize. She's horrid and unappreciative and I'd have you know that she does not speak for me or Faye and that Tristan would be equally, nay, even more horrified, were he to learn of how she treated you."

Poppy took Claire's hands. "You've nothing to be sorry for, Claire," she said softly, in an echo of that guidance given her by Juliet almost ten years ago. "You mustn't hold yourself responsible for the actions of others. And I am so very happy you are here. You and Faye."

Before their arrival, she'd dodged her family because she couldn't stand to see the pity or the know-it-all looks in their eyes. As miserable as the dowager baroness had been, her daughters had helped bring Poppy out of the misery she'd mired herself in with Tristan's leaving.

Tristan…

Pain returned; still present, but less sharp than in those earliest days.

"He misses you," Claire said softly, unerringly following Poppy's thoughts.

"Perhaps." Poppy was too mindful of her sister-in-law's sensibilities to ever provide the cynical truth: their marriage hadn't been a real one, and he'd left for something of much more importance than that hasty union. His honor.

"No, he…does. He asks of you often in his letters."

"I know," she said gently. He wrote, and on those pages proved his usual charming, Tristan self.

Sir Faithful hopped up; and crouching low, he faced the opposite end of the hall, and growled, announcing the visitor before he even turned the corner.

"Be nice," Poppy scolded as Caleb Gray started down the hall.

In fairness to Faithful, a few inches shy of seven feet, broad as he was tall, and in possession of long, black locks that he drew back, there was a rather primitively threatening aura to the gentleman… which would have inspired fear in creatures of two legs or four.

That was, if Poppy herself hadn't known the man.

He stopped before them, and earned a sharp bark from Sir Faithful. "Morning," he greeted, with that peculiarly flat tonality to his speech, marking him American. And without all the usual pomp of bowing and proper greetings.

"Caleb," she greeted warmly, eyeing the heavy leather bag in his fingers with a covetous longing. Caleb had been the other one to pull her from her misery.

Sir Faithful yapped loudly.

"Hush," Claire murmured, stroking the top of the wary dog's head, and like a sorceress casting her canine spell, he sank onto his haunches.

Poppy's sister-in-law cleared her throat. "Mr. Gray," she said crisply, without her usual charm and warmth.

Without a word of greeting, Caleb touched his fingertip to his brim in a dismissive exchange before turning to Poppy. "Time's a-wasting."

Claire stiffened. "Forgive me. I'll leave you to your work." She tapped her thigh twice and in concert the dogs jumped up.

"You are certain you won't join us?" Poppy offered.

"No. I'd not want to bore Mr. Gray with impressions of my floral arrangements." With that, Claire marched off; her army of dogs close at her heels.

"What did you say?" Poppy demanded as soon as the young woman was out of sight.

He lifted one broad shoulder in a shrug. "You know I don't lie, princess."

Poppy shoved an elbow into his side twice, eliciting the desired grunt.

"What was—?"

"The moniker and for being rude to Claire." Taking the bag from his hands, she grunted and adjusted her grip on the heavy weight of it, and started forward.

"You hired me because of my plain speaking." Yes, and after living in a society where all danced around meaning and truths with intricate steps, there'd been something all too refreshing in Caleb Gray.

"I *tried* to hire you," she reminded, not glancing back. "You proved too kind to accept payment."

Caleb laughed. "Kind ain't a term used to describe me. I was impressed by your skill," he said bluntly. "Had nothing to do with me being nice."

Yes, the papers and gossip circulating about the artist new to England had all spoken of his reputation as being an uncouth, unkind, and dangerous American.

All the reports had proven largely false.

At least, by way of her experience with him.

Poppy dropped his bag.

"Have a care, princess." He effortlessly hefted the satchel up and swung it over his shoulder before she had a chance to pillage through whatever he'd brought this day. "You've an ease in your command of the brush now."

She beamed. "Thank you."

"That is never a compliment in art." He started down the length of the ballroom, motioning to the murals she'd completed these past months. "Landscapes. Still-life. Nature," he continued, his deep voice booming off the walls.

"You say that as if it is a bad thing," she noted, lengthening her strides in a bid to match his longer steps.

"Always," he said automatically. "If there's no growth, and no variety, there is no art." At last, Caleb stopped, and Poppy's gaze slid beyond his shoulder, to that first rendering she'd ever added to these walls.

The mural...hers and Tristan's, nothing more than colors thrown upon the wall, that she'd not been able to bring herself to cover or repaint.

And she resisted the urge to rub the dull ache in her chest.

Caleb and his too clever eyes, however, followed hers. "I'm still curious about this one, princess."

"Artists must have their secrets. Wasn't that the first bit of advice you gave me?"

Caleb grinned, flashing a flawless, even white smile. "That was different."

"Why? Because you don't wish to share?" Poppy winked.

"Because you were demanding to know about my past."

Poppy smiled at his drawl. "I didn't *demand*, per se."

He snorted. "We'll not argue history. Our kind have never been on the same side of it."

"Fair enough."

"And princess?"

"Hmm?"

"Don't think I don't know that mural there has something to do with your fool of a husband."

She frowned. "Tristan isn't a fool." He was honorable and proud and, well, stubborn because of that pride.

"He walked away from you to rejoin the military?" Caleb molded the clay in his hand. "I've served in the military. Sane men don't do that. Especially when they have a wife like you."

There was so much contained in his words that she didn't know which to unpack first. In the end, Caleb diverted them safely back to his lesson. "If an artist isn't growing, he's not an artist."

"She."

"Anyone," he allowed. This time, he set his own bag down, with greater care than she'd shown that heavy sack.

Drawn as she always was by the fascinating items he brought for her to explore, Poppy fell to a knee. "What is it?"

"Ever hear of Jean-Antoine Houdon?" he asked, rummaging through the bag.

"No."

Caleb fished a small book from inside and tossed it at her chest. "Here."

Nearly pocket in size, the volume contained page after page of busts and statues. "He's remarkable," she murmured, holding the book close so she might better study the images.

"Houdon didn't see any use in small, witty pieces for no purpose other than dressing up a fancy lady's parlor." Caleb touched his brim. "Present fancy lady excluded."

She snorted. "Go on," she urged, continuing her study as he explained.

"Houdon saw sculpting for what it should be."

Poppy glanced up. "And what is that?"

"A return to the classical subject matter. Understanding and honoring the human form."

Poppy paused on a rendering of a tall, commanding figure; this man a leader, fully clad. "Who is he?" she murmured, turning the book out for Caleb.

"Washington. The first president of the United States and the reason you and I aren't both answering to King George now." Joining her, Caleb slipped the book from her hands and angled it so they might both see. "Houdon doesn't believe the subject has to be captured in nude to command the strength and beauty of the human form. See here." He touched a coarse, callused fingertip to the lines of the figure's stomach. "Fully attired, and yet, he captures the lines. Do you see?"

"I do," she said, running her eyes over the elegant specimen. A memory slipped in, as it so often did, of the night Tristan had made love to her in this very room. Splendorous in his nudity. Chiseled perfection represented in coiled muscles and the marks of bravery he wore upon his scarred flesh. And she resented him in that moment, along with her own body for betraying her with weakness…for this hungering to know those two weeks of bliss she'd celebrated in his arms. "One can see every perfection or imperfection of the form," she said softly as Caleb returned the book to her possession.

"Exactly. because Houdon knows that one has to have an understanding of the human form before one can effectively celebrate it."

Which is what she'd been attempting to do back with her study of Rochford. How naïve she'd been even in her artwork. "You've got to stretch yourself, Poppy."

She did a sweep of her transformed ballroom. "I rather thought I've done just that."

Caleb held a finger up. "If you think that, then you haven't come far enough." Reaching inside his pack he drew out a folded and wrinkled newspaper. "Here." He hurled it at her, and Poppy caught it in her fingers.

"What's this?" she asked, unfolding the pages of the unfamiliar paper.

"Left hand bottom of page three."

Mouthing those instructions, Poppy flipped through the newspaper. "And here I believed you not one to spend much time on gossip."

"It's not a gossip column."

The frown in his voice brought Poppy's head up. She peeked her head over the top. "I know," she whispered. "I was teasing."

He gave an impatient nudge of his chin, redirecting her back to the matter at hand. "We don't joke about art."

Unlike Tristan, who'd not only been endlessly fun to tease and who'd effortlessly given it right back. Yes, from appearances to personalities, the two men could not be any more different. There was an icy veneer to Caleb Gray. One that kept all people at bay, which she'd wager was deliberate. For as much time as they'd spent together, he'd been more of a mentor to her than a friend.

At last, Poppy found it. "Houdon is selecting four women for Académie des Beaux Arts," she read, glancing up.

"He's asked that I help him."

"Oh." He was leaving, then. That was what he sought to tell her. Another loss. Different than Tristan's but also sharp because of the brief friendship they'd known. Poppy held her hand out. "I wish you the best."

He snorted. "I'm not leaving, princess."

"You're not?" Confusion set in as she tried to follow the meaning of the newspaper then. "Then…?" She examined the write-up in the column, when she registered the silence…and its significance. Her head shot up.

He winked. "It's my hope that you are."

"English women are not permitted to receive free training." They could view art, sketch their own drawings of the required fruit and flowers, but as far as society was concerned, that was the extent of where artistic pursuits should start and end.

"I ain't seen any English woman sporting a pair of trousers." He glanced pointedly at her legs.

"That is different," she muttered, reluctantly turning over the paper.

"How so, princess? I'm afraid this is another one of those details about the English that my colonial brain can't make sense of."

She felt her lips pull in a smile. "It's… It's…" Only, how *was* it different?

I speak as though what you do is safe. You'd call me out, and yet, bold and spirited and proud as you are, you've hidden yourself away. In empty rooms of your sister's hotel, away from Polite Society. On your sketch-pad… Where no one will ever see your work or know what you do…

"You worried about your family disapproving?"

That query snapped Poppy back to the moment. "No," she murmured, toying with the corners of the page. "Not anymore." They'd quite come to accept Poppy for who she was. Even when they'd hoped she'd never find herself with a scandal to her name, neither had they sought to stifle her.

"You worried about your husband finding out?"

"Tristan?" she asked with some surprise.

"Aye. The missing man you married."

Aside from a question about an irate husband when they'd first begun her lessons, Caleb had not asked again about her husband, nor had Poppy volunteered information about him. Now, she forced herself to consider Caleb's question. There Tristan was again. Slipping in, as he so often did, when she'd spent weeks upon weeks trying to push the memory of him away. Because it was easier to exist, living under the illusion that their marriage had never happened. "He wouldn't mind," she said softly. He'd only ever celebrated her spirit…and then her pursuit of art.

"I know Englishmen, they always mind about everything."

Yes, she'd agree with him on that score. It was one reason she'd always been so hopelessly captivated by Tristan Poplar. He'd not looked askance at Poppy for fishing, or riding astride in breeches, or drinking from his flask. Instead, he'd treated her as an equal.

"Not my husband," she spoke from a place of truth. "We had an agreement."

Caleb barked his laughter, his broad frame shaking. "Now, that sounds perfectly English."

"What?" she bristled. She'd become accustomed to his frequent disparagement of the British way of life but her marriage was an altogether different consideration. He roared all the louder with his hilarity. "It is really harmless. He agreed that I should pursue art as I would."

"And what did you promise in return, princess?"

"To—" Her cheeks burned hot. For of all he could have sought that day, only one immediate one had come to him…which in itself should have been a harbinger to what a marriage to Tristan Poplar would be.

Caleb cupped a hand around his left ear, partially deaf from an injury he'd never elaborated upon, he leaned close. "What was that?"

"Watch his dogs. He wanted me to watch his dogs."

Caleb roared again, and she glared at him. "I'm so happy you find my marriage a source of amusement."

"Not your marriage, princess, just the foolishness of the men living on this continent."

And on that score, Poppy would only ever agree with him. "Even if I wanted to mentor with Mr. Houdon, there is nothing to say he'd wish to work with me."

"No." There was a pregnant pause. "But if he saw your work, then it might at least be a possibility."

"Oh, and I'll simply what? Invite the gentleman to come and view my art?"

"No," he said again. "*I* will."

She gave him a droll smile. Only, her heart beat an uneven rhythm…what he was proposing made this, all of this, her art and what she did, all the more real. It removed her from a place of sketching for herself, and instead, guided her work out so the world might view…and judge.

Poppy pressed her fingertips against her temple. But he was there, as he always was…Tristan and his urgings.

I'd have you know, your talent, the art you create…it is a thing of beauty and wonder. Don't hide that. Not anymore. Let the world see…

"He'll appreciate it," Caleb said, bringing her back to the moment.

"You seem confident." Which she'd gathered in the time they'd spent together could only come from a people who'd seen the British Empire crushed under the heel of their colonial power.

"I *am*. You've got talent. You simply were missing something."

She puzzled her brow. "And what was that?"

"Me."

Let the world see all of you...

Poppy drew in a breath. "What would it entail?"

"What, now? Now, we invite Houdon to a display of your work."

Caleb spoke of inviting a world-renowned artist into her home so that he might assess her work and speak to her talent—or lack thereof. All previous excitement left, replaced with nausea. About what he'd say...and the least of which would be the scandal. For if she did this, there'd be no doubting; regardless of her marital state, Poppy's holding an exhibit of her art work in her household would be met with one outcome—scandal. It would only further deepen the ire of her choleric mother-in-law, who'd remind her all over again that polite English ladies weren't artists.

"Very well." Poppy smiled slowly. "I'll do it."

CHAPTER 21

Tristan,
All these years, I believed I knew you, and yet, I find I'm still learning things new, such as your unexpected fascination with the weather. The skies have been clear here. Often cloudless. Most days there is a light breeze and as so, it is so very easy to forget that I'm in London and not in the country where I once wished...
Poppy

STANDING IN THE COURTYARD OF the Royal Barracks, the tall, granite-faced buildings made for an imposing presentation.

At another time in his life, standing there in charge of the meticulous exercises being carried out would have been met with excitement on his part. Military pursuits had, after all, proven the one endeavor he'd truly excelled in. In the months that he'd been there, Tristan had fulfilled those responsibilities flawlessly: training loyal, obedient, disciplined yet fearless fighting men.

He'd worked alongside and under officers of elevated rank, gentlemen of the peerage, whose admiration he'd earned, replacing the initial disdain and suspicion that had met him because of the crimes of his family. His name was on the path to restoration; and along with it, his honor.

In short, he was doing everything he'd set out to do.

Only to find himself...empty. Because of her. Because he missed her. Because he missed the two of them together.

In the distance, past the soldiers moving effortlessly through the intricate steps of a march, Tristan's gaze slid to a field of flowers.

Poppy.

Her name was a whisper in his mind, and a yearning in his heart.

She was everywhere. Every night as sleep eluded him…when he woke in the morn. Every moment of every day, she was there in his mind: smoking away at his cheroot, with a damn-the-world-attitude for all who saw her. Buried under bed curtains she'd been arranging because, in short, there was nothing Poppy couldn't do. Her standing beside him, reciting her vows, teasing him through the ceremony.

I want your mouth there…

And he was gripped by an all-too familiar hungering that entered with the mere thought of her. Like fire in his arms, she'd made love with the same abandon she lived every aspect of her life with.

And reminding himself that he'd gone for her and the babes they'd one day have…brought no solace. There was no satisfaction in knowing he did this for that future because his now was empty. For she wasn't in it.

Thrusting aside his melancholy, he surveyed the men, most ten or more years his junior, as they went through the motions of a drill.

From the corner of his eye, he caught the approach of his superior officer. The gentleman moved with a slight limp that he disguised nearly perfectly. So much so that Tristan might have missed it… if he'd not remembered Spicer suffering that injury years earlier. "You've got them in line nicely," Lieutenant-Colonel Spicer said, matter-of-fact in that deliverance. He clasped his hands behind him and continued to watch the infantry move through the steps. Five inches shorter than Tristan and three stone heavier, the man inspired fear in all the soldiers, and yet, Tristan had saved the older man from certain death. "They were a disgrace before, Poplar."

From the battle-hardened, taciturn lieutenant-colonel, that was praise, indeed. As such, there should be some sense of accomplishment. This is what Tristan excelled at. This is what he wanted. Wasn't it? "Thank you, sir."

"It's all about breaking them," his superior said crisply. "Making men into soldiers."

"It is about maneuverability, my lord. Well-drilled, they'll move confidently at speed without their formations and should the situation call for it, break up, and maximize the use of their weapons."

"The insolence of you, challenging me, Poplar."

"All a credit to my own training."

The ghost of a smile wreathed the weathered face of his superior. "That is true." He thumped Tristan on the back, and then as if the brief exchange had never occurred, the lieutenant-colonel was back in his familiar position; hands behind him, gaze forward. "You're adjusting to life back in the military?"

"Aye, sir," he said automatically. It was a lie. There was a tedium to what Tristan did here. He'd believed returning to the role he'd served in before would restore his honor, that it would fulfill him. Only to find an absolute emptiness in the course he'd set. There was a void because what he wanted—*who* he wanted—was, in fact, somewhere else.

Poppy.

Pain slashed through his chest and he resisted the urge to rub at that ache.

"No complaint with your accommodations?"

"None, my lord," he said quietly, thinking of the last place he'd all too briefly called home.

"Have I mentioned I've a rat infestation?"

"You've not, Tristan. We'll require cats, then. Sir Faithful won't be pleased, of course, but he should also dislike the alternative."

How composed she'd been when any other woman would have run screaming from the idea of a residence filled with rodents.

Lieutenant-Colonel Spicer snorted. "You would be the first gentlemen to serve with me who didn't bemoan his living arrangements."

Tristan followed his men's movements through their drill. "I've no reason to complain." Unlike the soldiers who slept six to a room, sleeping two to a bed and cooking in those same rooms where they slumbered, Tristan's position as an officer afforded him greater comforts: spacious rooms, his own bed. Eating not the grub scraped together but rather dining in the local taverns.

"That's always been your way though, isn't it, eh? Even when you had reason to gripe, you didn't."

Tristan briefly shifted his focus from the neat rows of soldiers in the courtyard. "Sir?"

"Villiers. Or St. Cyr, as he's known now."

Stiffening, Tristan retrained his attention on his men.

"Nothing to say about it?"

"I'm not certain what you'd have me say," he said carefully. What he'd done in battle had never been about attaining fame or notoriety. He'd simply done that which was right in service to his country.

"Most men would have wanted the matter righted. They would have wanted the world to rightly know that when on foot, they'd single-handedly fought off three French soldiers and saved not only one's best friend but one's commanding officer."

The man knew that. Of course it should have come as no surprise. Spicer had known everything.

"I was the reason you dismounted."

Yes, the other man pinned under his horse, he'd been trapped awaiting an inevitable death at the hands of the French. Sobbing and pleading, Spicer's screams for help had split through the din of cannon fire.

"You cut down three with nothing more than the edge of a bayonet. And then went back for Villiers, sobbing with his head in his hands."

Tristan's gaze landed on a pair of soldiers, beside one another in line: one dark, the other light, of like height and fresh from university, but only one of them with uncertainty in his gaze, as he periodically stole a glance of reassurance from the man beside him; they may as well have been he and St. Cyr as young men. "Not all men are meant for the military."

"No, that is true. Most would have wanted the record corrected."

As it was a statement more than a question, Tristan let Lieutenant-Colonel Spicer's words stand in silence.

The other man, however, would not be content with that. "Most would have wanted the world to know that it was, in fact, you who was the hero at Waterloo. Not Villiers."

Tristan looked over in some surprise. "How did you—?" He abruptly stopped talking.

"How did I know?" Lieutenant-Colonel Spicer did not let the matter die. "Villiers wrote me. He merely confirmed everything I'd already known." His superior, wholly focused on their regiment, spoke in his clipped, no-nonsense tones that may as well have been observations about the drills unfolding and not the past that had already occurred. "Changed my opinion some on Villiers. Not much. He was a terrible soldier and a lousy man for not having corrected the record."

He stiffened. "Either way, it was never about recognition," he said tersely. Saving lives and leading men to safety. That is what it had always been about. "St. Cyr is a man of honor."

"No," Spicer said casually. "But the man who'd defend him and stand by him for the mistakes he made is. There were some powerful people insistent that you not be granted the commission."

Grateful for that turn back to his own past and away from a discourse that betrayed his friendship, Tristan eyed the regiment. "Undoubtedly." Such was the treatment for those men whose families were guilty of great wrongs. And where that had once before left him with a bitter taste of regret and guilt, now Poppy's echo reverberated clear in his mind.

You are not responsible for your father's sins and crimes…

And with it, for the first time since he'd learned of his family's involvement in Northrop's disappearance, a lightness suffused his chest, healing and freeing.

Lieutenant-Colonel Spicer clapped a hand on his shoulder. "I don't give a rat's arse about the opinions of men who don't know a thing about character. It's why I demanded the commission go to you. You're more worthy than any one of those lords prancing around London; men who'd protect their arses rather than risk all on the battlefield…as you did."

Lieutenant-Colonel Spicer was the reason Tristan had received the commission then. Emotion flooded him. "Thank you, sir," he said hoarsely.

The other man blanched; the display clearly too much. "You're relieved for the day." Spicer grunted. "I pay my debts. If you require anything, Bolingbroke, you just need to inform me." With that, he marched off. "At ease," Spicer bellowed, striding forward, immediately commanding the in-sync soldiers.

The letter carrier arrived. "Letters for ya, Captain." The boy held out a small stack.

Tristan's pulse pounded. With a word of thanks, he took the notes tied together with a black ribbon.

Having been in Ireland now more than three months, Tristan

had become something of an expert on, of all things…the post.

In his time serving in the Cork Barracks, he'd gleaned the following: it took, on good weather days, three at most for a post from London to arrive.

Four on average.

And generally a week when weather was poor.

When he'd first arrived in Ireland, three days had been the average with which he'd received notes from his wife. Somewhere along the way, that had shifted.

Those letters still came, but with less frequency and it was never predictable when they would…or worse, would not…arrive. Oh, they always came. Just…infrequently.

And the handwriting had grown hurried.

And her parting address had gone through a decay.

"Ever Yours" had eventually become "Yours".

And then…

Poppy.

It was likely a matter of haste, more than anything which accounted for that change.

Because what was the alternative? a silent voice jeered… That any affection Poppy had carried, had also faded in his absence.

It was a possibility that entered anytime a note arrived from her, one that he thrust out of his consciousness. So that he didn't have to think about what it had been before he'd left. Or…what he'd truly yearned for.

"I love you, Tristan…I always have…"

That was what he'd longed to hear from Poppy…and it was very possibly words she would have had for him, had he stayed.

And how he'd given all that up…telling himself it was for her. For them.

You equate your honor with how the world views you and not with how you live your own life…

How right she'd been.

At his approach, a soldier saluted, and drew the door of the barracks open.

"At ease," Tristan commanded as he made for his offices. The minute he'd entered the rooms and closed the door behind him, he sifted through the notes.

St. Cyr.

Blackthorne.

Tristan's heart sank as he reached the last note.

His sister.

Claire.

Twelve days.

It marked the longest passage of time since Poppy had penned him.

Tristan,

I trust you are doing well. You know I am generally not one to complain; however, I must confess to annoyance that you should be able to make your escape from London, while Faye and I were called back to endure… Mother, here. As you can imagine, she's not taken well to being barred from most social events.

"No, she certainly would not." Tristan found his first grin since he'd reached the third note. He continued reading.

Poppy—

His heart sped up at the mere sight of her name.

Has been endlessly more patient than Mother deserves, and exceedingly kind to both Faye and I. She appears to despise all the balls and soirees as much as I myself do. Alas, she's been a sport, escorting us in the evening, and suffering the company of her dour art instructor during the day. One would think that foul temperaments and a lofty attitude is a requisite for the role.

I digress; you are missed. Be well.

Claire

Post Script: Despite all that, I still find you the greatest, most wonderful, most devoted brother.

Post Post Script: Next week, Poppy will be holding an art exhibit of her work in our townhouse. I find it inspiring. Mother is, of course, livid. I shall notify you of her success.

He scanned those pages.

Poppy was putting her work on display.

Pride, so powerful and potent sent his heart pounding.

He sank onto the chair at his desk, re-reading those words, and then he slid his eyes closed. In his time apart from Poppy, he'd lain awake, tortured by their argument. Haunted by the words he'd hurled at her in anger. Words that he should have only given to her from a place of caring. But mayhap in some small way she'd been encouraged by his urging. Tristan's lips formed their first real grin since he'd left her. Or, knowing his wife, she'd seen his charges as a challenge.

Tristan knew only one thing…he wanted to be there.

He stilled.

I need to be there.

He wanted to stand beside her when her work was on display, wanted to witness her receive the praise and adulation she so deserved.

If you require anything, Bolingbroke, you just need to inform me…

Tristan quickly folded the note.

There was *one* favor he needed.

CHAPTER 22

Tristan,
You were right…about so much. I have been hiding my artwork out of
fear of what the world will say. I've decided to not hide anymore. I wish
you could be here for it.
Poppy

THIS MOMENT SHOULD BE EVERYTHING in her world.

A hope she'd never even dared have, because well, she'd not allowed herself to dream wide—until Tristan had challenged her to do so.

And yet, though her ballroom was transformed into an art display, with her work on exhibit…for her family and the eventual guest, Mr. Houdon, the moment was somehow still incomplete.

Her throat constricted, and she attempted to swallow around it as she stared at the abstract colors she and Tristan had painted.

It is magnificent… Do you know, Poppy? I can't name anything that has made me feel that way…

Her eyes slid closed, and the ache of losing Tristan hit her all over again, fresh in its pain, and she had to look away from that work they'd created together. Before she'd known his intentions. Before he'd chosen another path. Before she'd known that she was not enough for him.

No, you always knew that.

You were the sister-like figure who'd become a friend but nothing more.

Across the room, her sister, conversing with Christian and his family, caught Poppy's eye.

Poppy flashed a smile that felt strained to her own muscles.

Prudence said something to her husband, and then slipped away from that happy tableau they'd been.

Which was, of course, that which Poppy had been missing. She was truthful enough to admit as much to herself. That she was the greatest of liars. That she'd done such a convincing job when she'd offered Tristan a marriage of convenience that she'd almost believed it herself.

Almost.

"I should think you'd be smiling more," Prudence said quietly, as she reached Poppy. "You've managed the impossible—you've earned Mother's approval."

They looked as one to where their Mother stood conversing with Caleb and Mr. Houdon. The regal dowager countess beside the wizened old artist and the broad bear of a man who'd become Poppy's mentor couldn't be a more peculiar sight.

"Yes, one could hardly believe it," she murmured.

Their mother had always railed at their love of art, and lamented at the time they'd spent sketching.

"You've done what I never have and never could do, Poppy. You've made your work into something not just for you, as I've done, but something that the world could and should share in, too."

She made a sound of protest.

"I'm not disparaging myself," Prudence interrupted. "It is the honest truth. I enjoy art. I always have. But I wouldn't have asserted myself to take control of Penelope and Ryker's hotel. Nor would I have dared paint a man nude."

"I didn't paint him nude," she said on a small smile.

"Attempted to." Prudence waved her hand.

Except… Her smile withered. For along with thoughts of Rochford came everything that had followed: her residence at the Paradise. Tristan. Her marriage.

Oh, God, when would her heart stop splintering? It wouldn't. Because she missed him still and hated herself for missing him. Because he'd not cared enough to stay, and yet, she should be breaking apart inside at the loss of him.

Prudence slipped an arm through hers. "Either way, it's all the same. Art was never something meant to be hidden away on a sketchpad for you. And I am so very proud of you for doing that which I, nor any other woman I've known, has done."

Only, Poppy hadn't realized all that of her own. Her husband had seen that, when she herself hadn't. She'd believed herself bold and daring in her work, but all the while she'd never had higher expectations for herself…because simply put, it had been safer that way.

I speak as though what you do is safe. You'd call me out, and yet, bold and spirited and proud as you are, you've hidden yourself away. In empty rooms of your sister's hotel, away from Polite Society. On your sketchpad…

In the moment, when he'd hurled those words at her, she'd been destroyed inside by the low opinions he'd had of her.

She realized now, in his absence. Acknowledged how very right he'd been. About so much. And he'd missed the moment. He should have been here for it.

"Why does it feel as though you're not as elated about this night?" Prudence murmured, giving her arm a light squeeze.

"I am," she said quietly, for it was possible to feel competing emotions all at once: a duality of pain and joy, so starkly different, and yet, capable of living together.

For the remainder of the night, Poppy went through the motions of being part of the moment with her family and the great artist Houdon. It was as though she observed another, watching herself, until at last all her family and guests had gone, and quiet remained.

Poppy remained there fixed on the small segment she'd painted with Tristan, that smattering of blue and green paint, those colors thrown together by she and Tristan, blended there in an unexpected harmony that had never been able to transcend their marriage.

"You showed yourself to the world, princess. Did you get burned?"

She glanced to the lone guest who'd remained. A kind friend and mentor, when it should have been another man. And yet, friend though he was, she couldn't very well bring herself to tell him she'd been burned long before, with her heart seared because of her loss. "No burns," she murmured as Caleb came forward with that small satchel he was never without.

He set it on the floor at her feet.

Poppy glanced down at it.

"Go on," he said gruffly.

Going to a knee, Poppy reached a hand inside. "It is a stone," she blurted.

He nodded. "You've experimented with fabrics and paints and charcoals. Never used stone before. It's time. All artists use stone."

"I didn't presume to be an artist," she said wistfully.

Caleb gave her a sharp look. "You're an artist," he said flatly, in the decisive tones of one who'd reached the conclusion and decided the matter was settled. "As long as you let yourself be." He shoved the sculpting stone at her. "You've painted every damn wall here, Poppy. You've painted every room. You've worked in your sister's hotel. It is time to grow."

"I don't…know what to do with it," she confessed.

Caleb slid himself into position behind her. "Here." Taking her hands, he guided them over the stone. "Close your eyes."

Poppy went absolutely still. No man, aside from Tristan, had ever held her close.

Only there was nothing sexual in Caleb's touch. Nothing suggestive in his hold that spoke of seduction or scandal. Because with Caleb, it was only ever about art…which is what had saved her from her misery when Tristan had left.

"Close 'em, princess," he ordered, and it was that all perfunctory business-like quality there that drove the tension from her.

And Poppy closed her eyes; she ran her hands exploratively over the hard surface, noting those details one missed when assessing it as only cold stone: the contours. The grooves. The imperfections. All perfect analogies to the human form. "Very good, princess. You've got to feel what it is to work with stone. You can't create the human form from it, if you don't understand your material." His voice broke through the spell and her concentration.

"And when do we begin my sculpting lessons?" she asked, craning her head back as he came to his feet.

"I'm done with your lessons, princess."

Her lips parted. "You're leaving."

Of course, it had been inevitable. He was an artist on tour, and not an instructor here solely for her pursuits. And yet, when he left there'd be another loss. This one different from Tristan's but painful in its own way.

Caleb ruffled the top of her head like she was a favorite sister. "Don't look so glum. I'm not the one leaving. Not yet."

She puzzled her brow. Then...

"*You're* leaving," he corrected.

"What?"

He reached inside his jacket and tossed a paper at her. It fluttered between her fingers but she caught it before the scrap hit the floor. Poppy unfolded the page and quickly worked her gaze over the words. "What is this?" she breathed.

"Houdon was impressed by you. Said you have talent and promise. I've secured your lessons with Houdon when you're ready to go."

Lessons with Houdon... Académie des Beaux Arts ... And truly for the first time since Tristan had gone, her heart soared. "Why are you doing this?"

"Because you deserve to go. Nothing says art belongs to men or that the art created by women should be hung in a parlor and forgotten."

If it was just a pastime, Poppy, you'd be happily sketching fruit bowls and floral arrangements like most every other lady in Polite Society. You wouldn't have taken on the responsibility of redecorating your sister's hotel...

Tristan's words pinged around her memory.

Tristan...whom she'd made an arrangement with. One that required her to fulfill a request he'd put to her. Reluctantly, she folded the page. "I... There is the Season. My sisters-in-law."

"And?"

"And I have promised to see them through the Season. After they are wed, perhaps..." *If they wed.* She'd not force them just so she might see her own future settled.

Caleb's disappointment was so palpable it stung.

"Think on it, princess. Because something tells me if you don't take this for you, someday you'll be having a whole host of regrets other than that husband you married."

"I don't..."

Except, her protestations died on her lips. And she hated that deep in her heart this man who'd known her a short time had gathered that truth she had hidden even from herself—all the regrets she carried for trapping her and Tristan in a marriage that wasn't.

CHAPTER 23

Tristan,
Some days it feels as though you've just left…and then other days, it is
as though you were never even here…
Poppy

TRISTAN WAS TOO LATE.

Or if one wished to be truly precise—too early.

Nearly six o'clock in the morn, and hours after Poppy's event had concluded. Dismounting from his horse, Tristan doffed his hat, and scanned the empty streets.

The windows of his townhouse revealed the darkness within. Traveling nearly two days straight, the last leg of his journey had been delayed—by a broken carriage axle. First by ship and then a carriage ride, he'd abandoned for a mount, he'd ridden like the devil, traveling for the better part of twenty-hours to get there.

To get to her.

Eyes bloodshot, Florence opened the door to greet him. "My lord," he said, his bushy white eyebrows skyrocketing. "Wasn't expecting you back." To the man's credit, he gave no outward display to the beard covering Tristan's face, or the stench of horse and sweat on him.

"Florence, so very good to see you," he greeted, as he entered. For it signaled that Tristan had returned.

He was home.

Home. How had he not seen that, until now? He'd railed at the idea of forcing Poppy to reside in the ramshackle residence. All the while failing to see that home was wherever he was with Poppy.

Tristan shrugged out of his cloak. "My wife?" he asked, turning over the dusty garment.

The older man took the garment. "Her Ladyship is in the ballroom." Even his butler had changed. His previous unkempt white hair had been neatly cropped. His slurred speech from too much drink had given way to more practiced, proper tones of one putting forth an effort with his words. "As she is most days, my lord." He said it as though Tristan should know. "Arises early, she does."

Poppy.

She was here.

So close.

And he was already striding through the townhouse, a townhouse that she'd since transformed; the covered portraits of his youth had since been uncovered and dusted. The floors and mahogany all gleamed from coats of varnish. Of course, everything she touched, she altered into a thing of beauty.

God, how he'd missed her.

He'd missed being with her.

And having her in his arms and in his bed.

And like a damned fool he was, until he'd left, he'd failed to realize how much he loved her.

Tristan staggered to a stop, skidding, off-balance upon the smooth flooring. He shot a hand out, catching himself at the wall. His pulse slowed, and then hammered away in his ears.

He loved her.

Since the moment he'd nearly trampled her, then a young girl, pressing him about his dogs, and reproaching him for hunting, he'd cared for her. But somewhere along the way, with all the times life had thrown them together, she'd matured, and he'd become hopelessly enraptured of Poppy Tidemore in all her spirited glory.

He didn't want a marriage of convenience with her—he wanted all that marriage entailed, with her at his side, battling every challenge, and damning whatever society said because as long as they had one another…it would be enough.

It was enough.

Tristan found his legs once more, and took off running.

The sound of her laughter reached him first: perfectly Poppy in its clarity and abandon. It called. Beckoned. The light within him and source of all his joy; the only joy he'd known these past three months.

He reached the ballroom.

Wholly engrossed in her task, her fingers flew over her page as she sketched. Unchanged in their time apart, absorbed by the work she loved. And he drank in the sight of her as she'd only previously existed in his dreams and waking thoughts.

Poppy.

He knew the moment she felt him there.

Her body, expressive like her eyes, revealed her every emotion. She went completely still. Her gaze locked on her book. Her fingers trembled.

His did, too. His entire body thrummed from the force of a jumble of emotions ricocheting inside.

Her shoulders tensed, and then ever so slowly, she picked her head up. Of course she did. She'd always been braver and bolder than he. Braver and bolder than anyone.

Time stood still and for the first time since he'd raced to her, having thought of everything he would say, he came up devoid of any words, making a mockery of the previous image of rogue he'd attained. For with this woman, there was only real emotion.

"Hello, Poppy," he said quietly, taking a step forward.

Poppy didn't blink. Those enormous hazel eyes. "Tristan."

He tried to make sense of that whisper; his name not quite a question, with shades of shock and confusion. Regardless, it pulled him forward, that soft contralto a song even when she spoke. Until he stopped on the opposite side of her art table, a slab of stone all that stood between them.

"I've found it, sweetheart."

Tristan's gaze slid to find the owner of the flat American accent…a man now approaching Tristan's wife. A man casually rolling forth endearments that should only fall from Tristan's lips.

Tristan's entire body coiled a primal reaction that came from the threat he'd not known was lurking.

And learned how wrong he'd been. There was something greater than mere stone between he and Poppy.

Nearly seven feet tall and all heavy muscle, the man who took up a spot beside Poppy would never be considered handsome. In fact, with a broad-hooked nose and large jaw he leaned on the side of ugly. But Poppy, Tristan's wife, the girl he'd known and the woman he'd fallen in love with, was never one who'd care about what a man looked like.

"Hello," Tristan said coolly, when no introductions or greetings were forthcoming from the pair. He started forward; sizing up the stranger as he walked, this unexpected competition for Poppy.

Why should it be so very unexpected? You left your wife alone, lonely… you yourself know what becomes of lonely wives.

And never had he despised himself more for having bedded such women, in good conscience. Without a thought to what had brought about that loneliness, or separation in those marriages.

At last, Poppy stood, her stool scraped along the marble floor. "Tristan, may I introduce you to Caleb Gray." She gestured to the towering figure at her side…as if there might be another man present, and therefore the matter required clarification.

"And should I know *Mr. Gray*?"

Either she failed to hear or note the deliberate emphasis he placed on that correct form of address for the man. Wagering man that he'd always been, he'd bet his very life it was the latter.

"He's an artist."

Tristan scraped his gaze over the long, black hair drawn back in a queue and the scruff on his face. A memory traipsed in of he and Poppy when life had been less complicated between them. *Your hair is long. You've scruff on your cheeks…and you're rumpled… Are you an artist…?* "Of course he is," he said, letting all the loathing and disdain he felt for the other man drip from his words.

Poppy frowned and moved closer to Gray: Gray, who looked mildly amused by Tristan's response and by his very presence alone.

And it was when Tristan knew…he was going to take the other man apart with his bare hands. Tristan was several inches shorter, and two stone lighter, but he'd defeated far bigger men in battle and those battles had never been over Tristan's wife. "Gray."

He'd give credit where credit was due. Gray didn't so much as acknowledge him with a greeting.

In the end, the only thing that spared Poppy's artist from a thrashing was being interrupted by a clamor of barking dogs. The sharp click of nails striking the hardwood floor announced Sir Faithful and Valor and Honor, and Tristan found himself surrounded by a swell of noisy dogs. The trio danced and circled Tristan, yapping excitedly, lapping his feet.

At least there was someone excited to see him.

Falling to a knee, Tristan stroked each dog, lavishing them with the attention they craved. All the while, his gaze remained fixated on his wife. She stared at him with stricken eyes that he could not make sense of. Just like any of this damned day. In the brief time they'd been apart, his wife had become an enigma. No longer transparent, her secrets only hers. The irony was not lost on Tristan. Before he'd gone, she'd wanted him to share his secrets with her; now he was the one searching for answers to hers.

His gaze slid to the man hovering close at her shoulder, a primitive claim that the American intended to stake.

Over my dead body.

That brought Tristan back to his feet. He slapped his leg twice and the dogs immediately fell quiet.

"I should leave you, princess."

Princess.

The bastard had affixed an endearment to Tristan's wife. This one somehow different from the previous, for now he'd tailored it to Poppy, a secret that they two shared. A mark of their familiarity. Nay, worse—their intimacy.

Narrowing his eyes, Tristan followed the other man's unhurried exit until he'd gone, and all that lingered in his wake was awkwardness.

Between Tristan and Poppy, when there never had been.

"Why does it not seem as though you're happy to see me, wife?" His question came faintly goading, even as he knew he was a bastard for it. Even as he knew he was the one who'd left and the mistakes his own.

"Stop it, Tristan," she chided, the adult of their pair, and it sent a guilty flush up his neck. "Of course I'm happy to see you. I…" Her voice faltered and her features, those delicate features, softened, in the first hint of tenderness since he'd entered. "I was not expecting you."

"I thought I might surprise you." Doffing his gloves, he beat the dusty articles against his leg. In the end, however, it had only been Tristan who'd been surprised.

"You've returned, then?" she exhaled her words on a single breath. Poised as she was on the balls of her feet, Poppy had the look of one about to take flight. At the thought of his being here?

"For three days." Now two and a half. "I've papers to deliver to the Home Office in London."

And just like that, she deflated, sinking back on her heels. "Oh."

He didn't know what to make of that "oh". It was the same opaqueness that had met him since he'd stepped into this ballroom. Prior to it, he'd almost believed her happy at the prospect of his being here. Only, she'd since returned to the task that had occupied her when he'd arrived. Back when she'd been smiling and laughing and not this serious, somber shadow of Poppy. Before him.

Tristan stood there, watching her as she organized a series of metal tools, cleaning one, and then setting it down. Reaching for another. An endless routine that she carried out, which heightened this horrible sense of his invisibility.

Then, he asked it: "Is he your lover?" That question that had haunted him the moment the American had come striding up to Poppy, and into Tristan's marriage. Nay, Tristan had opened that door long ago for the other man, and Poppy's artist had stepped right through.

Poppy ceased washing off that already gleaming instrument.

He saw the way she tensed and could decipher even less from the way her muscles bunched. "If you have to ask that, Tristan," she said softly, "you never knew me."

"You asked for me to give you a pledge of my faithfulness," he reminded her, as she reached dismissively for another instrument.

This time, Poppy glanced up. "Yes." She smiled sadly. "But that's because I *did* know you."

"Is that what you thought?" Frustration ripped that question from him. "That I couldn't be *faithful* to you? That I'm some manner of scoundrel incapable of honoring my vows to you?" He'd admired her all these years as a woman of character, strength, and spirit, only to be stung with the truth of the low opinion she'd carried for him.

Poppy sighed. "It wasn't about loyalty."

"What was it about then, Poppy? *Tell me.*"

"It was about *love.*"

Love. His heart thumped harder; that word he wanted from her but spoken as a vow, not as a single word that she left detached from his name.

"Or rather," she went on, staring at her interlocked fingers, "a lack thereof." When she lifted her eyes to his, the pain there squeezed the blood from his heart, leaving that organ hollow. "I loved you."

There it was…the past tense. He'd been expecting it, but even having prepared himself for it, it landed like a blow to the chest. "Loved," he echoed, in hollow tones, because he needed to say it aloud so that he couldn't deny to himself that she'd said it.

"Oh, Tristan," she whispered. "I'll *always* love you. Always. You were my first love. You captured my heart the moment we met."

"You loved the idea of me. The Earl of Maxwell with his dogs, who fished with you." And who'd fallen in love with her along the way.

"Perhaps," she conceded and that lance struck worse. "But Tristan…" She walked over, stopping so close they were nearly touching. "It was wrong of me to have expectations for you… or our marriage. I presented you one thing, and secretly expected another. It was wrong of me for so many reasons."

"Is that supposed to make me somehow feel better?"

She lifted her palms. "You were drunk when I asked you to marry me. How could I have ever held you to more from that beginning? It was wrong to expect you to set aside that which mattered most, your honor and career with the military, for me. I know that now."

She mattered most. Only, he'd failed to show her that. To let her see that with actions. "And this Gray fellow…" Trying to give some direction to the volatile emotion humming through him, Tristan beat his gloves together. "He makes you happy."

"Do you think I'm trying to hurt you by Caleb's being here?" Caleb. Not: Mr. Gray. Nor: My art instructor. "That I've set out to lash out at you?"

She had that wounded look again, and he shoved a hand through his hair. "No." She wasn't that manner of woman.

"I met Caleb at the Royal Academy for the annual summer exhibit. He offered to instruct me, and I said yes…not to hurt you but rather to do something I wanted. I should think you would be proud of me for not hiding my work away."

This was because of him. He'd encouraged her to share her work with the world. In that, however, he'd never foreseen a Caleb Gray there. More the fool he.

It took a moment to realize Poppy had started for the door. Sir Faithful and Tristan's own dogs—also strangers to him—hot at her heels. And as he watched his wife go, there should be some relief in what she'd confirmed: she and Caleb Gray weren't lovers.

But what was worse…had theirs been a sexual connection it would rip his still beating heart from his chest and destroy him completely, but would still be preferable to the truth…that what she shared with her American was, in fact, more. A relationship born of emotion.

"Do you love him?" There it was. Another question he forcibly made himself ask, not wanting the answer, and yet, needing it, too. It managed to freeze her in her tracks and keep her silent. With her back to him, he was ravaged by the inability to see the honest response, whatever it might be, reflected in her eyes. Forcing a calm he did not feel, he eased his way over toward where his question had frozen her in the middle of the ballroom. "Your American," he added, as if a clarification was needed, and yet, something was. Something to compel her to speak. To answer. So then he might know.

And be destroyed by her answer.

"He is a friend, Tristan. Nothing more."

He hooded his lashes. "I saw the way he looked at you," It was the same way Tristan himself did. "I saw the way he looked at me when I entered; that is a man who sees you as more than a friend."

"You're wrong."

Tossing his gloves down, he stalked over to her. "I've been wrong about so much." Most of it where she was concerned. All of it, really. "But I'm not wrong about this." Tristan slid a palm around her waist, drawing her near, allowing her to pull back. The slightest hesitation, and he'd set her away from him, mourning yet another loss. But she didn't. And he was emboldened by that willingness. "Is yours a friendship in the same way that ours is, Poppy?" he breathed against the teardrop-shaped birthmark. He flicked his tongue out, trailing the tip of it around that slight mark. Then, he suckled.

Her breath caught. "Stop it," she whispered; her chest quickening. "Y-You know that is not the case." Actually, he didn't. Hearing her say it sent a thrill coursing through him.

"Were you asking me to stop kissing you?" he removed her combs and let her curls fall free around them. "Hmm?" Tristan threaded his fingers through her luxuriant midnight strands; silken waves that gleamed.

She arched her head ever so slightly, allowing him better access to her slender neck.

He'd have her say it, though. "Stop 'this', Poppy? Stop what is right between us?" He teased the delicate shell of her ear, drawing the flesh between his teeth. "Or stop mention of your Mr. Gray."

Her lashes fluttered. "The…the…" *Please, God, let it be the latter.* "Latter," she moaned as he lightly bit her.

And triumph flared. Along with it, hunger and masculine pride. She wanted him still.

There was something inherently weak in her. She'd spent day after day crying for Tristan. She'd resolved to rein in her feelings and set herself on the path she'd laid out for them both that night at her sister's hotel.

Only, her body didn't care.

Nor did her heart.

Her heart still sang the same joyous celebration it had the moment he'd entered the ballroom. Rumpled, with the scent of horses clinging to him, his hair tousled.

Poppy wanted him still.

She wanted Tristan in every way and in the absence of the ways that she'd never have him, she'd take this.

Poppy opened her mouth for him and whimpered as he stroked her with his tongue. His kiss, a homecoming that stirred every nerve-ending. He tasted wicked; the hint of brandy and cheroots and she gripped that queue holding his strands back. Ripped it free, tossed it aside, so that she could run her fingers through those dark loose curls as she'd ached to do every day since he'd left, and the memory of his embrace had remained.

"Did you miss me?" he rasped against her mouth.

Except, she could not answer. His hands, he glided them over every curve; her buttocks. He sank them in her hips. And then he brought them up to palm her breasts through her thin lawn shirt. "Is that a 'no', then, love?" As if to punish her, he removed his hands and she cried out.

She panted. "You know I missed you, Tristan."

With a growl, he yanked her shirt free of her waistband, tossing it aside. Her undergarments followed suit. His eyes glittered with desire. For her…and this moment. Her body hummed in breathless anticipation as he lowered his head.

He teased both tips; circling them with his forefingers. He blew lightly, flicking his tongue over the bud tight with desire. Withholding that which she needed.

Poppy released a long moan; the sound wanton to her own ears. "Please," her entreaty ended on a sharp hiss as he took the pebbled tip into his mouth.

Tristan shoved her trousers down, and the cool air kissed her skin, a temporary balm on her flesh that burned with her hunger for him. He reached between them, and undoing the placard of his trousers, he freed himself; his length rampant and swollen and angry with need, and Poppy collapsed a shoulder into the Doric column at her back and took his length in hand—hot silk in her fingers.

Groaning, low and deep, Tristan closed his eyes.

She luxuriated in the feel of him and ran her palm over him.

"I can't," he rasped. "It's been too long." Burying his head in the crook of her neck, he slipped a knee between her legs, parting her, and she let them splay wider.

He settled himself between her thighs and she felt the weight of him there, pressed against her.

Poppy panted. Uncaring that the doors hung open. That anyone might wander past. Wanting only this moment. "Now," she ordered.

He sheathed himself slowly inside her. The slow drag of him was an exquisite torture that bordered between pleasure and pain.

She bit her lip hard enough that the metallic hint of blood tinged her mouth.

But Tristan was there; kissing the wounded flesh, lightly sucking the injury. "Please," she begged, but he tortured her still; drawing out and then in on one smooth glide, he sank deep inside her. Poppy cried to the heavens as he stroked her. Poppy sobbed his name.

She shook and shivered as he plunged deeper and deeper still. Over and over. Filling that place she'd ached every night since he'd left. That hungering having only grown in his absence, a yearning that could only be sated and stoked by this man.

Moaning into his shoulder, Poppy nipped him.

He grunted, thrusting hard, so hard that her back knocked against the Doric column, but only pleasure mobbed her senses.

"Poppy…" he gasped against her neck.

Through the cloud of his desire, she clung to her name, and the words to follow…wanting more.

Their bodies strained against one another; as they moved, their rhythm taking on a franticness that pulled Poppy higher and higher, to that glorious precipice she wanted to fall from.

And then as he thrust deep once more, she shattered, screaming and crying out from the force of her release. Blood rushed to her ears, muting his hoarse shout as he reached his own climax; pulsing inside her, and then they collapsed into one another. Gasping, and struggling to find a proper breath.

Her eyes still closed; Poppy lay her head against his chest.

She didn't want to climb down from this moment. She wanted to remain here, wrapped in his arms, where there wasn't just three days for them and a host of regrets and dreams for more.

Sir Faithful whined, and as one, Tristan and Poppy looked to the three dogs sitting in a perfect row, staring at them.

Poppy's shoulders shook with laughter as she buried her head against her husband. "I cannot face them."

"Naughty creatures, you are. Go," he scolded, and Poppy peeked to find them unbudging.

"Though, in fairness, I cannot blame them for wanting to w—"

Another laugh burst from her lips, and she swatted him. "Stop it."

They shared another smile and Tristan pressed a gentle kiss to her forehead that brought her eyes closed.

Invariably reality would always rear itself. This moment was no different.

Tristan straightened, and using his kerchief to gently clean Poppy, and then himself, he tucked himself back inside the front fall of his trousers, and stepped away.

Her legs still weak, Poppy rested a shoulder against the column, borrowing support from it. She made a show of righting her garments, and tucking her shirt back in the waistband.

This was one thing that had always made sense between them. It was everything else that hadn't ever been able to sort itself out.

"You're returning, then," she murmured.

"I..."

"Have to?" she supplied. "I understand." Unlike when he'd last departed, this time she did. He needed to do this for him. She wasn't enough.

"I'd have you know, your letters have been the only joy I've known in your absence."

How was it possible for words to prove both buoyant and heart-breaking all at the same time?

"I'm happy they've brought you comfort." She was unable to keep the rasp of bitterness from creeping in.

Brushing his knuckles along her jaw, Tristan guided her chin up. "Is he the reason your letters stopped coming?"

Once, she had craved a hint of Tristan's jealousy. Some visceral evidence that she mattered to him. She'd been searching for any crumb of indication that he cared. Now, she saw the truth: that sentiment had never been any mark of a healthy love relationship—like what her sisters had with their spouses. "My letters didn't stop, Tristan," she finally said. "They just came less frequently."

Tristan's nostrils flared. "Because of *him*."

"Because of me," she cried out. "Because of you." How could he still not see? How could he be so dense? "*You left, Tristan*," she enunciated each of those words, and gave herself back over to all the hurt and all the resentment that had tormented her at his leaving. "And when you left, I cried for days."

He reached for her. "Poppy," he said, his voice hoarse.

She shrugged away from him; his touch would only weaken her now. She'd have him hear and own all the truth. "For weeks I cried, Tristan." Her lower lip trembled and she bit it hard. "I would r-rewrite my letters to you because I'd stained them so very badly with my tears and I'd not have you see them."

He groaned. "I didn't know."

"Of course you didn't know." It was too much. She spun away from him, and hugged herself in a protective embrace. "You never knew. You never saw me."

He was immediately there; at her side, turning her to face him. "I *always* saw you."

A tear streaked down her cheek. "Not in the way I wanted you to."

"No," he said, so easily that he chipped off apparently the last piece of her heart that hadn't already been hopelessly shattered. "I saw the young girl racing in Hyde Park who just made me smile. And who teased me like no other." Another tear slipped down her cheek. Tristan caught it with his thumb, dusting it back. "I saw the young woman who didn't give a damn what anyone said, and could not fathom there was someone of such convictions." He gripped her shoulders. "I always saw you, Poppy. Never doubt that. I love you, Poppy."

Her breath caught. Four words twined together into a beautiful poem she'd lain awake dreaming to hear from him.

Only…she was not that girl. Not any longer.

"Why?" she asked curiously. "Is it because you think you're losing me?"

Is it because you think you're losing me…

Not: because you've lost me. And even as Poppy didn't recipro-cate his words of love, he took hope.

"Or are you worried over Caleb or—"

He pressed a fingertip to her lips. "There is no reason other than one: because I love you." His gaze roved each cherished plane of her face.

"I've an opportunity to receive instruction…in France."

His arm fell to his side. Of anything he thought she might say to his declaration, that had not been it. "Instruction."

"Art instruction," she said needlessly, but still necessary for his slow-to-process mind. "Women are forbidden from attending classes here, as you know. The Académie des Beaux Arts admits four women each year. Caleb believes I have talent." Tristan believed in her talent and long before that interloper in their marriage. "And he invited Jean-Antoine Houdon to view my works." She stared at him as if that name should mean something. As if any of this should make sense.

Tristan was only capable of shaking his head.

"Mr. Houdon, he is a renowned sculptor and he's helped secure one of those placements for me."

Tristan noted that mound of rock she'd been sitting with upon his arrival and found his way over to her abandoned work station. The tools. The stone. All new to her. Moments he'd missed while in Ireland. And how many more would he lose when he returned. He picked up one of the metal instruments, the foreign item cool in his hand.

"You'll be gone, Tristan," she reminded him, unnecessarily. From the moment St. Cyr had thrown the commission across his desk and hit him square in the chest, Tristan had thought only of being apart from Poppy. "As you said, in several years you'll sell your commission and we can have a marriage. But Tristan," she whispered, joining him. "I cannot sit here waiting for life to start. I don't want to. You were right. I want to stretch myself. I want to grow and share my work not as if it is some dirty secret that I should be shamed for." As she'd been with Rochford.

Everything was careening and out of sorts, and he couldn't slog his way through to the other side of reason. When he came out on the other side, there was just one thought. Tristan set the metal instrument down. "Are you going with him?" He himself heard the sharpness of that question.

"You aren't hearing me. This isn't about Caleb," she said gently. "This is about *me*."

And when she departed, taking all three dogs with her, Tristan was left uncertain which he loathed more: the absolute absence of "us" as a word to join Tristan and Poppy together. Or the sound of the other man's name that had tripped so easily from her lips.

The soft echo of returning footfalls brought him spinning around. "Oh."

"Goodness," Claire drawled. "For that reaction, one would think Mother had walked into the room."

"I'm sorry," he said tiredly; his rigorous travel, and the weight of all he'd discovered since his return, drained the energy from him. He sank onto the edge of Poppy's abandoned stool.

"Here." Claire held a flask out, and he wordlessly took the offering, removed the top, and drank deep.

"Why didn't you tell me?" Why hadn't anyone? Not St. Cyr or his sister-in-law.

"I mentioned her art instructor. Odd. Boorish."

Caleb Gray wasn't an art instructor. Art instructor implied little French fellows who spoke in nasal tones and oiled their hair.

"In fact, I wrote about him quite often," his sister said, tossing her curls.

"But you didn't mention…" The way he'd looked at Poppy; it was a look Tristan knew because it was the way he'd looked at Poppy long before it had ever been appropriate, so much so that he'd denied it from himself.

His sister knitted her brows together. "That he was an American?"

"That he is… who he is."

Understanding dawned. "Ahh. Yes, well, I would have expected Mother would have mentioned him to you."

"She did," he muttered. Tristan loosened his badly wrinkled cravat and tossed it aside.

"You just assumed it was Mother being disapproving."

He had. Now, he forced himself to remember all the notes she'd penned about Poppy and her "obscene work", as she'd referred to it. Poppy in breeches. Poppy who could not be bothered to work with a conventional instructor.

All the while, what she hadn't said was the truth: Poppy was spending her days with a tall, strapping American with unkempt hair and a beard, as all good artists should have.

Yes, Gray fit with all the images Poppy had of an artist.

Tendrils of jealousy unfurled, and he clenched and unclenched his fists.

"You needn't worry," his sister said softly.

"Who said I was worried?" He wasn't. He was terrified out of his goddamn mind.

"The vein is about to bulge from your temple." Claire rested a hand on his arm. "Poppy loves you."

His heart thumped hard. "How do you know?" he asked hoarsely. In his yearning, needing his sister to be correct.

"Because I see her smile when she reads your letters. And she smells them. Her eyes close and then when they open, they are only sadness."

Oh, God. His chest buckled.

"And with the cruelty she faces daily from Mother, she'd have to love you to stay here."

That snapped Tristan to. Poppy had married him, a worthless bounder, when she could have had any, and he'd saddled her with a heartless mother-in-law, and only after he'd hightailed it to Ireland. Restless, Tristan jumped up and began to pace. He'd assumed the only way to restore his honor was by the same acts of valor that he'd been recognized for after battling Boney. Only, Poppy had been right. Honor was not about how the world judged a person...it was about how a man lived his life. And he wanted to spend his life with Poppy.

He cursed. "God, I've been a fool."

"Yes, but in your defense, you had good intentions." Her eyes twinkled. "Alas, Hell is full of good meanings, but heaven is full of good works."

Tristan stared at the mural he and Poppy had painted together; her voice echoed in his ears.

You equate your honor with how the world views you and not with how you live your own life...

All this time, he'd connected his honor with the Maxwell title. He'd been so driven to restore his name. Failing to see until now, that it wasn't about the title he'd lost. He could be honorable on his own terms—honorable as Lord Bolingbroke rather than Lord Maxwell. He could care for his wife and his sisters and his properties—however unimpressive they may be. He could live a life he was proud of.

And he could do all that...*be* all that, with Poppy at his side.

"I know what I need to do," he whispered.

Claire wrinkled her nose. "Let us hope one of those things is a bath."

"I'll require your help with something."

"Anything."

But first...he was already striding across the floor. "Where is Mother?"

"The breakfast room. She was awakened the moment you returned." Claire cupped her hands around her mouth. "I have a feeling I'm about to enjoy this."

Ten minutes later, waiting in the breakfast room as his mother entered, it was clear who was not enjoying this.

His mother blanched. "Goodness, Tristan, you smell and look positively atrocious." He balled his hands, silent as she eyed the sideboard. "Where are the servants? It is those odd characters your wife insists on hiring—"

The servants Poppy paid for. "I want you gone," he said quietly.

"Street waifs, many of them," she continued, as though he'd not spoken. She reached for a plate.

"Did you hear me? I want your things packed, and I want you to return to Dartmoor."

The porcelain dish slipped from her fingers, and clattered upon the sideboard, but remained miraculously intact, much like the woman herself. "You aren't making sense."

"I'm not? Let me make it more clear for you then? I have spent these past months owning the guilt that belonged solely with you and father—"

"Hush," she whispered. Her terrified gaze flew to the door, and then back to Tristan.

"I have sought to restore honor to our name, and I've nearly cost myself the only happiness I've ever truly known." His wife. He'd almost lost his wife. Or mayhap he already had.

"Bah, what is happiness without one's standing in Polite Society?"

She'd never understand. And he'd have her nowhere near Poppy and neither would he force his sisters to suffer her company. "You're leaving," he repeated for a third time. "Claire and Faye will remain, but your days of ordering my wife around and speaking ill of Poppy and her talents are at an end."

His mother's brow shot up. "Th-this is because of your w-wife, isn't it?"

"This has nothing to do with anything Poppy has said about you and everything to do with what she should have said about you." Tristan walked off.

"Tristan?" his mother cried. "You cannot do this. Do you hear me? What are you doing?"

Hopefully winning his wife back.

CHAPTER 24

ONCE MORE, POPPY WAS PARTNER-LESS on the sides of a dance floor.

The great irony, however, was not lost on her, that she should find herself in the exact state she had for the better part of three years, while also having a husband.

Of course, one's husband would have to be present in order to have him as a potential partner.

His three days had really only been two and a half, and he'd since been gone a week.

It was not getting easier.

She'd believed she'd accepted her and Tristan's future for what it was: a man and woman who lived separate lives—for now—who would reunite in a few years and attempt to begin a life together as husband and wife.

"Mother will be horrified," her sister Prudence said. On the sidelines of Lord and Lady Smith's ball, Poppy found herself agreeing. "At your leaving to attend art school, but I am so very proud of you."

"Undoubtedly," she said, staring wistfully out at the dancers. "At least she'll pretend to be." The dowager countess, however, had beamed with pride during Poppy's art exhibit.

"Everything is in place," Pru murmured.

"Yes." She was set to leave in a fortnight. She'd promised Tristan his sisters would have a Season, and she'd honor that. Before she left, she'd see plans were in place for next year.

"I still find it atrocious that Tristan left his sisters' care to you," Prudence muttered.

Poppy frowned. "Claire and Faye are not a burden." And what was more… "He sent his mother away because she was unkind to me." He'd always been her champion: against Rochford. His mother. The unknown man he'd believed she'd been meeting at the last event they'd attended here together.

A wave of crippling pain swept her.

"I can forgive him somewhat, then" she said reluctantly. "But I still am not happy with him, Poppy, and nothing you say will make me forgive him." Prudence took a sip of her lemonade and her lips puckered. "Egads, this is awful stuff."

Lemonade.

Emotion stuck in her throat. Oh, God. This was too much. Lemonade, here at another of Lord and Lady Smith's tedious affairs. It was all an echo of another time.

"I cannot, however, forgive Tristan leaving you, still."

"He had to, Pru," she said tiredly; this same debate she'd had with her and Penelope at various points since Tristan's latest departure. "He is a captain in the King's Army."

"Fine. I'll even allow that. However, he cannot simply disappear and reappear, Poppy," her sister gesticulated wildly as she spoke, drops of pink lemonade splashing over the rim. "He is wreaking havoc on your heart," Prudence exclaimed, and slashed her hand at the air. Horror wreathed Prudence's face as she splashed Poppy. "Oh, hell," Prudence whispered, and Poppy's gaze slipped down to the wide stain drenching the front of her gown.

Pale blue and not white, and yet, how very much this moment was like another.

It was too much…

She needed to leave. The walls were closing in and crushing her heart in the process.

"Oh, please don't look at that," Prudence begged. "I'm so sorry."

"It is fine," Poppy assured. "I'll see to it."

"I'll help you."

"No. No. I'm fine. If you'll watch after Claire and Faye?" Her two sisters-in-law, social outcasts, pariahs amongst the other wallflowers, who looked as miserable as Poppy had been, and still was.

Only now, for altogether different reasons.

"You're certain?" Prudence called after her.

"Fine." She wasn't. Poppy weaved between guests, lords and ladies whose attention had at some point ceased to be fixated upon her, and had moved on to other subjects. In this case, her sisters-in-law. That was the way of the *ton*, though. One scandal to replace the next and there was a good deal less exciting about married Tidemores than the young girls she and her sisters had once been.

Poppy found herself walking these old familiar halls, wandering the same path she had as a young woman who'd dreamed of a future with Tristan. But this hadn't been it. The future had been the two of them together.

Out of sight of the ballroom, Poppy took off running, until her chest burned and her toes ached from the constraints of her heeled slippers.

She didn't stop until she reached the conservatory where it had all begun. Shoving the door open, she stumbled inside, the room a perfect replica of that night.

Poppy sucked in a shuddery breath and loosening the laces of her slippers, she slid them off. Freeing her feet from their miserable constraints, she flexed her toes. Her laces dangling in her hand, she wandered to the watering fount.

Sinking onto the ledge she stared down at her reflection in the lightly rippling water. Her lips quivered in a sad smile as she touched the front of her stained dress.

"I'm not adorable. Kittens and pups are adorable. And even if I was red in the face, which I am not, it would be with entirely good reason…

A sob ripped from her throat, and she bit her fist. But it was futile. Her body shook from the force of her tears, and she let them fall and accepted all she'd lost and all she wept for.

The happiness she'd wanted with him…

"Poppy, since when did you begin drinking lemonade?"

She didn't move. Those words, an echo of long ago, spoken so clear, in the now, by that same voice, and yet, it could not be… because he'd gone.

She'd waved him off once more a week ago.

"I don't drink lemonade," Poppy said softly. "Someone tossed it at me."

"Is your gown righted?" he asked, that deep baritone cascading over her like so much wonderful heat cast by the summer's sun.

"It is."

"Ah, that is unfortunate."

And for the first time since he'd gone again, Poppy smiled. "That wasn't what you said," she reminded, still unable to face him. Afraid this moment was a dream of pretend she'd crafted from her desire to see him.

"No. But that is what I wanted to say."

"And my stained dress?"

"I may have enlisted your sister's support," he called over from the doorway.

Prudence had known he was here.

"I may have sworn her to secrecy," he murmured, following her thoughts. Their thoughts had always moved in harmony. It was them, however, as people, who'd struggled to find a proper synchronization. Until now. "That is also how I would have rewrote that night for us, Poppy. Not a glass tossed at you by Lady Kathryn Delaney but an accident from a beloved sister calling me out for the fool I've been."

Another tear fell.

All these years, she'd believed the moment in Lord Smith's conservatory an afterthought Tristan had barely remembered, and yet, verbatim words that had fallen from each of their lips, were words he uttered now.

He was close. She felt him at her shoulder.

Then he was there. She caught his reflection in Lord Smith's pool.

He sank onto the stone ledge beside her, and waited, giving her time, and not again speaking until she at last looked at him. Tristan brushed the tears from her cheeks. "There remains so much about that night I wanted to do over, Poppy."

Her breath stuck funny in her lungs. "Our Marriage Pact."

"Our Marriage Pact."

She slid her gaze away, but he cradled her cheek, gently guiding her eyes back to his. "You misunderstand me. I wanted a do-over. I wanted to return in time to the damned fool I was and give you an entirely different list." He reached inside his jacket and withdrew a note.

She followed his movements. "What are you doing?" she whispered.

"A proper marriage pact needs to be written. May I?"

"Please." Through the watering of the fountain and her own beating heart she barely heard her own reply.

"I want to spend every damned moment of every damned day bringing your lips up in that saucy grin." With his spare hand, he touched a finger to the corner of her mouth. "This one. This one right here." Setting aside the list, Tristan held her eyes and recounted all those wishes. "I want to be with you, always. I want to share your bed and your dreams and your hopes. And a daughter, Poppy," he whispered. "I want a daughter just like you. One who has your spirit and smile and courage. Ten of them if you'd have it." She struggled to see him through the tears in her eyes. "I want a life with you in every sense of the word. And I want it now. Not three years from now."

Her lips quivered. "Your commission—"

Tristan ran the pad of his thumb over that trembling flesh. "I've called in a favor. My commanding officer at Waterloo has allowed me to trade my post for one with the Home Office in London… when I'm ready to accept it."

When he was ready to accept it? What was he saying? "I don't…I…but…"

"You helped me see that I was blinded by my own quest to restore my image in society. I'd lost sight of what mattered. I'll not have my pride be my ruin. Losing you would ruin me."

Poppy gasped.

"Because *you*, Poppy," he said gently. "You are what matters. Being with you. Having a family with you. And I want you to have your dreams and attend Académie des Beaux Arts because that is what you deserve. I'd just ask that wherever you go, you let me go, too."

A sob tore from her throat, and she fell into his embrace. Tristan's arms came up around her, and he touched his lips to her temple, her brow, kissing away the damp stains left by her tears. Then, he kissed her, claiming her mouth, and Poppy kissed him, willing him to feel everything she'd ever carried in her heart for him. "I love you, Tristan."

"And I love you, Poppy. I'd ask you for but one more thing?"

"Anything." She'd been his, as he'd been hers; their lives together ordained at that meeting.

"Forever."

And leaning up, she kissed him; offering him just that.

THE END

COMING MAY 2019

The Bluestocking,
Book 4 in the Wicked Wallflowers series.

Two damaged hearts learn there's a fine line between love and hate in a Wicked Wallflowers novel from *USA Today* bestselling author Christi Caldwell.

Gertrude, the eldest Killoran sister, has spent a lifetime being underestimated—especially by her own family. She may seem as vulnerable as a kitten, but given the chance, she can be as fierce as a tiger. Her adopted brother, Stephen, has just been snatched back by his true father, and she'll be damned if she relinquishes the boy to the man reviled throughout London as the Mad Marquess.

Still haunted by a deadly tragedy that left him publicly despised, Lord Edwin holds only hatred for the Killorans—the people he believes kidnapped his son. And not one of them will ever see the boy again. But when Gertrude forces her way into the household and stubbornly insists that she remain as Stephen's governess, Edwin believes he may have found someone madder than himself.

With every moment he shares with the tenderhearted Gertrude, Edwin's anger softens into admiration…and more. Is it possible that the woman he loathed may be the only person who can heal his broken soul?

OTHER BOOKS BY
CHRISTI CALDWELL

THE ROGUE WHO RESCUED HER
Book 3 in the "Brethren" Series by Christi Caldwell

Martha Donaldson went from being a nobleman's wife, and respected young mother, to the scandal of her village. After learning the dark lie perpetuated against her by her 'husband', she knows better than to ever trust a man. Her children are her life and she'll protect them at all costs. When a stranger arrives seeking the post of stable master, everything says to turn him out. So why does she let him stay?

Lord Sheldon Graham Whitworth has lived with the constant reminders of his many failings. The third son of a duke, he's long been underestimated: that however, proves a valuable asset as he serves the Brethren, an illustrious division in the Home Office. When Graham's first mission sees him assigned the role of guard to a young widow and her son, he wants nothing more than to finish quickly and then move on to another, more meaningful assignment.

Except, as the secrets between them begin to unravel, Martha's trust is shattered, and Graham is left with the most vital mission he'll ever face—winning Martha's heart.

THE LADY WHO LOVED HIM
Book 2 in the "Brethren" Series by Christi Caldwell

In this passionate, emotional Regency romance by Christi Caldwell, society's most wicked rake meets his match in the clever Lady Chloe Edgerton! And nothing will ever be the same!

She doesn't believe in marriage....

The cruelty of men is something Lady Chloe Edgerton understands. Even in her quest to better her life and forget the past, men always seem determined to control her. Overhearing the latest plan to wed her to a proper gentleman, Chloe finally has enough…but one misstep lands her in the arms of the most notorious rake in London.

The Marquess of Tennyson doesn't believe in love....

Leopold Dunlop is a ruthless, coldhearted rake… a reputation he has cultivated. As a member of The Brethren, a secret spy network, he's committed his life to serving the Crown, but his rakish reputation threatens to overshadow that service. When he's caught in a compromising position with Chloe, it could be the last nail in the coffin of his career unless he's willing to enter into a marriage of convenience.

A necessary arrangement…

A loveless match from the start, it soon becomes something more. As Chloe and Leo endeavor to continue with the plans for their lives prior to their marriage, Leo finds himself not so immune to his wife – or to the prospect of losing her.

THE SPY WHO SEDUCED HER
Book 1 in the "Brethren" Series by Christi Caldwell

A widow with a past… The last thing Victoria Barrett, the Viscountess Waters, has any interest in is romance. When the only man she's ever loved was killed she endured an arranged marriage to a cruel man in order to survive. Now widowed, her only focus is on clearing her son's name from the charge of murder. That is until the love of her life returns from the grave.

A leader of a once great agency… Nathaniel Archer, the Earl of Exeter head of the Crown's elite organization, The Brethren, is back on British soil. Captured and tortured 20 years ago, he clung to memories of his first love until he could escape. Discovering she has married whilst he was captive, Nathaniel sets aside the distractions of love…until an unexpected case is thrust upon him—to solve the murder of the Viscount Waters. There is just one complication: the prime suspect's mother is none other than Victoria, the woman he once loved with his very soul.

Secrets will be uncovered and passions rekindled. Victoria and Nathaniel must trust one another if they hope to start anew—in love and life. But will duty destroy their last chance?

⁕⁕⁕

ROGUES RUSH IN
A Regency Duet by Tessa Dare & Christi Caldwell

⁕⁕⁕

New York Times and *USA Today* Bestselling authors Tessa Dare and Christi Caldwell come together in this smart, sexy, not-to-be-missed Regency Duet!

Two scandalous brides…
Two rogues who won't be denied…
His Bride for the Taking by NYT Bestselling author Tessa Dare
It's the first rule of friendship among gentlemen: Don't even think about touching your best friend's sister. But Sebastian, Lord Byrne, has never been one for rules. He's thought about touching Mary Clayton—a lot—and struggled to resist temptation. But when Mary's bridegroom leaves her waiting at the altar, only Sebastian can save her from ruin. By marrying her himself.

In eleven years, he's never laid a finger on his best friend's sister. Now he's going to take her with both hands. To have, to hold… and to love.

His Duchess for a Day by USA Today Bestseller Christi Caldwell
It was never meant to be...

That's what Elizabeth Terry has told herself while trying to forget the man she married—her once best friend. Passing herself off as a widow, Elizabeth has since built a life for herself as an instructor at a finishing school, far away from that greatest of mistakes. But the past has a way of finding you, and now that her husband has found her, Elizabeth must face the man she's tried to forget.

It was time to right a wrong...

Crispin Ferguson, the Duke of Huntington, has spent the past years living with regret. The young woman he married left without a by-your-leave, and his hasty elopement had devastating repercussions. Despite everything, Crispin never stopped thinking about Elizabeth. Now that he's found her, he has one request—be his duchess, publicly, just for a day.

Can spending time together as husband and wife rekindle the bond they once shared? Or will a shocking discovery tear them apart...this time, forever?

THE VIXEN
Book 2 in the "Wicked Wallflowers" Series by Christi Caldwell

Set apart by her ethereal beauty and fearless demeanor, Ophelia Killoran has always been a mystery to those around her—and a woman they underestimated. No one would guess that she spends her nights protecting the street urchins of St. Giles. Ophelia knows what horrors these children face. As a young girl, she faced those horrors herself, and she would have died...if not for the orphan boy who saved her life.

A notorious investigator, Connor Steele never expected to encounter Ophelia Killoran on his latest case. It has been years since he sacrificed himself for her. Now, she hires orphans from the street to work in her brother's gaming hell. But where does she find the children...and what are her intentions?

Ophelia and Connor are at odds. After all, Connor now serves the nobility, and that is a class of people Ophelia knows first-hand not to trust. But if they can set aside their misgivings and work together, they may discover that their purposes—and their hearts—are perfectly aligned.

THE HELLION
Book 1 in the "Wicked Wallflowers" Series by Christi Caldwell

Adair Thorne has just watched his gaming-hell dream disappear into a blaze of fire and ash, and he's certain that his competitors, the Killorans, are behind it. His fury and passion burn even hotter when he meets Cleopatra Killoran, a tart-mouthed vixen who mocks him at every turn. If she were anyone else but the enemy, she'd ignite a desire in him that would be impossible to control.

No one can make Cleopatra do anything. That said, she'll do whatever it takes to protect her siblings—even if that means being sponsored by their rivals for a season in order to land a noble husband. But she will not allow her head to be turned by the infuriating and darkly handsome Adair Thorne.

There's only one thing that threatens the rules of the game: Cleopatra's secret. It could unravel the families' tenuous truce and shatter the unpredictably sinful romance mounting between the hellion…and a scoundrel who could pass for the devil himself.

TO TEMPT A SCOUNDREL
Book 15 in the "Heart of a Duke" Series by Christi Caldwell

Never trust a gentleman…

Once before, Lady Alice Winterbourne trusted her heart to an honorable, respectable man… only to be jilted in the scandal of the Season. Longing for an escape from all the whispers and humiliation, Alice eagerly accepts an invitation to her friend's house party. In the country, she hopes to find some peace from the embarrassment left in London… Unfortunately, she finds her former betrothed and his new bride in attendance.

Never love a lady…

Lord Rhys Brookfield has no interest in marriage. Ever. He's worked quite hard at building both his fortune and his reputation as a rogue—and intends to enjoy all that they can offer him. That is if his match-making mother will stop pairing him with prospective brides. When Rhys and Alice meet, sparks flare. But with every new encounter, their first impressions of one another are challenged and an unlikely friendship is forged.

Desperate, Rhys proposes a pretend courtship, one meant to spite Alice's former betrothed and prevent any matchmaking attempts toward Rhys. What neither expects is that a pretense can become so much more. Or that a burning passion can heal… and hurt.

⁂

BEGUILED BY A BARON
Book 14 in the "Heart of a Duke" Series by Christi Caldwell

⁂

A Lady with a Secret… Partially deaf, with a birthmark marring her face, Bridget Hamilton is content with her life, even if she's been cast out of her family. But her peaceful existence—expanding her mind with her study of rare books—is threatened with an ultimatum from her evil brother—steal a valuable book or give up her son. Bridget has no choice; her son is her world.

A Lord with a Purpose… Vail Basingstoke, Baron Chilton is known throughout London as the Bastard Baron. After battling at Waterloo, he establishes himself as the foremost dealer in rare books and builds a fortune, determined to never be like the self-serving duke who sired him. He devotes his life to growing his fortune to care for his illegitimate siblings, also fathered by the duke. The chance to sell a highly coveted book for a financial windfall is his only thought.

Two Paths Collide… When Bridget masquerades as the baron's newest housekeeper, he's hopelessly intrigued by her quick wit and her skill with antique tomes. Wary from having his heart broken in the past, it should be easy enough to keep Bridget at arm's length, yet desire for her dogs his steps. As they spend time in each other's company, understanding for life grows as does love, but when Bridget's integrity is called into question, Vail's world is shattered—as is his heart again. Now Bridget and Vail will have to overcome the horrendous secrets and lies between them to grasp a love—and life—together.

To Enchant a Wicked Duke
Book 13 in the "Heart of a Duke" Series by Christi Caldwell

A Devil in Disguise

Years ago, when Nick Tallings, the recent Duke of Huntly, watched his family destroyed at the hands of a merciless nobleman, he vowed revenge. But his efforts had been futile, as his enemy, Lord Rutland is without weakness.

Until now…

With his rival finally happily married, Nick is able to set his ruthless scheme into motion. His plot hinges upon Lord Rutland's innocent, empty-headed sister-in-law, Justina Barrett. Nick will ruin her, marry her, and then leave her brokenhearted.

A Lady Dreaming of Love

From the moment Justina Barrett makes her Come Out, she is labeled a Diamond. Even with her ruthless father determined to sell her off to the highest bidder, Justina never gives up on her hope for a good, honorable gentleman who values her wit more than her looks.

A Not-So-Chance Meeting

Nick's ploy to ensnare Justina falls neatly into place in the streets of London. With each carefully orchestrated encounter, he slips further and further inside the lady's heart, never anticipating that Justina, with her quick wit and strength, will break down his own defenses. As Nick's plans begins to unravel, he's left to determine which is more important—Justina's love or his vow for vengeance. But can Justina ever forgive the duke who deceived her?

One Winter with a Baron
Book 12 in the "Heart of a Duke" Series by Christi Caldwell

A clever spinster:

Content with her spinster lifestyle, Miss Sybil Cunning wants to prove that a future as an unmarried woman is the only life for her. As a bluestocking who values hard, empirical data, Sybil needs help with her research. Nolan Pratt, Baron Webb, one of society's most scandalous rakes, is the perfect gentleman to help her. After all, he inspires fear in proper mothers and desire within their daughters.

A notorious rake:

Society may be aware of Nolan Pratt, Baron's Webb's wicked ways, but what he has carefully hidden is his miserable handling of his family's finances. When Sybil presents him the opportunity to earn much-needed funds, he can't refuse.

A winter to remember:

However, what begins as a business arrangement becomes something more and with every meeting, Sybil slips inside his heart. Can this clever woman look beneath the veneer of a coldhearted rake to see the man Nolan truly is?

───── ⚜ ─────

To Redeem a Rake
Book 11 in the "Heart of a Duke" Series by Christi Caldwell

───── ⚜ ─────

He's spent years scandalizing society.
Now, this rake must change his ways.

Society's most infamous scoundrel, Daniel Winterbourne, the Earl of Montfort, has been promised a small fortune if he can relinquish his wayward, carousing lifestyle. And behaving means he must also help find a respectable companion for his youngest sister—someone who will guide her and whom she can emulate. However, Daniel knows no such woman. But when he encounters a childhood friend, Daniel believes she may just be the answer to all of his problems.

Having been secretly humiliated by an unscrupulous blackguard years earlier, Miss Daphne Smith dreams of finding work at Ladies of Hope, an institution that provides an education for disabled women. With her sordid past and a disfigured leg, few opportunities arise for a woman such as she. Knowing Daniel's history, she wishes to avoid him, but working for his sister is exactly the stepping stone she needs.

Their attraction intensifies as Daniel and Daphne grow closer, preparing his sister for the London Season. But Daniel must resist his desire for a woman tarnished by scandal while Daphne is reminded of the boy she once knew. Can society's most notorious rake redeem his reputation and become the man Daphne deserves?

TO WOO A WIDOW
Book 10 in the "Heart of a Duke" Series by Christi Caldwell

They see a brokenhearted widow.
She's far from shattered.

Lady Philippa Winston is never marrying again. After her late husband's cruelty that she kept so well hidden, she has no desire to search for love.

Years ago, Miles Brookfield, the Marquess of Guilford, made a frivolous vow he never thought would come to fruition—he promised to marry his mother's goddaughter if he was unwed by the age of thirty. Now, to his dismay, he's faced with honoring that pledge. But when he encounters the beautiful and intriguing Lady Philippa, Miles knows his true path in life. It's up to him to break down every belief Philippa carries about gentlemen, proving that not only is love real, but that he is the man deserving of her sheltered heart.

Will Philippa let down her guard and allow Miles to woo a widow in desperate need of his love?

THE LURE OF A RAKE
Book 9 in the "Heart of a Duke" Series by Christi Caldwell

A Lady Dreaming of Love

Lady Genevieve Farendale has a scandalous past. Jilted at the altar years earlier and exiled by her family, she's now returned to London to prove she can be a proper lady. Even though she's not given up on the hope of marrying for love, she's wary of trusting again. Then she meets Cedric Falcot, the Marquess of St. Albans whose seductive ways set her heart aflutter. But with her sordid history, Genevieve knows a rake can also easily destroy her.

An Unlikely Pairing

What begins as a chance encounter between Cedric and Genevieve becomes something more. As they continue to meet, passions stir. But with Genevieve's hope for true love, she fears Cedric will be unable to give up his wayward lifestyle. After all, Cedric has spent years protecting his heart, and keeping everyone out. Slowly, she chips away at all the walls he's built, but when he falters, Genevieve can't offer him redemption. Now, it's up to Cedric to prove to Genevieve that the love of a man is far more powerful than the lure of a rake.

TO TRUST A ROGUE
Book 8 in the "Heart of a Duke" Series by Christi Caldwell

A rogue

Marcus, the Viscount Wessex has carefully crafted the image of rogue and charmer for Polite Society. Under that façade, however, dwells a man whose dreams were shattered almost eight years earlier by a young lady who captured his heart, pledged her love, and then left him, with nothing more than a curt note.

A widow

Eight years earlier, faced with no other choice, Mrs. Eleanor Collins, fled London and the only man she ever loved, Marcus, Viscount Wessex. She has now returned to serve as a companion for her elderly aunt with a daughter in tow. Even though they're next door neighbors, there is little reason for her to move in the same circles as Marcus, just in case, she vows to avoid him, for he reminds her of all she lost when she left.

Reunited

As their paths continue to cross, Marcus finds his desire for Eleanor just as strong, but he learned long ago she's not to be trusted. He will offer her a place in his bed, but not anything more. Only, Eleanor has no interest in this new, roguish man. The more time they spend together, the protective wall they've constructed to keep the other out, begin to break. With all the betrayals and secrets between them, Marcus has to open his heart again. And Eleanor must decide if it's ever safe to trust a rogue.

TO WED HIS CHRISTMAS LADY
Book 7 in the "Heart of a Duke" Series by Christi Caldwell

She's longing to be loved:

Lady Cara Falcot has only served one purpose to her loathsome father—to increase his power through a marriage to the future Duke of Billingsley. As such, she's built protective walls about her heart, and presents an icy facade to the world around her. Journeying home from her finishing school for the Christmas holidays, Cara's carriage is stranded during a winter storm. She's forced to tarry at a ramshackle inn, where she immediately antagonizes another patron—William.

He's avoiding his duty in favor of one last adventure:

William Hargrove, the Marquess of Grafton has wanted only one thing in life—to avoid the future match his parents would have him make to a cold, duke's daughter. He's returning home from a blissful eight years of traveling the world to see to his responsibilities. But when a winter storm interrupts his trip and lands him at a falling-down inn, he's forced to share company with a commanding Lady Cara who initially reminds him exactly of the woman he so desperately wants to avoid.

A Christmas snowstorm ushers in the spirit of the season:

At the holiday time, these two people who despise each other due to first perceptions are offered renewed beginnings and fresh starts. As this gruff stranger breaks down the walls she's built about herself, Cara has to determine whether she can truly open her heart to trusting that any man is capable of good and that she herself is capable of love. And William has to set aside all previous thoughts he's carried of the polished ladies like Cara, to be the man to show her that love.

THE HEART OF A SCOUNDREL
Book 6 in the "Heart of a Duke" Series by Christi Caldwell

Ruthless, wicked, and dark, the Marquess of Rutland rouses terror in the breast of ladies and nobleman alike. All Edmund wants in life is power. After he was publically humiliated by his one love Lady Margaret, he vowed vengeance, using Margaret's niece, as his pawn. Except, he's thwarted by another, more enticing target— Miss Phoebe Barrett.

Miss Phoebe Barrett knows precisely the shame she's been born to. Because her father is a shocking letch she's learned to form her own opinions on a person's worth. After a chance meeting with the Marquess of Rutland, she is captivated by the mysterious man. He, too, is a victim of society's scorn, but the more encounters she has with Edmund, the more she knows there is powerful depth and emotion to the jaded marquess.

The lady wreaks havoc on Edmund's plans for revenge and he finds he wants Phoebe, at all costs. As she's drawn into the darkness of his world, Phoebe risks being destroyed by Edmund's ruthlessness. And Phoebe who desires love at all costs, has to determine if she can ever truly trust the heart of a scoundrel.

TO LOVE A LORD
Book 5 in the "Heart of a Duke" Series by Christi Caldwell

All she wants is security:

The last place finishing school instructor Mrs. Jane Munroe belongs, is in polite Society. Vowing to never wed, she's been scuttled around from post to post. Now she finds herself in the Marquess of Waverly's household. She's never met a nobleman she liked, and when she meets the pompous, arrogant marquess, she remembers why. But soon, she discovers Gabriel is unlike any gentleman she's ever known.

All he wants is a companion for his sister:

What Gabriel finds himself with instead, is a fiery spirited, bespectacled woman who entices him at every corner and challenges his age-old vow to never trust his heart to a woman. But... there is something suspicious about his sister's companion. And he is determined to find out just what it is.

All they need is each other:

As Gabriel and Jane confront the truth of their feelings, the lies and secrets between them begin to unravel. And Jane is left to decide whether or not it is ever truly safe to love a lord.

LOVED BY A DUKE
Book 4 in the "Heart of a Duke" Series by Christi Caldwell

For ten years, Lady Daisy Meadows has been in love with Auric, the Duke of Crawford. Ever since his gallant rescue years earlier, Daisy knew she was destined to be his Duchess. Unfortunately, Auric sees her as his best friend's sister and nothing more. But perhaps, if she can manage to find the fabled heart of a duke pendant, she will win over the heart of her duke.

Auric, the Duke of Crawford enjoys Daisy's company. The last thing he is interested in however, is pursuing a romance with a woman he's known since she was in leading strings. This season, Daisy is turning up in the oddest places and he cannot help but notice that she is no longer a girl. But Auric wouldn't do something as foolhardy as to fall in love with Daisy. He couldn't. Not with the guilt he carries over his past sins… Not when he has no right to her heart…But perhaps, just perhaps, she can forgive the past and trust that he'd forever cherish her heart—but will she let him?

THE LOVE OF A ROGUE
Book 3 in the "Heart of a Duke" Series by Christi Caldwell

Lady Imogen Moore hasn't had an easy time of it since she made her Come Out. With her betrothed, a powerful duke breaking it off to wed her sister, she's become the *tons* favorite piece of gossip. Never again wanting to experience the pain of a broken heart, she's resolved to make a match with a polite, respectable gentleman. The last thing she wants is another reckless rogue.

Lord Alex Edgerton has a problem. His brother, tired of Alex's carousing has charged him with chaperoning their remaining, unwed sister about *ton* events. Shopping? No, thank you. Attending the theatre? He'd rather be at Forbidden Pleasures with a scantily clad beauty upon his lap. The task of *chaperone* becomes even more of a bother when his sister drags along her dearest friend, Lady Imogen to social functions. The last thing he wants in his life is a young, innocent English miss.

Except, as Alex and Imogen are thrown together, passions flare and Alex comes to find he not only wants Imogen in his bed, but also in his heart. Yet now he must convince Imogen to risk all, on the heart of a rogue.

MORE THAN A DUKE
Book 2 in the "Heart of a Duke" Series by Christi Caldwell

Polite Society doesn't take Lady Anne Adamson seriously. However, Anne isn't just another pretty young miss. When she discovers her father betrayed her mother's love and her family descended into poverty, Anne comes up with a plan to marry a respectable, powerful, and honorable gentleman—a man nothing like her philandering father.

Armed with the heart of a duke pendant, fabled to land the wearer a duke's heart, she decides to enlist the aid of the notorious Harry, 6th Earl of Stanhope. A scoundrel with a scandalous past, he is the last gentleman she'd ever wed…however, his reputation marks him the perfect man to school her in the art of seduction so she might ensnare the illustrious Duke of Crawford.

Harry, the Earl of Stanhope is a jaded, cynical rogue who lives for his own pleasures. Having been thrown over by the only woman he ever loved so she could wed a duke, he's not at all surprised when Lady Anne approaches him with her scheme to capture another duke's affection. He's come to appreciate that all women are in fact greedy, title-grasping, self-indulgent creatures. And with Anne's history of grating on his every last nerve, she is the last woman he'd ever agree to school in the art of seduction. Only his friendship with the lady's sister compels him to help.

What begins as a pretend courtship, born of lessons on seduction, becomes something more leaving Anne to decide if she can give her heart to a reckless rogue, and Harry must decide if he's willing to again trust in a lady's love.

FOR LOVE OF THE DUKE
*First Full-Length Book in the "Heart of a Duke" Series
by Christi Caldwell*

After the tragic death of his wife, Jasper, the 8th Duke of Bainbridge buried himself away in the dark cold walls of his home, Castle Blackwood. When he's coaxed out of his self-imposed exile to attend the amusements of the Frost Fair, his life is irrevocably changed by his fateful meeting with Lady Katherine Adamson.

With her tight brown ringlets and silly white-ruffled gowns, Lady Katherine Adamson has found her dance card empty for two Seasons. After her father's passing, Katherine learned the unreliability of men, and is determined to depend on no one, except herself. Until she meets Jasper…

In a desperate bid to avoid a match arranged by her family, Katherine makes the Duke of Bainbridge a shocking proposition—one that he accepts.

Only, as Katherine begins to love Jasper, she finds the arrangement agreed upon is not enough. And Jasper is left to decide if protecting his heart is more important than fighting for Katherine's love.

In Need of a Duke
A Prequel Novella to "The Heart of a Duke" Series
by Christi Caldwell

In Need of a Duke: (Author's Note: This is a prequel novella to "The Heart of a Duke" series by Christi Caldwell. It was originally available in "The Heart of a Duke" Collection and is now being published as an individual novella.

~★~

It features a new prologue and epilogue.

Years earlier, a gypsy woman passed to Lady Aldora Adamson and her friends a heart pendant that promised them each the heart of a duke.

Now, a young lady, with her family facing ruin and scandal, Lady Aldora doesn't have time for mythical stories about cheap baubles. She needs to save her sisters and brother by marrying a titled gentleman with wealth and power to his name. She sets her bespectacled sights upon the Marquess of St. James.

Turned out by his father after a tragic scandal, Lord Michael Knightly has grown into a powerful, but self-made man. With the whispers and stares that still follow him, he would rather be anywhere but London…

Until he meets Lady Aldora, a young woman who mistakes him for his brother, the Marquess of St. James. The connection between Aldora and Michael is immediate and as they come to know one another, Aldora's feelings for Michael war with her sisterly responsibilities. With her family's dire situation, a man of Michael's scandalous past will never do.

Ultimately, Aldora must choose between her responsibilities as a sister and her love for Michael.

ONCE A WALLFLOWER, AT LAST HIS LOVE
Book 6 in the Scandalous Seasons Series

Responsible, practical Miss Hermione Rogers, has been crafting stories as the notorious Mr. Michael Michaelmas and selling them for a meager wage to support her siblings. The only real way to ensure her family's ruinous debts are paid, however, is to marry. Tall, thin, and plain, she has no expectation of success. In London for her first Season she seizes the chance to write the tale of a brooding duke. In her research, she finds Sebastian Fitzhugh, the 5th Duke of Mallen, who unfortunately is perfectly affable, charming, and so nicely… configured… he takes her breath away. He lacks all the character traits she needs for her story, but alas, any duke will have to do.

Sebastian Fitzhugh, the 5th Duke of Mallen has been deceived so many times during the high-stakes game of courtship, he's lost faith in Society women. Yet, after a chance encounter with Hermione, he finds himself intrigued. Not a woman he'd normally consider beautiful, the young lady's practical bent, her forthright nature and her tendency to turn up in the oddest places has his interests… roused. He'd like to trust her, he'd like to do a whole lot more with her too, but should he?

A MARQUESS FOR CHRISTMAS
Book 5 in the Scandalous Seasons Series

Lady Patrina Tidemore gave up on the ridiculous notion of true love after having her heart shattered and her trust destroyed by a black-hearted cad. Used as a pawn in a game of revenge against her brother, Patrina returns to London from a failed elopement with a tattered reputation and little hope for a respectable match. The only peace she finds is in her solitude on the cold winter days at Hyde Park. And even that is yanked from her by two little hellions who just happen to have a devastatingly handsome, but coldly aloof father, the Marquess of Beaufort. Something about the lord stirs the dreams she'd once carried for an honorable gentleman's love.

Weston Aldridge, the 4th Marquess of Beaufort was deceived and betrayed by his late wife. In her faithlessness, he's come to view women as self-serving, indulgent creatures. Except, after a series of chance encounters with Patrina, he comes to appreciate how uniquely different she is than all women he's ever known.

At the Christmastide season, a time of hope and new beginnings, Patrina and Weston, unexpectedly learn true love in one another. However, as Patrina's scandalous past threatens their future and the happiness of his children, they are both left to determine if love is enough.

ALWAYS A ROGUE, FOREVER HER LOVE
Book 4 in the Scandalous Seasons Series

Miss Juliet Marshville is spitting mad. With one guardian missing, and the other singularly uninterested in her fate, she is at the mercy of her wastrel brother who loses her beloved childhood home to a man known as Sin. Determined to reclaim control of Rosecliff Cottage and her own fate, Juliet arranges a meeting with the notorious rogue and demands the return of her property.

Jonathan Tidemore, 5th Earl of Sinclair, known to the *ton* as Sin, is exceptionally lucky in life and at the gaming tables. He has just one problem. Well…four, really. His incorrigible sisters have driven off yet another governess. This time, however, his mother demands he find an appropriate replacement.

When Miss Juliet Marshville boldly demands the return of her precious cottage, he takes advantage of his sudden good fortune and puts an offer to her; turn his sisters into proper English ladies, and he'll return Rosecliff Cottage to Juliet's possession.

Jonathan comes to appreciate Juliet's spirit, courage, and clever wit, and decides to claim the fiery beauty as his mistress. Juliet, however, will be mistress for no man. Nor could she ever love a man who callously stole her home in a game of cards. As Jonathan begins to see Juliet as more than a spirited beauty to warm his bed, he realizes she could be a lady he could love the rest of his life, if only he can convince the proud Juliet that he's worthy of her hand and heart.

ALWAYS PROPER, SUDDENLY SCANDALOUS
Book 3 in the Scandalous Seasons Series

Geoffrey Winters, Viscount Redbrooke was not always the hard, unrelenting lord driven by propriety. After a tragic mistake, he resolved to honor his responsibility to the Redbrooke line and live a life, free of scandal. Knowing his duty is to wed a proper, respectable English miss, he selects Lady Beatrice Dennington, daughter of the Duke of Somerset, the perfect woman for him. Until he meets Miss Abigail Stone…

To distance herself from a personal scandal, Abigail Stone flees America to visit her uncle, the Duke of Somerset. Determined to never trust a man again, she is helplessly intrigued by the hard, too-proper Geoffrey. With his strict appreciation for decorum and order, he is nothing like the man' she's always dreamed of.

Abigail is everything Geoffrey does not need. She upends his carefully ordered world at every encounter. As they begin to care for one another, Abigail carefully guards the secret that resulted in her journey to England.

Only, if Geoffrey learns the truth about Abigail, he must decide which he holds most dear: his place in Society or Abigail's place in his heart.

Never Courted, Suddenly Wed
Book 2 in the Scandalous Seasons Series

Christopher Ansley, Earl of Waxham, has constructed a perfect image for the *ton*—the ladies love him and his company is desired by all. Only two people know the truth about Waxham's secret. Unfortunately, one of them is Miss Sophie Winters.

Sophie Winters has known Christopher since she was in leading strings. As children, they delighted in tormenting each other. Now at two and twenty, she still has a tendency to find herself in scrapes, and her marital prospects are slim.

When his father threatens to expose his shame to the *ton*, unless he weds Sophie for her dowry, Christopher concocts a plan to remain a bachelor. What he didn't plan on was falling in love with the lively, impetuous Sophie. As secrets are exposed, will Christopher's love be enough when she discovers his role in his father's scheme?

Forever Betrothed, Never the Bride
Book 1 in the Scandalous Seasons Series

Hopeless romantic Lady Emmaline Fitzhugh is tired of sitting with the wallflowers, waiting for her betrothed to come to his senses and marry her. When Emmaline reads one too many reports of his scandalous liaisons in the gossip rags, she takes matters into her own hands.

War-torn veteran Lord Drake devotes himself to forgetting his days on the Peninsula through an endless round of meaningless associations. He no longer wants to feel anything, but Lady Emmaline is making it hard to maintain a state of numbness. With her zest for life, she awakens his passion and desire for love.

The one woman Drake has spent the better part of his life avoiding is now the only woman he needs, but he is no longer a man worthy of his Emmaline. It is up to her to show him the healing power of love.

A Season of Hope
A Danby Novella

Five years ago when her love, Marcus Wheatley, failed to return from fighting Napoleon's forces, Lady Olivia Foster buried her heart. Unable to betray Marcus's memory, Olivia has gone out of her way to run off prospective suitors. At three and twenty she considers herself firmly on the shelf. Her father, however, disagrees and accepts an offer for Olivia's hand in marriage. Yet it's Christmas, when anything can happen…

Olivia receives a well-timed summons from her grandfather, the Duke of Danby, and eagerly embraces the reprieve from her betrothal.

Only, when Olivia arrives at Danby Castle she realizes the Christmas season represents hope, second chances, and even miracles.

"Winning a Lady's Heart"
A Danby Novella

Author's Note: This is a novella that was originally available in A Summons From The Castle (The Regency Christmas Summons Collection). It is being published as an individual novella.

~★~

For Lady Alexandra, being the source of a cold, calculated wager is bad enough…but when it is waged by Nathaniel Michael Winters, 5th Earl of Pembroke, the man she's in love with, it results in a broken heart, the scandal of the season, and a summons from her grandfather – the Duke of Danby.

To escape Society's gossip, she hurries to her meeting with the duke, determined to put memories of the earl far behind. Except the duke has other plans for Alexandra…plans which include the 5th Earl of Pembroke!

TEMPTED BY A LADY'S SMILE
Book 4 in the "Lords of Honor" Series

Richard Jonas has loved but one woman—a woman who belongs to his brother. Refusing to suffer any longer, he evades his family in order to barricade his heart from unrequited love. While attending a friend's summer party, Richard's approach to love is changed after sharing a passionate and life-altering kiss with a vibrant and mysterious woman. Believing he was incapable of loving again, Richard finds himself tempted by a young lady determined to marry his best friend.

Gemma Reed has not been treated kindly by the *ton*. Often disregarded for her appearance and interests unlike those of a proper lady, Gemma heads to house party to win the heart of Lord Westfield, the man she's loved for years. But her plan is set off course by the tempting and intriguing, Richard Jonas.

A chance meeting creates a new path for Richard and Gemma to forage—but can two people, scorned and shunned by those they've loved from afar, let down their guards to find true happiness?

"RESCUED BY A LADY'S LOVE"
Book 3 in the "Lords of Honor" Series

Destitute and determined to finally be free of any man's shackles, Lily Benedict sets out to salvage her honor. With no choice but to commit a crime that will save her from her past, she enters the home of the recluse, Derek Winters, the new Duke of Blackthorne. But entering the "Beast of Blackthorne's" lair proves more threatening than she ever imagined.

With half a face and a mangled leg, Derek—once rugged and charming—only exists within the confines of his home. Shunned by society, Derek is leery of the hauntingly beautiful Lily Benedict. As time passes, she slips past his defenses, reminding him how to live again. But when Lily's sordid past comes back, threatening her life, it's up to Derek to find the strength to become the hero he once was. Can they overcome the darkness of their sins to find a life of love and redemption?

CAPTIVATED BY A LADY'S CHARM
Book 2 in the "Lords of Honor" Series

In need of a wife…

Christian Villiers, the Marquess of St. Cyr, despises the role he's been cast into as fortune hunter but requires the funds to keep his marquisate solvent. Yet, the sins of his past cloud his future, preventing him from seeing beyond his fateful actions at the Battle of Toulouse. For he knows inevitably it will catch up with him, and everyone will remember his actions on the battlefield that cost so many so much—particularly his best friend.

In want of a husband…

Lady Prudence Tidemore's life is plagued by familial scandals, which makes her own marital prospects rather grim. Surely there is one gentleman of the ton who can look past her family and see just her and all she has to offer?

When Prudence runs into Christian on a London street, the charming, roguish gentleman immediately captures her attention. But then a chance meeting becomes a waltz, and now…

A Perfect Match…

All she must do is convince Christian to forget the cold requirements he has for his future marchioness. But the demons in his past prevent him from turning himself over to love. One thing is certain—Prudence wants the marquess and is determined to have him in her life, now and forever. It's just a matter of convincing Christian he wants the same.

Seduced By a Lady's Heart
Book 1 in the "Lords of Honor" Series

You met Lieutenant Lucien Jones in "Forever Betrothed, Never the Bride" when he was a broken soldier returned from fighting Boney's forces. This is his story of triumph and happily-ever-after!

~★~

Lieutenant Lucien Jones, son of a viscount, returned from war, to find his wife and child dead. Blaming his father for the commission that sent him off to fight Boney's forces, he was content to languish at London Hospital... until offered employment on the Marquess of Drake's staff. Through his position, Lucien found purpose in life and is content to keep his past buried.

Lady Eloise Yardley has loved Lucien since they were children. Having long ago given up on the dream of him, she married another. Years later, she is a young, lonely widow who does not fit in with the ton. When Lucien's family enlists her aid to reunite father and son, she leaps at the opportunity to not only aid her former friend, but to also escape London.

Lucien doesn't know what scheme Eloise has concocted, but knowing her as he does, when she pays a visit to his employer, he knows she's up to something. The last thing he wants is the temptation that this new, older, mature Eloise presents; a tantalizing reminder of happier times and peace.

Yet Eloise is determined to win Lucien's love once and for all... if only Lucien can set aside the pain of his past and risk all on a lady's heart.

Only For Their Love
Book 3 in the "The Theodosia Sword" Series

Miss Carol Cresswall bore witness to her parents' loveless union and is determined to avoid that same miserable fate. Her mother has altogether different plans—plans that include a match between Carol and Lord Gregory Renshaw. Despite his wealth and power, Carol has no interest in marrying a pompous man who goes out of his way to ignore her. Now, with their families coming together for the Christmastide season it's her mother's last-ditch effort to get them together. And Carol plans to avoid Gregory at all costs.

Lord Gregory Renshaw has no intentions of falling prey to his mother's schemes to marry him off to a proper debutante she's picked out. Over the years, he has carefully sidestepped all endeavors to be matched with any of the grasping ladies.

But a sudden Christmastide Scandal has the potential show Carol and Gregory that they've spent years running from the one thing they've always needed.

ONLY FOR HER HONOR
Book 2 in the "The Theodosia Sword" Series

A wounded soldier:

When Captain Lucas Rayne returned from fighting Boney's forces, he was a shell of a man. A recluse who doesn't leave his family's estate, he's content to shut himself away. Until he meets Eve…

A woman alone in the world:

Eve Ormond spent most of her life following the drum alongside her late father. When his shameful actions bring death and pain to English soldiers, Eve is forced back to England, an outcast. With no family or marital prospects she needs employment and finds it in Captain Lucas Rayne's home. A man whose life was ruined by her father, Eve has no place inside his household. With few options available, however, Eve takes the post. What she never anticipates is how with their every meeting, this honorable, hurting soldier slips inside her heart.

The Secrets Between Them:

The more time Lucas spends with Eve, he remembers what it is to be alive and he lets the walls protecting his heart down. When the secrets between them come to light will their love be enough? Or are they two destined for heartbreak?

ONLY FOR HIS LADY
Book 1 in the "The Theodosia Sword" Series

A curse. A sword. And the thief who stole her heart.

The Rayne family is trapped in a rut of bad luck. And now, it's up to Lady Theodosia Rayne to steal back the Theodosia sword, a gladius that was pilfered by the rival, loathed Renshaw family. Hopefully, recovering the stolen sword will break the cycle and reverse her family's fate.

Damian Renshaw, the Duke of Devlin, is feared by all—all, that is, except Lady Theodosia, the brazen spitfire who enters his home and wrestles an ancient relic from his wall. Intrigued by the vivacious woman, Devlin has no intentions of relinquishing the sword to her.

As Theodosia and Damian battle for ownership, passion ignites. Now, they are torn between their age-old feud and the fire that burns between them. Can two forbidden lovers find a way to make amends before their families' war tears them apart?

MY LADY OF DECEPTION
Book 1 in the "Brethren of the Lords" Series

This dark, sweeping Regency novel was previously only offered as part of the limited edition box sets: "From the Ballroom and Beyond", "Romancing the Rogue", and "Dark Deceptions". Now, available for the first time on its own, exclusively through Amazon is "My Lady of Deception".

~★~

Everybody has a secret. Some are more dangerous than others.

For Georgina Wilcox, only child of the notorious traitor known as "The Fox", there are too many secrets to count. However, after her interference results in great tragedy, she resolves to never help another... until she meets Adam Markham.

Lord Adam Markham is captured by The Fox. Imprisoned, Adam loses everything he holds dear. As his days in captivity grow, he finds himself fascinated by the young maid, Georgina, who cares for him.

When the carefully crafted lies she's built between them begin to crumble, Georgina realizes she will do anything to prove her love and loyalty to Adam—even it means at the expense of her own life.

NON-FICTION WORKS BY
CHRISTI CALDWELL

Uninterrupted Joy: Memoir: My Journey through Infertility, Pregnancy, and Special Needs

The following journey was never intended for publication. It was written from a mother, to her unborn child. The words detailed her struggle through infertility and the joy of finally being pregnant. A stunning revelation at her son's birth opened a world of both fear and discovery. This is the story of one mother's love and hope and…her quest for uninterrupted joy.

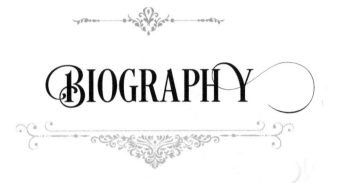

BIOGRAPHY

Christi Caldwell is the bestselling author of historical romance novels set in the Regency era. Christi blames Judith McNaught's "Whitney, My Love," for luring her into the world of historical romance. While sitting in her graduate school apartment at the University of Connecticut, Christi decided to set aside her notes and try her hand at writing romance. She believes the most perfect heroes and heroines have imperfections and rather enjoys tormenting them before crafing a well-deserved happily ever after!

When Christi isn't writing the stories of flawed heroes and heroines, she can be found in her Southern Connecticut home chasing around her eight-year-old son, and caring for twin princesses-in-training!

Visit *www.christicaldwellauthor.com* to learn more about what Christi is working on, or join her on Facebook at Christi Caldwell Author, and Twitter @ChristiCaldwell